By MJ Fields

Published by

MJ Fields

Copyright 2013 MJ Fields

This book is a work of fiction. The names, characters, places, and incidents are a product of the writer's imagination or have been used fictitiously and are not to be constructed as real. Any resemblance to person, living or dead, actual events, locale or organization is entirely coincidental.

This book is intended for adult readers only.

License Notes

This ebook is licensed for your personal enjoyment only. This ebook may not be re-sold or given away to other people. If you would like to share this book with another person, please purchase an additional copy for each recipient. If you're reading this book and did not purchase it, or it was not purchased for your use only, then please return to author and purchase your own copy. Thank you for respecting the hard work of this author

Other Titles by MJ Fields

The Love Series

Blue Love

New Love

Sad Love

True Love

The Wrapped Series

Wrapped in Armor

Look for **Wrapped Always and Forever** book three in the MJ Fields Wrapped series

coming in May 2013

A Young adult series is also in the works and will be available

In the Summer of 2013!!!

mjfieldsbooks@gmail.com
www.mjfieldsbooks.com
https://www.facebook.com/pages/MJ-Fields-books/514446948612589

Acknowledgement

I want to thank Stephanie for being my forever friend, second set of eyes, her tireless work, and for the constant encouragement.

A special thanks to Adreian for working on the music with me, I cant wait to share it with our readers.

To Laura BP for all the help and support your energy is crazy contagious

To Chris V, thank you for your work getting this website started and finished, soon.

To Karen thank you again for your friendship, encouragement, and support.

To my family who gives me enough love and support to continue working towards my dream. Mary, Suzanne, Sheila, Taylor, Faye, Emily, Erica, Tiffany you are all AMAZING

To Ally, my heart…I Love you more!

Table Of Contents

Chapter 1

Chapter 2

Chapter 3

Chapter 4

Chapter 5

Chapter 6

Chapter 7

Chapter 8

Chapter 9

Chapter 10

Chapter 11

Chapter 12

Chapter 13

Chapter 14

Chapter 15

Chapter 16

Chapter 17

Chapter 1

"Goodnight London I love you," Emma kissed her daughter's milky white cheek and pushed her brown hair out of her eyes as she tucked her into bed.

Her perfect little girl, who she would move mountains for, and the past seven years she had done that exactly. London hadn't come easy, Emma spent two years taking fertility drugs in hopes that someday she would have children. Something she assumed would come easily, and it did not. For years she felt like less of a woman and less of a wife. She cried each month when she menstruated. She was devastated each time she miscarried. She silently mourned, hiding in the bathroom holding her stomach wanting to hide the anger and self loathing she felt from those she smiled brightly for everyday. It always surprised her that no one could tell how she was feeling.

When Emma miscarried with her first pregnancy all her soon to be ex husband Troy could do was give her a cold hug, the kind you give an ex or an old acquaintance, one you really didn't like all that much. He acted as if he could have cared less, but was adamant that they would not be adopting. After they had London Emma wanted more children, and he refused.

Before they married they had discussed children, and after marriage he said he did not want them. Troy enjoyed his friends and her driving him from party to party or picking him up from golf, or whatever activity he had decided to do that always involved drinking.

Emma knew Troy for four years, all through college. He changed as soon as they said I do. His partying didn't change, but his need for all things except family did. The final straw was when she found out he had cheated. When she confronted him he didn't deny it. He told her it was her fault that she wasn't there for him like she was before they had a child.

Emma had checked through cell phone bills and credit card statements and found information that looked suspicious. She took his phone while he slept and made calls, two were women she did not know. Emma called the numbers and when they answered and she didn't say anything they would say his name with a knowing smile in their voice.

The next morning she confronted him about it. Troy looked at her and did not deny it, "So leave if that's what you want to do."

Emma remembered the evening three weeks after that conversation. London was in bed, and she had enough. He would come home and eat the meal she had made and set with their daughter on the couch never saying more than *thank you* when she gave him his food on a plate, as he sat not even looking in her direction.

"I don't like you drinking in front of her ever day," Emma finally confronted him.

"I don't care," he replied coldly rolling his eyes at her.

"No kidding," Emma quietly replied.

"I have to drink to be around you, I can't stand you, I haven't liked you in a very long time," he yelled.

"Well that makes two of us," she laughed.

"Then fucking leave," he screamed.

"You leave," she demanded.

"Oh if you did that would mean you'd have to get off your ass," Troy spewed at her.

Emma had gained weight over the years, but he had never mentioned it before. It stung.

"You know I agree with your indirect cut, our daughter certainly deserves better than a miserable drunk father and a fat mother. So get out," she yelled.

Troy left that day and was gone for two weeks. Emma filed papers for custody, and he wasn't happy.

"Thanks for the papers," Troy said as she answered the phone.

"I told you they were coming, I wanted us to work it out together and you wouldn't. What did you expect?" Emma asked. She had tried to sound strong, but the nervous quake in her voice gave her away.

Troy wanted to come home, and she said no. Emma had found a place for her and London to move into, she couldn't afford the house. Emma had stayed home and watched kids before and after school and a few over the summer while he worked at the bank twelve hours a day. He didn't want her to work, but she hated being scrutinized over every dollar she spent. She had always worked until London was born and she didn't want to miss a moment, this way she didn't have to.

Troy and Emma went to court, and he agreed to overnight Friday to Saturday and one night a week taking her to dinner. Emma felt it best that he not see her just every other weekend and this way she would only be away one night and not two in a row.

Emma moved into a half a house just inside the small village. She continued watching children and submitted resume after resume. She needed a job with benefits, and no one seemed to want to hire someone who had been out of the work force for seven years. Emma was going to be substitute teaching during the upcoming school year to make extra money.

~

London was used to taking end of the summer mini vacations and Emma scraped enough money up to get away for three nights. They decided on going to New York City, to site see and shop, and she knew they would have fun.

Emma walked into the bathroom of the hotel and wanted to scream. She sat on the ground and cried into a white hotel towel. This was not what she expected after eleven years of marriage and knowing that he would be coming down for the long weekend to take London to the shore for three nights drove her almost over the edge. Three nights without her daughter were going to feel like a lifetime.

Emma packed her bags and got things ready for the next day. She had gotten London a cell phone so that she could keep in touch, but really because she wanted London to be able to call if Troy drank. Per their separation agreement neither was allowed to drink when they had London. This was easy for Emma; she had not been able to enjoy an adult beverage since she could remember. But for Troy it may be harder.

~

Emma opened the hotel room door, and Troy looked her up and down. Troy was handsome, five foot eleven inches tall, and was built well. He had dark brown perfectly groomed short hair and blue eyes. He was dressed in jeans that were a bit tighter than he use to wear and a button up shirt with some sort of winged design. Emma smiled and stepped back allowing him to come in.

"Hey London," Troy walked into the suite and looked around, "Nice place Emma, I see my child support isn't going to waste."

Handsome until he opened his mouth that is, Emma thought.

Emma didn't respond, "Give me a hug," she said to her daughter, "Back seat and make sure you have your seat belt on. I love you more," she whispered in her ear.

"No I love you more," London smiled.

"Not possible," they both laughed, "Call me when you get there, have fun. Sunscreen, remember sunscreen."

"I think I can handle it," Troy snapped as they walked out.

~

Emma lay in the hotel bed and sobbed. When she couldn't cry anymore she decided to take a run in Central Park. Since her separation she had lost thirty pounds and was back to her weight before she had London. She loved running, walking, biking, or anything that kicked those endorphins in to overdrive. She needed it right now. She tucked her phone in her bra and threw a hat and glasses on and headed out the door. She had three hours before check out.

Emma jogged around the park and looked at all the people. There was so many. Coming from a small town it was nice to blend in. She wasn't stopped by people she knew asking her how she was doing; even those who had never had a conversation with her about her personal life before thought it appropriate to ask now. It was unbelievable the audacity of some people. She knew many just felt sorry for her, but that didn't make it any more comfortable.

Her phone rang and she slowed down and answered. "Hey sweet girl is everything alright?" she asked breathlessly.

"Yep, we will be there in thirty minutes, I just wanted to say hi," London giggled.

"Well hi to you," she laughed.

They hung up, and Emma started running harder, she didn't want to cry. She was always so stunned when she talked to London on the phone, London sounded so much younger. Emma chose to focus on what was happening now. Emma would be checking out of her hotel at eleven and going to stay with her college roommate, they had not seen each other in years. Lila worked as a publicity agency and was single and loved her very social lifestyle. They had always had such a great time together up until Troy came into Emma's life.

God just run faster harder she thought as she picked up the pace.

~

Brody Hines opened the door to his hotel room and grabbed the newspaper. The front page of the paper had the news of his separation plastered on it, still even after several months. He picked up the paper and looked at his soon to be ex-wife with another man and tore it in half and threw it out. He was blindsided, he never would have thought after three years of marriage she would have done this to him. He didn't even know she was unhappy. Ariel was a model and traveled a lot. Brody was a musician who had moved from Liverpool in England to New York seven years ago. They both enjoyed the lifestyle that their professions afforded them.

Brody hated his personal life being more important to his fans than his art. His song Blue Love had been at the top of the charts for five weeks, and it brought a lot of unwanted attention. Brody was six foot three and one hundred and ninety seven pounds. He had thick brown hair and light blue eyes. It wasn't easy hiding from the media who pounced whenever they saw him. It was even harder to not tell them to *fuck off* whenever they got in his face. Brody's new publicist tried to impress upon him that it would hurt his career. Brody was trying to listen and consider her recommendation, and it wasn't easy.

He was thankful that he and Ariel didn't have children, which he had wanted and she had wanted to wait. It was awful having the whole world watch as your life was falling apart, just waiting for you to break so that they could pounce. He grabbed a hat and glasses and walked out of his room and took the service elevator. He exited out the back of the hotel where none of those annoying photographers would be. He needed to get out of there. He hadn't felt like himself for weeks now, and he knew it was because he was held up in that room. He was going to run and hoped that his face now full of stubble, the dark glasses, and baseball cap would disguise him.

~

Emma's phone rang and she stopped and answered.

"We are here Mommy," London said cheerfully, "It is so nice right on the beach, and we are going to look for shells!"

"That's fantastic; can you find one for me?" Emma asked.

"I will find two," she laughed.

"Do you have sunscreen on?" Emma asked knowing Troy would have forgotten.

"Nope, Dad I need sunscreen," London yelled.

"Shit," she heard Troy say in the background.

"I love you more," Emma said.

"We love each other more Mom," London's voice sang.

"Okay have fun, call me later," Emma felt tears, she ran harder as the tears fell.

Come on she is having fun she thought. Emma rounded a corner and ran right into a man. She was knocked flat on her back. He knelt down on the grass next to her and helped her sit up. She couldn't breathe; the wind was knocked out of her. Being unable to take a breath made the tears slow down.

"I am so sorry," he said noticing her tears. "Are you alright?"

Emma caught her breath and wiped her face and laughed *nice accent she thought*, "I am fine. Sorry I wasn't paying attention," Emma saw his face; she was looking at the hottest man she had ever seen. His lips were full, teeth perfect, his jaw strong, and his hair looked like he had just rolled out of bed and definitely not after sleeping.

"Alright," he said uncomfortable as he picked up his hat and pulled it down over his head, "You know who I am, that is why you're laughing."

"Nope," she said, "I am laughing because I didn't expect the accent, and more so because I am on my butt in Central Park and no one seems to notice."

Brody liked her eyes and smile. He was unsure whether or not to trust that she was being honest. But something in her eyes was calming and made him feel better than he had in weeks, "So you don't know me from TV, magazines, or newspapers?"

"Let's see… if you are not on Disney or Nickelodeon I don't have a clue," Emma wiped her dirty hands on her shirt.

He smiled with relief and amusement as he offered his hand to help her up and she took it, "Thanks, so who are you?" she asked.

He grinned, "You'll figure it out someday," and ran off. *Damn I hope so* he thought.

~

Emma ran back to her hotel and took a shower. She checked out of the hotel to drive to Lila's building. She pulled out of the parking garage, and she checked out the yellow lined paper she had scribbled the directions on. Her GPS had become her arch rival, she was self admittedly technologically challenged.

Emma took the elevator to the tenth floor of the beautiful tall building and used the key that Lila had left for her with the doorman to let herself in.

There was a note on the counter.

Emma,

I will be at work until about seven. Make yourself at home. Then we are going out, you should meet me at The Spotted Pig 314 West 11th street, we can have drinks. Take a cab.

See you at eight,

Lila

Emma looked at her phone it was only one in the afternoon. She had seven hours to spend alone, a very unwelcome seven hours. *This isn't a good idea, if I were home at least I could clean or something* she thought. She preferred anything to being left alone to think about what had happened over the past year.

~

Emma walked in to the bar and saw Lila. She smiled and hugged her. "You look extraordinary," Lila said and hugged her, "Have a seat."

Emma took a deep breath and sat down at the table. She met some of Lila's clients; she really didn't know them but enjoyed the adult conversation. She excused herself and went to the bathroom secretly willing her phone to ring.

As she washed her hands it rang. "Hi Mommy, I am going to bed now. I had fun," London said with a smile in her voice.

"I am so happy for you!" Emma smiled as she spoke to London.

When they got off the phone she felt tears. She decided to walk outside to regain her composure before going back to Lila and her friends. She had her head down as she walked out.

Emma stood against the brick building not paying attention to the people walking in and out. Most people would be enchanted by the city and its surroundings. Emma just wanted to go home with her daughter and curl up on the couch watching a movie they had probably seen a hundred times, where everything ended perfectly. She took a deep breath and walked back in and made her way back to the table. A couple more people had joined the party and Lila was talking and laughing with them.

"Where did you disappear to?" Lila asked and grabbed her jacket.

"The bathroom, London called," Emma said forcing herself to smile.

"We are going to head over to a dance club, here is your jacket," Lila said handing the black coat to Emma.

~

Emma and Lila walked past security and made their way into the club. They walked through the crowd and up a set of stairs to the VIP lounge. Lila hugged and kissed a couple people on the cheek and ordered drinks.

Emma looked around like a deer in the headlights. The women were dressed in sexy dresses and high healed shoes. Emma looked down at her simple black dress and silver sandals. She immediately felt out of place and crossed her arms across her and looked down.

"You need to loosen up Emma," Lila smiled, "We are going to dance tonight."

Emma smiled and took a drink. More people began to enter the VIP lounge and Lila introduced them to Emma. The first was a man she recognized from TV. Emma wasn't sure exactly who he was, but she knew he was a celebrity.

"Brody this is my college roommate Emma, Emma this is my newest client Brody Hines."

Emma looked up and shook his hand. He also looked familiar.

"Nice to meet you," Emma smiled politely and looked at him and her face flushed.

Brody smiled when he saw her eyes, he knew exactly who she was, she didn't recognize him at all.

"You too," he said disguising his accent as he looked her up and down slowly.

"Let's go dance," Lila said to Emma as she handed her another drink and dragged her down the stairs.

The two danced, and Lila was having a blast. Emma was obviously uncomfortable and Lila laughed, "Been awhile since you've been out Emma? Come on have another drink, it'll loosen you up."

Emma drank a couple more vodka and cranberry's and started to relax and dance. Lila and Emma did a couple of shots and laughed as they danced.

Brody sat with his friends in the lounge away from the crowd. He could see the dance floor and watched as Lila's friend, Emma danced. He couldn't believe she was the one he had run into this morning. She was pretty, long caramel hair, green eyes, and the nicest most sincere smile framed by lips that he could imagine his against .

Emma and Lila walked back up to the lounge. Emma grabbed her bag and grabbed her phone. There were no missed calls, she was relieved that everything was alright but wanted to talk to London.

Probably not a good idea since you're buzzing, and it was ten o'clock at night, she thought.

"Emma come sit," Lila said pointing to the chair next to her, "Everything alright?"

"Yes everything is fine," Emma said putting her phone away.

"Have another drink," Lila tried to hand her another vodka cranberry.

"I don't know if that's a good idea," Emma smiled and she sat back.

"You are with me tonight, it's a great idea," Lila laughed and handed her another drink.

"I think I should drink beer, this is going to give me a hangover," Emma laughed.

Brody handed her a beer and smiled, "I think I owe you one."

"Thank you," Emma looked confused.

He laughed and turned away. *She has no idea who I am, that's a relief.* He thought.

"Who is that Lila?" Emma asked Lila.

Emma laughed, "Brody Hines, he is a singer, newly separated and he is a hothead."

"That's not true Lila," Brody laughed from behind her. "Just tell it like it is."

"Sorry Brody," Lila smiled and laughed.

"No that's fine, I have been called much worse," he smiled. "Emma is it?"

"Yes," Emma said embarrassed that he had heard her ask Lila who he was.

"I met you earlier today, at the park." he smiled, "I literally ran you over."

"Oh, okay, well thank you for the drink," Emma looked down unable to stop smiling.

"Did I hurt you?" Brody asked.

"No, I am fine," Emma blushed.

"Good, would you like to dance?" Brody asked.

"No I don't think that is a good idea," Emma looked away.

"You afraid you'll end up on the ground again?" he smiled.

"Yep that's it exactly," Emma giggled and walked to the bathroom.

When she came out of the bathroom Lila yelled to her from the dance floor. Emma and Lila were both intoxicate and they danced and acted outlandishly. Emma was having fun, and they were joined by Brody and a few others from the lounge. The music slowed down, and Brody grabbed Emma's hand and rubbed his thumb softly against the back of it.

"One dance?" Brody insisted.

"Sure why not," Emma giggled feeling a bit intoxicated.

"Do you like this song?" he asked as he wrapped his strong arms around her waist, and finally rested his hands on her hips pulling her a bit closer.

"Never heard it," she smiled, *wow this feels so…okay stop it* she told herself.

"Well do you like it?" Brody asked his eyes sinking into hers.

"It's alright, do you?" she asked nervously.

"I do," Brody spoke softly. "So what kind of music do you like?"

"Anything I can sing along with, most everything," Emma answered.

"But this one is just alright?" Brody looked confused.

"No it's nice," Emma's stomach churned and she felt dizzy. *Oh no she thought.* "Excuse me," she ran towards the back entry.

Brody followed her knowing she was not feeling well. He walked up to her after she threw up and handed her a tissue.

"Did that song make you ill?" Brody tried not to laugh at her.

"Thank you," embarrassed she looked away. "And no it wasn't the song; it was all the vodka and whatever else… mixed. I don't do this often."

"Should I get Lila?" Brody suggested

"No I will be fine, thank you for the tissue," Emma walked towards the door needing to get away from him.

Brody opened the door before she had a chance and looked down at her. He noticed her trying to avoid him. He smiled softly and his eyes crinkled as he tried to figure out what it was he was feeling.

"What's going on?" Lila asked smiling as she looked between the two of them.

"I think the song made your friend sick," Brody winked before walking away.

Chapter 2

Emma woke up at six in the morning. She didn't need an alarm anymore it was just something that happened naturally after seven years. She decided to go for a run and stop by and get coffee for her and Lila. She was back by seven thirty and sat looking at help wanted ads online.

"Good morning Emma, I was sure you would sleep in after last night," Lila laughed as she held her throbbing head.

"I don't sleep in, I wish I could," she laughed. "I brought you an iced coffee, I hope you still like the vanilla," Emma said handing it to her.

"I haven't had this since college Emma, thanks," Lila smiled and looked down at the paper, "What are you looking for?"

"A job," she laughed.

"What do you want to do?" Lila sat next to Emma.

"Probably something with my degree, my dream job would be flexible. I need to be able to available for London. She is at school from eight in the morning until three in the afternoon. I have done child care so that I am with her all summer as well. Maybe I should go back to school and teach, and then I would have summers off," Emma thought out loud.

"Yes and make crappy money. You always wanted to edit, why don't you try that?" Lila asked.

"I would have to move," Emma rolled her eyes. "We have made enough changes in the past six months."

"What about freelance work?" Lila asked.

"Benefits and a steady paycheck, I have a child," Emma laughed.

"Okay but I have some connections Emma, you could do it. I would like to help you." Lila hugged her.

"Okay I will look into it. Reading all day would be a dream," Emma smiled. *A dream… not a reality, she thought.* "I am going to take a shower."

When Emma got out of the shower she heard Lila on the phone.

"It's not the end of the world. This is exactly why you hired me, let me take care of this," Lila said and looked at Emma who was walking through the door. "Why don't you come over, the three of us can discuss this," Lila smiled nervously towards Emma.

Emma wondered what was going on. Lila hung up the phone and took a deep breath.

This is not good she thought, a hotheaded rock star and my best friend.

Emma answered her phone, "Good Morning baby girl!" she said smiling as she walked out of the room. They finished their conversation and Emma headed to the bathroom.

Lila opened the door and grabbed the pile of newspapers sitting outside her door in the hall.

Three of the four had Brody and Emma on the front page and the daily rages haven't even come out yet Lila thought

~

Emma walked out into the den as she was drying her hair. Her stomach flipped when she saw Brody was sitting at the table with Lila.

"Sorry to interrupt, I forgot my bag," she grabbed it and turned to leave.

"This doesn't even trouble you?" Brody asked in an irritated tone.

"I'm sorry are you talking to me?" Emma asked respectfully.

"Brody she hasn't seen them yet," Lila said, "Emma could you come sit with us please?"

Emma sat down and Lila handed her the newspaper. The first paper had a photo of Brody helping her up at the park on the front page. The next paper showed them dancing at the club. The last was him handing her a tissue after she had thrown up at the club. Her eyes widened as she looked at them. There was no mistaking that it was her in any of them.

"Why would someone do this?" Emma's voice cracked and she looked at Lila.

"Honestly?" Brody asked in his British accent. "Do you truly not get it?" he stood up and leaned against the window clearly agitated.

"Apparently not, and by the way I have been polite to you. However if you continue being rude that will certainly stop. Lila, what if Troy sees these. We have court in two weeks, what am I going to do?" Emma was panicked.

"Emma we will figure this out. It will be alright," Lila said comforting her friend.

"Excuse me I pay you a great sum to take care of this sort of thing for me. You would do well to remember that," Brody snapped.

"It won't be a problem. They have taken this situation and blown it way out of proportion. The truth will work it all out Brody," Lila said calming him.

"The truth?" Emma gasped, "And what's that Lila that I was drunk at a bar dancing with some, I don't know…him? That's not going to work well for me in court."

"Well my dear this is not all about you. I have a lot to lose here, do you understand? I can guarantee that I have far more to lose than you," Brody said ascetically.

"Oh really…" Emma began to speak.

"I am quite sure," Brody responded hastily, "So you will take care of this?"

"No you egotistical ass," Emma yelled at Brody.

"Now you listen here," Brody interrupted. "I don't know where you have been for the past five years of your life, but I am a platinum selling recording artist. The song you and I danced to last night was mine, and has been number one on the charts for five weeks in a row! I am going through a divorce and have a lot at stake . Honesty is always the best policy, but regardless of that, I will that I will not lose to my whore of an ex wife in court! Are we clear?" he snappped.

Emma jumped when he yelled, immediately aware that she was being intimidated by yet another self absorbed man. "You can go fu…" she started and Lila cut her off.

"Alright this is not helping, let's sit down and discuss this please Emma, Brody, please have a seat," Lila's tone was authorative just like always and both sat glaring at each other. "We can figure this out so that it works fine for both of you."

"How much do you want?" Brody looked at Emma.

"Are you for real? Well how about you go grab a stack of money and stick it up your...," her phone rang and she grabbed it and stood to walk away. "Hello is everything alright baby?" she asked.

"Oh I see she has a boyfriend already, just like every other woman. Can't wait for the ink to dry huh?"Brody walked past Emma.

"I love you more...yes we do. See you in two days. Remember sunscreen and call me later. I miss you more," Emma smiled as she felt tears forming in her eyes.

"Can you come sit down please Emma," Lila said softly knowing Emma was understandably upset.

"I need to use the bathroom," Emma walked down the hall and Brody brushed past her.

This was a mess, a big mess. She thought *Troy is going to have a field day with this.*

Emma walked into the den, she sat down looking at the ground avoiding Brody's harsh stare.

"Okay so I am going to talk and both of you are going to keep your mouths shut until I am done. Brody is going through a very hard time right now. His wife of three years, model," Lila began and Emma rolled her eyes and causing Brody to huff, "had an affair and is now living with another man. In three years they have accumulated assets and she wants half. Emma he is hurt, I know you understand that. Brody, Emma was married for eleven years. She is also going to be getting divorced. She signed off everything and walked away. She does have an amazing little girl with her ex, who also cheated on her. This is hard for both of you."

Emma's phone rang and it was Troy, "Hello is London alright?"

"Sure is, I just wanted to let you know that she will be meeting my girlfriend tonight at dinner," Troy said coldly.

"Troy we have discussed this, unless you are planning on dating her long term it is not necessary for London to meet her. It will just confuse her and…" he cut her off.

"I don't think that's any of your business, you have moved on. London and I read your piece in the paper a few minutes ago. By the way, that was confusing to her; she is actually upset with you Emma," Troy used that superior tone he took with her all too often.

"It's not what you think Troy; he is a client of Lila's. It was nothing, nothing at all. May I talk to London please?" Emma asked softly.

"No, she is upset with you, aren't you baby?" he snickered.

"First of all our agreement is that we can speak to her anytime we wish Troy. Second.. no forget it. This should not be discussed in front of her, she is a child, and none of this is her fault. I want to talk to her," Emma began shaking as she tried to keep it together.

"You will see her tomorrow. I have plans for the third night, she will be coming back to you. We can get her through this," Troy said in an antagonistic tone.

"You need to rethink this. She doesn't deserve, I mean she doesn't need to meet every woman who you bring into your life. Do you know what that will teach her Troy, you are her father first," Emma said softly.

"You did this Emma, you wanted this over," Troy said irately.

"Okay Troy, if that's the way you want to play this. Just thank God I don't feel the need to share with London the fact that you had numerous affairs. I won't try to make myself sound better and use my daughter to feel better about myself! you. London doesn't need to carry that burden," Emma said trying not to scream at him or cry or lose it in front of Lila and Brody Hines.

"Thank God you're wonderful, or were until this paper came. Talk to you tomorrow, have a great night, we will. Oh by the way we will discuss this in court," he hung up.

Emma sat and took several deep breaths before she stood up and left the room. She sat on the bed and cried softly. *Okay so you need to get it together it will all be okay. London is a very smart girl she will process this. I guess I should consider a law guardian.*

Emma walked back out, before she spoke she took a deep breath and tried to stop her lip from quivering, "Do whatever you need to do. I would however prefer that my being drunk doesn't come to the forefront of this mess," she turned and looked at Brody. "I am sorry you're hurting. Lila just let me know what you decide; I have to know for court."

"What did that asshole say Emma?" Lila asked, she had never liked him.

"He is playing games and using this situation to hurt, never mind. As far as all assets go buddy, I walked away from everything, to give my little girl normal which is far more important than material things. Best of luck Brody, it was great meeting you," Emma rolled her eyes trying to act sarcastically and walked away still fighting tears.

"Okay Brody, what do you want to do?" Lila asked.

"The truth, leave out the alcohol. Will you see that she is alright," Brody was conflicted as he watched Emma walk away and heard the door slam.

"Okay I will email you a press release when it's ready. Anything else," she asked. He was visibly upset. "You are going to be fine Brody."

"I know I will be," he said and looked in the direction Emma had walked.

He stood to leave and turned back and looked again towards the door Emma had slammed, "Talk to you soon."

~

Lila let Emma have about half an hour before knocking on the spare bedroom door. "Emma I wrote up a press release, would you look it over for me. You know edit it, like you did in college?" Lila asked sweetly.

"It looks great Lila thanks," Emma said drying her eyes as she made a few corrections.

"Are you alright?" Lila asked.

"No," Emma said honestly. "When things like this happen I wish I had just stayed, for London. I don't know which would have been worse for her."

"I think you did the right thing Emma. If you had stayed you would have become bitter and as much as you love that little doll of yours it would have spilled over on her."

"Lila it's not just spilling right now, it's pouring. My little girl is meeting slut of the week today. She is hearing him talk about my boyfriend in the newspaper, and that I ruined our marriage by moving out. My little girl," Emma began to sob, "did not deserve this."

Lila hugged Emma and didn't let go. "You are so strong. London is smart Emma; if she hasn't already she will figure his game out soon enough. Just don't stoop to his level."

"Thanks, I am sorry I was rude to your client. I don't get how you deal with people like that every day. Are they all so self absorbed?" Emma asked laughing.

"He is just angry and hurt. Just like you," Lila said wiping her tears.

"Except regardless of what they do, they have fans," she laughed. "It get's lonely Lila."

"You have me, I am your fan." Lila smiled. "Brody has people who seem to care but after all is said and done his true fan club is no different than yours. He has a handful of true friends. The rest either want something from him, like his ex-wife who would not have been half as popular on the runway as she has been if she wasn't attached to him or the ones waiting in the wings. He knows that. It's pretty hard for celebrities who have hearts and not just enormous egos. Imagine what it would be like to just need to break down and not be able to because you'd be seen. It is kind of like what you're going through with London. You can't fall apart in front of her."

"I guess," Emma said. Her phone made a musical sound alerting her to London's text.

-Mommy is that singer your boyfriend?

-Of course not London, he is a client of Lila's.

- Do you like him Mom?

- Well I don't know him well enough to make that judgment London. But he seems alright. The only reason those silly pictures were in the paper is because he is famous. Lila knows lots of famous people.

-Who else does she know Mommy?

-I am not sure London, but you can ask her when we see each other tomorrow.

-Cool, I love you Mom.

-Love you more!!!!

-We love each other more Mommy.

-Of course we do. Call me when you can.

Emma smiled, "Are you all better Emma?" Lila asked.

"Not all better, but that certainly helped," Emma smirked.

"Can we still go out tonight?" Lila said smiling.

"Sure, just don't let me drink. I hate throwing up," Emma laughed.

~

Brody walked into his new hotel room and his bags of belongings were all there. Lila had suggested it. He wished he could just go home. It sucked living out of hotel suites. He opened his laptop and read the email from Lila.

Date September 3rd, 2011

SUBJECT- The situation

Check this out and tell me what you think. I would suggest putting it on Twitter and Facebook. I will do a press release when you give me the okay.

The photos plastered on the paper this morning where interesting. My publicist invited a friend to hang out this weekend. I literally ran into them at the park, pretty comical. I asked her to dance, and she was deeply touched by my music, like the rest of you are. I think my song <u>Blue Love</u>, made her cry. So I gave her a tissue. I haven't moved on yet ladies, still healing. To the idiot who decided this was news…well there are many more important things going on in the world than my jog or a dance with a friend of a friend….Cheers

Brody.

Brody laughed *nice spin. So this is what he had been avoiding,* he never thought the idea of hiring someone like her, a publicist. *They always seemed so damn dishonest. Lila did what was asked of her. I like her.*

Date September 3rd, 2011

SUBJECT- The situation

To: Lila

Nicely done, I will put them online now. What are you up to this evening? I am doing an acoustic set at The Place, maybe you could drop in. You could bring your friend. I would like to apologize to her.

Brody

~

Brody Hines moved from England seven years ago. He grew up in Liverpool with his parents, brother, and sister. He was twenty seven and his music career had peaked in England, and he hoped to become even bigger in the United States. He worked hard and kept to himself. He knew that if he was a publicity junky his career would have taken off much quicker. He was tall and handsome. His brown messy hair and his large bluish green eyes could be mistaken for no one else. He did not blend in. He hung with his band, and they all kept pretty much to themselves. They went to small bars when they went out and watched local bands play. He enjoyed when they played original music but when he was drunk and wanted to dance it was always more fun to listen to and sing along with covers. Brody was drunk at an award show the night he met his wife. She was a tall leggy women and was handing out the awards. He won his first MTV music video award, and she handed it to him. When he left the stage he saw her and kissed her. They had been together ever since. His drunken moment of bravery, as he had always thought it was, ended up being just the type of drunken brainless moment he had avoided since his move to the United States. They traveled together and laughed a lot. When her career took off she traveled often. When he wasn't touring he traveled with her. When she wasn't working she went with him on tour. He believed she loved him, why else would she say she did. He would never understand why she would not tell him if she was unhappy. Or instead of breaking up she did this. He himself had plenty of opportunity to cheat on her but respected his marriage enough to not. He was hurt at first that quickly turned to anger. They had only spoken a hand full of times since she asked if they could fix this and at first he considered it. After a month passed and anger turned to disgust he told her no. Now Ariel was living with a different guy, not even the asshole she cheated with. They were speaking only through lawyers. His phone chirped, and it was Lila.

-After a lot of persuasion Emma finally agreed to come watch you perform…Lila

She hates me, he thought. He couldn't blame her, he was pretty heartless this morning. He knew what she was going through, sort of. *Eleven years of marriage, how old was she. It doesn't matter he thought,* as he tried in vain to wipe her out of his mind.

    -Alright, I wanted to apologize, that's all. It really is not a big production…Brody

~

Emma and Lila walked right past the security team. "Look at you Lila, all important," Emma laughed.

"I told you one day I would be, you should have known," Lila laughed as she flipped her hair.

They walked to a table marked reserved and sat and talked. Brody came on stage.

He smiled, "Thanks for coming out tonight," he said looking over the crowd. He quietly counted, "One two three, two two three."

The crowd clapped and cheered when the first song finished.

Brody smiled shyly, "Thank you".

He played three more songs. His voice was amazing and smooth. Each song was a story that pulled you in. Brody didn't interact with the crowd; there was no dancing or jumping around. His music felt like it was a part of him. You watched as he got lost in it, he closed his eyes a great deal as he performed. When they were opened he didn't look into the crowd, but over it. His guitar playing was for him as well. He cradled the guitar like he was keeping it safe and close. You could feel the love he had for his music. He didn't want to give it to you, but you could join him if you wanted.

Emma was lost in his music. She felt like she was looking through a window watching a very private and personal moment, one that she could not walk away from, one that Brody allowed you to watch from a distance. The wall he put up was infinite, yet not built of stone but instead shatterproof glass.

When he ended he stood and smiled, "Thank you, goodnight."

He said looking over the crowd. Brody glanced down and saw Lila and Emma sitting with his manager and a couple of his friends. Smiling slightly he walked off stage.

"Pretty good isn't he?" Lila smiled looking at Emma who was still staring at the stage with her mouth opened slightly.

"Yes. He is very, intense," Emma shook her head in agreement.

She noticed Lila trying not to grin.

Emma smiled, "I wonder if there is a Kids Bop version."

"I don't think so," Lila laughed.

Brody joined them at the table. He sat next to Emma.

"Thanks for coming. I wanted to say I am sorry about this morning," he whispered sincerely into her ear.

"Thank you, I am sorry as well," Emma looked away.

He smelled like heaven, clean with a hint of sandalwood, and his hot breath hit her ears making the hair on the back of her neck stand.

"So what did you think?" Brody asked.

Emma was looking the other direction, and he laughed.

"Emma," Lila whispered, "Brody asked you a question."

"I'm sorry, what was the question?" Emma face was heating up.

"Was it alright? The music, last night you said it was alright. What did you think?" Brody asked looking amused.

"Yes it was very good," she smiled and immediately looked away.

The waitress brought a tray of drinks and put a beer in front of her. She looked at it and glanced across the table.

"I wouldn't mix that with vodka if I were you," he tried not to laugh.

Emma shook her head and smiled, "Thank you."

Another band took stage and Emma sat back and sipped her beer. She smiled at Lila and the band began to play. Emma looked at Lila and bit her cheek trying not to laugh. Lila laughed and Brody smiled as he watched them.

"They are really bad," Emma giggled and Lila laughed.

Everyone at the table heard her and started to laugh. Emma's face turned red and she tried to stop smiling.

Emma excused herself and went to the bathroom. Her phone chimed and it was a message from London.

-Mommy I am scared, and I need you…London

-Can you talk? Can I call you?...Mom

"London what's wrong baby and where are you?" Emma asked as she answered the phone.

"In the bathroom upstairs. Mommy there's a lot of people here and bad things are going on Mommy," she cried.

"Lock the door, I will be there as soon as I can be, where is your father now?" Emma asked as she walked out of the restroom and grabbed her jacket off the back of the chair.

"What's going on Emma?" Lila asked.

She shook her head, and tears fell down her face, Lila followed her out the back door.

"Honey I will be there as soon as I can be, just stay in the bathroom. Did you lock the door?" Emma asked. "Okay good girl, is your phone charged up?"

Emma stayed on the phone trying to get a cab. None stopped and she began to panic. A black Limo pulled up.

"Get in," Lila yelled to her as she opened the door.

Emma jumped in and closed her eyes and pinched the bridge of her nose, "Hey London we are on our way okay? If your phone dies I wont be able to call you when I get there, so no games or music okay? I love you, it should not be long. Do you want to stay on the phone? Okay don't answer the door for anyone, do you understand. I am going to call every five minutes London, and I will be there as soon as I can but if you need anything call me. I love you more," She hung up and buried her head in her jacket.

"Emma what's going on?" Lila asked as she rubbed her back

"I fucking hate him!" she screamed and looked up at Lila

Emma was shocked when she saw Brody sitting in the car across from Lila. He looked down sensing her discomfort. He did not want her to feel anymore uncomfortable than she already did.

"Sorry," she said and tried to pull herself together. "He is having some sort of party and there are many people there that she doesn't know. Her father is apparently arguing with someone, and she is scared. I can't believe this Lila, he can't handle two nights?"

"We will be there in an hour, Jersey shore right? Do you have the address?" Lila asked.

Emma gave them the address and called London, "Hey sweet girl are you okay? Good … Okay …Soon baby very soon."

Emma sat back hiding her face with her hair rocking slightly back and forth trying to comfort herself.

"Emma we should call the police," Lila said.

"I thought the same thing, but I am afraid they will take her, or she will be scared. I don't want her to see her father get arrested she has already been through so much. What do I do?" Emma began to shake as she looked at Lila for an answer.

"I have a suggestion," Brody said, his tone was direct but bordered angry. "If you wait until we are almost there to make the call you'll be killing two birds with one stone. You'll get her out safely, and he won't have a chance in hell at court. But only if you feel that she is safe. "

"I agree with Brody Emma," Lila said

She looked out the window and tried to breathe, tears fell again, "Okay," she whispered.

Brody handed her a tissue.

She shook her head, "Thank you."

Emma stared out the window as she nervously knotted her hands together. It was so hard to keep it together but she had to. She closed her eyes and leaned into the leather seat and took deep breathes and slowly released them.

"We are thirty minutes away. Shall I make the call for you?" Brody voice was soft and calm.

"Yes please," Emma opened her eyes and called London.

"Mommy there is a fight, I hear people fighting," London cried.

"Okay you're still in the bathroom right?" she asked softly.

"Yes Mommy," London said crying harder.

"Okay we are coming London, and we are going to make sure you are safe. If someone knocks on the door don't open it, I will be there very soon. I am so sorry London. You won't have to deal with this again," Emma kept her voice steady and strong even though she was ready to fall apart.

They pulled in front of the beach house, and Emma opened the door, Brody grabbed her arm.

"Might I make a suggestion?" he asked as he pulled her back in. "Call her and have her flash the bathroom light so you know where to go, and if you could wait for the police, it may work out better for you in court."

Emma's hands shook as she dialed her phone and he grabbed them to steady her, Emma took a deep breath and settled down a bit. She looked up into his fierce eyes.

"Emma, you are doing great. Breathe okay like you were before. In and out slow and steady," Brody rubbed his thumbs up and down her hands, softly and gently. She did as he asked, "Very good Emma. Now call."

"London can you turn the bathroom light off and on really fast until I tell you to stop?" Emma asked.

Emma saw the lights flash and shuddered slightly, "Okay baby look out the window and you will see me." She stood outside and waved to her. "Yes honey you can ride in the limo" she laughed. "But you are going to wait until I get to you so I can come help you get your bags together. Yep Lila is here."

London's phone died.

"Her phone is dead" she started to feel panicked again.

"Emma you are here, everything is going to be okay," Brody voice was soft but his eyes looked angry.

"She can't see you, I mean after this morning and the paper and tonight, she can't see you. Oh God," she said grabbing her hair, "This is your car, I need to get a cab, Lila…" she started.

Brody interrupted, "I will sit in the front she will never see me, the Police are pulling in, get it together there are little eyes watching you now from the window up there," Brody said and pointed up.

"Thank you so much," Emma jumped forward and hugged him tightly.

She immediately felt odd and turned to Lila and did the same. She wiped her eyes and got back out.

The Police knocked on the door and no one answered. The music was loud. They walked in the door and Emma was disgusted with what she saw. She saw the stairs and started towards them.

"What the hell are you doing here?" Troy grabbed her arm.

"Getting my daughter," Emma tried to pull away from his grasp.

"She is asleep!" Troy yelled.

"No she had been awake for awhile now, she has been locked in the bathroom scared out of her mind waiting for me. Now let go of me!" Emma yelled and tried to pull away.

Troy pushed her down and ran up the stairs. Before he reached the door the Police apprehended him and brought him outside.

"London it's Mom, open the door baby," London unlocked the door and Emma walked in and grabbed her in her arms and hugged her tightly as they both cried.

"You are okay baby," Emma wiped her face. "You are going to hide under this towel so none of those weird people see you," she laughed as she put the towel over her head.

She grabbed London's belongings and hugged her all the way to the car.

They walked out, and Emma was giggling with London who was still under the towel, "Hey London you are going to hang out with Lila for a few minutes, if that's alright with her, so I can go talk to your Dad okay?"

Emma shut the door and turned around, straightened her clothes, and took a few deep breaths.

"Are you alright Emma?" Brody asked from the front window of the limo.

She jumped and laughed nervously, "Yep I am great, thank you so much for everything tonight, I am very sorry."

Emma turned around and stormed up to the house.

The Police had Troy in hand cuffs reading him his rights.

"Are you happy now Emma?" Troy yelled.

"I am happy my daughter is safe, not that her father has turned into someone I don't even recognize. You should be ashamed of yourself," she said and fought back tears, "Do you need me for anything," she asked the policewoman.

"We would like to get in contact with you later, we need your phone number. But right now you should get her home and to sleep," the officer said.

"Thank you," Emma handed them a piece of paper with her name, number, address, London's full name, and date of birth.

"Get it together for her and for yourself," she looked at Troy sadly before she walked away.

Emma jumped in the Limo, and London and Lila were laughing.

"What's so funny in here?" Emma smiled.

"Well London was just telling me how Troy googled my friend Brody, you remember him right?" she laughed, "Apparently London likes his music and thinks he is very cute. She also thinks he would make a perfect boyfriend for you, although Troy disagreed with her."

"Well I don't have time for a boyfriend, and even if I did, he is way too young. Maybe someday I will date someone my own age and from the same social circle," Emma laughed and hugged her daughter. "Are you alright London? Do you want to talk about tonight?"

"No Mom not now, alright?" London said with a sweet yet sad smile.

"Okay," Emma hugged her tightly.

"Mom you're squashing me," she laughed and tried to lighted the mood. "I want Lila to tell me all the famous people she knows."

"Well you already know that I know Brody, this is actually his car," she smiled.

"Is it really?" London asked elatedly. "How did you get his car?"

"Well he is my friend and your mom needed to get to you fast and he offered. Wasn't that nice of him?" Lila asked.

"It was very nice of him," Emma said and gave her a look, "So tell her more."

Within ten minutes London was asleep lying on Emma's lap.

"What do I do for someone like him as a thank you?" Emma whispered.

"Tell him," Lila tapped on the window.

"Everything alright?" Brody asked peering into the back.

"Yes, I just want you to know how much I appreciate your help tonight," Emma said. "If there is anything I can do for you please let me know."

"You are welcome. Your daughter looks just like you," he smiled. "Is she alright?"

"She is thank you," Emma said stroking her hair.

"London would love to meet you Brody," Lila said smirking.

"Alright anytime," he smiled. "By the way Lila, when is your birthday?"

"In February," Lila said.

"How old will you be?" Brody asked.

"Well I will be," Lila paused, "How old are we Emma?"

"We are thirty five, how can you forget how old you are?" Emma laughed.

"I am not sure," Lila said raising her eyebrow as she looked at Brody.

~

The car stopped in front of Lila's building. Emma stepped out with London draped around her.

Brody rolled down the window "Goodnight ladies."

Emma turned and smiled, "Thank you again."

"Goodnight Brody, by the way when is your birthday and how old are you?" Lila said loudly.

"I will be twenty eight in May," Brody scowled at her knowing she was in his head.

~

Emma was glad to be home. She was taking clothes out of the dryer when the phone rang.

"We just got back home an hour ago," Emma told Lila on the phone.

"How is she?" Lila asked concerned.

"She is well. Right now she is in her room playing." Emma laughed, "And I am drained."

"Have you talked to the Police, about Troy?" Lila asked.

"I did talk to the Police. They charged him with endangering the welfare of a child Lila. I am so sick to my stomach over it all. Why couldn't he just be better for her? One night a week I was certain he could handle. I was scared about the three nights, and then he changed it when he was upset. I guess he has court next week. I should go," Emma said softly so that London would not hear.

"Come stay with me that night, I will watch London," Lila offered.

"Alright, I will thank about it," Emma said.

"Hey I am sending you an email right now of jobs I think you should apply for, just to see you know," Lila pushed.

"Thanks I will look them over," Emma said gratefully.

~

London and Emma spent the next two days school shopping. London insisted on picking her own clothes out. She was going for retro rock star in the third grade. Emma was very amused by this, *she is her own little spirit,* she remembered; *at least he had not broken that.* London didn't ask about her father. She had not seen the Police there that night, and Emma was grateful.

The house was prepared and ready for the crazy school year to begin. Emma lay down and snuggled with London until she fell asleep. When she felt London's little body startle she knew she had fallen into a deep enough sleep for her to exit the room.

Emma opened her email finally to check out the jobs Lila had mentioned she was sending. She read through and decided to print them out. Her phone rang, and it was her mother.

They talked about what had happened while she was in the city and what London had gone through. Her mother was coming up to stay with London while Emma went to court.

"Honey I really wish you would consider moving back here. I don't mind driving to you at all, but you could have a much stronger support system here. After your divorce and custody hearing are done and you know what is going on I want you to please think about it," Caroline asked.

"I will, I just need to get through this first," Emma said softly.

Emma took the paper from the printer and read over the jobs. All were in the city, a thirty minute train ride from her childhood home in Tarrytown. Her head was spinning, she was overwhelmed.

I should just do it. London would have more opportunity living close to the city. She would have family who loved her. There were more jobs available. This is all too much, she thought.

Emma opened up her email again and saw another from Lila. She had told her that Brody had asked how she and her daughter were doing. He also asked for her phone number and email address. His court date was next week for his divorce.

Emma texted Lila.

-Tell him thank you again and good luck...Emma

-Em, I think he like you...Lila

-No I am sure he just feels vested in the situation after the newspapers and taking us to get London, there is a difference, and BTW he is a baby...Em

-Whatever you need to tell yourself...Lila

- Its reality, thank you for the ego boost...Emma

-Weird coincidence that your both going to court next week hu?...Lila

-Yes, coincidence. Leave it alone!!!...Emma

-Sweet dreams Em!!...Lila

-U 2...Emma

Emma spent the rest of the night emailing her resume to every company that Lila had suggested. Her dream was that one would pick her and let her work from home. It would allow her to continue parenting the way she wanted to.

~

Emma walked into Lila's apartment. Caroline was with London and Emma was glad. Not that she did not trust Lila enough to take her up on her offer, but this way she would not have to miss school. London didn't ask where she was going, down deep Emma knew that London was aware it had something to do with her father.

Emma decided to cook dinner for Lila who was supposed to be home at eight. She plugged her iPod into Emma's system and played some tunes as she danced in the kitchen. One More Night by Maroon 5 was playing as she cleaned up her mess and danced around and sang loudly. When the song ended she heard clapping and turned around to see Lila, Brody, and another guy she didn't know. Her face burned and she turned off the music and pulled her hair away from her face.

"Sorry," They all stood smiling, "I made dinner," she said trying desperately to change the focus "Will you be staying?"

Why on earth did I just ask that?

"Great idea," Lila said. "What do you say guys, a work dinner?"

~
They all sat at the large square dining table, Emma was still trying to recover from the awkwardness earlier. The others talked about Brody's court date tomorrow. The press had found out about his upcoming court appearance, and Lila was telling them how things would go down. The other man was Brody's lawyer Eli, he seemed young to be a lawyer but he was Brody Hines' lawyer, he must be good.

Emma began to clear the table as Lila and Eli coordinated tomorrow's plans and strategies for Brody to walk away unscathed by the divorce.

"Let me help," Brody grabbed the dirty dishes.

"Are you ready for tomorrow?" Emma asked while standing at the sink.

"Not particularly, but it will be nice to close this chapter of my life. And you Emma, are you ready for tomorrow?" Brody asked with concern in his eyes.

"Yes, it'll be nice to know what the next step is for London, and I," she said looking down.

"London is an interesting name. What made you choose it?" Brody asked curiously.

"Well," she laughed. "Her father and I had planned to go to London for our five year anniversary, but could not afford it," she looked at him feeling perplexed about whether or not he was just making small talk or truly wanted to know, she looked in his eyes, "We spent a lot of money on fertility treatments. Our trip plans changed. I made mention during an argument about money that the little one growing in my belly was better than ten trips to London. It kind of stuck."

He smiled, "That is wonderful."

"Yay, I think so too," she smiled as she put the leftover food in the refrigerator.

"So you like Maroon 5?" Brody tried not to laugh.

Emma smiled and giggled, "I guess so."

"May I see your music player?" he took it off the counter.

"Sure help yourself," Emma said cynically.

"Lots of Kids Bop," Brody said, and the way he pronounced the P in Bop made her laugh.

"Yes it is more appropriate for kids," she said and sat on the barstool at the massive kitchen island.

"Hmm," he said setting it down next to her.

"What's that supposed to mean? Hmm," she said jokingly.

"No Brody Hines music," Brody said astutely.

"Oh I guess not, I did enjoy your music," Emma said trying to save face.

"Apparently not enough to listen to it again," he laughed. "But Maroon 5 huh?"

"Alright do you want honesty?" Emma asked genuinely.

"Yes please do go on," Brody turning to her looking into her eyes totally focused on her.

"Okay I like music that doesn't make me feel like your music does," As soon as the words escaped her mouth she felt her face get red.

"Interesting Emma, how is it that my music makes you feel?" Brody asked sincerely.

"Well I had never heard your music before, I guess Kids Bop is not your thing," she laughed. "I like music I can sing and dance to, fun music."

"Yes I saw that earlier," he laughed.

Emma scowled at him.

"Okay that doesn't answer my question," he asked immediately expunging the humor from his voice.

"When Lila and I came to your show the other night," Emma said looking down. "It was like watching someone tell a story, a very personal story. When you came on stage you looked over the crowd, not at them. The entire time you sang you didn't make eye contact with the audience. The way you held your guitar was different. You cradled it, like you were holding a child or something that you held precious. It was like you wanted to share it but not like someone would share their cookies," Emma smiled and looked up. "More like an artist displaying their greatest piece of art for the world to see but with the red rope embodying it so no one could get close. I felt like you were saying look, hear, and feel from a distance, but don't come close. You close your eyes a lot when you sing. Which made me feel like it hurt you to share it," She smiled and looked down. "I personally felt like I was watching you through a window during a very personal moment. Your music is very intense. Beautiful but intense, and honestly it makes me uncomfortable," Emma took a deep breath and looked up at him.

He looked deeply in her eyes, "Thank you."

Her eyes widened, "Okay what does that mean?"

"Well that's very true. I am a very private person," Brody said.

She laughed and went to stand up.

"Don't leave yet, please. Tell me what made you laugh."

"Well you're a celebrity, your job is to perform for people. How can you be a private person and do what you do?" Emma asked and sat back down.

"I love music, and I am very good at what I do," he smiled, "Well most people think so anyway."

"I think your music is great," Emma raised her eyebrow, "I just said it seems very personal and private for you," her face softened. "Is it because you feel insecure about what is going on in your personal life?"

"Wow," he said and laughed.

"Sorry, I just know that after my husband and I split up I felt like I had failed. Every time I turned around someone would ask me how I was or wanted to know what happened. People at the grocery store would look at me differently. They even started asking in front of my daughter," she shook her head and smiled sadly looking down. "I stopped going to the store in our town when London was with me. I took her out of our local dance school and took her half an hour away, just so I didn't have to deal with the chit chat or the looks. So for someone like you, it must be just like that, except everyone knows who you are. Not just the people in your little town. And the way you were when you sang made me want to hug you or help you, knowing you're going through what you are. So your fans must feel so much pain for you. Which I am certain that makes you uncomfortable, embarrassed, and pissed off," she laughed. "on a much grander scale of course."

Brody looked at her thoughtfully, "I see, but add to that the letters, e-mails, and screaming fans who feel like they may actually be able to fix it for you. Or those who say they would like to take your mind off of it," he grinned seductively which made Emma laugh.

"I don't get those," she said jokingly.

"You are lucky then Emma," Brody said with a smile. "They are kind of freaky."

"Do you get unsolicited advice from everyone like I do?" Emma asked.

"Hordes of it," he smiled.

"Everyone else knows what you need, and how to fix it. When sometimes all you want to do is vent or just enjoy life and not think about it," Emma grinned.

"Exactly, and I am not sure how it is for you but in my case I feel like everyone needs something from me. Often I feel if I went on a sexual binge people may back off. That is deranged thinking isn't it?" Brody snickered.

"Maybe after your divorce you could come out," Emma laughed.

"Do you think I am gay Emma?" he asked seriously.

Emma smiled and tried to mask her amusement, "No, I just think that way the screaming fans would realize they had no chance."

"Or they would try to fix me," he said looking horrified.

They both laughed.

"What is going on in here?" Lila asked playfully.

"Divorce chatter," Emma said and smiled.

"So did you fix it all Lila dear?" Brody stood up.

"I think you will be just fine," Lila said shaking her head and walking out of the room.

"See even Lila is trying to fix both of us," Brody said as he winked at Emma.

"I kind of gathered that, sorry," Emma said as if she was annoyed.

"Best of luck tomorrow," Brody said extending his hand.

Emma shook it, "You too."

"Would it be awkward if I texted you to tell you how things went with me and you could let me know how things went for you, for London?" Brody asked earnestly.

"Not at all, it is kind of nice having someone who understands what I am going through. I hope you feel the same way," Emma smiled.

"I do," he looked at her intensely for a few moments and then looked away.

Emma and Brody walked out into the living room, and she said goodnight to Lila. She walked into her room and checked her emails. She had several responses from the companies she had submitted her resume to. Many asked for her to come in and interview. Emma was happy but knew from previous attempts at finding a job an interview meant that they may be interested.

"Hey Mom, how is my girl?" Emma asked.

"She went to bed after she talked to you. She is very tired," Caroline reported.

"It always takes her a few weeks to get used to the school schedule," Emma said softly. "So dependent on how court goes tomorrow, I may need to stay a few days for some job interviews. Would you be willing to bring London back home with you and I will meet you there?"

"Emma, you said home. Are you considering my proposal?" Caroline said with a smile in her voice.

"Dependent on court Mom," Emma said with reserve in her voice knowing if she said yes her mother would be pushing her to do it now.

"Well of course," Caroline said happily.

Emma skipped out in her pajamas to tell Lila the news.

"That is amazing Emma," Lila said hugging her.

"Celebratory dance party," Emma said and jumped on the couch and shook her fanny at Lila as she made a loud whoop, whoop, noise as if she were at a sporting event cheering on her favorite team.

Lila looked towards the bathroom, and Emma followed her eyes. Again Brody stood witness to her goofy ways.

"Listening to your happy music again Emma?" he joked.

She jumped off the couch and laughed. "No, Emma just got some good news. She put in a bunch of resumes and has to schedule interviews tomorrow," Lila said smiling. "I will be seeing much more of you if you accept an offer."

"What kind of work are you looking for?" Brody asked earnestly.

"Editor positions, entry level of course. It seems companies don't want to hire people like me who have been out of the workforce for seven years. Sorry again about the show. Goodnight," Emma smiled as she quickly walked to her room.

Chapter 3

Brody woke in his hotel room. He showered and shaved and grabbed the suit Lila had picked out for him. He was not looking forward to his pending court appearance. He had changed hotels again, and it seemed no one knew where he was. No slew of fans outside in the streets screaming for him. There were no packages delivered wishing Brody good luck today, or letters offering to take his mind off of the train wreck of a day. Brody was grateful to his new friend Lila and for her friend that seemed to be occupying his thoughts lately. *Emma was wonderful, kind, sweet, and funny. Even though, she didn't seem to have to try to be*, he thought and laughed to himself remembering the two incidents last night in which he caught her dancing.

Brody stepped out of the black town car wearing a gray suit and woven tie. He had on sunglasses, and he plastered his signature smile across his face. There were about a hundred women standing behind the police barricades screaming and yelling to him. Lila, his lawyer, and his manager followed him in the courthouse. He waved and walked past the masses trying to grab him. They may all mean well, but he certainly never asked for this, he wished his personal moments could be his own. Like Emma, he wished they could feel his discomfort and just sit back and watch if that's what they felt they needed to do, he thought.

He sat in the large court room behind a wooden desk next to his lawyer when Ariel walked in with her lawyer. He glanced up and immediately looked away. He expected to be angry when he saw her or disgusted as he was when he saw her in print with another man. From the day he left after the affair came to light, he had not been alone with her. Brody avoided all the calls and only answered text messages that concerned the divorce. Ariel was beautiful. She was almost six foot tall and extremely thin. Her long black hair was in a ponytail today. She wore a tan skirt and jacket, making her brown skin look even darker.

The judge looked over the paper work and asked if any changes had been made since the previous hearing. There had been none. His decision was that Brody would pay spousal support for the same number of years they had been married, at fifty thousand dollars a month. Ariel would get the New York home, and he would keep the one in Liverpool. No future earnings would be taken into consideration, the marriage had only lasted three years. Brody was to pay a three million dollar settlement. All parties accepted the decision and Brody and Ariel signed the paperwork. Brody was relieved that he would not have to sell the home in England near his family. He was not happy with spousal support, three million dollars and their shared home should have been enough. When they left the courtroom Ariel looked at him and smiled sadly as she walked into the arms of the man she was now shacked up with.

Brody walked out of the courtroom and looked down. He did not want to acknowledge the swarms of fans and press. He and his lawyer sat in the car as Lila worked her magic.

"It has been a rough few months for Mr. Hines. Although he adores all of you he needs his privacy, time to reflect, heal, and move on from this chapter of his life. Both he and Ariel came to an agreement today. Brody is currently working on a new album." Lila smiled as the crowd cheered. "Its release should be within the next few months. We will definitely keep you all informed, thank you for your show of support today."

Lila got in the car and looked at Brody, "Are you alright?"

"Sure, I just don't look forward to sitting in that damn hotel room. I am considering going home for a few months to finish the album instead of just a month," Brody said looking out the window.

The car dropped his lawyer off at the Manhattan office and started down the street. "I think you should stay with me Brody, just for a few days," Lila smiled. "Would you like to do that until you leave?"

"A few of my friends are coming in to the city tonight, to celebrate the demise of my marriage," he laughed. "Are you up for lots of company?"

"The more the merrier." Lila laughed.

~

Emma walked into the courtroom with the arresting officer and saw Troy sitting in a chair next to a lawyer. He looked up at her and scowled. Emma sat and waited for Troy to be called. They were the case on the docent.

"Mr. Fields you are being charged with endangering the welfare of a child, child neglect, and felony possession of a narcotic, how do you plead?" the Judge asked.

"Not guilty sir," Troy said and looked at Emma.

"Really, so you want to go to trial over this?" the Judge laughed. "Officer White could you approach the bench and remind Mr. Fields the evidence you have against him?"

"Yes your honor," Officer White said and read through the paperwork.

"You want to rethink that son? Your seven year old daughter locked herself in a bathroom and called her mother to come and get her when it was your responsibility to keep her safe. You threw a party with cocaine and alcohol for a rowdy group of townies. Mr. Fields you were so intoxicated that you didn't even know that she spent over an hour in the bathroom scared out of her mind waiting for her mother to travel from New York city to help her. Mrs. Fields, although it was incredibly stupid to wait to call the police, I can tell you it certainly helped to build a strong custody case for you. What is your visitation agreement?"

Emma handed him the custody paperwork, "Your honor I wasn't thinking of anything except getting to her quickly. It was a suggestion from a friend when we were almost there. I agreed because I knew Troy would not be happy if I showed up. I knew that London was safely waiting locked in a bathroom talking to me on the phone. I wasn't thinking," she whispered.

"So Mr. Fields, I could put you on the docket, and we are booking about two months from now, or you could get some help. Get your ass into a rehabilitation center and get better for your child," Judge Owen looked at him.

"I am not going to rehab," Troy laughed.

"Alright then I hereby order that your current custody agreement is null and void until after your trial for these charges," Judge Owen said looking at him, "Mrs. Fields visitation is at your discretion, I would suggest you contact your lawyer about this. There are several options including supervised visits."

"Your honor, I think you're stepping outside of your job description," Troy's lawyer said warning Judge Owen.

"No, I am merely telling Mrs. Fields to weigh her options. Case postponed until a trial date is set," Judge Owen stood up and walked out of the courtroom.

"You can't keep me from her Emma, she is my daughter. I have rights," Troy said in a superior tone she was so used to hearing.

"London has rights Troy, she has a right to be safe and loved. Get some help," Emma said as she turned to walk out.

"Don't you walk away from me Emma," Troy yelled after her.

"I am leaving to take care of my daughter Troy. Damn it could you do the right thing, please," Emma said pleading as she walked out.

Emma drove back to the city and parked in the garage at Lila's. She looked in the mirror and wiped the smudged mascara from her face and grabbed her bag. She had left a message for her lawyer so that she could figure out her next move. What a mess, London would be alright but Troy, what the heck was she going to do.
~
Emma walked into the apartment and saw a bunch of people. She didn't see Lila and tried to hide from the group of guys listening to loud music, laughing as they drank in the living room. Emma walked down the hall unseen towards the bathroom.

"Hello Emma," Brody said smiling as he walked out of the bathroom.

"Oh hi," she said pushing past him as she walked in the bathroom and shut the door.

Shit, Emma thought as she washed the makeup from her eyes and tried to pull herself together.

She called her mother, "Hello Mom," she said as her voice cracked.

"Emma, are you alright honey?" Caroline said in a deeply concerned tone.

"I will be, is London home yet?" Emma asked.

"Well you must have forgotten she had dance tonight, so she is upstairs getting ready. I will stay with her tonight and meet you tomorrow night," Caroline said.

"Oh how could I have forgotten," Emma began to cry.

"Emma you have a lot going on. She doesn't know you forgot, and we are enjoying our time. How did things go with Troy?" Caroline asked.

Emma took a deep breath and told her what had happened. Her mother agreed to support her in any way she could help, which Emma knew she would. Her parents were amazing. Emma knew how lucky she was to have them, especially now. Emma chatted with London and promised that they would do something fun when they saw each other in a couple days.

"Good luck with your interviews tomorrow Mommy," London said with a smile in her voice.

"How did you know about that London?" Emma asked.

"Grandma," she laughed.

"Of course she told you. It's not definite London, I am just weighing our options okay?" Emma asked cautiously.

"Mom, I am okay with moving if it would be better for us. Plus it would be fun to live with Grandma and Grandpa," London said happily.

"Oh Grandma talked about that huh?" Emma laughed.

She said goodbye and looked in the mirror again, *good enough* she thought.

Emma walked out of the bathroom, and Brody was standing against the wall in the hallway.

"Are you alright Emma?" he asked.

"How did things go for you today," Emma said changing the subject.

"As expected, it will be fine. Are you alright?" Brody asked again his voice was deeper.

Emma laughed, "I will be, I have to be."

"What happened?" Brody asked.

Emma wasn't sure if it was the accent that made him seem older than her at this moment, but it made her uncomfortable.

He could sense that. "If I am asking questions you do not wish to answer I apologize."

Emma knew she had made him uncomfortable and felt awful, "No need to apologize. I just haven't had time to process it all yet. The Judge left a lot of decisions in my hands. I just don't know what is best for London, I just need to figure it all out. And honestly I am tired of being an adult and trying to figure every damn thing out. I wish I could run away with my daughter and not deal with all the nonsense," she looked up when she heard the music start again, "You have a raucous group out there," she laughed, "You better get back to them."

"Emma, I did not consider that you would be here and in this state of mind," Brody said. "However you did mention needing a break from being responsible. This crew is the best at being rash. You should join us," Brody smiled.

"I would love to meet your friends Brody," Emma looked up at him.

"Oh, yes meeting my friends," he said looking confused.

Oh wow, that did not come out the way it was meant to. He must think I am into him. Why do I open my mouth? This silence is painful quick Emma fix it, she thought.

"If you don't want to share your people I get it," she smiled. "I have my people to."

"Emma that's not what I meant I just" Brody began.

"I know Brody," she laughed, her phone rang. "Give me a few minutes and I will come out. Hello this is Emma," she answered the call and walked to the room she had been staying in.

Emma woke up hearing yelling and a knock from outside the door. She jumped up and opened the door.

"Troy what are you doing here?" She asked still sleepy.

"Lila's friend huh?" Troy yelled.

"Yes, Lila's friend. Are you drunk Troy?" Emma pushed past him, "You need to leave."

"You're coming with me, we have a lot to talk about," Troy laughed pulling her arm.

"Release her," Brody said his eyes angry.

"Fuck you," Troy laughed.

"Enough!" Emma yelled, "Troy do you want the police to be called again?"

Troy laughed, "Why the fuck not, what else can you do to me?"

Emma's eyes felt like they were on fire, "Haven't you done enough?" She asked as tears started to flow down her face. "What can I possibly do Troy, to make your life any easier?"

"Take me back Emma, I will be better," Troy asserted.

"No," Emma said sternly looking down.

"How the hell am I suppose to fix this then, huh. How?" Troy pleaded.

"By admitting you have a problem and getting help, get help," Emma said and he hugged her.

Her body stiffened as he clung to her.

"I will, for us Emma," Troy said softly in her ear.

Brody looked at her and could tell she was disgusted. Emma took a deep breath and opened her eyes and saw the five guys standing there. *How freaking embarrassing* she thought and rolled her eyes.

The music turned off, and Lila yelled, "Is there a party here without me, you know I do have neighbors," she laughed and turned the corner and saw them all.

"Well hello Troy, how the hell did you get in here?" Lila asked pissed.

"Lila," he said and tipped his head. "Did you ever tell Emma what happened with you and I?"

"You mean when you tried to get me to go home with you, no I spared her the details. Emma we can discuss this later? In the meantime your ass needs to leave," Lila said to Troy.

"Can we please talk about this Emma, please," Troy pleaded.

"Lila can I have a minute?" Emma asked.

"Sure Emma. Come on boys," Lila said and they all left the hallway and went into the kitchen, all except Brody who walked into the bathroom.

"Emma, can we work through this. If I go to rehab can we be a family again," Troy pleaded?

"I think you should go to rehab Troy. As far as you and I are concerned I am sure it's over. However we have London so for the rest of our lives we are bound. You need to want to fix things for her and for you, do you understand?" Emma said in a concerned tone.

"If that will help us then that's what I will do," Troy said.

"You don't get it. London is your daughter Troy. She deserves to have a healthy relationship with you. For that to happen you need to be healthy," Emma said with pleading eyes.

"How about this, what are you going to do when I sit in rehab getting the help you think I need. What are you going to do for money without my child support? When I get out am I going to owe you all the back support and what about health insurance, do you ever think? Jesus Emma," Troy snapped.

"Here's the deal Troy. I want nothing if you're not getting a paid leave, I want nothing but for my daughter to have a healthy father. Get better Troy, we are done here," Emma said.

"What about visitation Emma when can I see her?" Troy asked.

"I talked to my lawyer, and she suggested supervised visits. But Troy if you think the nonsense you put her through the other day was alright? Telling her I had a boyfriend and trying to make her mad at me. Telling her I was at fault for this divorce and not that your several girlfriends played a major role in our marriage falling apart. She is seven years old, maybe while you are at rehab you could take a fucking course on growing up as well!" Emma yelled.

"You're pushing me Em, I wouldn't if I were you," Troy growled.

Emma laughed, "Time for you to leave."

"Why so you can go fuck the Rockstar?" Troy yelled.

"Oh yes, the same way I fucked you for the first four years we were together, remember that Troy," she looked at his eyes. "Oh and the endless blow jobs, I can't wait to get started on those. Oh and anal lots and lots of that, I never thought I would like it, but people change over the years. You certainly did. I think I will try it," Emma said seductively.

"You're a bitch Emma, you changed," Troy snarled.

"Yes I have, thanks to you," Emma said and walked him to the door. "Let me know what you decide. Did you drive?"

"No, why did you want to call the Police?" Troy said as he scowled at her and walked out.

~

Emma sat at the kitchen island drinking a cup of tea and saw Brody walk down the hall, he was trying not to smile.

Lila and the other guys walked into the kitchen, they all stood and looked at Emma. Emma laughed, "So he hit on you Lila?"

"Sorry Emma, I would have told you, but you had just miscarried, and I didn't want to upset you anymore," Lila said cautiously.

"Alright then. So what are we going to do tonight?" Emma forced a smile.

"I thought you already made plans Emma," Brody tried to hold back his amusement.

"No, I guess I could get ready for my interviews. You guys have fun," Emma said and turned towards the hall.

"Emma I am going to order dinner in tonight, the guys are staying to avoid the press. Don't go back in there, please. Have a drink with us," Lila begged.

"I don't want to interrupt," Emma said and smiled. Lila handed her a glass of wine, and she sat and listened to Brody and his friends talk as she thumbed through her music.

"Emma would you like to listen to Maroon 5 or Kids Bop?" Brody said and laughed as he handed her a beer.

"How about Brody Hines," his friend Joe asked.

"No, she doesn't care for my music," Brody laughed without smiling.

"I never said that," Emma said apologetically.

"What do you mean you don't like his music?" Joe said laughing.

"It's not fun enough, not Poppy," he laughed.

There's that P again Emma thought and smiled to herself.

She threw him a silly look, "Its great just not happy and upbeat."

"So music that you would make love to?" Joe asked.

Emma choked on her drink, and Brody laughed. "No, more like watching someone through a window as they have sex, right Emma?"

"Wow, that's pretty awkward if that's what you got out of our conversation," Emma said and laughed uncomfortably.

"No, awkward would be the conversation I heard while using the restroom, and you and your ex were talking…" Brody laughed obviously loosening up after a few drinks.

"Do tell," Lila giggled as Emma closed her eyes and tried not to laugh.

"Well apparently Emma is going to make some Rock Star very happy. Lots of sex, blowjobs, and possibly…" Brody started, and Emma threw a towel at him, he laughed.

"Emma dear were you talking about me?" he laughed.

"Troy brought it up, and I was trying to make him mad," Emma turned red.

"Well I think you succeeded," Brody guffawed.

"Were you spying on me?" Emma smirked.

"No, I truly had to use the restroom, when I went to leave that ass was being rude, and I was afraid he may hurt you," Brody said sincerely looking into Emma's eyes.

When he looked at her like that, she felt vulnerable and nervous. She cast her eyes down hoping to find something humorous to say to make her less uncomfortable.

"That is very sweet Brody, isn't it?" Lila said looking at his friends.

Joe smiled, "Brody man, you're pretty intense."

"Or pretty drunk," Emma smiled at them, trying to lighten the conversation that was now making her uncomfortable.

"I am not drunk," Brody said insistently and sat back. "I do not like him."

"Well me either," Emma laughed and stood up. "Anyone want a drink?"

"I do," they all said.

"Turn on some music," Emma yelled over her shoulder.

Emma handed out drinks and sat down and listened to the music.

Her foot was tapping, and Joe noticed, "You like this song Emma?"

"Yes actually it's upbeat," Emma smiled.

"It's Brody," Joe grinned.

"Okay, what changed from then and now?" Emma looked at Brody.

"I was younger," Brody said and sat forward and looked at his friends. "We had a lot of fun then huh?"

"Sure did, that was before," Joe said and laughed.

"Yes before," Brody laughed and ran his fingers through his hair.

"Before what?" Lila asked.

"Before that whose name we cannot mention," Joe laughed.

"Well then we won't," Emma laughed. "So why not live like you did then, happier times?"

"It was in England, five years ago. We were twenty three then," Brody smiled looking down. "So you two were thirty?"

Lila laughed, "I was, Emma was twenty nine."

"Happier times," Emma said and smiled as she grabbed her phone and sent a text to London.

-I miss you London, can't wait to see you.... Mommy

-Miss you to. I am having a great time with Grandma. I am tired and going to bed I will call you tomorrow...London

-Sweet dreams, make sure you say your prayers...Mommy

"Are you texting London?" Lila asked.

"Yep," Emma smiled.

"You know people in London?" Joe asked.

"Her daughter's name is London," Brody told him.

"How old is she?" Joe asked.

"She is seven," Brody and Emma said at the same time.

Brody smiled, "She is a beautiful girl Emma. You miss her."

"Thank you and yes very much," Emma said.

She looked at her watch, and it was only eight o'clock.

"Are we keeping you from something? Maybe a date with a Rock Star," Brody smiled making her uncomfortable.

"Hmm is Maroon Five playing here tonight?" Emma laughed, "Or no how about Pearl Jam."

"Eddie Vedor," Emma and Lila said and laughed.

"Isn't his music quite serious?" Brody asked.

"Yep, he was a favorite in college," Lila answered.

"Greenday," Emma laughed.

"Emma you're drunk," Lila laughed.

"Wow, I think I am," Emma smiled at her. "We should go out and dance Lila."

"Or we could dance here?" Lila stood up and flipped through her music.

"But who would be the lucky Rock Star," Brody said and looked directly into her eyes as he bit his cheek trying not to smile.

"Do you think you could play the part?" Emma smiled as she winked and laughed at him. He blushed.

"Emma!" Lila said shocked.

"I was joking," Emma laughed.

"Well that's a shame" Joe laughed, "Isn't it Brody."

Brody smiled seductively as he looked her up and down, "Sure is."

Lila and Emma cleaned up the coffee table and sat on the couch looking through a college yearbook. Brody, Joe, Quinn, and Max laughed over their shoulders as they showed them pictures.

"Well let's see your pictures from eleven years ago, I am sure they would be just as funny," Lila laughed.

"We were seventeen," Max laughed.

"Wow that makes me feel ancient" Lila laughed.

"No kidding," Emma smiled and laughed. "We could be their mothers!"

Emma and Lila laughed until tears came out of their eyes.

"Were you sexually active and menstruating at seven?" Brody asked, his voice and face suddenly turned serious.

Lila and Emma laughed harder.

"I don't think so," Emma said laughing.

"When did you have sex for the first time?" Brody asked.

"Are you always this serious?" Emma looked at him shaking her head trying not to laugh.

"Just curious," Brody looked intense.

"Well I was in high school, it was after my junior Prom," Lila laughed. "Emma here made Troy wait two years before she put out. So that was thirteen years ago right Emma?"

"Yes," Emma laughed. "I tormented him, perhaps that's why he turned out to be an ass."

"Oh now it's your turn guys let's have it," Lila said.

"It is not something I would like to share," Brody said biting his bottom lip trying not to smile.

"Too private? Maybe you should sing it then," Emma laughed.

"Well my dear Emma, I was thirteen. So by my best guess, I had sex for the first time before you. Making it impossible that you could be my mother, do you understand?" Brody said searching deeply in her eyes.

"I do, you were a slut," Emma laughed, and everyone joined in which broke Brody's intense look.

"I was not," his smile hit his eyes.

"Thirteen? Did you even know what your penis was for at that age?" Emma said laughing.

"Apparently I did, I still do. I think anyway, it has been a very long time," Brody snickered.

"You're a Rock Star hot stuff, get out there," Emma laughed.

"You first Emma," Brody smiled.

"I am not divorced, oh, and I am a Mom," Emma laughed.

Brody smiled at her, "But I should just go have sex with anyone willing?"

"Well, not anyone, I mean I am sure you can be picky," Emma said and Lila and her giggled, "Besides if you just had sex with anyone willing you would probably never finish your album, you would be a very busy boy."

"Thank you for the ego boost," Brody's eyes expressed amusement.

"No problem. I had a lot of fun tonight, thank you all. I am going to bed," Emma smiled. "Goodnight."

Emma walked down the hall and into the bedroom.

"What is going on with you Brody?" Joe asked.

"Whatever do you mean," Brody asked in a serious tone and took a drink.

"Emma, do you have a thing for her?" Joe asked.

"I find her interesting, refreshing actually. As far as a *thing* goes, I would not say that," Brody said deep in thought.

"You wouldn't but those of us watching what goes on with you when she is present would beg to differ," Lila smiled. "On that note, goodnight everyone."

~

Emma walked into the midtown office building and had butterflies in her stomach. She rode the elevator to the twenty second floor. The doors opened and she stepped out into the lobby of Writes House and looked around. The brunette behind the desk asked if she could help her and she sat and waited to be called for her interview.

Emma's interview went well. She had three more that day all of which made her feel uneasy, not because she felt like they did not like her, but because she did not want life to change for London. She wanted something to be normal.

~

Emma walked into Lila's apartment, and Brody was sitting at the counter with his IPad, looking serious.

"Hello Brody," Emma said as she walked past him.

"Oh good afternoon, I didn't hear you come in, how did your interviews go?" Brody turned towards her.

"They went fine," Emma said softly.

"Why do you look bewildered?" Brody pulled out the chair next to him and patted it for her to sit.

Emma sat and looked up at him, "I guess because I am, if any of them offers me the job it would mean I would have to move."

"And did you not expect that?" Brody asked.

"Well," Emma said looking down in deep thought, "I guess, I just don't want to do that to my daughter. She has already had to make a lot of changes."

"Children are resilient right?" Brody asked.

Emma laughed, "That's what they say. I think they just have no choice. The adults make the decision not taking into consideration what they want or need," Emma laughed knowing she was getting too serious. "But it's my job to figure out what is best for her, and I will."

"What are your options?" Brody asked.

"Well, I could stay where we are and hope to get enough substitute teaching jobs to pay living expenses, dance tuition, oh, and I promised piano lessons. I could continue being there for everything which I have been fortunate enough to do, even after the split, or I could take whatever offer I am given and move with my parents until I find a place, and depend on them to pick up my slack," Emma said shaking her head.

"Or you could run away with your daughter, you had mentioned that before," Brody smiled.

Emma laughed, "That to. Lots to figure out. So what's next for you?"

"I guess I am going back to my house in Liverpool to finish my album and breathe," Brody said looking confused. "After I wrap some things up here," he said as he sat back.

"Well I truly wish you the best Brody Hines," Emma said with a smile.

He leaned forward and looked intensely in her eyes, and she couldn't pull her eyes away from him. *Oh he is beautiful* she thought as she took a quick sharp breath.

"Emma, are you alright?" Brody whispered.

Her eyes widened, and she shook her head yes. He took her hand and kissed it.

Holy shit she thought as she looked down.

"Am I making you uncomfortable?" he asked.

"God yes," Emma gasped nervously.

"Can I hug you Emma?" Brody asked softly staring at her making her more uncomfortable.

Sure at least then I wouldn't have to feel you staring at me. She shook her head yes, and he stood and wrapped his arms around her.

"I want you to be alright, I just don't know why?" Brody whispered.

She wrapped her arms around him, "Thank you."

Damn he smells good, and he is so damn gorgeous, and oh boy this isn't good, she thought. She felt him pulling away and lifting her chin.

"Emma I want to kiss you," Brody said.

Emma opened her eyes just in time to move her face so that his kiss landed on her cheek.

"Oh, oh, I am extremely sorry," Brody said releasing her and stepping back looking dismayed.

"Oh, please don't be like that, please," Emma grabbed his hand.

"No, I overstepped, I just thought… Damn it," he said uncomfortable.

"Oh Brody please don't make this awkward, I have enjoyed getting to know you," Emma pleaded.

"I don't know how I can avoid awkward after that," he started walking towards the door.

"Please don't go," slipped out of Emma's mouth before she could stop it.

He turned and looked at her. His face was a cross between mad and confused.

"Emma, I thought there was something…. I am sorry," he confessed.

She watched him grab his jacket and felt panicked.

She didn't realize until that very moment that she truly liked him, no she needed him, "Maybe I messed up," she said loudly and gasped.

"Emma," he breathed out as he turned around, "You are confusing me."

"Well you just confused me, and now you're leaving?" She asked.

"Do you want me to stay Emma?" Brody searched her face.

"Yes," Emma said softly.

"But how do we get past that?" Brody asked motioning to the spot he kissed her.

"I don't know, maybe try it again," she looked down.

He walked to her and wrapped one arm around her waist and lifted her chin with the other, she was trembling.

"Emma you're shaking," he said and kissed her cheek.

"Sorry," she said breathlessly.

"You don't have to," Brody said softly as he stroked her hair and pulled her closer to him.

"I want to," Emma said softly.

"You're sure?" he searched her eyes.

She quickly closed them and whispered, "Would you just shut up and kiss me?"

His lips lightly touched hers, and she kissed him lightly back, she let out a breath, and he kissed her again. His light kisses made her head spin, and they became longer and firmer. *Oh this is nice, this is really nice*, she thought. She felt him start to slow and pull away. Emma's eyes were still closed as she caught her breath.

"Was that alright?" he asked softly in her ear as he held her closely.

"Uh huh," Emma let out a breath.

She looked up at him, and he was looking into her eyes. She closed her eyes and grabbed his face lightly and kissed him. Brody moaned and kissed her. She kissed him harder, and he returned her kiss. He gently kissed her top lip and then her bottom, and she gasped as he kissed down her neck. He returned to her lips and gently pulled at Emma's bottom lip with his. She opened her mouth, and his tongue gently entered hers. Emma closed her lips around it and lightly pulled her mouth down his tongue. He breathed hard and grabbed her face and kissed her hard, and she gasped. He moved down her neck and she could not restrain the moan that escaped her mouth. Brody lifted her and pulled her legs around his tall lean muscular body. She held tightly around his neck as he walked towards the living room and he pulled back and looked at her.

"Emma," he started, and she pulled his hair gently towards her.

She kissed him as he pushed her against the wall. Emma let out a breath and kissed his neck and bit lightly down. He moaned and walked to the chaise lounge and laid her down. He was on top of her, and she wrapped herself around him and pulled his face to hers and kissed him again and again.

"Oh Shit," Lila said as she walked in the apartment and saw them making out on the chaise.

He stood up and clenched his jaw and turned away from Lila. Emma saw the bulge and bit her cheek trying not to smile. He gave her a frustrated sexy smile and walked down the hall and into the bathroom.

"Oh Emma I am so sorry," Lila said in shock.

"Excuse me please," Emma said turning a hundred different shades of red and went into the bedroom.

She shut the door and buried her head in her pillow.

"Sorry about that Lila," Brody said trying not to smile when he returned to the living room.

"I don't think you are," Lila laughed.

"Where did she go?" Brody whispered.

Lila laughed, "The bedroom, I think you should go see how she is."

"Did she look upset to you?" Brody asked with deep concern in his voice.

"I'm not sure, you should go find out," Lila said turning away so he could not see her smile.

Brody knocked on the door and didn't wait for her to answer, "Emma are you alright?"

"Um, yes," she said trying to hide the smile from her voice.

She felt the bed move as he sat next to her. "Why are you hiding your face then Emma?"

"Well Brody," Emma said using her best English accent and laughed, "I am embarrassed."

"Why is that?" Brody lay down next to her.

He is laying in a bed next to me, he so hot, and he is lying down next to me. She thought burying her face even further in the pillow as she giggled.

"Emma are you and I twelve?" Brody laughed.

"No, but I just kissed you, and I liked it," Emma said and looked at him in shock.

He gasped mimicking her expression, and they both laughed.

"You also bit me," he said teasingly. "No one has ever bit me before," he smiled and pulled her into his arms, "and I liked it" he whispered gruffly against her neck.

"Lila is here," she said as he continued to kiss her neck and moved back to her lips.

"Mmm," he moaned.

They kissed passionately, and Emma pulled back quickly, "What time is it?"

"I don't care," Brody kissed her again.

Emma pulled back and smiled, "London is going to be here at seven," she said pulling away and leaned over and grabbed her phone. "One hour and I get to see my little girl."

"I would like to meet her," Brody smiled. Emma's face fell, "That's not alright with you is it?"

Emma took a deep breath, "Yes you're Lila's friend."

"And London's extremely beautiful mother's future lover?" Brody laughed knowing it would make her uncomfortable. "Oh I am sorry, do you think she is a tad young to hear that?" Emma's face was crimson, and her jaw had dropped. "Emma I was joking, I would never tell her of my intentions, I have not even told her mother yet."

He smiled and kissed her.

Emma sat staring at the bed as he stood up, "Brody I…" she started.

"Don't worry. I will behave," he smiled.

"But," Emma began and looked at him smiling, "You are being silly."

"Do you prefer the tormented chap you've known for a week now?" Brody laughed.

"Well no, but which one are you? I am confused," Emma said looking down.

Brody sat next to her, "Tormented was when I knew I was wildly attracted to you when I ran into you at the park, than amused at the club, then angry the next day, then poignant that I could have hurt you by being self centered, then truly intrigued by how you care for your child and said you felt about my music, and yesterday with your ex I was angry and felt protective, and then particularly turned on by your confession of what you might want to do to some Rock Star," he laughed. "Then last night Emma, you are lovely. I have not felt this way about anyone and I mean anyone in years, if ever. And now I want to kiss you again."

"Okay," she said and closed her eyes.

He kissed her, and she kissed him back. He pulled her closer and they held each other tightly as they caught their breath.

"I want to know how you are feeling right now Emma," Brody said gazing in her eyes.

Her phone chimed.

-Mommy we are about thirty minutes away!!! <3 London

-I CANT WAIT TO SEE YOU!!!!...<3 Mommy

"To be continued Emma? By the way, you need to do something with your hair, you have sex hair," he laughed and kissed her then walked out the door.

Emma showered and threw on some Khaki cargo pants and a button down shirt. She toweled off her hair and walked into the kitchen. Lila, Brody and Brody's friends all looked at Emma.

"Hey Emma," Joe smiled knowingly at her.

"Hello." Emma said and looked panicked at Lila, "London and Mom should be here soon. I think I am going to get a room tonight."

"Why would you do that?" Brody pushed her hair behind her ear and looked deeply into here eyes.

"Well, I know you are all having a great time, and I don't want to interrupt that," Emma smiled.

"First of all no, you are staying. My friends leave in an hour for the airport. Lila said you all have plans tonight. Secondly Emma, I promise I won't behave badly," Brody smiled, and his friends laughed.

Emma was shocked and walked away. Brody followed her and grabbed her arm.

"You told them!" she snapped.

"Lila knows and well," Brody said looking embarrassed "They knew how I felt before any of this happened, from the moment they saw how I looked at you Emma, come now don't be angry at me," Brody said and hugged her.

"Brody, my little girl is going to be walking through that door any minute. She has been through hell. I have not seen her in three days, and that is a first. I can't put her through any more. I am sorry Brody," Emma said and pulled away.

"Emma please listen to me. They will not say anything, I would not do that to you and they are my closest most trusted friends. Please understand that. I will leave Emma if I am making this difficult," Brody looked down.

Emma took a deep breath visibly relaxing, "Is that angry or tormented Rock Star?" Emma said and smiled. He looked up at her confused. "I am sorry I just can't hurt her, and I don't want you to hurt either, just don't leave," Emma said and heard the door bell.

She smiled and grabbed his face and kissed him. She pulled away and saw Lila and the guys standing there.

Of course, she thought. Brody followed her eyes.

"Not a word," he warned them.

Chapter 4

"Mommy," London yelled and jumped on Emma, and both fell to the ground, "Oh sorry."

"You missed me a lot huh? I missed you more," Emma kissed her face like a crazy woman.

London laughed and squealed, "We missed each other more!"

Emma grabbed her and picked her up and twirled her around, "Are you ready to have fun?" London smiled and shook her head. "Come in Mom, sorry," she said and hugged her mother.

London was staring at Brody and smiling. Brody was doing the same. Emma laughed, "London this is Brody Hines, Brody this is London Fields."

"Pleased to meet you Brody Hines," London reached out her hand.

"The pleasure is mine London," Brody kissed her hand.

London laughed.

"You talk funny," London smiled, "You don't sing that way."

He laughed, "I have an accent because I lived in England for a very long time."

"Near London?" She asked.

"Yes, and did I hear you say you heard my music?" Brody squatting down looking in her eyes.

"Well my Dad Googled it, and I listened, it was alright, a little sad, but good. Friends at school said they saw pictures of you and my Mom, and well they have your albums on their MP3 players now. Do you play a guitar?" London asked.

"Yes and piano," Brody said smiled as he listened to this little girl talking as if she were an adult.

"I am going to learn piano," London motioned to her grandmother. "By the way Brody this is my grandmother Caroline, Grandma this is Lila's friend Brody," London said with a sheepish grin.

Emma looked at her curiously. And Brody laughed.

"Nice to meet you Caroline," Brody shook her hand.

"Pleasure to meet you, Lila your friend is a doll. Emma would you be offended if I left now, I have missed your father," Caroline said and winked.

Emma looked shocked.

"Um alright Mom, thank you," she hugged her.

Emma's parents had been married for thirty six years and were still deeply in love. Emma never realized it could be any different.

"Mom I am going to take my things down to your room, then use the bathroom alright?" London said as she walked towards the hall.

"What the hell just happened?" Emma said finally able to speak.

Lila laughed, "I am not sure."

Brody shook his head, "London is a doll. Very smart and well spoken," he smiled as he passed by, "And your mother, well she is a treat," he whispered in her ear.

"Holy shit," Emma said loudly.

"Mom, that's a bad word," London said as she returned.

"I am sorry honey, but it's a grown up word…" Emma started.

"I know if adults decide to use vulgar language, they can. It's a sign that their vocabulary is lacking," London laughed as she walked in the bathroom.

Emma laughed, "Eating those words right now." Brody walked back in smirking, "Are you enjoying yourself?"

"I am a great deal," Brody flashed her a big perfect smile and his eyes twinkled.

Emma looked at him and took a quick breath, he looked at her as if he was confused and then smiled with his whole face. *Oh Emma, you are going to be so much fun*, Brody thought. He winked at her.

"Mom, so what are we doing tonight?" London bound down the hallway.

"What would you like to do?" Emma grabbed her hand and sat on the couch.

London sat down, "Dinner and a show?"

"What would you like to see?" Emma asked.

"Wicked, Dad was supposed to take me and well that didn't work out," London said and looked upset briefly, "But the show must go on right?"

"Absolutely," Emma hugged her. She closed her eyes and took a deep breath and swallowed. "We will see what we can do, but no promises. It's Friday night who knows if we can get tickets," Emma got up and grabbed her laptop and walked back out, London wasn't there.

Emma walked in the kitchen, and London was sitting on a stool next to Brody talking to his friends.

"You disappeared on me," she kissed London's head.

London smiled, "I was just meeting Joe, Max and Quinn. They are going to fly back to England today. Nice to meet you all," London jumped down, "Mom I am going to shower, to get ready to go out," Emma sucked in her lips not to smile. "So if Brody's friends are leaving he should go with us, wouldn't want him to be lonely without them. Lila said she would go," London disappeared down the hall.

"She has grown up so much Emma," Lila laughed.

"Yay when did that happen," Emma wondered out loud. "Last weekend," she said quietly lost in thought.

"Emma she seems fine," Lila said.

Emma looked up and forced a smile on her face, "I suppose."

"So Brody are you going out tonight?" Quinn asked.

"Oh he couldn't, he would be seen," Emma shook her head. "That must suck."

"Potty mouth," London said from behind her, "Is there Halloween in England?"

"Yes, it is not as immensely celebrated as it is here, why do you ask?" Brody asked with amusement in his voice.

"Well we could dress you up, no one would even notice," London said raising her eyebrow.

"Oh yay? What would I be?" Brody smiled.

"Maybe Glenda," London laughed loudly.

"I am sure that would go unnoticed, a six foot tall man in women's clothing in New York City? Not as odd as one would think London," Joe laughed teasingly.

"Drag queens?" London asked.

"London, did grandma teach you that?" Emma asked shocked.

"Mom do you remember recess?" London raised her eyebrow and putting her hand on her hip. "So Brody, if you would like to join us I will come up with something, think about it," London said as she walked to the bathroom.

"Who is that and what has she done with my daughter?" Emma looked down. "You don't have to go," Emma said to Brody.

"I think I want to," Brody smiled, "Unless you would prefer I don't come along."

"No, that's not what I was saying, I just don't want you to feel like you have to," Emma said sincerely.

"Emma dear, if he didn't want to go he would not go," Max smiled. "I think he like's your daughter," he laughed.

Emma smiled, "Alright then, I am going to go see about tickets."

Emma was searching online when the guys were leaving. They came in to say goodbye.

"It was nice meeting you all," Emma said and hugged each of them.

"I am certain we will see each other again," Joe said and gave her a big kiss. Emma laughed.

"Alright London, it's not looking good for tonight, unless we want nose bleed seats" Emma said showing her the computer.

"What about tomorrow night? Front row center?" London smiled.

"Sure London, we can stay with Granma and Grandpa tomorrow night," Emma grabbed London and pulled her on her lap and hugged her.

"No way, you are staying here, we can hang out all weekend. I don't have anything pressing going on," Lila said and snuggled into them, "Where are we going to dinner London?"

"I don't care, where do you think Brody?" London smiled.

"What kind of food do you like? Mac and cheese, chicken nuggets?" Brody asked.

"Processed food? No, we don't do that, it's full of chemicals. I like chicken, veggies, and pasta. How about you?" London asked.

"Chicken nuggets and Mac and cheese," he laughed. "I am not a good cook."

"We can teach you, right Mom?" London asked.

"Well not everyone wants to learn how to cook London," Emma smiled.

"Do you cook London?" Brody asked.

"I can cook some things. Pasta, eggs, toast, oatmeal, and I help make cookies. Mom's chocolate chip cookies are the best," London exclaimed.

"Well maybe you could cook us dinner, breakfast for dinner sounds good right?" Brody asked.

"I am in New York City, I want to go out," London audaciously said.

They all laughed, "Where to London?" Emma asked.

"Tavern on the Green, I saw it in a movie," London smiled.

"Let's see what we can do?" Emma said and looked up the number. "Do you both want to come?"

"Off course," London said looking at Brody and then Lila, both accepted with a smile.

"Okay then," Emma smiled.

~

They ate dinner at Tavern on the Green. Brody decided he didn't have to dress up. It was a place he knew he could go and not be bothered. When they left they took a horse and carriage ride through Central Park and when they returned to Lila's apartment. London was fast asleep. Emma tucked her in and kissed her. She waited for her little sleepy shake that she had done since infancy that let Emma know she was in a deep enough sleep to leave the room without her waking up.

Lila and Brody were sitting on the couch talking when Emma walked out.

"Is she asleep?" Lila asked.

"Yes, she is. Thanks for going with us tonight and for dinner, although I am annoyed by that just so you know, Brody," Emma said sternly.

"Then you're going to be truly annoyed with Lila, she got four tickets for Wicked tomorrow," Brody laughed.

"I am perfectly capable of taking care of myself and my daughter," Emma said and her face turned red.

"Emma, I wanted to. We wanted to. It's not charity, so stop acting like that and sit with us," Lila said as she patted the couch next to her.

"I have to check my email," Emma said and started to walk away.

Brody grabbed her hand, "Here use mine."

Emma thanked him and sat and opened her inbox. She smiled and read.

"What are you smiling about?" Lila said.

"I have an offer," Emma said, "And if I were ready it would be a fabulous offer, look at this."

Lila read, "Emma, you need to think about this. Sleep on it, this could be huge for you and London."

"I would have to move London… again, I would be away from her for a lot of hours. I want to be able to work from home, to work when she is busy. She doesn't have someone she can count on to fill my void," Emma said. "I can't do that to her. It would change everything, again."

"Emma don't think like that, don't do it to her. Do it for her," Lila said softly.

Emma felt her eyes burning and excused herself and went to the bathroom and cried. She was overwhelmed, completely overwhelmed. Emma knew what living paycheck to paycheck meant. She had never had to live not knowing when she would get support or knowing there was money coming in from somewhere. Now she was waiting to be called in to work when someone was sick, in order to get paid. Emma stood up and washed her face and walked back out.

"Everything alright Emma?" Brody stood and gazed down at her, she smiled. "Hmm, that's a fake smile," he said softly, "It's alright to be upset."

"Welcome back deep Brody," she smiled.

"Anytime Emma," he said and kissed the top of her head.

"Emma I am not trying to interrupt your moment, but you should look at this," Lila said and handed her the iPad.

Emma read her email. Writers House had offered her a job, it was a flat salary plus commissions. Emma would be required to come in three days a week for six hours a day with the possibility of less office time dependent upon performance. Emma's starting salary would be eighty five thousand a year. Tears started to roll down Emma's face, and she smiled. Emma looked at Lila.

"It's almost perfect," she smiled softly.

"Emma, do it for both of you," Lila said.

"It will change her whole way of life," Emma said quietly looking down.

"Emma, is that such a bad thing?" Lila said.

"Probably not," Emma hugged her knees.

Brody looked at Lila, he was trying not to react. His eyes wide and jaw set. Lila smiled at him.

"Do what you have to do," she laughed, "both of you, goodnight."

"Goodnight," Emma said softly and cleared her voice. She sat up and grabbed his iPad and read the rest of her emails as he sat at the edge of the couch knee bouncing and foot tapping. "You are very noisy, occupational hazard?"

"God Emma are you alright," he said finally breathing out.

"I am, are you?" Emma laughed quietly when she saw that his face mirrored what she was feeling inside.

"No, not really," Brody said and threw himself back into the couch.

Emma sat down the iPad and turned towards Brody.

"What's wrong?" She asked concerned.

He laughed, "Emma you were crying, which means you are not alright?"

"I will be, just have to figure it out," Emma laughed trying to make light of the situation.

"And you don't like to, and you're hurting," he said intensely.

"Brody are you going to be okay?" Emma said nervously.

He took a deep breath and looked down shaking his head, "What the hell is it with you?"

"I am not sure what you mean Brody, but you need to breathe," Emma said and grabbed his hand gently.

He laughed, "This is not happening, I want to make sure you are alright not the other way around. I should leave you alone, I am not making this any easier, for fuck sake you feel like you have to take care of me," Emma looked down and scowled. Brody grabbed her and pulled her onto his lap and held her.

She didn't breathe, he kissed her head and pushed his forehead into hers, "I need you to be alright, or I am going to kill that bastard."

"You would not fare well in prison," Emma hugged him.

Brody hugged her tighter, "No?"

Emma laughed, "No."

"This is hard for you, I know how damaged I felt after Ariel screwed around. I didn't have a beautiful little girl to take care of and Emma I have never known a person in my life who put another human being's well being ahead of their own dreams and desires, until now," Brody sighed sweetly, "But after meeting her, I get it. Your daughter is precious."

"Thank you, I am a Mom, and not any different than many people who have kids. We all want what's best for our children. I am just highly aware that everything I do affect's her and that will affect the rest of her life, nothing special," Emma said. "So Brody Hines, tell me about your family," Emma said looking up at him.

"Not much to tell, you could Google it," he smiled.

"I prefer to hear it from you if you want to talk. If not I can Google it," Emma laughed.

"Do you need to know Emma?" Brody swallowed hard.

Emma looked at him, "Not if it's going to hurt you."

"Emma, how do you feel about me now?" Brody asked.

"Well, I have to say I am confused. I know I care about how you feel, but honestly I care about how everyone feels," Emma laughed.

"No, how do You feel about Me?" He asked with an intensity that made her stomach flip.

"Well I like you. I like to be around you. I like that you seem to like me. I like, how you seem to like my daughter. I like your music, even if you don't believe me," she laughed, "I like your sense of humor, have I said enough. Have I answered your question?"

"What don't you like about me?" Brody asked pulling her hair back away from her face.

"That your making me feel uncomfortable, right now, by asking a lot of questions," she paused hoping he would change the subject, and he didn't, "I don't like your age, I feel like Mrs. Robinson, I don't like that I am attracted to you. I don't like that I feel drawn to you. I don't like that you're a celebrity."

Brody smiled and lifted her chin and kissed her gently.

"I like to kiss you," Emma said and kissed him hard taking his hair in her hands and pulling his face harder into hers.

He tastes so damn good, not like alcohol or like gum trying to mask alcohol. His taste was hot and sweet, *and I want more* she thought.

He pulled her up and she sat on his lap straddling him, his lips never leaving hers. His kisses became harder and more possessive, she pulled back to breathe, and he kissed down her neck and back to her ear. He moaned as he pulled at her ear and she became intensely aware of his excitement.

"I think we should stop," Emma said and pulled further back and he put his hands up, and she fell backwards. Emma was leaning backwards holding herself up with her hands on the floor laughing.

"What is this scar from?" Brody asked as he kissed her stomach.

Oh God she thought.

"Brody, please" she whimpered as he kissed her stomach and licked her belly button, "Oh," she let out and he pulled her up and smiled a hot sexy smile that made her feel like she was going to explode right there.

"Stop smiling at me," Emma said raising her eyebrow as she stepped off him.

He smirked as he watched her try to get herself together.

"Cut it out" she whispered. "I thought you were curious about my feelings Brody."

"I was until I found your belly button," he said and pulled her back down and kissed her.

"Oh no," Emma said smiling. "No, no no," she told herself as she stood up.

"Emma, sit back down here," he said and pulled her onto him.

"Brody as much fun as it is sitting here on…you, I need to go to sleep," Emma kissed him and sat back and smiled.

"Are you sure Emma?" Brody said kissing her.

"Brain yes, body No," she said breathlessly as she stood up. "How many people have you slept with?"

"Um, I am not sure?" Brody said confused.

"I have had sex with one person," Emma said sitting next to him, Brody laughed uncomfortable. "And you don't even have a number."

"I'm sorry. I can tell you I have had sex with seven people in the seven years I have lived in the U.S." Brody said shaking his head.

"And the…" she held her hands up counting, "Seven years before that?"

"Emma, they were very busy years," Brody expressed his amusement while uncomfortably shaking his head.

"Did you use condoms?" Emma asked.

"Really are we having the sex talk Emma?" Brody responded tilting his head slightly to the side.

"Do you want to make… fuck me Brody?" Emma inquired in a straightforward tone looking him in the eyes.

Brody gasped in shock from her curt statement and smiled, "Yes I do want to have sex with you."

"Have you been tested for STD's?" Emma crossed her arms and raising her eyebrow.

Brody grabbed her with one arm around her waist and held the back of her head tightly to his face and kissed her, and she melted, he pulled away leaving her panting.

"Do you want me Emma?" he whispered in her ear and kissed her neck.

"Uh huh, I want you…too, yes." Emma breathed out.

He laid her down on the couch and kissed her as she lay there letting him, and her head was spinning, "Oh please… not now."

He kissed her mouth and sat up, "Okay Emma, I had sex with at least twenty women before moving here."

"That's a lot," Emma whispered and sat up keeping her eyes closed.

"I was tested a year ago, free and clear. I will do it again if you need me to," Brody said looking at her, "Emma open your eyes, do you need me to get tested?"

"Uh huh," she said and opened her eyes.

"Have you been tested?" He laughed.

"Yes, every year since London was born, oh God I hope she didn't wake up, what time is it?" Emma reached across him to grab her phone. "It is two in the morning?"

"Time flies" Brody smiled.

"My daughter gets up every morning at six thirty, you won't be laughing when I have her wake you up," Emma said trying to make him nervous.

"Well then…. I am going to have a shower," Brody said and kissed her gently as he whispered in her ear, "and jerk off."

Emma tried to hide her smile, "Really? Can I watch?"

"Are you serious?" Brody tried to hide the excitement in his voice.

"No, I think you can handle it," Emma tried to stop smiling as she stood up "Pun intended," she said and gently kissed his head.

"No one has ever told me no Emma," Brody said quietly, "It's going to make me try that much harder."
"Get tested, good night music man," Emma said as she walked into the bathroom.

When Emma finished in the bathroom she started to walk out, and he pushed her gently into the bathroom, "I need to check something out, I am fairly certain I don't need to be tested for this," he said as he reached under her shirt and squeezed her breast gently as he kissed her.

"Nice," he said and pulled her in to kiss him.

He held her against him, and she felt her bra unsnap. In one swift move, he lifted her shirt and bent down and took her breast in his mouth and took the other in his hand. She leaned against the counter, and he lifted her up and sat her on it. His mouth was full, and he sucked and tugged gently at her erect nipple as he used his fingers mimicking his movements on the other breast. Emma felt her body begin to burn.

"Oh God," she moaned and he tugged harder, it was almost painful if not for the pleasure she felt.

"You have to stop," she moaned as her hand rubbed his stomach. "Brody I need you to stop, because I don't think…oh God…I don't think I will be able to… please."

He released her and kissed up her neck to her mouth.

He looked in her eyes, "You need to leave," he laughed deeply through clenched teeth "before I tear the rest of your clothes off and take you in the shower."

"Sorry," Emma said.

He kissed her again, "Don't be, get out," his laugh dark and jaw clenched.

"Thank you," Emma said and kissed him. "Good night," she said as he pulled his shirt off looking into her eyes intensely.

He dropped his pants, and her eyes widened. *Brody… commando*, she thought, and damn he was perfect. *Wipe that stupid grin off your face Cheshire cat* Emma thought.

"Emma, five, four, three, two…" he counted down pausing briefly between numbers and she grinned.

"Goodnight," Emma said closing the door.

Chapter 5

"Mom, let's make breakfast, "Emma opened her eyes.

"What time is it?" Emma asked.

"Almost seven, I slept in," London smiled.

London turned on music and she and Emma danced around the kitchen to Kids Bop, Payphone was playing as they fried eggs and made toast. London was singing and when the chorus started they both sang and danced.

Here is my silly smiling girl, Emma thought.

Beiber's *Boyfriend* played as London buttered her toast and Emma took her hands and twirled her. Next was Train's Drive By, London knew it was one of Emma's favorites, and they danced and sang loudly laughing.

Brody walked up to London and twirled her as he sang. When the song ended London looked at him and curtsied. Brody bowed and kissed her hand. Emma was smiling as she plated the food. London changed the song to Just The Way You Are. Emma smiled.

"Mom." London said, "You're not singing it to me."

"I don't do well in front of an audience," Emma smiled. "But for you London…"

Emma started singing. Brody joined her, and London laughed.

"Mom," London said looking at her when the song finished, "I love you."

"I love you more," Emma said kissing her and twirling her around.

Lila came out, "Its Saturday and seven thirty in the morning."

"Good morning Lila," London said and jumped down and hugged her. "I made you breakfast."

Lila smiled, "Well then seven thirty is perfect."

Brody cleaned his plate and thanked London, "I have a few things to do this morning, I will see you ladies later?"

"Where are you going?" London asked.

"London that's none of our concern" Emma scolding her softly.

"It's fine Emma, I have a doctors appointment," Brody smiled and briefly glanced up at Emma and raised his eyebrow.

"On a Saturday, you must be sick," London said and jumped up to feel his head, Brody laughed. "No, you're not warm," London giggled. "But my friends think you are hot."

"London," Emma said shocked.

"Emma she is fine, and apparently her friends have great taste," he winked at London as he made his way to his room.

"Mom I am going to shower," London said when they finished dishes.

"Okay," Emma said and smiled remembering that just six months ago she insisted on bubble baths, and she had to help her wash her hair. Emma now only insisted on scrubbing her scalp three times a week.

Brody walked out and smiled at Emma, "Good morning," he said and kissed her.

"Good morning," Emma said trying not to look at him as she smiled looking down. He laughed, "You have a doctor appointment this morning?"

"Why do you sound shocked, you kind of insisted," Brody smiled as he lifted her chin and kissed her gently.

"I am pretty bossy huh?" Emma smiled.

"You're wonderful," Brody said and kissed her again.

"Okay thank you," she said trying to will her way out of his arms.

The shower turned off, and he slowly kissed her again and let go.

"Emma I am leaving to go to England in three days," Brody said and looked hurt.

Emma felt a lump in her throat and smiled, "To finish your album right?"

"I would love for you to come Emma," Brody said. "I know you can't, but I want you to know that I want you and your daughter to come."

"Thank you," Emma said. "How long will you be gone?"

"Three weeks and six days," Brody answered softly.

"Okay then," Emma smiled.

"Forged smile," Brody said and stepped towards her to kiss her.

"Mom," London yelled.

"Coming," Emma said, "Good luck today."

~
Emma helped London get ready, and they had decided to go shopping. To Emma's delight London was on a mission to pick out a disguise for Brody to wear at the show that night. They went and got Pedicures and ate lunch. London all but begged to ride the subway and Emma didn't cave.

They returned to Lila's at three in the afternoon, three hours before the play. Brody and Lila were looking at something online.

"Hello, are you excited about Wicked?" London skipped up to Lila and Brody.

Brody smiled, "I need to talk to your Mom first okay? Emma may I have a moment," he said as he walked towards the bedroom.

"I don't think that's a good idea, London is…" Emma started.

Brody smiled, "Trust me," he said pulling her in to the room he was staying in, "sit please."

"Okay," Emma blushed.

He smiled and shook his head as he sat next to her and showed her a website with a picture of the four of them taking the carriage ride. Brody was sitting next to London, and both were beaming.

"Well you both look great," Emma took a deep breath.

"Does this upset you?" Brody asked. "Her privacy being violated, those scum taking pictures of her?" he said in an angry tone.

"I don't like it, I bet she will," Emma smiled as she looked up at him.

"What about your divorce Emma?" Brody looked apologetically at her.

"I am not worried, he kind of sealed his own fate with that one, I hope anyway. I don't know, are you alright with it?" Emma looked confused.

"I am never alright with my privacy being invaded," Brody scowled. "I am not alright with hers or yours being invaded either."

"Alright but really what can we do about it?" Emma asked.

"I don't think it's a good idea for me to go this evening Emma," Brody said.

"Oh," she said shocked.

"That upsets you?" Brody took her hand gently in his.

"Well London kind of went crazy on a disguise today," Emma laughed. "But she will understand I suppose."

He smiled and shook his head. "She did?"

"Yes, it was actually kind of funny," Emma smiled.

"Do you want to discuss this with her or maybe I could tell her my doctor wants me to stay in for a few days?" Brody asked.

"I don't lie to her Brody. I answer her truthfully with age appropriate answers of course, hoping that will help her do the same in years to come," Emma smiled.

"Alright then," Brody stood up.

Emma smiled at him, "Can I kiss you? I mean…sorry that was stupid, this is obviously a poor idea, I mean quit while you're ahead…."

"Are you done Emma?" Brody scowled, and she shook her head yes, "would you like to know what the doctor said?"

"Sure, what did he say?" Emma's face started to turn red.

"All the test results came back, and I am healthy. Blood work was rushed so I should know in a couple days," Brody said looking in her eyes and she knew he was trying to figure something out.

"Oh, a few days?" Emma asked.

"Yes, why?" Brody asked.

"Well I will be home, and you will be in England right?" Emma asked.

"Oh so we have to wait until everything comes back?" Brody asked confused.

"Well yes," Emma smiled and looked away.

"So no condoms?" Brody asked.

"I am allergic to latex," Emma looked down.

"Good to know," Brody said.

"Are you monogamous? I mean..." Emma started and he interrupted.

"Emma do you want me to be?" Brody tried not to laugh.

"No, I want you to have sex with lots of other people while you...you know what this is irresponsible. Let's just forget it" Emma said and stood up.

"Emma," he said grabbing her hand and pulling her onto him, "I haven't had sex in months. I am particularly choosey now, and I am choosing you, I trust you."

"How do you trust me? How am I supposed to trust you?" Emma said standing back up.

"Have I given you reason not to?" Brody asked seriously.

"You didn't tell me about your past," Brody looked hurt, "I am sorry, but you should know the only person I did this with was Troy. I made him wait two years. I knew him truly well. I am not trying to hurt you. I'm just, not like that. I already feel like, I don't know a week is truly too soon."

He looked down and didn't say anything.

"Okay this is a bad idea, I'm sorry." Emma stood up and walked out.

She walked into the living room, "Hey London we need to chat," Emma said looking at her smiling.

Brody walked out and looked at Lila, his eyes wide and confused.

"Ok some silly person took pictures last night, see right here?" Emma said showing her. "I am sorry. Does it upset you?"

"No, it's kind of cool," London smiled.

"Ok so it bothers me, and it bothers Brody that someone would invade your privacy. He isn't going with us tonight," Emma said.

"But we got him all this stuff mom, it was going to be fun," London was upset.

"Sorry London, maybe I could wear it?" Emma smiled and hugged her.

"Does he know it's not his fault Mom?" London whispered.

"I don't think so London, but we are not going to cause a scene, it will be fine," Emma said and hugged her closer and closed her eyes.

"I need to use the bathroom," she whispered and stood up and walked away.

"You alright London?" Lila asked.

"I am fine," London said and smiled just like her Mom did when she was upset, and Brody noticed.

"Sorry London," Brody said. "It's not your fault, it's those people who took the pictures."

" It's not your fault," London repeated. "But why is my Mom upset?"

"I don't know," Brody said looking down.

"Are you sorry about that?" London asked and looked at him raising her eyebrows.

"Well if I upset her I am truly sorry about that," Brody said softly.

London smiled at him, "She will be fine, she always is."

London's eyes looked into his for a while. He didn't turn away and they both ended up smiling. When her mother came out she looked at her and smiled.

"We should bake cookies," Emma said and smiled at London as she grabbed her hand and pulled her into the kitchen.

Lila looked at Brody, and he looked at her and shook his head.

"What's going on?" Lila asked quietly.

"She isn't ready Lila, and I am," Brody said sadly.

"Emma will never think she is ready. They have been separated for over a year. She hasn't dated or hooked up or done anything that wasn't well planned, perfectly and precisely," Lila smiled.

"I get that, she just wants to know things Lila, things that I have put behind me and am not ready to bring back. Is it not enough that I care for her? I went and got tested for disease today Lila what is that about?" Brody said shaking his head as Lila tried not to laugh.

London skipped in the room, "Do you need anything at the store, Mom and I have to get a few things," she said waving the list.

"I need a lot of things at the store, how about we go together and let your mother start getting ready to bake," Lila asked and walked in the kitchen and told Emma they would be right back.

~

When they left Brody walked into the kitchen and hugged Emma from behind.

"Brody, please don't," Emma said softly and tried to turn around.

"Please just stay," he said holding her firmly. "So my past is not something I enjoy talking about, at all. However you are important to me so I will let you know a few things. My mother died when I was twelve. I was withdrawn, my father was not home very much at all. My brother moved out, and my father's much younger girlfriend moved in. I left and lived with my Aunt and Uncle for a couple years and then started singing and partying and having lots of sex. I am not proud of who I was then or the amount of sexual partners I had. I hooked up with a seriously wild partner, and we partied hard. She died and I moved here," Brody said, and she could hear him trying to breathe calmly. "I understand that sex is different for you than it has been for me, young, dumb, and reckless. All physical," he said, and she heard the smile in his voice, "You as a sign of love or something special."

"We went from your life to sex awfully fast," Emma said softly.

"Emma yesterday and last night, I thought that meant you wanted me as badly as I want you, and today you are ready to walk. I am confused," Brody said still holding her.

"You're going to England. I am going to try to fix this mess that I have made of my life so that my daughter can have a good life," Emma said and turned to him, "Brody wanting you and doing the right thing… I don't know they don't seem to fit."

"Maybe not when your head is spinning Emma, when your feet are planted solidly where they are meant to be. It will fit perfectly. It will feel as if they were supposed to be there forever. You may not want to hear this Emma, but I know I fit perfectly with you. It was not planned, I did not search for this, I did not even know I wanted this or even that I would immediately feel this ever with anyone. It just showed up and I literally ran into it, and I feel like I have been chasing you ever since. Emma I want more than one night, I want you to know that. I am not going on a European sex campaign. I am going to finish my album. After that, I am going to take a break, a long break. When I return I would love to see where this leads. I know you're used to making all the plans and decisions, but I also know you don't like it. I want you now and when I get back and no one in between. I don't need you to promise you'll be here waiting when I return, I know you would be. I do not need you to put it into words. It is visible in your face, your kiss, the way you look at me. You feel the same way I do. If things were not messy would you have given us a chance? Emma turn the hurt off and feel it, feel what we have both been trying to avoid that has only grown deeper."

She stood on her toes and kissed him, and he sat her on the counter and kissed her back, he pulled back and smiled. "What did that mean?"

"I want you to dress up all stupid tonight and go with us," Emma kissed him again. "I need to figure my life out, and I do believe you think you want this."

"I don't think Emma, I know. Emma what do you want?" Brody asked.

"A happy life," Emma said, and he hugged her.

"Alright then, me too," Brody kissed her gently.

They heard the door open and London ran in with the chocolate chips and real butter.

"Mom you look happier. What did you do Brody?" London smirked.

"Well London, I agreed to go tonight, for you," Brody picked her up and spun her around.

London smiled and let out a belly laugh that Emma had not heard in months, one that she missed terribly.

"What do you say, shall you let me see what magnificent outfit you have picked for me?" Brody laughed.

~

London stood in the hallway waiting for Brody to come out of the bathroom. Brody walked out and smiled at her. He wore baggy army green pants and a light pink shirt and matching green blazer.

"I kind of like this," Brody smiled.

"How about the hat, wig, and glasses?" London grinned.

"I thought I should save those for later," he said. "Are the cookies done?"

"Looking good Mr. Hines" Emma laughed. "Put on the glasses."

He put them on and Emma smiled. *He looks good in glasses, kind of like Clark Kent.* Emma thought. He looked at her and wondered what she was thinking.

"Thank you Emma," he smiled. "Where are those cookies?"

"Lose the glasses and I will give you some," Emma said seriously and turned around.

"I think Mom likes the nerd look," London whispered, "Maybe you should leave them on, I mean if you want to?"

"What do you think I should do London?" Brody whispered back.

"Whatever you want to," she said, and belly laughed again.

Emma turned and smiled, "What's so funny?" she asked as she put cookies and milk in front of them.

London looked at Brody and smiled, he raised his eyebrow and peered over the glasses at her. "Thank you for the cookies Emma," he said seductively.

She looked shocked and turned around, "You're welcome. I am going to get ready."

Brody and London laughed as she walked out the door.

"You like my Mom don't you?" London asked.

"She is very likable," Brody answered and took a bite of his cookie.

"But you *really* like her right?" London asked with her eyes wide.

"I *really* like this cookie," he smiled giving her the same wide eyed look.

London rolled her eyes and groaned.

"Can you keep a secret?" Brody whispered.

"Yes," London whispered back.

"Yes, I do. But don't tell her please," Brody said quickly and smiled at her.

"Brody, I think she knows," London smiled.

"Okay so what should I do?" Brody whispered.

"Well I am only seven, so I am not sure, but don't treat her like my Dad did," London whispered softly. "He was, well is not nice to her."

"He loves you though, the best he knows how, right?" Brody asked and put his arm around her.

"I guess," London said, and tears began to form in her eyes. "Mom doesn't think I know but that night when you let them take your car to get me, he was doing drugs, and when we left the Police were there and well I haven't talked to him since."

Brody picked her up and hugged her, "London, I think you should tell your mother these kinds of things. She loves you and only wants what is best for you."

"I can't," London hugged him back, "It will hurt her."

"Well, it hurts you not to talk about it right?" Brody asked.

"I guess," London said and sat up and wiped her face. "If you tell her you love her I will tell her about that, I go first. That way she get's bad news then happy news, is it a deal?"

"Oh I don't know," Brody said nervously. "Don't you think I should tell her I want to be more than friends before I lay that on her?"

"Maybe," London laughed and hugged him, "I would not want her to faint."

They were laughing and hugging when Emma walked out in the kitchen.

"What's going on here?" Emma asked and saw London's red eyes.

"London needs to tell you something," Brody said and smiled gently at her. "Go on," he smiled at her.

London told her everything she had told Brody, and more. London had tried to go back into her room to grab her favorite stuffed animal, the one she had that smelled like her mom, and there were several people occupying her room. London cried and so did Emma. Brody hugged them both and tried to control the emotions he was feeling.

After awhile London looked up at Brody, "A deal is a deal, now it's your turn."

Brody smiled and shook his head, "Hey Emma, I like you a lot."

He smiled. London scowled at him and he took a deep breath, "I want to be more than just Lila's friend," London laughed, and he looked at her. "I want to be more than just your friend."

"Brody I don't think now is a good time to discuss this," Emma said nervously.

"Mom seriously? You like him too!" London laughed. "You two should grow up," she said jumping down and laughing, "I am going to get ready, deal with this like adults please."

Brody smiled softly at Emma, "Are you alright?"

"No, what am I going to do for her?" Emma said and started crying.

"She is incredibly smart and has you Emma, do what is best for her," Brody hugged her.

"Thank you," Emma said and pulled away.

"Don't think Emma, tonight we are going to a show. We are going to have fun. Tomorrow I would like to help you figure this out. And you are going to let me," Brody said and kissed her, "No arguments."

Chapter 6

On the ride to the show, Emma tried not to think about how much pain Troy had caused London. She looked at Brody in that goofy wig and suit and glasses and listened to him talk to London who obviously adored him. Emma felt very comfortable and at ease with him. She still didn't like that there was such a big age difference, especially since she was the older one. But he actually seemed more mature in different ways than she was. Brody was decisive and didn't seem to go back and forth or be led by feelings, except for anger when it came to Emma, which was a quality she loved about her own father. He even did something he loved. Not because of fame but because it was what he was passionate about. He was soft and caring, but took control when he felt he needed to. Emma smiled as she looked at him, London nudged him, and they glanced at Emma. He smiled at London as he pulled her attention away from Emma's now red face to the different landmarks they passed. He looked over at Emma who was still looking at him. She raised her eyebrow and smiled shaking her head when she was able to look away.

After the show, Brody carried London to bed, and Emma tucked her in. Lila had already gone to bed when they walked out of the bedroom.

"Did you have fun Emma?" Brody smiled.

"I did, it was a great show. Did you?" Emma tore her eyes away from him as he took off the hat and wig.

"I did. Emma are you allergic to lambskin?" Brody asked matter of factly as he walked towards her.

"No, I don't think so," Emma said confused. "Are you allergic to anything?"

"Cats, they are hideous creatures. Okay so I am not in reality allergic I just don't like them, and it's easier to say I am." Brody was in mid sentence when she kissed him.

"Emma" he gasped and pulled gently away. "If that continues, I may turn a color that matches my eyes."

"I'm sorry" Emma turned away.

He took her hand and led her to the room he was occupying.

"Lay down, I want to tell you a story," he smiled.

Brody laid next to her, "Once upon a time there was a beautiful princess who had a beautiful daughter who just happened to be named after a beautiful city," he began, and she giggled.

"Well that beautiful princess had been locked up in a tower by a dreadful ogre whom we shall call...hmm Roy," he kissed the back of her head.

"He did not know what he had, and he lost sight of what was perfect and precious right before him. The princess finally escaped his evil clutches and vowed to keep the little princess safe. She suited up, full armor and carried with her a sword. She fought the Ogre and won, but she could not believe it so after she had fought off the Ogre... Roy, she fought off her feelings for any other that came to her. One day a tall, handsome, Prince came to her, wanting badly to be part of her life. Did I mention he was handsome?" Brody said with a smile in his voice, "Oh and smart, the Prince was handsome, and smart, extremely smart."

"Hot," Emma said and giggled.

"Well if you say so, but this is my story Princess, I mean Emma, so please quiet down," Emma laughed, and Brody cleared his throat. "Where was I?"

"The Prince was hot," she said grinning.

"Thank you, now do be quiet. Okay so this Princess she let no one in. She fiercely protected what she loved. With every day that passed, the armor she wore became heavier and began to rust. After many months it began to weigh her down to the point that she did not realize she was breaking underneath it," Brody said with sadness in his voice.

"Well the Prince desperately wanted to save her. He vowed that regardless of how much time, and how blue he may turn," Brody smiled, "he would strip her of that armor so that she could shine, so her radiant light could help those she loved shine even brighter in her glow. The end." Brody said and kissed her head.

"That was a remarkably nice story," Emma smiled and yawned.

Brody laughed.

"Sorry," Emma laughed. "What time…" Emma began to say.

"It's almost midnight, I think I may start telling you a story about a white rabbit with a giant pocket watch," he laughed and rubbed her back.

Emma rolled to her side and smiled as she ran her fingers through his hair.

"You are truly sweet you know?" She smiled and sat up, "I am going to bed," Emma smiled and kissed him.

"You're in bed, stay for a bit. Please?" Brody asked.

"I can't, allergies," Emma smiled.

"I asked you to lay down for awhile Emma, not if I could have sex with you until the sun peaked over the horizon. Making you scream my name as you had orgasm after orgasm and finally caved and begged me to never leave your side," Brody smiled seductively at her.

"Oh and you are not allergic to lambskin, so allergies are not going to work," he said as he grabbed a condom out of his pocket and handed it to her.

Emma blushed and looked down at the floor with her eyes wide. She took a deep breath.

"Oh," was all she could manage to say.

Brody laughed, "Still not going to happen is it?"

"I want to I truly do, just not while my daughter is in the next room," Emma said quietly. Brody smiled at her. "I am leaving in the morning, and I don't know when I will see you again, and I don't know…."

"When do you want to see me again?" Brody propped himself up on his elbow.

Every morning, every day, she thought, and it hurts.

Emma smiled, "When will you be back? When are you leaving?"

"Well I was going to leave on Wednesday and be gone for a month," Brody said watching her.

"That's a long time," Emma said looking sadly. He smiled at her, "Why does that amuse you?"

"I am not amused Emma, I am glad you think that's a long time, I do as well. You can come with me," Brody said wishfully thinking, "So can London."

"Well London is in school, and I have court next week and we have known each other a week," Emma said quietly.

"A week and three days," Brody smiled as he looked at Emma and gently kissed her nose, "I will just keep chiseling away at that armor," Brody smiled and sat up, "One day at a time," he kissed her and pulled away from her lips.

Emma grabbed his face and kissed him again and moved so that she was sitting astride him, "I am scared, and I keep thinking I am going to wake up from a dream. You can't be real Brody, this is too much," Emma said and kissed him harder.

"Emma, I think you're awake, I know I am," he said, and she pulled his shirt over his head and kissed his neck, he moaned and sat back pulling her with him. Emma sat up and pulled her shirt off, and he watched as she un-hooked her bra.

"Emma you are so beautiful," he said as he watched her.

"Please don't talk right now," Emma kissed his chest and stomach. She moved lower and unbuttoned him.

"Emma," he moaned as he took her breast in his hand and tugged lightly at her nipple.

"I don't know how this works, you're going to have to do it," she said breathlessly handing him the silver foil package.

"Are you sure?" he sat up opening the package as she pulled his pants down.

She swallowed hard and shook her head yes. Brody flipped Emma on her back and kissed her neck and up to her lips. He moved back down to her breast and she whimpered. His hand pushed her cotton pajama pants down, and his hand moved between her legs. He looked up at her and watched as her back arched in response to his touch. He lightly kissed down her stomach and moved to her thighs. Oh wow, she thought as he skillfully kissed and licked and sucked between her legs. He eased his finger into her, and her body moved towards his touch. She tried to stay still and she couldn't. She pulled his hair and finally breathed out, she felt her toes curl and quickly started closing her legs. He reached his long sculpted arm up and caressed her breasts again, but his grasp was much firmer now and she felt her body start to release months of frustration. Brody was well aware of what was happening and continued as her body tensed.

"Brody, please" she whimpered as she tried to close her knees," he looked up at her and his eyes were full of desire as he continued. "Brody I already…"

"And you will again, you taste delightful Emma, I want more of you," his voice as deep as his lust filled eyes watched her as he slid a second finger into her, his thumb circled and pressed on her sweet spot. She felt her body pulse. How is this happening she thought, it never had before. He kissed up her belly and tugged at her nipple with his teeth as he slowly eased into her. She grabbed him and held him tightly. He moved slowly into her.

"Emma," he whispered into her ear as he tugged at it with his teeth and gently pushed into her further. "You are so tight, we will take this slow, awe you are so hot and wet," he moaned as he eased into her slowly and gently.

He watched her face and saw her tense up. He sat up on his knees and pulled her legs over his strong thick thighs. He held himself with one hand as he slowly fed his large thick penis into her as he watched. His other hand continued to stimulate her rubbing his fingers gently across her still pulsing sex. His jaws clenched as he watched and he licked his lips.

"Emma you are beautiful," he whispered easing himself into her.

"Brody," she moaned as her body pressed into him, "Please."

Brody pulled her hips to him.

"Almost, FUCK Emma," he moaned.

Emma couldn't take it she wanted all of him. Her body pulsing and throbbing with desire. She sat up on him and winced in pain and felt so full she wanted to scream, she bit down on his shoulder, and he pushed harder into her. He kissed her cheek and made his way slowly down her neck, and she gasped. Brody looked at her his eyes full of heat and her face flush. He moved faster and harder until he felt her quake. He continued as he watched her face relax and she gasped. He thrust into her as his mouth opened and he growled out her name when he released.

He lay on top of her and tried to calm his breathing. Emma closed her eyes, and the only thing she could think was *the end*.

"Emma, are you alright?" Brody asked as he lay next to her. She shook her head yes, and he pulled her head to his chest. "The sun has yet to peak over the horizon," he said with a smile in his voice.

Emma smiled, "What…" she began.

"Two in the morning," Brody smiled as he rubbed her back and kissed her head. "Not going to let me have you again?" Emma laughed softly as she fell asleep.

Brody held her as she slept. He let Emma sleep for an hour before he began kissing her neck, "Brody," she smiled.

"It's three thirty, and I will just need you to lay still for thirty minutes or so," Brody said as he rolled her to her back. He winked and crawled under the covers. She melted within minutes. He came up and reached for his pants and grabbed a condom, "You alright?"

"Uh huh," Emma said trying to breathe.

"Good," Brody lifted her up, so she straddled him and thrust deeply into her, she bit down hard on his shoulder. He flinched.

"Sorry," Emma breathed out and pushed him back and moved up and down him slowly watching his eyes closed slightly.

She closed her eyes and moved faster as he watched her. He grabbed her hips and guided her, her face flushed and he laid her back and moved swiftly. Emma pulled back to stop.

"Emma don't pull away," Brody demanded in a husky voice.

"I am going to scream or bite you," Emma said angrily.

He kissed her and grabbed the pillow, "I think if you bite me I may scream, use this," he smiled as he lay her down and continued slowly moving. "This okay?"

"Perfect," she gasped as he continued his slow powerful thrusts into her.

"You are perfect," Brody moaned and moved faster and harder. Emma dug into his muscular ass and felt her toes curl as she arched her back, Brody smiled seductively and handed her the pillow. He knew she was ready, and he hastened his powerful thrusts until she yelled his name into the pillow, he released moments later.

"I don't want you to leave Emma," he said breathlessly as he held her tightly against his naked sweaty body.

"I kind of have to, London will be up soon," Emma sluggishly sat up still trying to catch her breath.

"That's not what I mean Emma," Brody said softly as he sat up and gently rubbed her back.

Emma turned and looked at him as she pulled her bottoms on.

"I leave today," she thought out loud.

Brody hugged her, and at that moment she felt like she was supposed to be there and it scared her.

"Brody I am..."

"So am I," he said rubbing her back. "I need you to know how I feel Emma," Brody started.

"Please not yet, please," she begged softly.

"Alright, I don't think I have to even say the words Emma, you already know. And you feel the same, I know you do. Your body knows too Emma," Brody said and kissed her head.

"I can't," Emma said and pulled away and stood up composing herself. "Thank you Brody, you are amazing," she said as she walked out the door.

Brody felt frozen. He sat for a long time trying to figure out what that meant. Well that was a first, he thought to himself. Brody was not used to women leaving him, especially not after sex, he was the one who left. *Chip that Armor away*, he thought as he threw himself back on the bed and groaned in frustration. He set his alarm and finally fell asleep trying to think of what he could do to keep her.

Chapter 7

Emma woke and saw the sun and stretched as she sat up alone. She heard music when she opened the door and walked down the hall. She turned the corner, and London and Brody were laughing as they made breakfast.

"Good morning," Emma said as she walked in.

"Almost afternoon Mom," London laughed and hugged her.

"What…" Emma started.

"It's nine thirty Emma, good morning," Brody said and turned around and flashed her a smile. "Sit, London taught me how to make breakfast," he brought her a plate, "London be a dear and grab the juice?" he kissed Emma's head when London's back was turned, "Sex hair," he whispered, "I like it, especially knowing I put it there," he winked at her as Emma blushed and looked down.

~

Emma was almost finished packing and London looked at her, "If I take a shower now can I skip it when we get home?"

"That's a fabulous idea, then we can get in our PJ's and snuggle and watch a movie," Emma said and answered her phone. "This is Emma," she said and smiled as she watched London walk out the door. "I would love to, yes see you at 7:30," she hung up, "Hey London guess who will be your art teacher tomorrow?"

"Cool," London smiled knowing it would be her mother as she shut the bathroom door.

Emma brought the suit cases to the foyer, she heard Brody on the phone.

"No, just change the flight for Thursday please...no I will wait to make that change... open ended," Brody said grabbing Emma's hand as she walked by stopping her.

"Yes thank you," he said ending his call. "I am leaving Thursday after I know how court went," Emma started to interrupt and he put his finger over her lips, "Stop, please, and I am staying in a hotel half an hour from your town in case you need me. I have a meeting tomorrow and should arrive Tuesday morning if you want to see me I will be there."

Emma looked at him and down deep she fought the desire to smile, "Okay," she said and took a deep breath.

"I am fighting the need to ask you if that makes you happy or upsets you. I don't want you to feel like you need to plan or over think it, but what you want is important to me. You want a happy life, that's what you told me. I am going to do my best to make sure that's what you get, Emma I...," he started, and she knew what was coming and kissed him sucking his lower lips so that his mouth opened and he held her tightly as their tongues danced.

He pulled away and smiled at her, "You are impossible."

"We have to leave soon, I am working Monday. London has dance from four until six. You should stay here, you have a lot going on," Emma said knowing it was the right thing but desperately wanting what he had proposed.

"Plans are already in place," he winked and kissed her head and walked away. "Good morning Lila."

"Good morning," Lila said giggling as she looked at Emma's red face. "Brody you're scheduled for the Today show tomorrow before you meet with your record label."

"Why?" Brody bruited.

"You have a number one song, you are going to sing in the Plaza before you run away from your adoring fans," Lila said insistently, "We will tell them the carriage ride was a friend if asked, is that alright?"

"No, London doesn't need to be discussed on national television," Brody said protectively.

"I could always skip school and go with you," London laughed as she ran out and stood next to him.

Brody flashed her a smile, "And what would we tell them?"

"The truth, you love my Mom, and I don't know maybe someday you'll be my," she paused and looked at Emma who's jaw dropped, "Piano teacher."

Brody laughed, "Your mother may have a heart attack if I ever dare say something like that."

"London, please say your goodbyes," Emma said firmly as her neck started to heat up.

London hugged and thanked Lila and walked over to Brody and threw her arms around him and kissed him, "I like you Brody Hines."

"I adore you London, and I will miss you very much," Brody whispered and hugged her tightly closing his eyes.

"Lila thanks so much," Emma hugged her.

She looked at Brody and smiled, "Nice to see you again."

"London come here and help me get an elevator," Lila said rolling her eyes at Emma.

"I will see you soon Emma," Brody hugged her and kissed her lightly on the lips. Emma smiled, and her eyes felt heated, he noticed immediately how she was feeling exactly the same as he was, "I will see you Tuesday night."

"You don't have to, Brody this is stupid," she said widening her eyes and blinking hoping to stop the impending tears.

He smiled and hugged and kissed her again, "Poor timing, but not stupid. I will be figuring things out on my end. Oh and I am falling in love with you. There I said it and you couldn't stop me," he gazed at her with a sexy half smile.

"Brody, my feelings are no different. I just don't know how to trust, or believe, that all that will matter after a few years. London is waiting," Emma reached up and softly stroked his soft stubble and kissed him.

"Well sometimes you just have to have faith," Brody said and took her hand and kissed it as he led her to the door.

~

Emma and London walked into their home, and both looked at each other and smiled.

"Mom is it weird that I miss the city?" London asked.

"Do you miss the city London?" Emma smiled.

"Ya and I miss Brody, he was fun. Do you?" London smiled.

"I missed our couch, let's watch a movie, pick one out, I will make popcorn," Emma smiled back.

Emma's phone chimed

-I miss you Em…Yours, MM

-Who is this?...

-Music Man...I miss you.

-We just got home, feelings mutual...Em

-See you Tuesday...MM

-We shall see, sweet dreams...Em

~

Emma woke and was excited for her first day subbing. She missed Brody, especially after the highly erotic dream she had just woke up from. She grabbed her phone,

-Good Luck today Music Man...Em

-Good morning. I am extremely glad you are thinking about me. I miss you Em. Have fun at school today, I never understood the desire to teach, wasn't thirteen years enough?...MM

- I did seventeen years. Do great MM, BTW, me2...Em

-hmm...MM

Emma hit the DVR to record the Today show. She smiled and shook her head.

~

Brody was on stage with his band, and they played Blue Love. Matt the host came on stage as the crowd of women screamed and cheered.

"That is a great song, where did the inspiration come from?" Matt asked.

Brody smiled, "Well you know," and he laughed nervously.

"Alright Brody, I get it. So how have you been since the divorce?" Matt asked.

"I have been fine, life goes on," Brody gave a dazzling smile.

"Any truth behind the rumors?" Matt asked.

"Probably not, there usually isn't," he answered.

"So you're going home to finish your album?" Matt asked.

"I am," Brody replied, "I only have a couple to record and one that I just started working on about my favorite city in England," Brody beamed.

"One more song?" Matt asked.

"Absolutely," Brody smiled and winked at the camera.

They sang Over It which was a new song released that day.

Matt walked back on stage, "We have to ask Brody," Matt said, and Brody raised his eyebrow. "Who was the little girl in the carriage?"

Brody took a deep breath and looked towards Lila.

"She is a friend of my publicist," he countered in a guarded tone.

"Does she have a name?" Matt asked.

"She is a minor, someone's child. Let me ask you something Matt, you have kids right? What are their names and would you want them on national TV or magazine's or online without your consent," Brody stated rather than asked.

"Actually I would not," Matt laughed, "I need something for the fans Brody, something personal from someone they admire," Matt looked at Brody and Brody shook his head and looked down. "Alright how about something like what is your favorite candy?"

"M&M's," Brody grinned and raised his eyebrow.

"Really?" Matt responded and laughed.

"Absolutely," Brody smirked, "melts in your mouth."

"Well everyone we got something out of Brody Hines, thanks for stopping by," Matt shook his hand.

"Thanks so much everyone!" Brody yelled to his fans and flashed his stunning smile.

Brody got in the car, and Lila smiled at him, "M&M's Brody?"

"Yes, they are insanely addictive and delicious," Brody smiled sheepishly.

~

Emma and London went for a walk after school, when they came home Emma made dinner, and London did her homework. She looked at her phone willing it to ring, and it didn't. No call, no text, nothing. London showered and read Emma a story about a Princess, and Emma couldn't help but think of him. He was in her head, and nothing seemed to be able to get him out.

Emma went downstairs and grabbed the remote and skipped through the Today show until she saw him. He looked amazing, she laughed when she noticed the pants and wondered how he could have thrown together something that made them look good and laughed to herself when she realized nothing he wore could look bad, he even looked hot in those glasses. When the song finished she saw the anchor Matt walk on stage, and she worried he would be shy like he was onstage the night she and Lila went to see him sing. He was smiling and happy, and she snickered when he talked about his favorite city in England and was almost certain he was talking about London. She watched cautiously when he was asked about the carriage ride. He did extremely well, she could tell he was angry but pulled it off well. She could not believe the M&M comment but was not sure if she was assuming correctly. She rewound and played it over and over, like she did her favorite songs when she was younger.

Her phone rang, and she smiled.

"Hello this is Emma."

"Hello Emma, this is Brody," he said with a smile in his voice.

"Oh I wasn't sure which man with a British accent would be calling at this hour," she joked.

"I am sorry Emma am I calling too late?" Brody asked.

"I was joking," Emma said trying not to act overly excited that he had called.

"Did you catch the Today show?" Brody smiled.

"I recorded it, does that sound bad? Like creep you out?" Emma asked softly.

"No, are you busy? Can you watch it now while I am on the line with you?" Brody asked.

"Why?" Emma spoke as she covered her eyes, *good lord he can't even see me* she thought.

"Just want to see what you think," he said with a smile in his voice.

"Ok," she laughed and paused for a minute. "I have already watched," she laughed, "Three times."

"Okay Emma that makes you sound a little creepy," Brody laughed.

"I just had to make sure you did well, ya know in case you needed feedback," Emma said trying to defend herself.

"I love that you watched it Emma, now tell me what stuck out the most to you," he asked in amusement.

"Really?" Emma asked embarrassed.

"Yes really," Brody said in a particularly self assured voice.

"The pants were nice," Emma chuckled. "You made them look good."

"Did I?" Brody said laughing, "Emma is that all?"

"Did you hear him ask me about my favorite candy?" Brody asked trying to sound serious.

"Yep," Emma said.

"Did you know that I liked M&M's?" Brody asked.

"No," Emma said smiling to herself.

"Can I tell you a secret? Neither did I," Brody laughed, "But now it's my favorite candy."

"Well I will have to remember that," Emma said trying not to giggle like a teenage girl.

"Do I need to spell it out for you Em?" Brody asked.

"Well I guess not," Emma said.

"So you know I was talking about you?" Brody asked.

"I do now," she smiled.

"Good, did London see it?" Brody asked.

"No!" Emma said sharply.

Brody laughed, "I am sure she would not get it."

"Well I certainly hope not," she said and laughed, so hard tears were falling.

Brody laughed, "I miss you."

"I miss you Brody," Emma said still laughing.

"I love you Em," Brody said smiling.

"Oh I love you Bro..." she stopped.

"Emma did you just call me Bro?" he snickered. She sat with her hand over her mouth, "Emma?"

She cleared her throat, "I am here, sorry."

"Hmm, I will see you tomorrow? I want to come see you after court. I also want you to know that my lawyer is going to meet yours tomorrow and be at court with you," He began without missing a beat, "Have you decided on which offer you will be accepting?"

"Brody, can we please talk about something else," Emma said calmly.

"Sure, M&M's?" he asked.

"Or how about that you are leaving in a few days for a month," she said in a remarkably dry tone.

"Do you have a problem with my Lawyer meeting yours?" Brody asked.

"I don't know why that is necessary," Emma answered.

"He is the best, and you and London deserve that, I don't want to argue with you," He said in an authoritative tone. She said nothing and he took a deep breath and said sweetly, "Emma I am in love with you, I want you and your daughter to be happy, please accept that."

"Ok," she whispered. She had tears building, and her voice cracked. "Brody I can't be your project, I can't feel like all of these feelings you're expressing are because you feel sorry for me or my situation because I will be okay. You don't have to do this. And you have to promise me," she said finally stopping to take a breath, "that when you realize this is just because you and I have both been through hell lately, you'll just tell me and not string me along. I can't do that. So please promise me."

"Are you done Em?" Brody asked in a clipped tone.

"I guess," Emma said feeling like a child.

"Chipping away," he whispered as he leaned back breathing deeply trying to regain control. "Good, so have you looked over your offers?"

"No," she pouted.

"So what are you waiting for?" Brody asked.

"Tomorrow Brody, to see what I am allowed to plan, to know that I can breathe again, to know my daughter is going to be safe," she said, and the dam finally broke, "is that what you wanted to know Brody?" Emma said harshly. "I lived many years with someone who enjoyed lording over me and making me feel like nothing, someone who loved me broken, so he felt better about himself."

"Emma I am sorry, I am so sorry." Brody sounding devastated. "Can I talk to you tomorrow?"

"Sure. Goodnight Brody," she hung up feeling awful about snapping at him.

~

The next morning Emma dropped London off at school and went home to get ready, she didn't tell her that they had court today. She did not want it to affect her.

Emma walked into court and saw her lawyer talking to a extremely sharply dressed man. Emma's lawyer Joan waved her over. "Emma this is Eli, he is your friend's lawyer. Is it alright that he discuss this with us?"

"Sure," Emma felt insecure.

They sat in a conference room, and Joan started the conversation. "Emma and I have discussed what she would like to happen today. She will be going for sole physical custody, supervised visits and the divorce to be finalized. We are pushing for Mr. Fields to agree to rehab. Emma is not asking for alimony and would prefer that child support be suspended while he is in rehab if he is not going to be paid from his employer. The other thing is that Emma is considering moving back to her hometown in order to pursue a career that will enable her to provide for her child. We will wait until we get a feel of how this is going before we spring that on them. Do you have anything to offer Emma?" Emma shook her head no, "Eli?"

"I am just here to offer advice if things start turning in a direction undesirable by your client," Eli looked at Emma, "Not to change your mind about anything."

"Thank you," Emma said softly

~

Emma walked down the courthouse stairs and past her car. She walked until she reached the park next to the lake. She walked to the end of the dock and hugged herself and crouched down and closed her eyes hugging her knees. She cried quietly until she couldn't cry anymore.

"Em," she heard softly behind her, and she stood up and turned around.

She wiped her eyes and smiled softly.

"Hi," she said.

Brody walked slowly up to her and bent down and wiped her face and smiled.

She closed her eyes and whispered, "I am so sorry."

Emma wrapped her arms around him, and he wrapped his around her, holding her tightly against him kissing her gently on the head while he gently swayed back and forth soothing her.

"You need a few more moments or are you ready to get out of here?" Brody asked taking her hands.

"I don't know," Emma smiled and shook her head.

"Well my little white rabbit, I don't know what time London gets out of school, but it's one thirty," he smiled.

"Oh," she said shocked. "Oh wow, I need to go." Emma said and looked at him.

"Can I go with you?" Brody asked.

Emma looked at him confused, "Do you want to?"

"Yes, or I wouldn't have asked. What is with you?" he laughed and she scowled. "Emma men are not that complicated, we don't ask if we don't want. I want to take two beautiful females to dinner."

"What if people see you Brody?" Emma asked.

"You're divorced Emma, so am I," Brody smiled.

"I am divorced," Emma smiled, "I have sole custody of my most precious gift, and the man I thought I loved for fifteen years is going to rehab," Emma started crying again, and Brody looked at her with deep concern, "These tears are not because I am sad, it's a release," Emma said and smiled. "I want to scream!"

"Then do it!" Brody laughed. And she raised her hands in the air and screamed. Brody picked her up and spun her around and kissed her.

"I love you Princess."

Emma wrapped her arms around his neck, "You too Brody."

Chapter 8

Brody pulled on a hat and sunglasses as he pulled in the pickup driveway at London's school. "Right here?" he asked. Emma shook her head yes, "How is she to know where to meet you, there are a lot of little people running around out here. Don't they have a system?"

Emma laughed, "She knows our car. You are truly paranoid."

"Oh yah?" he laughed. "I am going to get out and wait for her, how do you feel about that Emma?"

"You wouldn't dare," Emma laughed.

Brody opened the door, and Emma laughed.

He looked at her as if to say I am going to do it, and she laughed, "Chicken."

"Wrong thing to say Em," he laughed and took his hat off and stood outside the door and leaned against the car with his arms crossed in front of him.

Emma watched for the aide that walked London's class out to the pickup lane. She saw London and her whole body seemed to smile. She started towards the car, and the aide made her wait.

Brody bent down and looked in the window, "Is that normal Em?"

"Yes, they don't know you're here to pick her up, you don't have permission," Emma opened the door and walked around the car and waved.

The aide walked over with London, "Sorry I didn't see you, wow," she said as she looked at Brody, "You're," she stopped and couldn't finish her sentence.

"I am London's ride today," he smiled at London.

London ran up and jumped in his arms and hugged him.

He opened the door for London, "Off you go, buckle up. Thank you for seeing to it that she is safe. Ready Em?"

They sat and waited in line to pull out, and everyone was looking at them.

"London I would like to take you to dinner, where would you like to go?" Brody asked.

"The cafeteria, so they can all see that I didn't Photoshop that picture online." London said annoyed.

"Is there a bathroom in the school that I could use?" Brody said in the same irritated tone London used.

"Yes," London smiled.

"Could you show me where it is?" Brody asked, "Em could you park across the street and we will meet you there?"

"Do you think that's a good idea Brody?" Emma asked to caution him.

"If London does, do you London?" Brody glanced in the mirror.

"Yep," she opened the door, he got out and followed.

"Hop on my back London," Brody said bending down, "Tell me where to go."

"Okay, left. Hey could you lose the shades?" London pulled them off him and putting them on herself, "I look way cooler in them."

Fifteen minutes later London and Brody walked across the road towards Emma smiling. *This is not good, she adores him, when it ends it's going to break her again.* Emma thought.

"Did you find the bathroom?" She smiled and Brody looked at her with concern.

"We sure did," London smiled.

"Everything alright Em?" Brody whispered when he got in the car.

Emma smiled, "Sure. Hey London, you have dance in an hour, so we need to eat fast, where to?"

"Let's go home, I need to get my stuff. Then maybe we can go out," London said smiling.

"Alright," Emma said and pulled out. "Please excuse any mess Brody, we haven't been home a lot."

He is going to hate it, Emma thought. *It's nothing like what he must be used to. Nothing like Lila's place.*

They walked past the landscaped yard into the back screened in porch, it was small but charming. London and Emma took off their shoes, and Brody followed suit. They walked into the kitchen, and he looked around and smiled.

"This is enchanting Em," Brody said.

"It's quaint," Emma agreed.

Emma opened the fridge and grabbed some fruit and cut it up as London ran into the other room, and Brody heard her little feet pitter pattering up the stairs.

"Are you hungry?" Emma asked.

Brody smiled when he noticed the bag of M&M's sitting on the counter, Emma looked in the direction he was smiling at and blushed.

"Your face is red," Brody hugged her from behind and placed his hand low on her stomach.

"I wonder why," she said softly.

"Well actually I am ravenous," Brody whispered and grabbed a strawberry. "What can I do to help?"

Emma smiled, "Nothing, not right here or right now anyway," and shook her head as she pulled away and looked up at him.

London came out, and Emma put a small plate of strawberries and kiwi in front of her and London grabbed her book bag and took out her homework folder.

"Do you have a lot of homework?"

"Just spelling and a book to read you," London said.

"Okay," Emma said and grabbed a brush and brushed her hair as London wrote her spelling words and Emma pulled her hair into a tight bun forgetting for a brief moment that they were not alone.

"So this is our life, a little different from yours huh?"

"It's wonderful," he smiled.

"I forgot I have a roast in, so is it alright if we eat dinner here after dance?" Emma asked to hope they would agree.

She did not feel like going out after the day she had.

"Sure," London said. "Is that okay with you?"

"Sounds great," Brody answered.

"Alright then time for us to get going," Emma said filling up London's water bottle. "Grab your bag."

Brody sat in the car while Emma walked London in. he smiled when he saw her come back out.

"So what shall we do for two hours? What do you normally do?" he grabbed her hand.

"Well, I read or walk or get groceries. I think that would be a bad idea with you," she smiled.

"Alright then, we have two hours. Do you have any books?" Brody said laughing.

"No, I forgot them," Emma smirked.

"Well I think I may have a couple, I believe they're in my hotel room that just happens to be about two miles back, shall we go get them Emma?" Brody asked looking serious.

"Brody do you truly have books in your room?" Emma whispered breathlessly.

He smiled, "Well depends, I do have a book reading app on my iPad," he whispered back.

"Oh," Emma took a deep breath.

He took her hand and kissed it. "Em I understand if you don't want to be alone in a room with me."

"You do?" Emma asked.

"No," he laughed.

"Ok, you drive," Emma said and got out.

They walked into his room, and Emma was more nervous now than she was the first night she had spent with him.

"Em are you alright?" Brody asked.

"No," she said and her eyes widened.

"Well come sit," Brody said as he patted the seat next to him. Emma sat next to him wringing her hands, and he smiled. "Alright, let's see what we can do to relax you." He pulled her into him and she trembled. He kissed her cheek, "Been a rough day huh?" Emma shook her head yes and felt her face flush. He wrapped his long arms around her and held her. She finally started to relax, and she let out a deep breath.

Emma's phone rang, and she jumped up and grabbed it out of her bag.

"Hello," Emma said.

"Emma we need to talk about what happened today," Troy said.

"Okay Troy what is it?" Emma said as Brody rubbed her back.

"I want to see London," Troy said softly.

"Well I think we kind of talked about that at court," Emma said.

"Yes we discussed supervised visits, I also agreed to give you custody thinking you might do the right thing, by the way how is Lila's friend?" Troy said, "He picked my daughter up at school today?"

"We picked her up, I was there," Emma said defending herself.

"So you're not fucking him Emma?" Troy asked.

"Troy, you called asking about London please don't do this," Emma asked kindly.

"Are you fucking him?" Troy demanded.

"At this moment no, I am not fucking him," Emma snapped.

"And what about London, you said no one meets her until, holy shit Emma are you going to marry him?" Troy asked.

"Wow Troy, no, I just got divorced no plans on doing that again anytime soon, listen when you want to talk about our daughter call me," Emma said and hung up.

Her phone rang immediately.

"Yes Troy?" Emma asked.

"I want to see her before I go to rehab, I am going Saturday. I want a day possibly a night. We can get adjoining rooms at a hotel, I will pay for it. This weekend Emma," he paused, "Good, I didn't hear a no, I will text you the details, goodbye," Troy said and hung up.

Emma turned and looked at Brody, "What just happened?"

"I think you just agreed to spend an evening at a hotel with your ex," Brody said calmly.

"No, Brody it wasn't like that," Emma hugged him.

He smiled, "So if I act pissed off you hug me?" he laughed.

She grabbed his face and looked at him like she was mad and then closed her eyes and took a deep breath and leaned her forehead into his chest.

"Brody I am struggling, I can't make everyone happy," Emma started.

"I know Em, I was joking. I think you should call your lawyer and get her advice," Brody said. "Just a suggestion but, please."

She looked up at him and smiled *if this is nothing more than a distraction I will take it right now.* Emma kissed Brody and turned and sat on his lap. She kissed his neck and pulled his shirt over his head.

"You sure about this?" Brody whispered.

"Yes," Emma said lifting her arms as he pulled her shirt over her head. He kissed down her neck, and she stood and took off her skirt.

"Emma get over here," Brody said in a seductive heavy voice.

~

Emma and Brody picked up London, and they dropped Brody off. Emma had asked that she have a couple hours to talk with London alone about everything that went on today. It was a rough night, although London was well prepared for the divorce it still upset her. She was more upset about the fact that Troy was demanding time when he had not even called her since the night everything happened at the beach. She wanted to see him before he went to rehab, but not overnight, unless she was allowed to stay in the same room as Emma. Emma's parents were planning to come up and stay with London during the visit and Emma would stay the night with the adjoining door shut and locked. Emma had never been afraid of him, but lately she had no idea who the man she had been with for fifteen years was.

When London went to school Emma decided to surprise Brody and drove to the hotel and knocked on the door, he smiled when he opened the door, and she jumped in his arms.

"Good morning," Brody said squeezing her ass.

"Good morning is it alright that I am here?" Emma asked nervously.

"Of course, how did things go last night?" Brody inquired as he gently kissed her and she slid down his body as he ushered her in the suite.

"Alright, what did you do?" Emma asked putting her bag down and looked around.

"Wrote," he said smiling softly.

"Do you write all your own music?" Emma asked finally stepping back from his embrace.

"Most of it, where are you going?" Brody asked laughing as he followed her into the bedroom.

"In here," Emma smiled tossing her shirt off.

"Well then," Brody said and grabbed her and kissed her.

They stayed in his room all day making love and talking. She told him the plans for Friday night, and he was relieved that her parents were coming to stay.

Emma picked up London, "Where is Brody?"

"I am pretty sure he is at his hotel writing, he leaves tomorrow for England," Emma said.

"When am I going to see him again Mom?" London asked as the phone rang.

"Hello, you are on speaker," Emma said answering.

"Is London available?" Brody asked.

"Hi Brody!" London said excitedly.

"How was school?" Brody asked.

"It was alright, lots of drama. Everyone was talking about you," London said.

"Is that alright with you London?" Brody asked concerned.

"It was alright except the stuck up girls said you're only being friendly to me because you want my mom," London said.

"Really? They must not know you very well. You are extremely likable," Brody said with a smile in his voice.

"They also said that you wouldn't stick around that you would leave my Mom just like my Dad did," London said in an angry tone.

"Well that pisses me…" Brody began.

"Okay Brody I think London, and I need to talk, can we call you later," Emma asked.

"London, I am leaving to finish something I have already started. After that we will see what happens, I have to tell you that I would never leave if I didn't have to, or if your mother got incredibly sick of me. I am extremely boring once you get to know me," Brody laughed. "Em could you to come to my hotel and have dinner after dance?"

Emma was annoyed by what the girls had said to London, but what did she expect, "We can."

"I will text you the address," he laughed, "oh and the room number, I would not want you to get lost."

Emma looked in the rear view mirror at London who was smiling, "Is that alright with you London?"

"Yes," London laughed.
~
London read her mother her book on the way to the hotel. When she finished she wrote her spelling words. She finished the last of her homework as they pulled into the parking lot of the hotel.

"Good evening ladies," Brody said meeting them outside in the hall.

London ran up and hugged him, "Hi Brody!"

"Come in, dinner will be here soon, I ordered for you. I hope that's alright," Brody smiled, "Good evening Emma."

They returned home from dinner with Brody at eight thirty, half an hour after London's normal bedtime, Emma tucked her in and waited for her to fall asleep. She got up and folded laundry and thought about her day with Brody and quickly realized how much she was going to miss him.

Her phone chimed

-I want to see you, may I come over…MM

-Sure…Emma

Emma finished laundry, and she heard him pull in the driveway.

"Hey," she smiled opening the door to the back porch, "Come in."

He smiled and walked in, "This doesn't freak you out does it Em?" Repeating what she had said to him about the DVR'd Today show episode.

"No, should it?" Emma asked confused.

"Not at all, I just want to talk," he hugged her.

Great, she laughed to herself.

"Come in," she said and took his hand and walked towards the door.

They sat on the couch, and she played with the hand she was holding. His hands were large and strong, double the size of hers. They were soft and well taken care of. She smiled as she looked at them and gently rubbed them.

"Em?" he asked curiously.

"Oh sorry," she let go of his hand. "You wanted to talk?"

"Ya, I guess," he laughed bewildered shaking his head and smiled at her.

"Your hands are nice," Emma said blushing, "okay?"

Brody smiled, "I have never heard that before, Thank you?"

"Okay," she blushed, "So let's talk."

"Have you decided on which offer you will take?" Brody asked. Emma sat back and rolled her eyes and he laughed, "I think you spend a lot of time with children Em."

"I have not decided, but am leaning towards," she paused and grabbed a notebook and scribbled down four places.

She ripped the pieces apart and folded them. Emma tossed them on the coffee table and spread them around and pushed them into a messy pile.

She closed her eyes and grabbed one, "Here tell me Brody what I have decided."

Brody took the paper and smiled, "Well it says here that you will do whatever I ask," he laughed. Emma tried to grab it, and he held it high above his head, "you wrote it Em, so you better follow through," he laughed trying to keep the paper away from her.

Emma laughed as she grabbed for it again. Brody wrapped her in his arms and kissed her neck, "I want to know," Emma laughed.

Brody smiled seductively at her, "All decisions have been made, just go with it. Now quiet, enough talk, let me kiss you," he smiled and kissed her.

She climbed on his lap and grabbed the back of his head and pulled his hair towards her and kissed him. Brody grabbed her bottom and pulled her tighter against him. His mouth was hot, and his hands had not moved from her ass as he gently squeezed it. Emma kissed his neck and he started lifting her shirt.

"We should go in the bathroom, just in case, we can lock the door," Emma panted.

He stood and carried her through the kitchen and sat her on the counter in the bathroom. She lifted his shirt and kissed his chest, she undid his belt and then his buttons.

"You are so amazing," Emma said looking down at him, "Did you get your tests results back yet?" she asked licking her lips.

"Yes, all clear," he said and unclasped her bra.

Emma pushed him gently away, grabbed him, and looked down. She slide off the counter and onto her knees and took him in her mouth.

"Emma" he moaned, and pulled back, she bit down softly, and he stopped.

She continued slowly and felt his hands move to her head, and he leaned against the counter. She loved hearing him try to control his breathing, and when she looked up he was watching her. His mouth was opened and his eyes filled with desire.

"You should stop Emma," he said as he tensed up. She grabbed behind his thighs and squeezed as she moved faster "Emma damn, oh suck harder, fuck you need to stop."

Brody groaned looking down, she winked and shook her head slowly from side to side and continued until he spilled into her mouth and moaned loudly. Emma swallowed quickly and stood up. His eyes were closed as he breathed heavy.

Emma giggled softly and nudged him over with her hip moving him away from the sink. She cupped water in her hands and swallowed it. Emma grabbed her toothbrush and brushed her teeth, he moved behind her and wrapped his arms around her waist and hugged her as he kissed her neck.

Emma smiled and grabbed her shirt, "What did the paper really say?" She asked pulling her shirt over her head.

"It said take that off," Brody said softly as he kissed her neck. Emma smiled. He handed her the paper.

Emma read it and smiled, "Alright then."

"Alright then," Brody smiled. "You are quite sure?"

"Yep, I am going to try extremely hard not to over think this. I have tomorrow night to get Troy used to the idea," Emma said laughing.

Brody's eyes changed, he looked annoyed. "How are you going to do that?" he asked walking away.

Emma followed him to the couch. "How do you suggest I do that?"

"Not like that," he said his voice ominous.

"Like what?" she asked confused.

"The way you just convinced me to give you that piece of paper," Brody said staring at the floor.

"You are kidding right?" Emma was disgusted.

He looked at her and saw that he had upset her, "I leave for three weeks tomorrow afternoon."

"Ok, so then you think I am just going to go crazy on my ex because I," Emma stopped, "That's comforting, what will you being doing for three weeks?"

"Em, I am just unsure," he started and she interrupted him.

"Are you?" Emma asked, "That's fine, it was fun for the week and a half, I think you should leave Brody," Emma stood.

"Emma sit," Brody said pulling her down and wrapping his arms tightly around her as he tried to hold her still.

"I am pissed at you," Emma seethed.

"I am pissed at me too, that's not what I meant. You had just, well I don't want you to ever do that again with anyone other than me Em," Brody said apologetically.

"Listen I am not like that, at all! Is that what you think of me?" Emma asked looking at him.

"No, I should not have said anything, but that was amazing Emma and so has every other moment I have spent with you. I am going to be going a hundred miles an hour, getting this album done when I would rather be here with you. I wish you could come with me, both of you," Brody said apologetically.

"Well we can't," Emma said softly.

"Em should I leave?" Brody asked.

Emma was confused, "I guess if you want."

"I just thought you," he began.

"Over thinking things Brody?" Emma whispered.

"I don't want to leave you, ever," Brody admitted.

Emma looked at him and took a deep breath, "You have to do this right?"

"I sure do," Brody sighed.

"Well then it's not something to stress about if you have no choice," Emma said coaching him.

"Emma you have to be here when I get back," Brody spoke with urgency in his voice.

"You don't have to worry about me, I will not be going anywhere," Emma spoke softly.

"Thank God," he kissed her neck before he pulled her up and dragged her to the bathroom.

~

"What time…" Emma started to ask when they finally walked out of the bathroom.

Brody laughed, "That's going to be quite difficult for me to answer when I am over the pond, ten thirty at night Em."

"We were in there for an hour and a half, no wonder I am having trouble walking," she giggled.

He smiled, "I am going to miss your laugh."

"Please stop talking like that, will you come over tomorrow morning and spend the day? Maybe we could use my bed and not the bathroom counter if you want to," Emma blushed.

"Sounds perfect," Brody said between kisses. "Get some sleep tonight Princess."

"You too," her hands wrapped around his waist and her head snuggled into his chest.

"Emma, I love you," Brody said holding her tighter.

"Me too," she replied sadly.

He pulled away and looked down at her, "That makes you upset Em, why?"

"I have so much to get through, so much to do and I would rather just stay like this, and you're leaving. I know you have things as well and I may sound like a child, but I am afraid of what is to come," she closed her eyes and shook her head.

"I believe in us Emma, I know it sounds childlike as well but I feel it here," he said taking her hand and holding it against his heart.

Emma smiled and hugged him tightly as he stroked her head, "I should go," he said kissing her head. Emma did not lighten her grip at all.

"The sun has not come up yet," Emma smiled as she spoke softly.

"Hmm Emma I want to stay," Brody moaned, "you and I would both be spent by eight in the morning."

"When does your flight leave," Emma asked pulling away, she kept her hands on his hips.

"One o'clock from Rochester and then four from JFK," he said as his hands lightly caressed her cheek.

"When can you be back?" Emma asked taking his hand from her face and kissed each finger and finally licked his middle finger and drew it into her mouth.

"God Emma," he breathed as he watched her and felt his desire grow quickly.

"Bathroom now," Emma said grabbing his hand and pulling him back in.

Emma sat on the closed toilet as she undid his pants, his hands found their way up her shirt, and he tugged at her erect nipple. She released his hard thick erection from his jeans and licked her lips as she stroked him gently. She licked the purplish tip and her grasp became firmer and motions faster. She took him in her mouth, she needed to do this. Never had she felt such desire and need to please someone and not for him but for her. She felt her sex heat, and she moaned as she sucked harder and faster. She stopped to breathe and licked the throbbing veins underneath his hard shaft. He leaned into the wall and she took him completely in her mouth, it touched the back of her throat, and he threw his head back and clenched his teeth, she knew he was nearly there. He looked down at her his nostrils flared, his eyes full of heat and she looked up at him as he tensed and stood back. She opened her mouth and held his hard shaft and milked him into her mouth as he watched until he was empty.

"Fuck Emma that was amazing," Brody said trying to relax and bent down taking her breast in his mouth and spreading her legs as he rubbed her wet and throbbing sex. She moaned, "Em come for me, your wet and hot and I want you to come Emma, come now," he said and shoved two fingers into her and his thumb rubbed her clit. He bit down on her nipple as he squeezed the other with his fingers and she lost control as she started to yell out and he put his mouth over hers to soften the moans. He continued his thrusts into her even when she tried to stand and she came again.

"God Brody," she whimpered.

"I know Em," he said as he slowly pulled his hand back and licked his fingers, "Mmm."

That is oddly a turn on, so hot, she thought, and she took a quick breath. Brody looked at her and smiled seductively.

"You are extremely tasty Em," he said as he kissed her.

"Time for you to go," Emma said and stood up against him.

"You kicking me out?" Brody asked in her ear as he licked her lobe.

"No," she sighed "Just trying to remember who I am."

"I know who you are," he said continuing to lick down her throat, "you are mine."

Emma willed herself to lean back and smiled, "Well then, as much as I am enjoying this, reality is…"

"Reality is I have to leave, or your daughter will find out," Brody gently kissed her head. "But here," he said placing his hand above her rapidly beating heart, "there is room for us both," he placed her hand on his, "I am sure I am ready for all of what you bring Emma, forever," Emma's face started to burn and he beamed, "I love you Emma, see you at eight thirty."

How could he be so sure, there is so little he knows about me. Forever was a long time, and he was younger in years even when he makes me feel like I am less mature. He had to know everything, tomorrow I will tell him. When he leaves he will have time to realize as amazing as this has been, he deserves more. How could I let this happen so soon, how could I have fallen in love with him? Well I get it he is amazing but how could he fall for me. It's not real. We are each other's rebounds, nothing more.

~

Emma opened the door and he stood smiling, Emma looked down. Brody wore a pair of dark jeans, a gray button down shirt, and a white tee. His blue eyes sparkled and her insides heated from just looking at him.

How could it be possible that he could get better looking every day?

"Are you going to ask me in?" Brody grinned.

"Of course," Emma said snapping out of her ache for all things Brody, "I made you breakfast."

"I had M&M's in mind," he whispered in her ear as she walked through the door.

Emma laughed, "I think we should sit, eat, and talk, there are things I want you to know."

"Alright, you sound serious. Are you alright?" Brody asked cautiously.

Emma smiled and set two plates on the table and sat across from him. She looked up and forced a smile.

"Brody where do you see yourself in three months," she asked as he took his first bite of his omelets, "Don't answer that keep eating, I want you to just listen…"

Brody swallowed, "Emma I can answer."

"No, I don't want you to, I want you to know some things. You asked me about the scar on my belly. I had surgery a few years ago. I have one ovary, no uterus, I won't be able to have any more children. Besides I am too old to anyway. I am overly protective of my daughter and always will be. I was not always an only child. I had an older sister that was taken at a shopping mall and never returned. I have extremely low self esteem, which means I will get fat again. I am just taking a step towards a career, so I have no retirement. Frankly I have nothing to offer you and I want you to leave today and find someone who will be able to give you everything you deserve in life. I mean I would love to spend the day in my bed fucking you until neither of us could walk and then drop you off at the airport and kiss you goodbye knowing that what we had was amazing. We have been exceptional rebound material for each other but love? Brody love doesn't last, not between two people who are so different," Emma took a deep breath and chewed the food she had stuffed in her mouth.

She took a deep breath and sat back. Her head still hung low as she tried to avoid looking at him. *Okay Brody say something please say something*, she thought trying to will him to speak.

"Please say something," she finally whispered.

"Thank you for breakfast, I am ready for you to show me your bed now," Brody said, his voice was different from ever before.

He pulled her chair out and she stood unsteadily and he grabbed her waist. She walked up the stairs and to the end of the hall. When they entered the room painted in soft rose, he looked around and then back to her. His eyes went from dancing at the door to dangerous in the bedroom. She had not seen this look before and she wasn't sure what he was feeling, she started to speak, and his mouth crashed into hers.

He pulled away after his fast hard kiss, "You are done talking for awhile, you just fucking floored me down there. If I wasn't leaving you for three weeks in just a few short hours, I would fuck you until you were about ready to come. But you wouldn't, I would not allow it after that shit down there. And that would continue until I couldn't take it anymore and then you would suck me until I came in your mouth. I would walk out that door and you would be left here to wish I had not left, or you chased after me. Emma your clothes are still on, get them off," he growled, and she jumped.

Holy fuck he is so hot and rude, and why do I still want him so badly, she wondered. Brody grabbed her shirt and pulled it over her head and next her pants. She stood still, her heart beating harshly like a wild bird wings wings against her chest. He ripped her under ware off and rubbed his nose in them and moaned. *Oh fuck me, I think I am going to come right now* she thought and she squeezed her thighs together and moaned.

"Not yet Emma you'll come when I tell you to," he said and took her bra straps off her shoulders and bit her neck and turned her around, unsnapped her bra and it fell to the floor, "Lay down if this gets too intense let me know, bend over."

Emma did as she was told, and he rubbed her sex, "All ready for me Em, good," he slipped his finger into her gently and then harder until he heard her breathing change. She squeeze around his finger and he pulled it out. He flipped her to her back, and she gasped. He avoided eye contact and pulled her up to sit kneeling down in front of her he spread her knees wide, he put two fingers into her mouth, "Suck."

Emma obeyed.

He pulled his fingers away from her mouth and slid them in her, she moaned, "Brody, please."

"Quiet," he said as he continued to pleasure her.

Emma looked down and saw his jaw clenched and the wild look in his eyes as he pulled his hand away and licked and nibbled and sucked between her legs. Emma was on the edge again and he stood up and kissed her.

"Please Brody," she whimpered. He pulled her up the bed and kissed her hard and roughly kissed down her body until he reached her sex again and licked and tugged until again she was on the edge, he pulled away. He looked at her, she had tears in her eyes, and finally something snapped. His eyes changed to her Brody.

"Emma," he whispered and took a deep breath.

Her tears started flowing, and he kissed them away. Finally, she breathed and kissed him back. He lay on top of her and gently eased into her and slowly, softly made love to her until they both came.

Emma rolled to her side putting her back to him. Brody sat up and pulled his pants up.

He sat on the edge of the bed with his elbows on his knees and hands in his hair, "I am going to take off."

She let out a breath and sat up and grabbed her shirt, "I will walk you out," she whispered.

"No need," Brody said coldly.

"Fine," Emma said and grabbed her clothes and quickly walked past him, dressing as she walked down the hall.

As he came down the stairs, Brody heard her in the bathroom crying.

He knocked on the door, "You alright?"

"NO, I am not alright, but you can leave you proved your point to yourself, whatever the fuck it was," Emma yelled.

She heard the door open and waited a few minutes and walked out with tears pouring down her face, she grabbed a tissue and blew her nose and screamed into her hands. She turned and he was sitting at the table with his arms crossed over his chest scowling at the ground.

Brody peered up, "I'm sorry."

"For what?" Emma asked to trying to get it together.

"Everything you have been through. Your sister, your shitty self esteem, that you can't have more children. I am sorry you don't believe me when I say I love you and that the past almost two weeks have left you still doubting what I tell you," Brody quietly said.

"But not about what happened upstairs," Emma gasped.

"No. I took control, so you didn't have to. I let you come, and I should not have. If you were not spending tomorrow night with your ex, I would not have let you. You would have been so worked up that all you would have thought about was how badly you needed me to fuck you that none of your doubts would have mattered, so no. I told you to tell me if it was too much and you didn't," Brody stated unemotionally.

Emma gasped, "Why would you do that to me when you say you love me?"

Brody raised an eyebrow, "You are not allowed to act pissed Emma, you were ending it down here."

"So why are you still here," Emma tried to use the same detached tone he had used with her, "Do you need to fuck me senseless again?"

"If that's what you want, but no I wanted to say I was sorry," he said coolly.

She could see the bulge in his pants growing, *shit why do I still want him because I love him, because he rocks in bed, because he is still here when anyone else would have just left*, she thought.

"Fine I will be upstairs waiting to be fucked again, even though that is a nasty word!"

When he walked in the room, she was sitting on the bed in a t-shirt looking down. Brody climbed in behind her and sat against the head board and grabbed her and pulled her between his legs and held her, leaning her back into him.

"After we made love Emma this is what should have happened, I should have held you. I don't regret taking you to the edge over and over, but I do regret not ending it like this, I was pissed." Emma didn't respond, but she put her hands on his knees. "Em what happened with your sister?" he asked softly.

"She was kidnapped and killed," Emma said in a straightforward tone.

"My God I am so sorry," Brody kissed her head.

"Yay me too," Emma sighed.

"And your surgery," he asked quietly.

"Cysts and the fact he wouldn't have more babies. I couldn't deal with the pain knowing it was not going to be rewarded with a bundle of life," she laughed softly.

"Em I don't need to have a child," Brody whispered softly in her ear.

"That's not a decision you should make in an hour or two. You will be a great father someday Brody, London adores you, I know you'll be such a wonderful father," Emma felt tears building in her eyes again.

"You're beautiful Emma, you should see you the way everyone else does, you should never worry about what you look like. The day I ran into you my breath was taken away immediately, you left me breathless," he kissed her again. "You are more than I could have ever imagined, I wish you knew how deeply I feel for you. So as far as me wanting more Emma, you are my more, I love you."

"Please, I won't hold you back, right now, even after your nonsense here earlier..." Emma began.

"You liked it, tell me it was awful Em..." Brody nuzzled into her neck.

"I like you Brody, I love you and want you to be happy without resentment. I love you enough to let you have everything you deserve without me holding you back, I hope you understand," Emma took a deep breath trying not to cry.

"Not going to happen, stop your nonsense or I will fuck you senseless Em," he lightly bit down her neck. Emma moaned, "You liked me being in control Emma?"

"I didn't like how detached you seemed. It was like you left me, where did you go?" Emma asked.

Brody took a deep breath, "Skirting the question Emma, did you like it?"

"Yes I did," she whispered.

"Good to know, might we do that again. If I promise to stay with you, not act so detached." Brody's hand rubbed across her shirt and the other down her sex. "Hmm I guess that's a yes. Oh Emma you are going to love this, trust me. I am going to take you right to the edge, and I promise not to let go, you trust me Em?" Emma turned and looked at him. He looked like a kid on Christmas morning, and his excitement made her hot and anxious all at the same time, she shook her head yes and he watched her eyes widen. "Perfect, I am going to need a few things."

Brody stood up and opened her closet and grabbed three scarves, he looked back at Emma and winked. Her heart was pounding, and her mouth watering as he took off his clothes and stood naked in front of her. His legs were long and muscular and his ass should be the front cover of his next album. It would be a number one hit even if not one song was on it. He grabbed his iPhone out of his pocket and plugged it into her Bose on her nightstand. He looked at her and bit his lips pondering a thought and then grinned devilishly and raised an eyebrow. Emma giggled.

"Emma don't you dare laugh," he warned her.

Brody gently tied her arm to the headboard and kissed her and tied the next.

"Close your eyes," he breathed and kissed her. Emma was tied and blindfolded when she heard the music start. She giggled when she heard Nine Inch Nails start until he bit down on her very alert nipples and pulled them almost painfully away from her body, she whimpered and immediately felt pleasure shoot between her legs.

Brody's fingers lightly skimmed over her breasts, and she breathed heavy, he teased her with his hands the entire song and she was about ready to make him stop. Her breathing was heavy and she was already wet when Zeppelins Whole Lot Of Love filled her ears and she tried to relax, she felt her legs spread, and his tongue crashed into her, and she yelled out his name. She realized immediately that the more intense the music got the more intense her pleasure was *Damn he is good my music man* she thought and enjoyed his slow, pleasureful, torture. *Damn this is a long song*, and she was ready and wanted to come so badly. Cold Play Paradise started, and he stopped and moved back to her breasts.

"Hey Music Man," she whimpered "I need you inside me please," she felt him pull away, and the door closed, "Fuck," she said and stomped her foot. Her feet both quickly were raised above his shoulders as he once again used his impressive oral skills to bring her to the edge. "Brody, please, please," the music changed, and it was Blue Love, he lowered her down and she yelled out his name and she came hearing his voice. She felt her arms release and she sat up and went to remove the blindfold, and he gently grabbed her hands and slide behind her and took it off. She turned her head and looked at him, he kissed her and lifted her onto him, her back to his chest as he helped her move up and down his massive erection he muttered her name and said over and over, "I love you Em, forever."

"Oh Brody, I love you," she said and turned so he wouldn't see her cry. She moved up and down him with urgency and need. He tried to slow her, but she wouldn't, they both finished together. Brody laid down and pulled her onto him. His song was repeating, and he was holding her tightly. She turned and buried her head into his chest. He felt her tears and tilted his head to look at her.

"What's wrong Em," he asked sweetly as he wiped her tears.

"I need a shower," she said and stood up and walked to the bathroom.

He waited until the shower turned on and he cleared his throat as he walked in.

She peeked out of the shower, "What are you doing?"

"May I?" Brody asked.

"Sure," Emma said and held the curtain open.

They kissed and washed each other until the water ran cold. Emma had never felt so loved before. Brody was amazing in every way. She watched as he dressed and smiled, he looked up at her through his long lashes as he buttoned his pants and shot her an embarrassed half smile as he shook his head. She sat on the edge of the bed and watched him throw his shirt over his shoulders and started to button it.

"Please don't," Emma said.

"What?" Brody chuckled.

"Leave it undone, please. Just until, we leave, please" Emma asked feeling her face flush.

"Anything for you Princess," he swooped down and kissed her.

"Can we lay here and just hold each other?" Emma asked boldly.

"Yes, I have an hour before I need to leave," Brody grabbed her and pulling her towards him.

"Okay I have to leave a few minutes before to stop and get gas, where are you dropping off your car, the hotel?" Emma asked.

"No, Emma, I am going to drive to the airport. I would rather you not drive all that way by your self," Brody kissed her head.

"No, Brody, I need to say goodbye to you, I am taking you," Emma's voice broke, and she started to shake.

"Emma I can't let you drive like this, to emotional," Brody softly stroked her hair.

"No, you can't make all the decisions, it's not fair, I want to go with you," Emma was now sobbing.

He sat up and held her tighter, "This is why Emma, no more fighting. Please, I can't have the woman I love, or London's mother driving in this emotional state. Not a request and it is my final decision, out of love Emma."

Emma held tightly to him and cried until she fell asleep in his arms. He watched her sleep, and she woke with more tears. "Emma please don't cry."

"Okay," she wiped away her tears, "I am going to fix you lunch."

Before he could argue she had jumped up and run downstairs, she returned with lunch. They sat on the bed, and he ate and she nibbled.

When she had finished she decided that he had dominated her most of the day, and it was her turn. She started to undo his pants, and he shook his head no. "You can't tell me no."

Brody kissed her gently, "Emma I have thirty minutes, and I want to spend them holding you, not coming in your mouth and knowing I can't return the favor for three weeks."

"Are we keeping score because if we are I am down by about at least thirty," Emma smiled.

"Are we keeping score Em?" Brody laughed.

"And if its basis were intensity well I don't think I could ever make up for that, I am sure I have had more with you than I did the entire time I was married," Emma said laughing hysterically.

"Good to know, so no worries about tomorrow night then?" Brody asked cautiously.

"No, Brody none," she said looking him in the eyes.

"How about the next three weeks," he asked sadly, she shook her head no and took a deep breath.

He held her tightly, "None for you ever, do you understand, ever."

Emma shook her head yes as she fought tears.

Emma walked him to his car and held his hand tightly.

"So how do we do this?' she asked breathlessly.

"I am going to kiss you, and you are going to return my kiss, it's not goodbye, it's see you soon," he pulled her in and kissed her, she kissed him back.

"I love you Em, see you soon," Brody said softly.

"Brody thank you, I love you. Drive safely, have a safe flight," she paused and took a deep breath, "See you soon."

Brody stood back with his hands on her hips, he looked down at her and winked.

He took a deep breath, "Em there are some packages on the porch, one for you, one for London, I love you," he started the car and looked out the window.

He held up something, and she looked closer. It was her panties from this morning. He held them to him nose and took a deep breath, Emma shook her head and smiled. He pulled away looking in the rearview mirror, he saw her watching him with tears falling down her face and her hands over her heart.

Half an hour later her phone rang, a picture of him holding her as she slept popped up as her picture ID, she smiled.

"Thank you for doing that, I hadn't even thought about taking a picture of us and well, it's perfect," she gushed.

"Have you opened the packages yet?" Brody asked.

"No, I figured I would wait until London got home," Emma said quietly.

"I thought you would say that so listen, one has something she shouldn't see, grab the small rectangular box out of the smaller bag and open it with me on the phone," he chuckled.

She did as he asked and gasped, "Brody."

"Yay, glad I remembered," Brody laughed.

"Why did you buy me a vibrator?" Emma whispered.

"Just in case three weeks was too long, and well I want to hear you Princess, it's really more for me, we can have phone sex. Or if you're bold enough we can Skype," he chuckled.

"I will have to think about that," Emma said embarrassed. Brody laughed. "It's kind of small in comparison to what I have grown accustomed to."

"Oh yay?" Brody asked in a sexy voice.

"Most definitely," she laughed, "It's also not attached to the hottest man on earth or that mouth that makes me melt."

Emma heard horns, "Damn it," Brody yelled.

"What's going on?" Emma asked with concern in her voice.

"I am very distracted by my favorite candy right now, and well I do come from England, we drive on the other side of the road," he laughed.

"Oh God Brody you need to pay attention," Emma gasped.

"I agree, you are extremely diverting, I will call when I am safely in the airport, love you forever Em," Brody said and hung up.

~

Emma sat and stared at the picture on her phone. His face was perfect. His big blue eyes set perfectly and his eyebrows thick and masculine. His nose was strong and in perfect proportion to his face. His bottom lip was plump and begged to be sucked. His square jaw line made her take a deep breath thinking of that mouth and the magic he made happen with it. His hair brown with hues of copper was messy and begged for her hands to be in it. Brody's white perfect teeth and a smile that would forever outshine any other. In the picture, he took he was biting the corner of his lower lip and the way he held her reminded her of how he held his guitar the night he sang at the club in the city, like she was precious to him. Emma felt tears form and set the phone down and hoped that she was right.

Emma did the breakfast dishes and decided to put away laundry. She cranked up Rusted Root and danced around the room. Her phone vibrated in her pocket, and she jumped. It was her doctor's office reminding her of her annual appointment scheduled for Monday. Emma grabbed the laptop and checked her email. Emma had a response, she could start her job in two weeks. Emma took a deep breath and was not looking forward to her discussion with Troy about this.

Her phone rang, and the song Blue Love played, she smiled and answered.

"President of Brody Hines fan club," she spoke in her best English accent.

He laughed, "Em I am here and should be boarding in ten minutes, do you have time to chat?"

"I am particularly busy you know, but yes I am all yours," Emma said softly.

"And I yours Emma," Brody's voice sounded sad.

"Hey guess what? I start my new job in two weeks," Emma said with a smile in her voice trying to cheer him up.

"That's great news Em. You'll be very close to the city and to me when I return. Where will you be staying?" He asked.

"My parents have a place in Tarrytown. There is an apartment above the garage, small but very reasonably priced. I will look for a place after a month or so," Emma smiled.

"Please don't buy anything until I return, I would love to help you pick something out. Promise I can please?" Brody asked calmly.

"Sure if you would like," Emma said anxiously.

He laughed, "I miss you already."

"I miss you more," Emma said softly.

Brody knew that was what she had said to London when she wasn't with her and at that moment he felt more loved than he had when they made love, "Emma you have no idea what that means to me."

They sat for a moment in silence.

"Well you mean a lot to me Brody," Emma choked out.

"Well Princess I think I should let you go, you have to pick London up right?" Brody asked thoughtfully.

"Yep, will you call me when you land at JKF?" Emma asked.

"Of course, and before I leave and when I arrive in England," Brody said softly, "Love you Em."

"Fly safe, I love you," Emma quietly said.

"See you soon," Brody said with a smile in his voice.

"See you soon, Music Man," Emma responded and hung up.

~

London and Emma sat at the table and ate a snack. "You miss him Mom?"

"I do, and you?" Emma asked.

"Yep," London replied as she ate a grape.

The phone rang, and London grabbed it and answered, "Nice picture."

"Well hello London how was school?" Brody asked hoping she would let it go.

"It was fine. We miss you," London grinned.

"Did you get your gifts?" Brody asked.

"No, what gifts?" London replied happily.

"Sorry I wanted to wait until you were on the phone," Emma said and went and grabbed them. "Alright London you first."

London opened a box and screamed, "Thank you so much!"

Brody laughed, "You are very welcome, I guess you like it?"

"I love it!" London exclaimed.

"I am glad, I added some music and photos for you to check out when you have time, there are a couple more things in that bag London," Brody said smitten.

Along with the iTouch there were gift cards to purchase music, a stuffed bear, and a concert sweatshirt from his last tour that he signed, To London with big hugs Brody.

"This is too much, thank you Brody," London spoke in a sing song voice.

"Your turn Emma," Brody laughed.

Emma opened a package with a brief case in it, "Thank you Brody this will be perfect for work."

"Look inside Em," Brody suggested.

She opened it and inside was a Mac Book Pro and an iPad, "Brody this is too much, I can't accept…"

"Emma it's more for me, there's Skype installed already," he giggled. "Keep going."

Emma opened an envelope with a note, he had picked out new business attire for her, and it would be shipped when she and London had moved. Along with it was a Pottery Barn book and a note attached that he had picked out bedroom furniture for her and London also to be delivered.

"I don't know what you are looking at, but the clothes have been picked out. The furniture also but if you want something else by all means change it," Brody said cautiously.

"I love it Brody," London laughed.

"Brody this is way too much, I won't accept it, I can take care of us," Emma said softly but firmly.

"Em I am making this decision, if we need to talk about it we can later. My flight has been called ladies. See you soon, Emma I love you," Brody said and heard London gasp, "I adore you London, take care of each other until I return."

"Mom, say it back," London whispered.

"You to Brody, see you soon," Emma responded uncomfortably.

"London will you take me off speaker and give your mother a moment please," he said gently.

Emma took the phone and walked into the bathroom, "Brody that was all too much."

"No, Emma it wasn't enough, but it will be soon. Once more I love you," Brody said in a firmer tone.

"Brody I love you I just don't want London so vested in us, what if…" Emma started.

"If I could I would be there right now dragging you back up those stairs, we are good Emma. We both know it so stop. I love you Em," Brody said more forcefully.

Emma let out a breath, "I love you Brody, fly safe and see you soon."

"Much better Emma, see you soon. I love you, more," Brody hung up.

Emma and London sat on the couch and played with their new electronics. London was going through the music, and every Kids Bop album was on the ITunes account. London was so delighted she almost could not sit still. Emma smiled softly at her.

"Mom he shouldn't have done this, right?" She asked trying to contain herself.

"No, he shouldn't have, and I will pay him back, it's too much," Emma said as she hugged her.

Emma clicked on the photos and shrieked, "Mommy look," she handed it over.

Emma flipped through the pictures, there were ones of the carriage ride, of them at dinner, and of the night they went to the show. All pictures of London and Brody. There was one other of when Emma was doing London's hair for dance.

"London they are amazing, I don't think you should share these with anyone, he is very private."

"I know Mom, I promise. I shouldn't let Dad see them, he will get mad huh?" London stated.

"You and Dad are going to hang out tomorrow. Just hang out he and I will talk about the move, my job, and everything else. These are not choices that you need to be worried about okay. The only thing I want to know is that you want this, if not we can figure it out here."

"Mom, I think it will be perfect," London hugged her.

"I will be happy wherever we are together. If we hate it we can always come back okay?" Emma asked.

~

Brody sat in first class waiting for the other passengers to board when he noticed Ariel walk into the cabin. She sat next to him, "Hello Brody."

"Ariel, what are you doing here?" Brody asked coldly.

"I have a shoot in London, you are going to finish your album right?" She asked.

"Yes," he said and turned away.

"Brody, I miss you," Ariel said placing her hand on his leg.

He laughed as he pushed her hand away, "We are divorced, you got what you wanted. Keep your hands off me Ariel."

Brody stood and walked past her and asked if there was another seat.

"I am sorry Mr. Hines the flight is booked," the blonde flight attendant informed him.

"How about coach?" he asked through his teeth.

"I am sorry," she said nervously.

"Fuck!" he yelled.

Brody sat down, "Brody are you seeing that woman, the one in all the pictures?"

"That is none of your fucking business," Brody said looking straight forward.

"Good choice for a rebound, she is the total opposite of what I know you like," Ariel began, "Very safe."

"Are you quite finished?" Brody asked as he stood up and walked past her again. "Miss could you kindly go ask another passenger to switch with me, I will not spend even a second next to her let alone seven bloody hours."

"Mr. Hines we need to take off, I will see what I can do when we are safe to move around," she assured him.

Brody took his seat and buckled his seat belt. He put his ear plugs in and listened to some new music. He was exhausted from the past couple days. Brody fell asleep. He woke, and Ariel was smugly sitting next to him.

~

Emma was asleep in London's room when her phone vibrated, she jumped up and smiled when she saw the picture.

"Hang on one second please," she said with a smile in her voice.

She kissed London and covered her up and walked out closing the door.

"You're there safely," she said softly.

"I am, I miss you," Brody said in a deep tone.

"See yah Brody," Ariel said as she walked by.

"Bitch," he snapped.

"Brody is everything alright?" Emma asked.

"No, I spent seven hours and forty five minutes in a damn plane that had no extra seats sitting next to my ex wife," Brody said furiously.

"Oh," Emma said and then was silent.

"Emma, I had no idea. I truly don't think it was planned on her part either, how could it have been I changed my damn flight. You believe me right?" Brody asked.

"Sure," Emma answered quietly.

"Please don't," he whispered softly.

Emma cleared her voice, "What time is it there?"

"Five AM," he answered, "Emma I didn't know, and I love you. You can trust me, just like I do you. I need you to remember that neither of us were the reason our marriages did not work. I will never hurt you."

"Okay Brody, I love you. I miss you, and I wish you weren't so far from me," Emma said softly.

"Thank you. I feel the same. So we should have talked about this when I was there, but the time difference, it's midnight there right?" Brody asked.

"Ya, it's okay I am glad you called. I am glad you are safe," Emma whispered.

"Thank you," Brody said sincerely, "Alright at eight thirty your time it's one thirty my time, will that work for you?"

"Sure," she yawned.

"Sleepy Em?" he asked.

"Yes very I was worn out today or yesterday, but in a particularly good way," Emma giggled.

"I was too, I slept the entire flight. Why don't you go to bed and I will call you at one thirty my time," Brody suggested?

"Hey you need to sleep Brody," she laughed. "Why don't you call me before you go to bed so I can say goodnight to you. It's the weekend, I can manage. Besides I am going to be stuck with my ex tonight as well, hearing your voice will make it better."

"Anything you want Emma, I love you, sleep now," Brody said soothingly.

"Goodnight, love you," Emma said and waited for him to hang up.

~

Emma spent the morning cleaning, a chore she had neglected all week since she had been preoccupied. She called her mother and told her she would like to start moving some of their things on Sunday, Caroline was ecstatic. Emma packed some of their things in boxes. She was grateful that she had not pulled out any of the holiday decorations and winter items, at least they were already boxed.

   Emma and London had talked extensively every night about the move and what the change would mean to London. London was very happy to be able to have her grandparents there every day. Even though they lived so far away they were extremely close. Emma knew how lucky she was to have parents that were such a strong presence. London would be going to the same school that Caroline worked at. Caroline was a librarian. She would be taking her to and from school every day. Emma knew Caroline would keep her safe; she had lost a child to a deranged convict that held a vendetta against Henry, Emma's father, who at the time was a detective. Emma was three when her sister was taken from the mall in Florida. Elizabeth was five and beautiful and full of life. Had she been in the stroller she would have been safe. Caroline and Henry were at the department store buying bedding and turned for two seconds, and that was all it took. Elizabeth was never found. Emma's family moved from Florida to New York running from a constant reminder of the beautiful child that was now in heaven with the angels. Neither blamed each other, what would have normally tore a family apart bound them even tighter together. It also made them cling tightly to Emma and shower her with more love than any one child could ever wish for.

   ~

   Emma's phone rang bringing her back to the here and now. She saw the picture ID and smiled.

   "Brody you should be sleeping," Emma answered.

   "I missed you Em, and I needed to warn you that there are some pictures popping up on the internet of Ariel and I. Lila was going to call you, however I prefer to do it myself. Now don't get the wrong idea but could you get online and Google my name, it should pop up," Brody requested.

Emma opened the link and saw the first picture. Brody looked annoyed as he spoke to her. The next he was asleep, and she was holding his hand, the next Ariel's head rested on his shoulder and her hand high on his upper thigh as they both slept, and the last was his head resting against hers.

"Emma can you say something?" Brody asked gently.

"Sure, they make my skin crawl," Emma said quietly, "I wonder if London's friends have said something to her yet, which would upset her, she certainly doesn't need anymore stress than she will be dealing with over the next few weeks. This is too much Brody…"

"Ok I agree Emma, I didn't ask for this rubbish either. I hope you know by now I would not want to hurt her, ever," Brody said urgently. Emma didn't know what to say, so she said nothing. "Are you still on the line Emma?"

"Yes," Emma said and he sensed the distance in her voice.

"I love you, and I am so sorry. Emma when you move no one will know, she won't have to deal with this. I am sorry," Brody said softly.

"You didn't wake up when she was laying on you, or her hand was…" Emma spoke in a whisper.

"No, Emma, I told you I was exhausted. I have no idea how she ended up on the same flight, and I can assure you I tried to get the seat changed," Brody spoke in almost a whisper.

"Okay, I will figure out how to deal with it for her. Brody I think this needs to slow down," Emma said with a quiet laugh.

"No, you just need to trust me. And I need to let you know when shit like this happens because it will Emma. Fuck," he yelled.

Emma swallowed, "Can this just be between us and not London."

"What's that supposed to mean Emma?" Brody asked in an agitated tone.

"Well, you shouldn't have said I love you in front of her for starters. You shouldn't be buying her things or me for that matter. Brody we have only known each other for two weeks this is all moving fast," Emma said nervously.

"You are kidding right?" Brody asked in an angry tone. Emma didn't respond she was trying not to cry. "Fine Emma, maybe in three weeks we can discuss this, have a good fucking time with prince fucking charming tonight," he yelled and hung up.

Emma sat and cried, all she wanted was to get through the next few weeks and be strong for her child. Maybe this is exactly what was supposed to happen, she thought trying to calm herself down when her phone rang again. It was Brody, and she pushed decline and walked away. She received a text minutes later.

-Emma, please call me back I am sorry, please don't do this. I can come back now and walk away from all this, I love you…MM

-I am trying to get things done around here. Don't come back, your work is important, and so is my sanity. I need to be strong for her Brody, please understand that…Emma

-Your sanity and your daughter are important to me Emma, and BTW two weeks was enough for me to realize that…MM

-I am having a seriously rough day Brody, very emotional. Please understand that I am going through some things. You need to focus on your album, and I need to focus on here. Please call me tonight and please excuse my extremely jealous nature…Emma

-Whatever you need, but as previously determined you don't need to control everything. You don't like being the one to always make the big choices. I however, love every part of taking care of you and making choices for you, all of which have your best interest at heart. If I remember correctly, twenty four hours ago, you quite enjoyed it as well. Stop being difficult Emma...MM

-How is it you made me go from angry and jealous enjoying my miserable existence to hot and damp in two seconds. By the way your going to have to stop being so bossy, I am someone's mother...Emma

Emma's phone rang, and she answered.

"Much better Emma," Brody said seductively.

"No, not actually," Emma breathed out.

"Hmm, I did buy you a gift to take care of that for now," Brody said in a deep voice that made her hair stand on end.

"Brody I am truly busy I can't be, stop, please this is too much," Emma said exasperated.

"I love you," Brody said softly, "I need to hear you Emma I want you to make yourself..."

"Brody I won't and you need to stop," Emma said in a whinny tone.

"You will before three weeks is up or I am going to torment you when I see you again," Brody laughed. "Are we all better now?"

"Yes, I love you," Emma said tenderly, "I do trust you, I just wish you were like the UPS man or something. I also want to know how she knew."

"Delivering you a package," he moaned.

"Brody!" Emma snapped.

"Sorry Em, I don't know how she knew, and I don't care. She did ask me about you and I ignored her. I will never give you a reason to not believe my package is yours alone. This is going to get easier, I promise," Brody assured her.

"Before you called I was thinking about Elizabeth, my sister I told you about. Is your ex sane Brody, I mean I don't have to worry about London's safety do I?" Emma asked anxiously.

"She isn't crazy, or never gave me the impression she was anything but a gold digging whore. But I will look into it if it makes you feel better Em," Brody said calmly.

"How did she know you where on that flight?" Emma questioned.

"I don't think she did Em I think it was coincidence," Brody told her even though he questioned it to. He didn't want her to worry.

"Okay, please be safe Brody. I have a feeling that I can't shake," Emma's tone was tense.

"When do you move Em?" Brody asked.

"Next weekend, why?" she asked.

"Do you have a security system?" Brody asked.

"No, Brody you're scaring me," Emma said.

"No, you're fine Emma, I just think you would feel better, less on edge. I am going to get one installed while you're at the hotel. London won't know, and you'll feel better," Brody said in his bossy voice.

"Okay that's not necessary" Emma scowled.

"Not up for discussion. I love you, see you soon," Brody said with a cheerful tone in his voice.

"I love you, see you soon," Emma said and waited for him to hang up.

"Emma, Skype tonight, bring that gift," his voice was hot and steamy, and he hung up.

~

London and Emma walked into the Hilton, and Troy met them at the front desk.

"Daddy," London smiled and ran up and hugged him.

Troy looked shocked, this wasn't the normal greeting he received from his daughter.

"Hello London," he said stiffly, "Hello Emma," he said and quickly looked away.

"Hello Troy," Emma smiled politely to him, and he looked confused. "Hey London would you check out the window Grandma and Grandpa will be here soon."

London turned and looked at her and rolled her eyes and nodded back to Troy. Emma smiled and laughed.

"What is going on with her she seems, I don't know different," Troy asked flustered.

"She is happy Troy. And she loves you and probably missed you, it's been almost two weeks since she has seen you," Emma said with a soft smile.

"I expected her to be pissed," Troy snorted.

"Well she wouldn't be pissed, she would be hurt," Emma said correcting him.

"Of course she would be, especially if that's what you told her to be," he said rolling his eyes.

"Let's not do that, please. Have fun with her Troy," Emma said sadly.

"Mom they are pulling in," London beamed.

"Cool wait for them and then help Grandpa grab the bags," Emma said smiling, "Dad and I are going to talk for a minute."

"About what Emma?" Troy asked sarcastically.

"Well for starters, we will be moving next weekend…" Emma began.

"With Brody Hines," Troy said angrily through his teeth.

"No, Troy, with my parents," which seemed to relax him a bit, "I got a great job and start the following Monday. I only have to be in the office three days a week, the rest I will work from home. London is excited to be going to the same school as Mom works at. Do you have any questions or concerns yet or shall I go on?"

"What kind of job did you get that's so excellent you're going to move to Tarrytown and uproot London that you only have to be in the office three days a week Emma, sounds like a crock of shit to me," Troy laughed.

"Well it's a junior editor's job and the starting pay is excellent. There are commissions and bonuses. Honestly it's a dream job," Emma smiled.

"Really, well that's great, how much is great money Emma. Do you plan to live with your parents forever?" Troy laughed.

"Well Troy, I will be starting at a little less than you make. I assume that I can afford my own place at some point. Living with them is absolutely fine with me for as long as it's necessary," Emma smiled.

"Sounds perfect Emma, everything you deserve right. So how is your love life? How is your Rockstar?" Troy said flippantly.

"Brody is in England finishing an album for three weeks Troy. He has nothing to do with what happened with us. Nothing at all," Emma said looking sadly at him.

"No, but you've let him into London's life haven't you?" Troy said in a bitter tone.

"Well London saw him when her weekend with you ended abruptly, and she had a lot of fun with him. Troy she is so much fun I wish you would just enjoy her. You're her daddy, always. She is one person in your whole life who will never hate you regardless of how much you screw up," Emma laughed and elbowed him gently, "Do the same for her, love her, have fun with her, find yourself again Troy, please."

Troy looked at her like he was lost, "But never us again Emma? We were good together."

"Troy I wish nothing but happiness for you, always. You hurt me, I can get past all of it for London, but never for us as a couple, only us as parents to the most amazing little human being on the planet," Emma smiled, "That's what I wish for anyway."

Troy watched her and shook his head, "I fucked up. I loved you Emma, I truly did."

"Okay, so what now Troy. What will you choose for London?" Emma asked feeling her eyes fill up.

Troy reached over and wiped her tear away, "Emma I want to be the man I was, I don't know what happened I truly don't. Please forgive me," he pulled her towards him and hugged her.

"I can't be anymore but..." Emma cried.

"I know Emma. I see that, just help me get better for her, please. She is the best part of us she truly is," Troy said and held her tighter.

"Daddy, please don't cry," London said and sobbed, "Please."

Troy closed his eyes and took a deep breath and pulled her into the hug he shared with Emma.

"Hey what do you say we head up the suite? This is kind of embarrassing," Troy laughed and held her hand and held Emma's hand with the other.

"Emma your father and I are going to grab some dinner, call us if you need us," Caroline smiled.

Emma, Troy, and London ate dinner in the suite and talked about the move. Troy seemed happier than he had been in years. "Daddy, you know everything that went on the other weekend?"

"Yes London, I am so sorry," Troy said and leaned forward like he wanted to hug her but stopped himself.

"Well it was bad, really bad and scared me. I did not feel safe, please don't do that to me ever again," her voice cracked and she started to cry, "Please!"

Emma gasped and looked at Troy who looked horrified. Emma gently pushed his back so that he moved towards her, and they hugged and both cried.

"I am going to get better at being your Dad London I promise you that, Mommy and I aren't going to fight anymore. And I am choosing you right now London over anything else, I choose you."

"Oh Daddy, thank you!" London continued to cry.

Emma cried and closed her eyes, *why now you asshole, why now* she thought.

Troy looked over at Emma, "London my hope is to be half as good a parent as your Mom. And our marriage failing was all me, not her. I want you to know that she has been nothing less than what I knew she would be when I married her."

"Daddy Brody loves her," London said looking him straight in the eyes, "And he is very nice to her."

"Wow London," Troy laughed uncomfortable and looked at Emma, who looked down. "Well she deserves to be loved, I kind of sucked at it."

"Yes you did," London said. "Mom are you mad that I said that?"

"No, London, I want you to be honest with both of us but always considerate," Emma said, "And sorry Troy, but something's even adults can't emotionally handle so just be kind alright?"

"Your mom thinks I can't tell she is in love with him. She seems to forget I know how easy she is to love, but I get it. I won't interfere. I know she deserves to be happy," Troy laughed, "So how about we hit the pool?"

"Sounds good, can Mom come?" London asked.

"Whatever you need until I have earned your trust London," Troy smiled.

They swam and laughed and had a great time. Caroline took pictures and talked with Emma about the move. After Emma and Troy tucked London in, he apologized to her parents and promised to get the help he needed.

Emma went to her adjoining room and showered and threw on the sweatshirt Brody had left and a pair of shorts. She decided to lay down and rest her eyes while she waited for Brody to call. Emma woke to a knock on the door, she opened it.

"Emma you left your phone out here," Troy said and handed it to her.

"Oh, oh God Troy I am sorry," Emma said shocked.

"Nice picture by the way," he laughed and shut the door.

"Brody?" Emma laughed.

"Em," he said and laughed too, "Wow that's kind of like getting busted by your parents doing it in the car."

Emma laughed as she covered her mouth, "Okay it's not funny," she chuckled, "He has been wonderful today."

"Oh well thank God your ex who is sleeping in the next room has been wonderful and we have been found out?" Brody laughed a belly laugh and Emma couldn't help but fallow suite.

"God I love you," Emma said laughing.

"Emma, do you realize how loud you just said that?" Brody gasped jokingly.

"Well it's been one heck of a night. After we talked and hugged and cried and London hugged and cried with us, which by the way is the first since our separation, we actually talked, and he told her she would be first in his life. He also told her how perfect I was. Do you know what she told him? She told him that you loved me and said it looking him right in the eye. She also told him that you were nice to me, like warning him. And he said that he could tell I loved you too and deserved to be happy. So Brody I think me being loud is a moot point," Emma laughed again.

"London said that to him?" Brody asked with a smile in his voice.

"Yep she sure did," Emma laughed, "Do you know how exhausted I am?"

"I am sorry Em. Does that mean no Skype tonight?" he chuckled.

"Brody that's not going to happen, sorry I want the real thing" Emma said softly.

"Emma you'll have it soon," he whispered.

"Tell me about your day," Emma said as she laid back in her bed.

"Compared to yours mine has been pretty dull," Brody answered.

"No raunchy photos that I may come across that you need to warn me about?" Emma asked.

"None, I stayed locked in my room writing. Two more songs to finish up and then to the studio for a week if I am lucky, then onto interviews for another week. Followed by a flight home and directly into you," Brody said and Emma moaned, "Emma don't do that."

"Sorry," Emma giggled.

"So I finished a song today, I would like your opinion on it, or approval I guess. May I email it to you?" Brody asked taking a deep breath.

"Yes, please, I will boot up my new iPad now," Emma said cheerfully.

Emma opened her email, and it was there, she giggled, "Can I open it now?"

"Please do," Brody answered jovially.

Date September 23rd, 2012

Honest opinion expected. If it's to much let me know.

Love ,

MM

London

Once cold and broken not knowing where to go. Pain unbearable when I let you go.

Dulled the memories where did it all start,

Where it all began when she broke my heart.

Falling down sitting broken for years and years

waiting to begin still waiting for the tears.

I return to you hoping you can give me strength to do what is right

stop this painful bitter internal fight.

Chorus

In your rain, I fall to my knees

In your light, I beg you oh please, oh London oh, oh, London

The sky lights up from your light the clouds break and I know it's finally right.

The fog it's lifting could it be oh could it be

That light from London's eyes is shining for me.

The brilliant light you come from is where I need to be.

Opening oh opening up the ground beneath my feet,

The warmth of her smile it's my hearts heat.

Memories not so dulled by the pain anymore,

Through her eyes I see what I left behind, now I ache to explore.

Standing, watching, learning, feeling what was buried deep inside.

The love that I shoved so far away burns so bright it can no longer hide.

I return to breathe you in again to make it up to you.

To remember what once was peaceful when I first felt love.

Pain felt for years never came from I fall again looking above

Chorus

In your rain, I fall to my knees

In your light, I beg you oh please, oh London ooohhh London

The sky lights up from your light the clouds break and I know it's finally right.

The fog it's lifting could it be oh could it be

That light from London's eye's shining for me.

The brilliant light you come from is where I need to be.

"Brody it's beautiful," Emma said softly.

"Would you like me to explain it?" He asked.

"Please do," Emma said.

"The first verse is about my mother's passing and how angry I was at her for leaving. The chorus is about this trip actually, and about your daughters love for you and dependency on you to keep her safe which I didn't feel as a child. The brilliant light that you come from part of the chorus is you. The next verse," he said taking a breath, "Is about when I realized why she left before she passed, for months Em, she lived here in London with my Aunt and we never knew why she left, let alone that she was dying and was trying to keep that pain from us. I only realized that when I saw that you would jump in front of a damn train to stop any pain that may come to your child regardless of the pain it would cause you. My mother loved me enough to not want me to watch her suffer Emma. My father told us she left us and never the truth. And then he fell apart."

"Brody when did you find out all of this?" Emma asked deeply concerned.

"Today Emma, I spoke to my aunt today," he spoke, and his voice shook.

"Oh I don't know what to say. I am so glad you have an answer and that it brought you what I hope is peace. But I am sorry I can't be there with you. Talk to me please, where is your head right now?" Emma asked.

"I don't know Emma," he laughed, "We are both nasty messy right now."

"But I am here for you don't forget that Brody, please," Emma said nervously.

Brody took a deep breath, "Do you know it's only eight o'clock in the evening, and I am literally as exhausted as you sound."

"You should sleep," Emma said in her maternal voice and Brody laughed, "Please tell me what you need form me."

"Emma I need you to go to sleep and take care of London," Brody said in an authoritive tone.

"What can I do to take care of you?" Emma asked softly, "I love you Brody don't shut me out."

"I am not Emma, go to sleep, see you soon," Brody hung up.

Emma cried herself to sleep.

In the morning, she woke up and sent him a text.

-I don't want to shut down, but last night was confusing. You confused me by sharing your music and then something truly personal and not letting me any further in. I hope you are alright, you can trust me I am here…Emma

Emma didn't receive a response and spent the day with Troy and London. Troy helped them load her parent's vehicles with boxes and even helped load the storage trailer. The three of them went out to dinner and then to visit his cousin Tessa to let her know what was going on.

The night passed and still no word from Brody. Emma googled him and saw pictures of him walking in the park with three women, another of him walking out of a cemetery with dark glasses and his hair was wild. He had on a black t-shirt and loose jeans. The last was a picture at a bar sitting next to a blonde and next to her was Ariel.

Damn it, damn it, damn it. What was I thinking? I can't do this, I won't do this. Focus damn it, Emma's head screamed. *Coincidental plane trip to London together what the hell ever!*

Sunday London and Emma attended the early church service and said goodbye to their friends. They took Troy to the rehab center and said tearful see you soons. Emma and London went to the movies and out to dinner and returned home for their normal Sunday routine.

Emma went to bed that night and cried, still with no response from Brody.

~

Emma sat in the exam room at her OBGYN's office and waited. She looked at her phone and still no call. The doctor did a breast exam and felt a lump in her left breast. A mammogram was scheduled for Wednesday.

Emma drove home feeling nervous but knew he was just being overly cautious, she was only thirty four, ands he was sure it was nothing.

Emma busied herself with packing and getting London together with a few friends and family members before the big move. London was so excited and busy that she didn't sense the unease in Emma.

Wednesday Emma sat in the small white office looking at the photos on the wall as she waited for the doctor to go over the results with her.

"Hello Emma I am Dr. Green," the tall gray haired man said shaking her hand.

"Hello," Emma said nervously.

"Emma we found a tumor that is one point six centimeters in your left breast. I would like to schedule a lumpectomy; we will be able to remove it without having to do a mastectomy, so that is something very positive to focus on right now. I am suggesting that while we do the lumpectomy we also do a biopsy of two lymph nodes because that's how cancer usually spreads. This will tell us if we need to do any other treatments like chemotherapy or radiation. Emma do you need to take a break?" Dr Green asked.

Emma shook her head no.

"Alright, I am going to refer you to an oncologist and a surgeon," Dr Green spoke in a professional tone.

The dam broke and Emma began to cry, "Are you telling me I have breast cancer?"

"Yes Emma, but we won't know what we are looking at until we remove the mass," Dr Green said, "May I please call someone for you Emma?"

"I am divorced, I have an eight year old daughter. I am moving and starting a new career on Monday," Emma said wiping away the tears.

"Okay I am going to make a couple calls now Emma, and you are going to sit here and think about strength. You are going to be fine alright?" Dr. Green told her.

"Thank you," Emma said.

Dr, Green set up the appointment for Friday, there was a cancellation, so they pushed her right in. They would leave a day earlier than planned, London was excited about skipping school and Caroline and Henry knew what was going on, and they were truly supportive as always.

On their drive to Tarrytown Emma smiled as she looked in the rearview mirror at London who was happily singing along with her iTouch.

"Hey baby girl could we talk for a minute?" Emma asked smiling.

"Sure Mom, what's up?" London responded.

"I have to have a little procedure in the morning, so you'll hang out with grandpa while I go to the surgery center," Emma explained.

"Are you alright Mom?" London asked worried.

"I will be just fine, it's just a test nothing like the operation I had two years ago. In fact, I will be home that night and still be going to work on Tuesday as planned, just a little detour from our original plan, no big deal" Emma laughed.

"Does Brody know?" London quizzed her.

"No honey, no one but you and your grandparents, it's kind of private okay?" Emma explained.

"When did you talk to Brody last Mom?" London continued the quiz.

"Well I think it was Saturday, we have both been busy," Emma smiled.

"Okay good, I like him," London said stating her opinion.

"Well you know we are very different and just because we hung out a few times does not mean he is right for me," Emma reminded her.

Her phone rang through the cars blue tooth system and announced Brody's call.

"Answer it Mom!" London cheered.

"Hello this is Emma, and you are on speaker," she said.

"Hello Em, hello London," Brody said sweetly.

"Brody I miss you!" London laughed.

"I miss you too. I have been busy. London are you skipping school?" Brody asked in an accusatory tone.

"Yep, mom's idea, we are moving today instead of tomorrow, I guess mom has.." London started.

"Brody this is kind of a bad time can we speak later?" She asked shooting London a goofy face.

"Sure, when can I phone you?" Brody asked.

"We should be there in two hours, then you can talk to her alone," London laughed.

"We are going to be truly busy this weekend getting things straightened around, how about Monday?" Emma asked trying to keep it together.

"Em, please, I need to speak to you," Brody said sounding wounded.

"Alright then Monday works best for me, talk to you then," Emma said and hung up.

"Mom are you mad at Brody?" London asked.

"No, not mad, just busy," Emma smiled.
~
Caroline and Henry had unpacked all of Emma and London's things and put them away. London had decided she wanted to sleep in the house and not the apartment the first night which Emma agreed to, that way she could unpack the remainder of the stuff that they had brought along after London was in bed. She decided to call Lila and tell her that they had moved and what was going on.

"Emma," Lila answered the phone, "How are you?"

"We are home now, almost moved in. The storage trailer will be here in the morning. I need to ask you a favor," Emma asked softly.

"Anything, you know that," Lila said kindly.

"Well, Brody kind of flaked on Saturday and didn't return a text after that, he called today and well, I can't do this with him Lila. There is so much going on," Emma said and began to cry.

"Emma, you should hear him out," Lila started.

"No, he should leave me alone Lila, I need to get through something, and I can't waste my energy on this puppy love nonsense," Emma said pulling herself back together.

"Emma..." Lila began.

"No, please Lila, I need to tell you something and I need you to be strong for me," Emma said sternly.

"Ok I am listening," Lila said soothingly.

"I have an appointment tomorrow, to have a procedure. A lumpectomy, I have breast cancer," Emma started.

"What?" Lila said shocked.

Emma explained everything and made her promise not to tell her client any of it. While they were on the phone Brody called three times and Emma ignored each call. When they got off the phone she received a text from him.

-You should know I am not going to stop trying to contact you Emma, so answer your fucking phone!...MM

Her phone rang again, and it was him, "Brody, please stop calling," Emma said softly.

"Will you just listen to me Emma! I fucked up, we had a pretty deep conversation, and I thought you needed space to deal with..." he began.

"I do need space, a lot of it. So thank you for being so very aware of what I needed and still need," Emma started.

"No, Emma you need to listen to me so just SHUT UP for five minutes," he yelled.

"See I knew that age thing was going to be an issue, DON'T YELL AT ME!" Emma snapped.

"I am coming home, maybe if you could just…" Brody started.

"No, you finish what you went there for, right now Brody I don't need nor want this distraction. If you come home I will refuse to see you, do you understand Brody, I am done," Emma told him.

"You're done Emma? Wow that's great, just fucking great. Glad I could fuck you through your slump!" Brody yelled.

"Oh yes thank you for making me feel even more worthless than you already have," Emma responded in an exasperated tone.

"Frustrated Em, good! Damn it what the hell happened?" Brody asked.

"Let's see we talked about some really important things on Saturday morning. You realized Troy knew and that my daughter was vested, you are struggling with something, I said three stupid meaningless words to you and you didn't respond. When you and I finally actually opened up to each other you flaked. I can't do that to me, and I won't do that to London!"

"You need to get…" he started, "Emma I will have my album done by Wednesday I have been busting my ass to finish it so I could get home to you. I am cancelling my interviews and will be home no later than next week. Is that acceptable?"

"No, don't Brody, please don't cancel anything. I just have things to work through, please stay. I am going to be pretty busy for awhile," Emma whispered.

"Emma," Brody said sadly, "Don't push me out, please. I love you Em."

Emma cleared her voice, "I can't, not now and not ever."

"I love you Emma," Brody repeated.

"I am begging you to just leave it alone Brody this will never ever work. Please," Emma begged, "I can't do this."

"No, Emma you won't do this, you love me, that doesn't change in a week," his voice cracked.

"Well that's where you are wrong I don't. I mistook lust for love. It was exactly what I needed at the exact time I needed it. I am sure if you dig deep enough you'll find the same holds true for you. I am sorry, but you and I are finished, I am so sorry, Goodbye Brody," Emma said sternly.

"Don't hang up Emma, I won't call again," Brody said firmly.

He heard her take a deep breath and she hung up. Emma pulled her knees to her chest and cried. *It hurt so bad to lose him, even more than ... no ,no, no, pull it together*, she told herself, *I don't have the time do this.*

Chapter 9

"Your test results will be back by Wednesday, we were able to remove the entire tumor. You should rest for a week, no lifting over ten pounds for a week okay Mrs. Fields," Dr. Spandard said.

"Yes thank you, may I go home now?" Emma asked.

"Yes the nurse is bringing the wheelchair now," he smiled softly.

Emma stood at the hospital entrance and looked at her father and began to cry, "Dad everything has to be alright."

"Emma I know it will be," he kissed her forehead.

Emma slept the rest of the day in her bed. London and Caroline made sure she was well taken care of and pampered. Her phone chimed alerting her to a message.

-Seems I am not the only one making the gossip sites, is this why we are done Em? Are you really no different than the rest of them?...Brody

-Well hello Brody. Interesting that you can go five days without any contact and then when I say I am done you get awfully chatty...Emma

-Answer the damn question Emma...Brody

-Brody the man I am holding is someone I will love forever, very handsome and strong isn't he...Emma

-Who is it Emma...Brody

-Who is the Blonde in your lovely shot and why was Ariel there? Pointing fingers is a sign of someone hiding things, best of luck…Emma

-Just answer the fucking question, how long have the two of you been together…Brody

-Well about thirty four and a half years/ He is the only man I have ever needed in my life, my father…Emma

-Good…Brody

-I am going to change my number, I sent all your gifts to Lila. LET IT GO!!!...Emma

-You took the gifts I gave London?...Brody

-I bought her a new one…Emma

-With child support, classy…Brody

-Better than prostitute payment…Emma

-You said it…Brody

-Yep and I returned it…Emma

-I guess I could recycle the gift to the next single Mom I hook up with…Brody

Emma shut off her phone and fell back to sleep, when she woke Lila was sitting in her room watching her.

"Hi," Emma yawned.

"Good morning," Lila smiled, "How are you feeling?"

"Sore, very sore," Emma said holding her chest.

"Not as feisty as last night?" Lila chuckled.

"What?" Emma asked confused.

"A very angry Rockstar with a funny accent called me last night and sent me a whole page of text messages and insisted I deal with it," she laughed.

"Oh I am to be dealt with?" Emma laughed.

"Apparently, you may be a liability," Lila said in an English accent.

"Yes I may just lose my mind, being the unreasonable women that I am. Do me a favor, tell him I said maybe he should have gagged me the day he tied me up and fucked me into submission," Emma said annoyed.

Lila gasped, "Did he really and before you answer that can I really tell him you told me that?"

"Absolutely, just don't tell him I loved it," Emma laughed.

Lila sent Brody a text, and they both snuggled on Emma's bed and laughed waited for a response.

-She said WHAT!!! Lila she is going to be a problem, let her know that her mouth wasn't running when she was on her knees in her bathroom sucking the life out of me. No, don't Lila I thought I could trust her what the hell am I going to do now?...Brody H.

-She has been my best friend for nearly fifteen years, she will not be a problem, just don't fuck her up Brody...Lila

-It was never my intention to do so…Brody

-Okay what else can I do for you today?...Lila

-Tell her to start acting her age and that her place is with me, and that regardless of what she thinks I know she loves me…Brody H

- you actually want me to do that?...Lila

-No she asked for space, more like demanded it, I should have listened to her. Lila I do love her…Brody H

-Well maybe you should start by not hanging out with the women in your photos online. Especially Ariel!!!...Lila

-Wasn't planned, BTW the blonde is my sister…Brody H

-I am a bit busy now maybe I could call you later…Lila

-Are you with her now?!?!...Brody H

- Later Brody okay...Lila

Lila's phone rang, and it was Brody.

"Hello," Lila answered.

"Are you?" Brody asked.

"Yep," Lila said without expression.

"Good put me on speaker," Brody insisted.

"As you wish," Lila said.

"Since it seems fair to discuss our private affairs with Lila, I want you to know Emma that if I was there right now this would be a non issue so cut the crap. When I do get home I will find you and tie you up in pretty little bows and fuck you until you beg me to stop, even then I won't. Remember what I said about not letting you finish so that you know where you are meant to be so that you don't flake out and feel that you need to be some sort of warrior Princess and take on the world alone. I love you, you love me and those pretty words are not the only thing that my mouth was made for Em, do you remember that. I do, I remember your taste, your intoxicating scent, your perfect tits and the very warm tight place that took me forever to work into. I also want you to remember I am going to tag that ass as well. Now as you sit there wet with desire and need for me, remember that the pulsing you feel deep inside is mine to take care of. Got it Em?" he waited for a response, "Okay good, your not being defiant. You know your place. Now I am going to take a hot shower and jerk of as I suck on the panties I took from you when I left, so I can taste you Emma, my favorite candy. You may want to open up that gift in the box and use it a lot because I am not going to let you come for days Emma, see you in a week. Ask your Mom for two nights off cause you're going to be tied up for that long so that I can fuck your brain straight!"

"I can give her three days Brody," Caroline said breathlessly from behind Emma.

"Mom?" Emma gasped.

"Good lord Emma say yes!" Caroline snapped, "Your father and I are taking London for ice cream while you rest, we will bring you back some."

"You're an ass Brody!" Emma snapped.

"Your ass, see you in a week. Good day to you all. I love you Em see you soon," Brody said and hung up.

Lila and Emma looked at each other and laughed, "Emma is he really like that?"

Emma's face turned red, "That and more, he is a bad ass Rockstar."

"And you're going to let him walk?" Lila said.

"I am, I need to get better, I can't expect that he could hold up to that forever," Emma said trying to laugh it off.

~

London's first day of school was amazing. Even in just the first grade they were going to learn Spanish and had the option of taking a musical instrument after school one or two days a week dependent on their capability. London would start piano on Tuesdays and Wednesdays and Emma would be able to pick her up from them. Thursdays Emma could work a little later so that she could learn all that she needed to with hopes her career would take off.

Wednesday she went to her appointment after work. They had gotten everything, and there was no sign of cancer in her lymph nodes. She was ecstatic and she and Lila went out for a drink before getting on the train.

"Your boyfriend called last night, he is wrapping up his interviews this week," Lila smiled smugly.

"He isn't my boyfriend, and I hope he is doing well, I haven't googled him in a week, so I have no idea what he has been up to. I am going to get going and hug my little girl. Thanks for celebrating with me. One more visit and I will be ready to honestly celebrate," Emma hugged her and left.

On Friday Emma met with a new oncologist Dr. Marcus Slain, he was in his late thirties and stood six foot tall. He had jet black hair and piercing green eyes.

"Hello Emma I am Dr. Slain and would like to talk to you about a few things would you have a seat."

"Yes, please I think I need one," she said as she sat, he smiled at her. "I thought everything was fine."

"Right now it is and very well could be forever, would you like a drink Mrs. Fields?"

He walked to the mini fridge set in the cherry wall unit in his impressive office. He took off his lab coat and threw it across the back of the large black leather chair that sat behind his desk. He was particularly handsome and well built. His black pants and blue shirt were obviously expensive and made to fit his body perfectly.

"Mrs. Fields?"

"I am sorry please call me Emma and yes I would love a drink," she said smiling.

"Do you have a husband or boyfriend that could be here while we discuss this further, Mrs., I mean Emma?" He felt a bit uncomfortable.

"No, neither, I do have an eight year old little girl and would love to be able to know that I will be here to see her children and her children's children. Do you have kids?" Emma asked.

"No, I don't yet," he smiled.

"Are you married or dating anyone?" Emma asked and her face turned red when she noticed that he was uncomfortable, "Oh I am sorry, please excuse me I just read that if a doctor felt vested in his patient he would do more to… I am sorry I will be quiet now."

"Emma" he said and sat in the chair next to her, "I can assure you that I will not forget you and will do everything in my power to make sure you see your grandchildren. I am single, I just moved here from Boston, and my work is my life. I will take care of you."

"I have a friend that I want you to meet," Emma smiled, "She is also married to her career, and if anyone can show you this crazy town she can."

"Are you trying to set me up or are you still trying to make sure you get the best possible care," Mark laughed?

"Both, so back to me, what do you suggest I do?" Emma asked.

"I would like to try a very light dose of radiation targeting the area around where the lump was. This would kill any harmful cells that may become problematic in the future. It is not one hundred percent but nothing is. I want you to think about it. I would like to do some more photos of your left breast and then set up some appointments to do the radiation," he said and looked at her, "Are you alright Emma?"

"Yes just dizzy, when do we start. I just started a new job and I…" her voice broke, and she started to cry.

"Listen," he said grabbing her hand, "How about you take my card, I will put my cell phone number on the back, you can text me as soon as you can wrap your brain around this. I hope you're not driving, I can give you a ride."

"No, a friend is picking me up, I just have to wait downstairs," she said wiping her tears.

"I will walk you down, you are my last appointment today," he said grabbing her jacket, "How are you healing?"

"I think good, aren't you supposed to check?" Emma said.

"Ya I am sorry I just got a little side tracked by my new patient Emma Fields, who has an eight year old daughter and just started a new job who is way too young to be going through this and is trying to set me up, how did I do?" Mark smiled.

"And now your new patient is going to flash you," Emma laughed and so did he.

Emma and Mark were waiting out front when Lila pulled up front and jumped out.

"Hey Emma," Lila smiled, "Did you meet a hot new friend, you know the Rockstar will be heart broken."

"Emma, is this the friend you were talking about?" Mark said, and his eyes twinkled.

She shook her head yes, "Lila this is Mark, Mark this is Lila."

"Pleasure to meet you Mark," Lila smiled.

"The pleasure is all mine," he laughed.

"Not yet but it could be," Lila laughed as she stepped back into the car.

He laughed, and Emma looked at him, "She is all bark and no bite."

"That's too bad," Mark looked past Emma and towards her. "Give her my number, PLEASE," he said with pleading eyes and hugged Emma, "Call me as soon as you have time to process it alright."

"Come on London's waiting," Lila yelled.

"London?" he asked.

"That's my daughters name," Emma smiled.

"Alright two more bits of info about my new favorite patient, making you absolutely unforgettable," Mark smiled as he opened the door for her, "Very nice to meet you Lila."

"Nice Emma," Lila laughed.

"That is my new oncologist, Dr. Mark Slain. And he wants me to give you his number," Emma laughed.

"Well I guess I could call him, for you that is, you know take one for the team," Lila said in a sexy voice.

Emma laughed, "Maybe he will tie you up in bows."

"Hmm one could only wish. Speaking of bows, your boy has two interviews that will be aired tonight, you should watch them," Lila grinned.

"Lila I need to keep focused, this is not over yet. I will be seeing the good Dr. for awhile. Just think he's already seen my tits, even touched them, yours could be next," Emma winked.

~

Emma and Lila walked into the house with dinner on the table.

"I could get used to this," Emma smiled as London hugged her gently so she wouldn't hurt her.

Caroline had been researching recipes that had cancer fighting ingredients. She made sure that most everything was high in vitamin D which was linked to slow the growth of cancer. As well as green vegetables, tonight it was Brussels sprouts.

As they ate, Lila made mention that Brody had a couple interviews that would be aired tonight and winked at Caroline. Emma thanked Lila and wrote down Mark's number.

"Call him, he is as married to his career as you are, and hot as hell. His eyes twinkled when he looked at you Lila," Emma smiled and hugged her.

After London was asleep Caroline brought over laundry and turned on the TV.

"I will fold them just sit and relax and watch TV with me," Caroline smiled.

Emma was almost asleep when she heard Brody's voice and jumped. Caroline smiled and looked at the TV.

"Welcome Back Brody Hines" Gordon the host said.

"Good to be here," Brody said and flashed his sexy smile.

"So as per your Publicist we have to avoid any talk of your personal life except what is on this card," Gordon laughed as he crumpled it up and threw it over his shoulder.

Brody licked his lips and his eyes narrowed a bit, "Well we just feel the less personal the better," he said sitting back.

"Well let's get all the personal stuff out of the way first, we can time it if it will make you feel better. Let's do thirty seconds of rapid fire questioning. You can skip three. Agreed?" Gordon smiled.

"We shall see, shoot," Brody smiled.

"Boxers or briefs?" Gordon asked.

"Neither," Brody smiled.

"M&M's really your favorite?" Gordon asked.

"More than you'll ever know," Brody answered.

"Miss your ex wife?" Gordon asked.

"Hell no!" Brody laughed.

"Anyone new in mind?"

"Yes," Brody gave a half smile.

"Have you sealed the deal?" Gordon asked.

Brody raised his eyebrow "Skip."

"Do you want to seal the deal?"

"I believe in abstaining until marriage," he chuckled.

"Will you remarry?"

"Sure, if she would have me."

"How long would it last?" Gordon laughed.

"Forever," Brody said deep in thought.

"Do you like top or bottom?" Gordon laughed.

"Hmm, top," Brody said.

"Vanilla or mix it up?"

"Skip" he laughed.

"Do you want children?"

"I love children, doesn't matter either way."

"Now look at the screen and tell me which is more your type, A B or C."

Brody watched as the pictures came across, one was of Ariel, the second of Princess Kate and the third of Emma from the first time he ran into her at the park.

"Skip, are we done here?" He asked annoyed.

"Yep, thirty seconds are up, thank you for playing that with us. After the commercial break we will return to talk about Brody Hines' new Album, to be released a week early. And to discuss a new charity he has founded. Stay tuned," Gordon stood and smiled at Brody as Brody looked at the ground.

~

"He is very handsome Emma," Caroline said softly.

"Mom, please I need to get through all this," Emma said looking down.

"Do you love him?" Caroline asked.

"In a perfect world without cancer or ex's he would be wonderful, possessive and…" Emma started.

"Domineering is the word I think you're looking for dear," Caroline giggled.

"Mom I am sorry about that," Emma was embarrassed.

"Don't be sorry, enjoy him," Caroline laughed and Emma joined her.

They heard his voice again.

~

"So Brody tell us about your new Charity," Gordon said.

"Well it's called London's Child. It is to raise money for families, mainly orphaned children whose parents have died of terminal illness. So that, they don't have to fend for themselves. This is Rebecca, my sister," he said looking into the camera and Emma gasped, "She will be running a home here in London for kids who have lost a parent. A lot of times when someone dies the other parent struggles, and it's the children who are failed. Be it to drugs or alcohol or just the demands to work more to replace income, those children lose. We want to help them, as many as we can."

"Is there a reason behind this?" Gordon asked.

"Actually it's personal. But I will share. My mother died of cancer when I was young and well, to put it mildly, I lost my way for awhile. Until the past few weeks, I didn't realize how much I needed my mother. There you have it," he smiled shyly.

"So what else are we going to do today Brody?" Gordon asked.

"Well I would like to wrap some gifts that Rebecca and I bought that we will be donating to the charity for Christmas. We want to wrap them up in bows," he said grinning and looked at the camera. "Pretty little packages, if anyone cares to donate a gift the address will magically appear on the screen."

~

Caroline laughed and looked at Emma who was crimson and crying. "What's wrong Emma?" Caroline said and hugged her.

"His mom died of cancer, he was alone and scared and sad for many years. Now I have cancer and that's just yet another reason I can't be with him, and I love him Mom, I do," Emma cried.

They sat snuggled up on the couch and watched Brody laugh while he tied the gifts Rebecca wrapped in bows.

~

"So what do you do when you run out of ribbon?" Gordon laughed holding up the empty roll.

"Improvise, like use a scarf or I don't know socks, whatever you can get your hands on I guess," Brody laughed as he tided up the bows.

"Wow bows make you happy," Gordon laughed as he took his tie off and handed it to Brody to use to make a bow.

"I love bows," Brody said trying to hide his amusement.

"And M&M's" Gordon laughed as his assistant brought out a bag.

Brody shook his head and bit his cheek as he tried not to laugh but failed miserably, it was a darker deeper laugh, "Yes nothing makes me happier than bow's and M&M's, nothing in this whole world."

"So we could set you up in a chair with a bowl of M&M's and a box full of ribbons and that would be good for you?" Gordon laughed.

"Oh it would be like I imagine heaven to be, I could stay cooped up like that for at least two days," he laughed, and looked at the camera, "Maybe three," he said and his eyebrow raised.

"Alright so you have a surprise for us tonight Brody, why don't you tell the audience," Gordon smiled.

"Tonight we are going to release our title track. All proceeds will go to London's Child," Rebecca Hines shared, "And Brody and the boys are going to sing you the title track."

Emma sat and watched him as he sang. Just like the first time she saw him perform, it was like watching a private moment, one that she was part of. Her heart ached when she remembered the Night Brody and she had talked about the song and how open he seemed. She was reminded how quickly that changed and how cold he became, and she knew she could not go through that again, ever.

"I think I may love him too Emma, on that note I will leave you and go find your father," Caroline laughed as she took the empty basket and disappeared out the door.

Emma received a text at midnight

-I hope you caught the show. No reading between the lines Princess, I will have you in bows…Brody

- Think deeply Brody Hines of what happened after you opened up to me about that and let this go…Emma

Her phone rang, and she ignored it.

-Please Emma I need you …Brody

- The interview was comical, now all your crazy fans know you don't wear undies The foundation you started with your sister is beautiful, and you should be very proud of yourself. Your performance was amazing. Take care .... Emma

-Don't patronize me…Brody

-I am not, you did great…Emma

-I hope you can see I have been busy Emma this trip has been far from pleasurable…MM

-Brody please, I don't know how to end this, but I can't do this to me or to you…Emma

-Then don't Em, just don't..MM

~

Emma sent Dr. Slain a text message with a few questions.

-Do you work near the office...Mark

-A few blocks away...Emma

-Meet me for lunch? Tell me where you want to meet I have an hour and a half. We can chat...Mark

"Thanks for meeting me," Emma said as she smiled at Mark Slain.

"No problem, I know you're working at a new job, and after work you have your daughter to tend to so I can be flexible," Mark smiled. "So what do you think?"

"Well how often do I need to do the treatments, how long do they take, how will I feel, what are the side effects?" Emma bombarded him.

He smiled and sat down and took her hands in one of his, "First I want to do another Mammogram; next we will start with treatments three days a week for seven weeks. Unless you want to try twice a day for a week. The side affects vary. There is armpit and chest pain, fatigue, lowered white blood cell counts, and can cause lung and heart issues."

Emma realized how hard she was squeezing his hand and let go.

"Sorry," Emma said and looked horrified.

Mark hugged her, "You're fine."

"What do you suggest I do, I mean which treatment plan?" Emma asked.

"Well you have to make that choice, you may have no side effects. one week treatment plan will obviously hit hard and fast, but if it were me I would do that. But I didn't just start a new job or have a London," Mark smiled sweetly.

"Well maybe I can see if I can spread my hours between five days instead of three and work that out, I want this done," Emma said decisively.

"Good, listen we can start Thursday or Friday, and you would go until Monday or Tuesday. It's up to you but three of those days you would have off of work. Maybe you could stay with your friend in the city?" Mark smiled, "I could come by and check on you."

Emma laughed, "I will think about it."

Mark walked with Emma back to her building and answered more questions. She hugged him and thanked him and went back to work. She spoke to her boss and was given permission to work from home both Thursday and Tuesday. Emma was extremely grateful. She texted Mark and let him know, and he would set things up. Lila insisted she stay there, and Caroline promised to bring London on school days. Lila would occupy her on the weekend at her place.

~

Emma was scheduled at eight in the morning and four in the afternoon on each day.

Thursday the good doctor brought her back from each appointment and walked her in. "You have my number Emma anything you need or are concerned about, let me know," Mark said sternly.

"Thanks so much, I think I may be concerned at around eight tonight if you would like to stop over and have dinner," Emma smiled.

"You're a doll, we will see. Go get some rest," Mark said and gave her a quick hug.

Emma walked into the bathroom to examine her breast. There was a small incision which was healed and nicely except for the pink mark it left behind to the left of her areola. Her once perfect breast now marked for life. It wasn't a huge change, her breast was still the same size as the other, but if you looked close enough you could tell that a small dent would forever be there. The incision was low and horizontal so that if she wore a tank top it would not be noticeable. But Emma knew she would never feel completely comfortable the way she had felt with Brody, completely naked and tied up allowing someone to explore every part of her. It had taken her years to feel confident enough to wear a bathing suit let alone be in her birthday suit. She made Troy turn off the lights and still used covers most of the time. It was never like that with Brody, he made her feel beautiful and desirable, and now he was gone. Tears fell down her face as she looked at herself. London would be here tomorrow so today she could cry, and so she did.

She was asleep when Lila came home to check on her. It was eight o'clock and she had been asleep for three hours. Lila saw her phone flashing missed calls. She grabbed it and walked into the hall. Lila returned Caroline's call and told her that Emma was asleep, and they decided it would be best to let her sleep. She answered the phone when Mark called and told him she was asleep, and he offered to come over, she accepted his offer.

They were chatting in the living room when Emma walked out.

"Oh hey what time is it?" Emma asked.

"Eight thirty, you should call London, she is worried about you," Lila smiled.

"How are you feeling Emma?" Mark asked and felt her head and immediately took her pulse.

"I am fine just tired," Emma said with a forced smile. "Is that my phone?"

"Yes I am sorry, I returned your calls, I didn't want to wake you. All except one," Lila said giving her a sad puppy dog face.

"Give it a rest Lila," Emma said and walked away to call London.

Friday was the same except London would be there at seven, and she was extremely excited. Lila had rented some movies and Mark was stopping again. Friday ran into Saturday and Emma was getting more tired every day. By noon on Sunday she was exhausted, and her body ached. Her breast was red and hot and extremely uncomfortable. Caroline had come to get London and Emma thought she had held it together wonderfully for her daughter, and now she was going to bed.

~

Caroline pulled into the driveway, and London screamed and jumped out of the car and ran towards her Grandfather and a man Caroline couldn't tell yet who he was.

"Brody," London screamed and jumped in his arms.

"Well hello there London, have you missed me?" Brody said laughing.

"Of course I have, more than you could ever imagine," London squeezed him tightly, and he felt her little body shake and could tell immediately that she was crying.

"Miss London what is wrong?" Brody whispered.

"I missed you Brody," she sobbed.

"Well you were with me the whole time," he breathed out and closed his eyes.

"Brody, mom is not here, she is in the city, and she..." London began.

"Brody Hines, what brings you here?" Caroline interrupted.

"I just returned from London, and I missed it so much that I figured I would stop by and see someone who outshines the whole city itself," he smiled and twirled her around.

"Well why don't you come in for a little bit, it's almost London's bedtime, but I think we could bend the rules this once," Caroline smiled and patted his back. "Henry you have met Brody?"

"I have, he pulled in a couple minutes before you did," Henry smiled and kissed his wife.

London was still wrapped around Brody, and he held her as tightly as she held him. "I brought you some things from the city that was named after you," Brody said and pulled her away and looked in her eyes still full of tears.

"Okay Miss London, I don't know what is going on, but I am going to fix it, so you don't have to worry anymore."

"I love you Brody," she whispered.

"I love you more," Brody said softly.

"That's what Mommy says," London said with a smile on her face.

"And I learned it from her, she is very smart. Just like you," Brody set her down, "Are you going to be okay?"

"Are you going to see my Mommy?" London asked.

"Do you think I should?" he smiled.

"Yes," London said sticking her nose in the air.

"Well then I guess I should then," Brody said and kissed her nose.

"London, your Mom is going to be busy for a few days, three to be exact Brody," she said giving him a knowing look. "Maybe you should wait until then."

"No Grandma she needs…" London started.

"London my sweet, sweet girl," Caroline smiled "Your Mommy needs a few days okay?"

London started to cry, and Brody fought the urge to destroy something. "With all due respect ma'am…"

"Watch yourself Brody," Henry sneered, "My wife and granddaughter are standing right here, and our daughter, our little girl needs just a few more days without a bunch of..."

"Okay Henry. Thank you," Caroline said and wrapped her arm around his waist.

"Shit Grandma, that's what he was going to say, and Brody isn't shit, he loves her and she loves him," London screamed and ran to Brody crying.

"Oh London," Brody said picking her up and held her. His eyes narrowed, and jaw clenched as he shook his head. "Is she at Lila's?"

"Yes and she is sick Brody really sick," London sobbed.

"What is wrong with her?" he growled.

"It will be her decision to tell you if she feels like it," Henry answered with piercing eyes.

"Grandpa..." London yelled.
"Shh it's okay, your Mom would do the same thing to protect you. Caroline, Henry could I please read London a bedtime story and hang out until she falls asleep?" Brody asked politely.

"Yes you can, Brody come with me," London said jumping down and grabbed his hand and pulled him into the house. "Come with me to our place, I can get my PJ's."

Brody walked up the open stairway behind London that lead to a beautiful open floor plan. It was about sixteen hundred square feet, the living room and kitchen was separated by a large granite island with a stovetop and a grill built in, there were four cast iron barstools. There was a large dining room pub style high top table and six chairs and four bay windows, two of which had window seats. The others set up as office areas. One was clearly where Emma worked. Brody walked over and grabbed the sweatshirt he had given her that was hanging over the back and smelled it, he could smell her sweet scent mixed with his and he felt tears fall down his face. He loved her and something was horribly wrong, and he had been told he could not go to her.

FUCK he thought *I don't give a shit what they say, there is no way I will spend three more fucking days without her.*

London gave him a tour, and he noticed she had not gotten the furniture he had given her, and when he saw the garment bags he knew Emma had not touched the clothes.

"How does your Mom like her new job?" Brody asked.

"She loves it," London smiled.

"So she isn't feeling well?" Brody asked, and London looked over his shoulder.

"She will be fine," she said and smiled.

"Okay miss London let's get you into bed, tell me where," Brody smiled and took her hand.

Brody waited until London was asleep. He knew she was because Emma had told him about the little shake she did before she fell into a deep sleep. Emma was right she knew her daughter so well, and he knew it took a lot to keep her away from London. As he lay with London in his arms he took his phone and searched the web and found many pictures of Emma with a man, all involved hugging. He immediately was pissed and when he saw Lila in one of them he felt betrayed.

He couldn't move, he didn't want to, he adored her daughter and thought there was no one else but Emma for him, forever. He fell asleep holding London, Caroline went into the room and took a picture and texted it to Emma.

-He loves you Emma, and she loves him, please don't over think this...Mom

Brody woke up to London giggling, "London, I am so sorry I can't believe I fell asleep, you Mom is going to be so angry and your Dad well…"

"Good morning Brody," Caroline smiled as she walked in the room, "Did you sleep well?"

"Caroline I apologize.." Brody started.

"I didn't have bad dreams last night Grandma," London said and took his hand and pulled him up.

"I know, that's the first time in almost a week," Caroline smiled at her and winked at Brody, "Breakfast is ready and then showers and school for you Miss London."

~

It was ten o'clock when Brody's car pulled up in front of Lila's building. He still had the key and let himself in. He walked down the hall and the bathroom door opened and Emma was standing in a towel fresh out of the shower looking like hell.

"Brody," she whispered and started to fall.

"Emma," he yelled as he grabbed her and held her in his arms.

"I am so sorry," she whispered.

"Emma?" Brody looked up and saw the man from the photos.

He was pulling his shirt over his head, "Emma are you okay?"

"Who the fuck are you and what have you done to her," Emma tried to pull herself up, and her towel dropped and Brody grabbed her and looked down and saw the scar and the red swollen breast, "What the fuck did you do to her!"

"Please stop, please. Mark the towel, please cover me up," Emma said softly.

"Mark? Emma is that what you want, someone to fucking leave marks on you?" Brody yelled.

"Brody, please I don't feel well," Emma said and closed her eyes.

"Brody Hines?" Mark looked at the angry man holding Emma, "I need you to go put her on the bed and let me make sure she is alright."

"Fuck you, get the fuck out of my way you sick bastard. Emma I am going to get you help but whatever he did to you, you need to tell me, Em come on Princess talk to me," Brody said holding her tightly, "If anything happens to her I will rip your fucking throat out Mark!"

"Brody, he is my doctor," Emma choked out and closed her eyes again.

"In any other situation Mr. Hines I would not be telling you shit but you need to do as I asked, go set her down now," Mark snapped. Brody gave him a challenging look, "Do it now and then call Lila."

Brody did as he asked out of sheer panic that he was going to lose her. He watched as Mark checked her heart rate and breathing. He grabbed his bag and set up a saline drip and put an IV in her arm.

"Did you call Lila?" he asked looking at Brody.

"No, I didn't. I haven't decided if I am going to let you fucking live or not," Brody sneered at him.

Mark smiled and grabbed his phone, "Lila I know you're busy but there is a very angry Rockstar here threatening my life could you come back home? Thanks."

Emma started to wake up, and Brody grabbed her hand, "Brody why are you here?" she asked weakly.

He didn't answer he just looked at her and kissed her hand. He heard Lila and Mark walking towards the room.

"Brody this is Mark Slain. Mark this is Brody Hines."

"Lila what the fuck is going on?" Brody growled at her.

"Emma is sick, and Mark is her doctor," Lila said sitting on the bed next to Emma, "Emma you have had an exciting morning, how are you feeling?"

"Like hell," Emma smiled, "What ti…"

"It's ten thirty in the morning," Brody answered, and Emma started to laugh.

"I need my phone I need to call…" Emma started to say as she was sitting up with Lila's help.

"London is at school, your parents are fine, here's your phone," Brody said in a detached tone.

"I missed a message from Mom," Emma whispered and looked at it as Lila looked over her shoulder.

"Where were you last night Brody?" Lila laughed.

"That's none of your concern," he answered as he scowled at her.

"Brody, damn it!" Emma yelled and started to cry.

"We are going to give you two a moment, Lila let me get you breakfast," Mark said taking her hand and walking out the door.

"Emma you need to tell me what is going on," Brody said firmly.

"How could you do this, I told you that we were done. Tell me why you would do this to her?" she said and handed him the phone.

Brody looked at the picture and narrowed his eyes, "I went to see you and London was upset, I read to her and waited to feel the little shake, and I was going to leave but she was so upset Em," Brody couldn't control it anymore, "look at me Em, you are fucking me up," he said and cried with his head in his hands.

"I am so tired Brody, so seriously tired. I don't want to talk about this anymore, but you are giving me no choice. So listen because I will not say it again. I have breast cancer. I found out the Monday after you left. You had not returned my text, and I honestly don't have it in me to make things right for anyone else but me and London. I thought I had lost you. I had to move, I started a new job, I was told I had cancer. It's a lot Brody, and I can't do it anymore. I need to attack this and get better. I have had my breast cut open, sewn shut and am now going through a extremely intense course of radiation," Emma closed her eyes to think and fell asleep.

Brody caught her before her head hit the pillow and pulled her into him and laid down with her head on his chest as he cried.

Mark walked in the door at three o'clock, "Emma, you need to be at the hospital in an hour for your treatment," he said, "I can take you, or you can meet me there."

Emma sat up and looked at Brody sadly, "Give me a minute, thank you Mark. I have to get ready."

"I will take you and I will help you," Brody said and stood up.

"I don't want you to. Didn't I just tell you I couldn't do this?" Emma said covering herself.

"No, Em you fell asleep," he said pulling her up and grabbing her clothes.

"I don't want you to see me," she snapped.

"Em I have seen all of you, stop, I am not going anywhere," Brody said pulling her shirt over her head.

"No, you haven't not seen the new and improved me," she sneered at him.

"Yes Em your towel dropped, and I saw you, your beautiful. Feet in please," he said kneeling down holding her yoga pants.

"Why are you here!" She yelled.

"I love you Em, I am here because I love you. Can you walk or shall I carry you?" Brody asked standing in front of her.

"I can walk," Emma slowly walked into the living room, and Mark removed her IV, "Mark I will take that ride please."

"No, you're riding with me Emma, which hospital?" Brody asked Mark.

"No, damn it!" Emma yelled.

Brody swooped her up and walked out the door, "Emma shhh," he said and kissed her.

Mark and Lila followed.

~

While Emma received her treatment Brody stood outside the room starring at the floor. "Brody are you alright?" Lila asked.

"Lila I don't want to talk to you right now, I am very pissed that she has gone through all this and you could not even tell me!" he snapped.

"Well be pissed then you asshole!" Lila snapped.

"I will," he glared at her.

Emma was being wheeled out, and she looked up at Brody and scowled. He looked at her and shook his head and followed her out. His car was waiting, and he grabbed her arm and helped her up and into the car. He looked back and saw Lila and Mark standing behind him, "Get your ass in here Lila," he snapped.

"Fine!" Lila sneered at him, "Mark will we see you later?"

"Of course," Mark said and hugged her, "Hines you need to be nice to her."

"You're lucky your breathing Doc," Brody snapped.

Mark looked at Emma and smiled, "You need to rest, one more day okay, and this is done. I will be over in a few hours."

"Thank you so much Mark, for everything," Emma smiled politely.

"Anything for my favorite patient," he said and winked.

"You're pushing it asshole," Brody said under his breath.

Mark laughed as he shut the door.

"Brody," Emma said.

"I'm right here Em," he said and grabbed her hand lovingly.

"I need you to let this be, I can't do this with you anymore," Emma said sadly.

"Well let me think about that," he said and sat back still holding her hand, "No sorry Emma but that's not going to happen."

Emma began to cry, and he pulled her into his arms and held her. "Lila I will be staying at your place until she is better, can you deal with that?"

Lila shot him a dirty look, and he returned it.

"She was following my wishes, be nice to her," Emma snapped.

"Fine, sorry Lila," he managed to say.

~

Emma and Brody laid in bed, she slept, and he held her. Her phone rang, and he answered it.

"Good afternoon London," he said with a smile in his voice, "I am here, no she isn't happy with me, but she will get over it, no she isn't mad at you she saves her anger all for me, isn't that sweet," he said and laughed.

He felt Emma stir and grabbed her cup of water as he held the phone with his shoulder against his ear.

"Drink Em," he whispered, and she did as he asked, "She is awake would you like to talk to her? Okay I will talk to you soon, I love you too," Brody handed Emma the phone and looked away.

"Hi baby girl..I am feeling great better everyday…Yes tomorrow night I hope to be home with you..I miss you very much…okay…I will pick you up after piano…I love you more…yes we do… you have been having nightmares?..Okay you don't have to tell me just sleep good tonight please…no I don't think that's a good idea, maybe Grandma could sleep with you…Okay I love you, see ya soon," Emma hung up the phone and drew her knees to her chest and cried.

Brody pulled her into his chest and wrapped his arms around her and kissed the top of her head.

"Don't," Emma snapped.

"Are you feeling up to having a chat Emma?" Brody asked in a deep serious tone.

"No, I would like for you to leave, how could you do that to her, she thinks you're some sort of damn hero because she didn't have a nightmare last night, she wanted you to come stay again. Do you know what you have done?" Emma yelled, "Do you!"

"Emma I…" Brody began to explain.

"And you tell her you love her, what the hell are you thinking, she is not a toy Brody, she is a little girl, she doesn't need you to confuse her, she can't handle it, I can't handle it, and I am an adult!" Emma yelled weekly.

"Are you finished Emma? Are you going to give me a chance to speak?" Brody snapped, "When I showed up at your place last night I expected to find you there, she ran from the car and jumped in my arms, which by the way, when I left here was just fine with you! Emma she was crying and shaking and scared and worried about you. She told me you were sick Emma, she tried to tell me what was going on, and your parents cut her off, she got angry," Brody laughed, "She even said shit…twice."

"She what?" Emma tried not to smile, but he sensed the amusement in her voice.

"You father started to say you didn't need my shit right now, and your mother stopped him, London just filled in the blank.." Brody said with a smile in his voice.

"Twice?" she asked.

"Yep, twice. Well then she was angry, you know the way you get with me, and she cried and I couldn't leave her, my intention was to wait until she did that little shake thing you told me about when she falls asleep, but I laid there and watched her sleep and she looked so peaceful and well, I screwed up and fell asleep. It wasn't to be hurtful to either of you. I am sorry," Brody said and hugged her a little tighter.

Emma didn't reply, she couldn't.

"So then I came here and well you know the rest. Emma, please talk to me, please," Brody said urgently.

"You didn't say it back, or text back and I won't let myself get in a situation like that, ever again. I am not angry Brody I just need you to leave us alone, let us get our lives to the point where they resemble normal. London will always be mine, not for a few months or ten years, forever. I need to be the best me I can be and I knew Troy and I couldn't be together anymore or I would lose myself and then London would suffer, and Brody we were together for fifteen years, but I did it. And I know it's better for her, even though right now she is scared and having bad dreams," Emma said trying not to cry, "But you and I Brody, can't happen. I love her too much to let her be broken again."

"That Saturday morning when we talked, and I pulled away from you, well I was scared. I shared more with you in that hour than I have ever shared with anyone in my life. I had just found out about my mother and found my sister, Emma it overwhelmed me. And yes I was scared. But I knew I needed to figure it out so that I could return strong for you, and your daughter. I am sorry that hurt you and I am so sorry that my break down or break through as I believed it was happened when you got sick Em. But you should have told me. I would have never let you go through this alone Em," he said stroking her hair.

"Brody that's my point, you feel obligated and you are not. I don't want that for you, I want you to find someone to love and have babies with and not have to worry about breast cancer or ex-husbands who will always be there, I love," Emma stopped.

"You love me enough to let me go, that's what you were going to say Emma. Well that's very noble of you however, I love you more because I will never leave you, you are mine forever. When you allow yourself to believe that and stop being so damn selfless you'll get it. And I will be sitting right here. Now take a drink and go to sleep, you need to rest," Brody demanded and handed her water.

Emma took a drink, "It's not up to you," she said and handed him back the water and sat up.

"Okay turn and look at me Emma," he said helping her, "Tell me your pissed at me, tell me you hate me or blame me, get it out of your system."

"I was angry Brody, very angry at myself just as much as I was at you. But I stopped being angry. None of this is your fault it's a wake up call," Emma said looking in his eyes.

"I will never be able to tell you or even put into words how sorry I am Em, but you know it here," he said and touched her chest.

Emma immediately started crying, "Don't, don't touch me not there, not ever!"

"Emma don't do that, don't think for a minute that changes how I feel here," he said and put her hand to his heart.

Emma closed her eyes and let the tears fall, and he pulled her onto his lap and cradled her. "You need to sleep I know that. But do me one last favor," he said and pulled her chin up, so she was looking at him. He wiped her tears and kissed her gently, "Tell me that you don't love me and tell me you don't feel the same way I do about you," Emma didn't respond. And he kissed her again. "Sleep now Emma."

Brody woke up as Emma was getting out of bed, "Do you need something Emma?" he said as he jumped up.

"I need a shower," Emma said softly.

"Okay how about a bath? I will draw you one, sit please I will be back in a minute," Brody said and kissed her.

He ran a bath and added bubbles and lit the candles.

"Alright where are your night clothes?" he asked.

"In the top drawer but I can get them Brody," Emma pouted.

He smiled at her, "No I want to. Emma is this right?" he asked holding up a t-shirt and cotton pajama bottoms.

Emma blushed, "Yes."

Brody giggled, "Alright then."

"What's so funny?" Emma scowled.

"You should be wrapped in satin bows Emma, not cotton," he smiled and tried not to laugh.

She rolled her eyes at him, and he walked into the bathroom and went to help her out of her shirt and she slapped his hand. Brody gasped and looked at her with a shocked expression.

"Did you just strike me?" he asked.

"Yes!" she snapped.

"You won't let me help you?" he asked confused.

"No, I won't," Emma responded, "You should leave."

"You keep saying that Emma and you know I am not going anywhere," Brody said and hugged her.

"I don't want you to see Brody," Emma said shyly.

"Okay for now, but just your breasts right?" Brody asked.

"Brody I am not feeling all that hot lately, I don't think it's a good idea," Emma said looking at the ground.

"Princess I didn't bring the bows with me," he smiled, "I just want to help you get in the bath, I don't want you to fall or get hurt," he said pulling her pants down and she closed her eyes. He looked up at her, "Is this alright Emma?" she shook her head yes and let out a deep breath. "Emma."

"Brody, I can't," Emma said with a shallow breath.

"I know, but the fact that you want to is so hot Emma," Brody said and hugged her. "I am going to turn around, and you can slip into the tub, carefully," he whispered in her ear.

"Brody," she stopped and shook her head hoping to snap out of this mood, "Thank you."

"Emma I love you, it's a privilege to be here," Brody said and turned around.

"Brody damn you," she moaned.

"Get in that bath Emma," he said through clenched teeth.

He heard the water move, "Okay I am in, could you please grab me a wash cloth, please."

Brody grabbed two wash clothes and handed her one as he put the other in the water, "What are you doing?"

"I am going to help you," Brody said.

"No, you are not," she laughed. He looked at her and smiled, "What?"

"You laughed Emma, I haven't heard you laugh in weeks," he smiled and looked away. "First I am going to wash your feet and make my way up to your hair, if it makes you uncomfortable just tell me to stop, I will let you wash your breasts. Just lean back and relax Em."

Brody sat on the edge of the tub with his back to her and washed her feet. He started at the tips of her toes and carefully washed between her toes. He moved to the pad of her feet and she giggled, he turned around and smiled at her, "Stay still please."

He moved to her ankles and moved up her calves, gently rubbing them up and down. Emma leaned further back and he saw her toes curl, and he took a deep breath and stopped. He took the other calf and did the same thing and her toes curled again, he looked over his shoulder and her eyes were closed, and she was biting her bottom lip. He stopped and stretched. He took her left leg and slowly moved up behind her knee to her upper thigh and he felt her body tighten, and she whimpered softly. He could feel himself hardening. He washed the other leg, and she whimpered again. He finished her right leg.

"You need a break Em," he asked in a husky tone.

"No," she said in a whisper.

He cleared his throat and stood up, which startled her. "I do," he said and looked at her.

Emma laughed, "I guess so."

"It's not funny Emma," he growled.

"Are you embarrassed Brody," she smiled.

"No, you got me hard and worked up, are you embarrassed Em?" he smiled.

"Oh so it's my fault?" Emma laughed.

"Let's see, your beautiful naked body is laying in a tub full of water, and bubbles with candle light flickering over you," Brody started.

"All of which you did, so I would hardly call that my fault," Emma smiled brightly.

"No, you got me there Em, but as I worked my way up your legs and your whimpering and moaning and your toes are curling, that's all you," he said in an accusatory tone.

"Then don't help me," she snapped as her face turned red.

Brody smiled at her, "We aren't finished yet if you could be so kind as to not moan and whimper or…"

"Breathe Brody, shall I stop breathing to?" she interrupted.

"No, not ever," Brody said seriously.

"Now shut up and wash me," Emma said and laid back smiling.

Brody took a deep breath and began washing her legs, "Brody you already did that spot, time to move up," Emma smiled.

"Emma keep quiet please," Brody said shooting her a dirty look.

Emma laughed, "You can stop Brody. I can do this, I feel better now."

"You feel better because I am here Emma, because you know I love you and because you know you love me too." Brody said and continued to wash her moving up. He washed between her legs gently, applying the right amount of pressure in the right spots. Emma moaned, and he rubbed a little harder, "Emma I am going to make you come," he said as he slowly slipped a finger inside her and she moaned loudly, "Is this alright?" he asked, his voice gruff.

"Oh God yes," she whimpered.
"This is not why I am here Emma, I am here because I love you, but you seemed to be happy and I want you to be happy Emma forever, but if you don't want this just say stop."

"I love you Brody, don't stop, please don't stop," Emma moaned.

"I am going to give you more than you could have ever hoped for in every way," he said and slipped a second finger into her and moved his hand faster until he felt her body tense up, "Emma I want you to come for me, this is mine all mine, so you need to listen to me and believe me when I tell you I will love you forever, don't push me away ever again, if I upset you tell me if you feel me pulling away," he said slowly pulling his fingers out of her, "Tell me I am, we can be perfect together. We will be perfect together." He moved back into her with more force, "Now come from me Emma, for us, come now," he said and pressed his thumb down on her sweet spot and her body did as it was told to do. "I love you Princess."

Emma was completely relaxed for the first time in weeks. She was happy and smiled as her orgasm finally finished. "I love you Brody, I love you more."

"We love each other more Em," he said and kissed her head. She lay in the bath and he continued to wash her, washing her stomach, and when he got to her right breast he stopped, "May I?" he asked.

"No, please not yet," Emma said sadly.

"Okay, can you sit up and let me wash your hair," Brody said and kissed her head gently.

"I'm sorry," Emma said.

"Emma we will get there okay, when you're ready, don't be sorry," Brody said as he rubbed shampoo into her scalp, "Does this feel good or is it too hard?"

"It feels good. Brody I owe you one, I would like to…" Emma started.

"Emma love, please don't finish that sentence, you'll have a lifetime to do that. Besides I need you to eat food and I would probably fill you up, it's been a long almost three weeks," he chuckled.

"Exactly, I want to Brody, it's not fair to you," Emma said sadly.

Brody rinsed her hair and put conditioner in her hair, she moaned as he rubbed it in, "Em, right now I need you to be quiet, or I am going to take you into that room and have my dinner."

"Hmm," she laughed.

"You just wait, when you are feeling better you are in so much trouble," he said and rinsed her hair. "Alright you're finished."

He grabbed a towel and helped her up, he looked down and grabbed her bottom, "Lots and lots of trouble," he said, and she leaned into him, "Em are you tired?"

"No, Brody I am wet with want for all things you," Emma said and smiled as she turned around.

He gave her a shocked look, cocked his head to the side, and then frowned. He grabbed her clothes and opened the door.

"Off to your room wench, you need your rest, I need you well and wet understand?" Brody said and kissed her quickly.

She sat on the end of the bed, and he put her shirt over her head. He grabbed her panties and she slowly lifted her leg to put her foot through, spreading them enough to give him a peak, he looked up at her, and she raised her eyebrow.

"You are playing with me Emma, and in your condition I won't wear you out," he spread her legs and licked her, she moaned, he used his tongue and circled her sweet spot, and she began to pant and pull his hair. He nibbled lightly on her inner thigh and plunged his tongue deep into her, and she came again.

"So easy to please wench," he winked.

"Emma?" they heard Lila coming down the hall.

He quickly grabbed her panties and wiped them between her legs and bit his lip. He grabbed her pajama bottoms and pulled them up and swiftly placed her on the bed and covered her as the door opened. Lila opened the door, and Brody turned away from her.

Emma looked and saw his erection and gave him pouty lips, he smiled and bent down and kissed her.

"I am going to shower," he said and raised his eyebrow, he pulled her panties out of his pocket and dragged them across his nose and Emma burst out laughing.

"I won't be long, I love you Em."

Lila turned back to face Emma, "You look better. Did you two figure it out?"

"He did," Emma said, "And I am going to blindly follow."

"Emma did you two have sex in your condition?" Lila snapped, "You're exhausted!"

"No, Lila we didn't have sex," she said and grinned.

"Good, you better wait," Lila ordered.

"I don't have a choice," Emma pouted.

"Emma, did he turn you down?" Lila laughed.

"Well kind of," Emma smiled.

"What's that mean?" Lila asked.

Mark walked in the room and scowled.

"Yes what does that mean? You need rest especially if you think you're going back to work on Wednesday."

Brody returned with a towel wrapped around his waist drying his hair.

"She isn't going back to work Wednesday," Brody said giving her a dirty look.

"Yes I am. I am feeling much better now," Emma smiled, "Only one more day of treatment and I will be able to put this all behind me."

"Emma you're going to need to take it easy for awhile. Not exerting any unnecessary effort," Mark said shooting a nasty look at Brody.

Brody laughed, "Doc she doesn't even have to move, I got it all covered."

"Brody," Emma scolded him.

"Emma I won't put you in any danger this asshole needs to understand that," Brody glared at him, "Even though I am confused as to how it's any of his fucking business!"

"Brody put some pants on, and a shirt and then you can come back in here, now!" Emma yelled.

When Brody returned Mark was finishing up with her vitals.

"You seem to be doing better Emma, which surprises me," Brody brushed past him and sat behind Emma on the bed pulling her back so that she rested between his legs against his chest while he glared at Mark. "You look more rested."

Mark started to get the IV ready.

"She needs to eat something, that's probably not helping her appetite at all Doc," Brody snapped.

"Fluids are more important, and she is not drinking enough," Mark responded in the same tone.

"She has drank six twelve ounce cups of water today, she needs food. Em what sounds good?" Brody asked sweetly.

"I don't know soup something with chicken broth, but something with substance sounds good," Emma smiled up at him.

"Well I am happy your appetite is returning, Lila could you order something. I can go pick it up," Mark smiled.

Brody was texting, "I got this, already ordered, and they are going to deliver."

Lila smiled at Emma and shook her head.

"Well there are other things I would like to discuss in private with my patient if you could see yourself out for a few minutes," Mark said trying to dismiss Brody.

"Em love is it alright if I stay?" Brody asked nuzzling his nose into her neck.

"It's okay Mark, I have kept enough from him already," Emma said softly.

"Alright so let's talk about sex," Mark said sitting on the bed, "Emma it may take your body awhile to desire being touched. Especially your breast. Sexual intercourse could be problematic, physiologically you may hinder the production of lubricant making intercourse uncomfortable." Emma felt Brody shift, and he held her tighter. "In some cases the patient would not resume sexual contact for up to a year. But some as soon as a month have reported their desire return."

"Emma you are not only mysteriously intoxicating in bed, you're a medical mystery as well," Brody whispered in her ear.

"Is there something you need to say Brody? Is he pressuring you Emma?" Mark snapped.

"No, he wouldn't do that, please go on," Emma said trying to hide the humor in her voice.

"I would suggest you wait at least a week before you try anything that may make you uncomfortable," Mark suggested.

"I have a couple questions Doc, let's start with what if she wants to have sexual intercourse. Will it slow her recovery?" Brody asked.

"No, it won't slow it unless she feels pressured to have sex and then she could become withdrawn and uncomfortable, the physiologically effects could be even more harmful," he answered.

"So if for instance she is in the bath and someone is washing her feet and she moans and her little toes curl, and she says she wants to have sex it should be allowed?" Brody asked, and Emma looked down.

"I suppose it would be fine, but I would hope that person would exercise caution so that she did not exert herself too much," Mark replied.

"So manual stimulation or oral stimulation leading to orgasm is better than intercourse?" Brody asked.

"Yes I would think so," Mark said his face growing red.

"Okay now let's say she wanted to go down on someone, is that too much exertion?" Brody asked in hopes of making Mark more uncomfortable.

"I don't see why not. However, that is highly unusual for even a healthy woman to just want to give a blow job, unless she felt like she had to please her partner because he was ridiculously insecure, and if that was the case their relationship wouldn't last anyway," Mark said sarcastically.

"Let's say her partner wanted to please her in every way possible and took every precaution to ensure she was not able to exude any energy at all. I don't know like tied her up and ravaged her body," Brody asked and smiled.

Emma and Lila both gasped loudly.

"Well I'd say if he had to tie her up to get laid that would be enough to make her run and scream for the hills. Very unhealthy need for control," Mark said cautiously looking at Emma.

"What if she wanted him to?" Emma asked, and Lila laughed loudly.

Mark looked at Lila.

"Why don't you two just whip them out and see whose is bigger right here and right now?" Lila laughed and so did Emma.

Mark looked confused.

"Brody, Mark adores Emma, he is a good doctor. Mark, Brody is head up his ass in love with Emma and she is scared to death of being hurt after her divorce, but she is madly in love with him too."

"Do you want to fuck Emma Doc, do you intend on wooing her and sweeping her off her feet?" Brody asked seriously.

"No, Brody I actually am going to help Emma get well and stay well. My sexual intentions are for her friend," Mark sneered at him.

"Good glad that's cleared up," Brody said, "So now that I don't want to throw you out the window and I hope you realize I love her, tell me what I need to do."

"Make her happy and not just sexually Brody. Be her partner, not her captor. Hold what is dear to her as closely as she does and just love her," Mark smiled and looked at Lila, "Whip it out and see whose is bigger?"

"Well you were both acting like seventeen year old boys!" Lila said defensively and Mark laughed.

"What's this tying her up shit about?" Mark asked.

"Oh God could we please not do this," Emma begged.

Brody laughed, "You are going to eat Princess, the food is on it's way up. Do you want to sit at the table or in bed?"

"The table please," Emma said and stood up.

After dinner, Emma and Brody brushed their teeth and went into her room.

"You want to call London?" Brody asked.

"Yes," she smiled.

"Should I give you a few minutes alone?" Brody said kissing her head.

"No stay," Emma sat and dialed the phone.

"Mommy!" London yelled.

"London you sound happy," Emma smiled.

"I am because I know he went to see you and you are going to be just fine," London said laughing.

"London I am glad you are happy, but you need to know I would have been just fine with or without him. I love you, and you love me, you have to remember that okay, life is what you make it. Just like before Brody when Daddy left we were very happy right? And we smiled and laughed all the time, as a matter a fact I think we laughed at least a zillion times a day right?" Emma asked.

"Of course Mommy it's just, I don't know I think he makes us even happier, like we match and fit perfectly together," London said trying to come up with the right words.

"We complement each other, or as Brody may say…" Emma started.

"We harmonize perfectly, I love you too London," Brody said.

"You're still there?" London asked.

"Is there anywhere else I should be?" Brody asked, "Besides with you of course."

"Brody we need to talk in private sometime okay?" London asked.

"What?" Emma laughed, "Are you two ganging up on me?"

"I love Brody Mommy, I love you, and I love you with him, that's all you need to know," London laughed.

"I look forward to it, actually maybe I could cook you and your mother dinner at your place tomorrow, I learned a few things in London while I was there, some new tricks to impress you with," he laughed.

"Sound like a plan if the warden okays it," London laughed.

"London you're breaking my heart," Emma said sadly.

"I was talking about Grandpa, he was rude to Brody last night!" London snapped.

"Yes well about last night London," Brody shook his head no, "We will talk about it when I get home," she scowled at

Brody, "Be nice to Grandpa he was being protective of me, I love you more London..."

"So do I..." Brody chimed in.

"We all love each other more, goodnight love birds," London said and hung up.

Emma and Brody snuggled into bed.

"I should have told her a story, damn it," he sulked.

"Call her I am m sure she would love it," Emma said and kissed him as she rubbed his stomach and laid her head on his chest, "You make me happy, well most of the time, except I do have to say I was livid when you made that crack about child support Brody. I think I am still mad."

"I was being hurtful because…" Brody began.

"I hurt you?" Emma asked.

"Yes and we need to figure that out. It isn't healthy, and I do it often. Not just with you. I need you to know I have a remarkably bad temper," Emma laughed, "Emma I am being serious here," Brody said honestly.

"Brody I know that, not that it was my first hint but when you threatened to rip Mark's throat out well I kind of got it," Emma laughed.

"I would have you know, that's the not so funny part to that," Brody was serious.

"Well we need to work on that too," Emma said and kissed him again.

"You seem at peace Emma," Brody said hugging her tightly.

"You have that effect on me, which has me at a serious disadvantage you know," Emma laughed.

"Good," Brody said and rubbed her back.

"You like me weak? Is that why you want to tie me up?" Emma asked and looked at him with a great desire for him to answer her truthfully.

"They honestly don't fit together at all. But it's late, I am tired, and you have to rest, just trust me Emma I can't have you any other way but completely. I love you Princess, sleep, now!" he snapped.

Emma smiled and fell asleep. Brody lay and waited to know she was asleep and smiled when she shook, just like London had. He got up to use the bathroom and make a few phone calls. When he finished with his calls he got up to get a drink. Mark was in his boxers in the kitchen.

"So I can't have sex and you can?" Brody laughed.

"Brody I am sorry about earlier, I didn't react the way I should have to you. I hope you can accept my apology," Mark said with genuine concern.

"Forgiven, I am sorry as well," Brody smiled.

"Good, I kind of think we will be seeing a lot of each other," Mark laughed.

"So is there anything I can do for her?" Brody asked.

"No, she was very fragile and you come here, and she is already doing much better. Just don't let her down," Mark warned.

"Alright I need Lila at the top of her game. She is magic with people and the press, treat her right Mark," Brody warned.

"I will, as long as she will let me," Mark laughed.

"Emma is asleep, do you think you could put the IV in just to be on the safe side?" Brody asked.

"I think that's a good idea. I will do it now," Mark said.

"Alright I will be in soon," Brody smiled.

~

"Emma I am going to put your IV in, just a little pinch okay," Mark warned.

"Where is he? Did he leave, where is Brody?" Emma yelled still half asleep.

"Did you miss me Em?" Brody laughed.

"It's not funny, don't do that to me again. Don't you leave me again," she cried.

"Okay," Brody said and sat next to her, "I am not going anywhere."

Emma curled up in his arms and fell asleep. Mark looked at Brody and shook his head slowly back and forth. Brody took a deep breath and sat against the headboard stroking her head and her back.

~

Emma woke feeling much better than before.

"Good morning," Brody said looking down at her. "Would it be alright if I used the bathroom?"

Emma laughed, "Of course."

Mark walked in and took out the IV, "Wow when did you put that in?"

"About midnight," Mark smiled, "Look at you all bright eyed. Last day of treatment Emma, and then never again ok?"

"Of course, hey you're certainly good at the IV thing I didn't even wake up," Emma said holding the gauze tightly to her arm to stop the bleeding.

Brody said as he walked in, "You woke up, to yell at me," he said and bent down to kiss her.

He sat and looked as she took the gauze off, "Much better, you do kind of resemble a heroin addict," he laughed.

"I didn't yell at you," Emma said looking at her arm, "Ya that's kind of gross huh?"

"You yelled at me Em, I kind of liked it. You told me I could never leave you again. Which makes me wonder how that's going to work tonight," Brody said getting up to get his clothes.

"Did I?" she asked.

"Yes Emma you did," Mark laughed, "I think you like him," He winked, "See you in an hour, don't be late," he said to Brody.

"I will have her there, thank you Doc," Brody said and smiled at him.

"Wow did you guys make up?" Emma smiled and stood.

"Yep, for you anything, plus it helped that he was sneaking out of Lila's room," Brody said, and his jaw dropped in mock shock.

Emma smiled, "I love you."

"You better," Brody smiled.

Emma scowled at him and walked to the dresser to grab her clothes.

"Emma love, I was being silly. I love you more," he said reaching around from behind and kissing her neck.

"Sorry, I am moody," Emma said as she reached up and ran her hand through his hair.

"That time of the month?" he laughed.

"Brody, do you remember me telling you I had a hysterectomy a few years back, and I could not have more children," Emma asked.

"Of course," he said and kissed her neck again.

Emma turned around and rubbed her hand down his stomach and pulled him by the waist band into her and bit his ear and whispered, "That means there is no that time of the month."

Brody's breath snagged, "Ever?"

"No, not ever," she kissed his chest and rubbed her hand slowly down him and she felt him harden, she squeezed him hard, and he jumped, "Don't joke when I say I love you, it pisses me off."

Emma let go and started to pull away, he pulled her tightly to him, "I think I like you pissed off."

She laughed out loud, and he smiled, "Which one of us is going first?"

"You were scrubbed down last night Em, why not wait until tonight?" Brody winked.

"I will be home tonight Brody," Emma said.

"Yep, I will be there too Emma, you told me I could never leave you again so I won't, be back in ten minutes," he yelled and walked back in. "It is okay if I shower right? I mean technically I am not leaving you," he winked.

"Emma how will your boss feel when I come to work with you tomorrow?" he laughed walking down the hall.

Holy shit, note to self never scream don't stop while having sex, Emma thought and smiled thinking about sex with him.

Chapter 10

Brody's car pulled into the driveway, Emma was asleep on his lap. He didn't want to wake her, so they sat until London ran out and opened the door.

"Hello London," Brody whispered and patted the seat next to him.

London jumped in and sat quietly next to him, "I have missed you."

"I missed you and Mommy too, she is still tired?" London asked, "You can give it to me straight I can handle it."

Brody chuckled, "She is just resting, she seems much better than when I first saw her."

"Good because I was scared Brody, really scared," London said sadly.

"Well I understand that I was too, but I talked to her doctor and I know she is the strongest person I have ever met. Do you know she could have done this over seven weeks, and only three times a week and she decided on the harshest treatment plan so that she could be here for you? That's how much she loves you London, so much that she will do anything. You are her happy place. With you is where she wants to be," Brody kissed her head, and London leaned into him.

Caroline opened the door and smiled at them, "Welcome home," she said as she snapped a picture.

Brody smiled, "Thank you."

"London why don't you come in and help me set the table?" Caroline smiled.

"May I stay here until she wakes up please?" London asked respectfully.

Caroline smiled and shook her head yes and shut the door.

"We might have to wake her up soon, she will be upset," Brody kissed London's head.

"Hey," Emma smiled and looked at London.

"Hi Mommy," she smiled.

"That's all I get?" Emma sat up and hugged her daughter, "I have missed you all the way to the moon and back."

"Well I have missed you half way to heaven and back," London replied.

"Only half way?" Emma asked curiously.

"Yep," London said as her bottom lip quivered, "I don't want you to get all the way there Mommy."

Emma held her tighter as she cried, "Oh London I am not going anywhere, not for a very long time."

"Pinky promise Mommy," London asked sobbing.

"Of course London," Emma said holding her face in her hands and kissing it all over.

London laughed and looked at Brody, "Oh sorry."

"No, I feel honored to be here London, that was beautiful. Absolutely beautiful," Brody said looking at her in awe.

"Alright you two let's go eat, I am hungry," Emma announced and scooted off his lap stopping to whisper in his ear, "Thanks for the seat," and kissed him quickly.

~

"Nice to see you again Brody have a seat right here," Caroline pointed to the chair next to Henry.

"Hello Brody," Henry said looking over his reading glasses.

"Hello Henry nice to see you," Brody said and smiled.

"Uh huh," Henry said as he continued reading.

"Hi Daddy," Emma said and smiled.

"Hello Princess," Henry said and stood up and hugged her and spun her around, and Emma laughed.

Brody smiled at their interaction, and Caroline noticed that he was pleased.

They ate dinner, and Henry watched the way Brody looked at his daughter. Brody walked over with Emma and London so that London could get ready for bed. He helped tuck her in and kissed her goodnight. London had asked to sleep in Emma's bed with her.

Brody fell asleep on the couch waiting for Emma to come out. He woke up when Caroline walked in.

"Are they sleeping?" Caroline whispered.

"I think so," Brody said sleepily and sat up.

"I brought over some fresh sheets and a blanket if you would like to sleep in the spare bedroom, I will make up a bed for you," Caroline offered as she walked in the spare room.

"Let me do that," Brody smiled.

"Brody do you love my daughter?" Caroline asked.

"More than I thought possible," he said as he tucked in a corner of the sheet.

"What are your intentions?" Caroline asked.

"They're simple, I don't ever want to be without her. I love her. I am the person I know I am supposed to be with her," he laughed and shook his head, "I want to spend forever with her, after a little over a month I already know that."

"Okay, you do know you're going to have to warm Henry up to the idea right?" Caroline snickered.

"Yes, about that, any tips?" He asked.

"She is his Princess Brody," Caroline smiled.

"We may be at odds with that one, I have called her princess for over a month now. She never mentioned that was her Dad's pet name," Brody smiled, "Do you think we could arm wrestle over it?"

"You could try," Henry said walking in with pillows.

"I am sorry sir," Brody said as he sat down.

"So you want to arm wrestle over my Princess?" Henry said giving him an intimating glare.

"No, sir, I want you to like me. To trust me with your daughter, I want you to know I am in love with her, and I would like to marry her when she is ready, preferably soon. I want to start forever with her," Brody looked up at him.

"I see, and you think you are ready for that responsibility? Taking care of my daughter and her daughter, keeping them safe and happy? You're a musician how is that family friendly," Henry was interrogating him.

"That's enough Henry," Caroline said soothingly.

"I would like your blessing sir, and with all due respect I need you to know that either way I will ask her and she will accept. We love each other," Brody said looking him in the eye, "Now if you will excuse me I need to make sure that Emma has a drink."

Carolina looked at Henry as Brody left the room, "She loves him, you need to accept that."

~

Emma felt herself being lifted out of bed, she opened her eyes and smiled, "Hello Music Man did you miss me?"

"Of course," he smiled and kissed her head, "You need to drink."

Brody handed her a glass of water as she looked at him smiling, "I also need a bath, and you are going to give me one."

"Oh am I now? Drink up Em. You are insistent on going to work tomorrow, so you need to rest, understand?" Brody stated.

"So I should go un bathed?" Emma scowled.

"No, but you need to take a quick shower and get yourself back in your bed. You need rest," Brody took her empty glass into the kitchen.

"I need you, I want you, and if you won't have sex with me for a week I want you in my mouth," Emma stood up and walked towards him.

"Em not tonight, okay. I want you healthy and rested," he kissed her.

She reached down and grabbed him, "And I want you in my…"

Henry cleared his throat loudly, and he sat up. "Daddy what are you doing here?"

"I am sleeping on the couch to make sure Brody behaves himself, I guess I needed to be more concerned about you," Henry scolded, "Go take a shower Emma and get into bed, alone!"

"See you in the morning," Brody smiled and kissed her cheek.

He looked at her and his eyes widened, and he made a face that said uh oh busted.

"Daddy I am grown women…" Emma stomped.

"Get your ass in the shower Princess," Henry said sternly.

Emma stomped into the bathroom, and Brody walked past Henry, "Goodnight sir."

"My name is Henry use it. Troy is only breathing because of London if you hurt my daughter I will hurt you. But you have my permission. When were you thinking of doing this?" Henry asked looking up from his paper.

"Tomorrow night," Brody smiled.

"Make it hearts and flowers, she deserves nothing less. And remember I am sleeping right here," Henry said and laid down.

"Thank you so much, Henry. Good night," Brody said and walked into his room.

~

Brody woke to London giggling, "You know I could get used to waking up to that sound," he smiled opening his eyes.

Brody grabbed her and tickled her.

London dove on him and hugged him. He looked up and Emma stood in the doorway watching them with a smile on her face.

He winked at her, "Good morning Emma, did you sleep well?"

"I did and you?" Emma asked.

"Well you know," he said and stood up.

"I am going to drop London off at school, and head in to work, will I see you tonight?" Emma asked.

"Give me fifteen minutes and we can drop her off together, and I will drop you at work," he smiled as he walked by.

~

"You do know I am perfectly capable of driving," she said when London was walking into the school.

"Are you grumpy this morning Emma?" Brody laughed.

"No," Emma said and looked out the window of the black Limo.

Brody reached for her hand and kissed it gently, "I love you Emma, tell me what is upsetting you."

"Nothing," Emma smiled.

"Are you not feeling well," he asked moving next to her and feeling her head.

"I am fine," Emma said moving away from him.

"Em come now tell me, is it me, am I smothering you?" Brody asked nervously.

"It's definitely you and you can't say things like that," Emma said and threw her head back in frustration.

Brody thought about what he had said and looked at her.

Her face was flush, and she squirmed in her seat, "Emma, you miss me?"

"Stop, please. Just don't touch me," Emma said sadly.

"Emma come here," he said and pulled her closer, "You need to come Emma?"

"Brody, please don't say things like that," Emma murmured softly.

"Be quiet please, and stay very still," he whispered and kissed her neck as he pulled her onto his lap. "I like the skirt, but these need to go," he said and ripped her underwear, Emma gasped, "Shh," he said running his fingers lightly over her. "Emma you're wet for me, see what I can do for you, just the thought of my fingers here," he said and slowly pushed into her, she whimpered.

Brody closed the privacy glass and turned up the radio, "You still need to stay as quiet as you can, but Clive can't see or hear us. It's just you and I Emma and I am going to make you come all the way to work," Emma pushed into his hand, "Be still

Emma, he moved his fingers, and he could already feel her body tighten, "So soon Emma? Should I make you wait?"

"Brody, please," she said and moved her hips to him.

He removed his fingers and kissed her. He pulled back and licked his finger, "You taste so good Emma," he said and slipped his finger back into her, and she moaned loudly. He pulled it out and rubbed it across her bottom lip, "See how you taste, I can't get enough of it, I need to lick you, suck you, and I want you to come for me, I want to taste you," he said as he slid two fingers in her. Emma moaned loudly and tossed her head back. She was on the edge and he started to withdrawal, and she grabbed his hands and pushed into him. "Okay Em, you need me, tell me."

"Brody I need you, I love you, and I want to come for you please, Brody," she panted.

"Emma I love you and I want you to come for me, Come now!" Brody whispered loudly in her ear and moved faster and harder in and out of her until he felt her body relax. She tried to pull back, and he continued to move his fingers. He laid her down and moved between her legs, "I can't wait for you to come again I want to lick you dry. Come baby I want all of you."

When she was finished, she sat up and looked at him, "Brody."

He smiled, "I know Emma, rest now please."

"I need you, I need to feel you please," Emma said looking at him.

He smiled and kissed her head, "Drink this water Em."

"I want you to feel as satisfied as I do right now, let me..." Emma said with begging eyes.

He smiled, "You can please me tonight love, okay, now rest until we get you to work."

"I need you now please," Emma said and straddled his lap.

"Emma not now," Brody moaned.

"But I..." Emma started.

"Emma, I want nothing more than to tie your hot wet ass up in bows right now and fuck you so hard you can't walk for a week, I am doing this for you, you need to stop now. I will take care of this," he said and shoved her hand down his pants. "You feel how bad I want you?"

"Brody," she moaned and gently took hold of him.

"Emma, I need you to want this every single day, every minute. I want you to think of how hard I am for you. I need you desperately right now, but you need to rest. I won't let you until I know you're ready. Until I know you can handle the three week's worth of need for you that I have been denied," Brody said as his hand worked up to her right breast, "And this is mine, and when you're ready so is this," he said and gently rubbed his finger across her shirt over her left breast. I want all of you forever. I want you to know that I will make sure you're taken care of and loved and fucked thoroughly every time you need me. I am denying myself to take care of you Emma, and I want you so bad it's painful. That is how deep my love for you is."

"I am so sorry," Emma said and started to cry.

"Don't do that Em, don't be sorry, I'm not. When you are truly ready we will both know alright? I promise you when that happens you'll never be sorry again. I need those ripped panties, I brought you another pair," he said and reached in his leather bag, "They kept me company for three weeks, and yes they are clean, I saw to it myself," he said and licked his lower lip.

Emma looked at him and gasped as he put her feet through the leg holes. "I don't deserve you."

"Emma we are perfect for each other, and yes you do deserve all I am going to give you. I know I will never tire of you," he smiled, "I hope you feel the same. We are here love, can I come by for lunch?" he smiled devilishly.

"I would love to say yes, but I don't think I could handle it, I think work is going to be the best place for me to rest because when I am with you I can't think about anything but how you make me feel. And I am not just talking physically Brody Hines, you make my head spin," she quickly kissed him and hopped out the door, "I love you more," she said and shut the door.

Emma's phone chimed while she was on the elevator, a text from Brody.

-we Love each other more…MM

-so sweet…Em

-I wouldn't want you upset all day, last time I didn't return with the proper response you were a little upset. I do not want you to be upset with me. And I don't think it's possible for you to love me more, just saying. I will have your lunch delivered. Don't respond I have control issues and must have the last word. All my love…MM

-Oh Brody, you can't control everything…Em

-Is that a challenge?...MM

- Sure is…Em

-You are in trouble someday very soon…MM

-Not if I get you first, I love you, going to work now. All hot and bothered with visions of bows dancing in my head…Em

Emma was glad to be back to work, but even happier that the day had ended. She walked out of her building after work and her phone chimed, a text from Brody

-How about a picture now?...Em

-Emma right now I need to wrap up a few things, and you are distracting the hell out of me...MM

-I am going to take you in my mouth and suck you so hard...Em

-Emma please love I don't have time for this right now...MM

-And then I am going to let you watch as you come in my mouth...Em

-Just so you know I am at your place, and your mother is baking cookies, me walking around trying to hide a hard on is not an easy task...MM

-Well then I am going to have your driver stop and pick you up on my way to get London ...Em

-Please not now, I am trying to bond with Henry. Hoping someday he will like me...MM

-Fine you win, I love you...Em

Emma and London walked into the apartment above the garage. It was lit up with candles, flowers, orchids, and tulips everywhere. Silk bows adorned everything they could, all silver and white.
-Emma, my car is there I had some things to wrap up. Go pick up London, I made an appointment for you both at the spa for manicures and pedicures. I should be there when your finished, I love you...MM

-UUGGHH I have thought about that car ride all day, maybe I can take care of myself on the way to pick up London, never tried that before…Em

-Don't you dare, they're all mine…MM

-Silly boy you gave me a toy, who was that for…Em

-Your not talking to a boy Em, and that was for Skype, for me, it better be unused…MM

-You better ask Lila, I sent it with the other gifts…Em

-I will be stopping by to pick those things up and tossing that one. How wet are you right now?...MM

-None of your business, if you had come pick me up it wouldn't be a question…EM

-Oh Emma, your being defiant…MM

-How hard are you right now?...Em

-I will show you soon enough…MM

~

Emma and London got out of the car feeling very pampered. Emma wondered where everyone was. They walked up the stairs into the apartment.

"Mommy did you do this?" London gasped.

"No," she said when she could finally speak, "I have never seen anything so beautiful."

"Well I have, two things actually," Brody walked out of his room.

He was dressed in a grey suit and black neck tie, "London I would like to steal you for a moment would you come with me?"

Brody winked at Emma who was still looking around at the beautiful room full of flowers, and took London's hand and lead her into her room.

"Well London I have a very important question for you. A few actually, I would like to ask you how you feel about some things ok?"

London stood with her eyes wide open and looked nervous as she pushed her long black hair out of her face and shook her head yes.

"Do you know how much I love you and your mother?" She shook her head yes and smiled shyly "do you think you feel the same way about me?"

"Yes" she answered.

"We'll how would you feel if I asked your mother to marry me?"

"I would be happy," London smiled.

"Okay because that would mean I am marrying into your family so technically I would be marrying all of you. And since you are my favorite person in the family I want you to know how much you mean to me. So," he said getting down on one knee, "I have one last question for you, London Fields will you please accept this ring," he smiled and pulled out a small box and opened it revealing a small platinum ring with a beautiful diamond set in the band, "do you accept London?"

She laughed and hugged him tightly, "Yes!"

Brody hugged her and placed the ring on her finger.

"Now if your Mom says yes I won't feel so sick to my stomach," he said and took a deep breath.

London laughed, "You will be just fine, take a deep breath and think about something that makes you happy, that's what I do. Thank you so much Brody."

"Thanks London, that helped a lot. Your Grandma is waiting for you, if you could give me a few moments alone with your Mom I would appreciate it," Brody said walking out the door with her hand in his, "off you go now."

"Brody is everything alright?" Emma said searching his face.

"Yep, could you have a seat please Emma," he took her hand and led her to the chair. He grabbed his guitar and started to play.

"I wrote this song the day after our last awkward phone call a few weeks ago while I was in London. I want to play it for you if I could," Emma smiled, and he played and sang.

Wrapped in Silk

Soft caramel fanned across my breathless chest,

the scent intoxicating as the warmth of her breath.

Your wrapped tight around me and me wrapped in you,

A lifetime like this makes my heart, not so blue.

When I sit alone it's your smile your heart your love I miss,

A deep burning desire, the taste of your kiss.

I close my eyes, and I feel you beneath me,

holding me high you never deceive me.

Wrapped in my arms, my heart feels so full.

Wrapped is my heart. loves light never dulls.

Wrapped in silk, as your body should be always,

Wrapped in my kiss, I could live on your love every day.

Wrap you in silk from head to toe,

Wrap you in my love topped with soft silky bows.

More precious to me your smile each day,

The roads once traveled are now far away, the wounds unaware for your love they have healed,

My need for you I have never known the confusion it caused not even real.

Years of pain my heart hid in fear,

Weeks of a need unfamiliar brought down to tears.

I tried to let go, willed myself to run

Chains were let loose replaced with smooth silk, without you could have never been done

I won't let go I won't let go

Forever is not long enough.

I promise you my heart a life without pain I promise you a life where all dreams come true if you'll say the same,

Wrapped in silk, wrapped in silk, forever with me wrapped in your silk.

He looked at her the entire time and when he finished she stood up and walked over to him and kissed him and grabbed his guitar and put it on the floor.

"Did you like it Emma?" Brody chuckled.

"I loved it, and now I want you," Emma loosened his tie as she kissed him straddling his lap.

"Emma I can't wait to have you, but I need to ask you something first," Brody pulled back, "Could you get up for a minute love?"

"No," she kissed him again.

"Alright then, can you give me a second?" Brody said, "Please I have something to ask you."

"Can it wait an hour?" she asked unbuttoning his shirt, and kissing his neck.

"Not really," he moaned.

"Sorry, control freak I need you and London is with Mom," Emma said frantically undoing his pants and kicking off her shoes.

"Emma I think you should…" Brody started as she pulled up her skirt and lowered herself slowly onto him.

"You still want to talk Brody," Emma whispered in his ear.

"Actually, I really have to, it shouldn't take long, fuck Emma you are so hot," Brody said pushing further into her as he reached in his pocket and grabbed the ring.

"Oh God," Emma moaned.

"Emma slow down give me a second please, Emma, please," he moaned and grabbed her hips stopping her, "Emma I had this whole thing planned, and this was not part of the plan but fuck, you are amazing, Marry Me Em, please Marry Me," he showed her the ring.

"Fuck me Brody and then we will talk," Emma kissed him.

She wrapped her arms around his neck and stopped moving, she put her head on his shoulder and started to cry.

"Emma," Brody smiled as he sat back. "Give me an answer please."

"Boy did I screw that up," she said as he wiped the tears off her face, "I'm sorry."

"Sorry for what Emma?" Brody asked searching her eyes.

"This was all so beautiful, and I wanted to win a stupid game," Emma said and laughed.

"Emma, this is actually pretty perfect, I am shocked that I proposed when I was deep in you however, I am still waiting for an answer Emma," he kissed her.

"Sorry, I am just shocked and embarrassed. I ruined this I am so sorry," Emma said.

Brody shifted nervously, and Emma moaned, he laughed and kissed her softly, "Do you need more time Emma if you do I understand. I knew you might think this was all too soon, and I can give you as much time as you need, I know without a doubt that I will love you until the world stops spinning, so if it's time you need I am not going…"

"Yes," Emma said and hugged him.

"Yes what? Do you need more time?" Brody asked nervously.

"I will marry you, of course I will marry you," Emma said and kissed him, "But not because of cancer or..."

Brody stood abruptly and walked with her still on him to her bedroom. He pulled his pants off.

"Your parents and London are waiting for us, so I am going to do this quickly, on all fours love." Brody slowly entered her and wrapped his arm around and used his hands on her sweet spot, "This has nothing to do with cancer Emma, I ordered this ring the Monday after I left, I paid for it and picked it up the night before I left to return to you," he started moving faster, and she moaned. "This is because you are mine and I am yours forever Emma because I love you," he moaned and she tensed up, "Come Emma, it's been awhile and I need to fill you, come now!" he instructed, and her body did as he asked. He continued as he held her up and finally finished.

"Brody are you sure," Emma asked softly.

He laid on the bed and pulled her over to him, "I am Emma, are you?"

"I need to show you something," she said and slowly, nervously pulled up her shirt, "Can you deal with this?"

He bent over and kissed her gently and then kissed her breast, "You're going to kill me Emma," he said and sucked gently on her nipple, "Of course, honestly Emma it's not even that noticeable and they taste exactly the same. And trust me they have the same kind of effect on me as they did before," he smiled and looked down. "Thank you Emma, so much, I love you and will forever."

Emma smiled, "You have no idea how much you mean to me."

"I do Emma because if it's half as much as you mean to me we are good, so good" Brody said as he pulled her up, "Thank you Emma, for saying yes and for trusting me with you and London, and allowing me to see what I already knew was perfect," Brody said and gently touched her breast.

Emma stood looking at him, *how could he love me how could this beautiful man love me*, she thought and stared at him.

"Emma we have to go love," he smiled, and they walked down the stairs.

They walked in the kitchen and her parents and London were standing there.

"So let's see the ring!" Caroline yelled.

Brody looked at Emma and laughed.

"Mommy you didn't say yes?" London asked and started to cry.

"Yes I did London, I just um," she started and looked at Brody for help.

He gave her a look egging her on and laughed, "She wanted to see you first, honestly, I think she wanted to know that you had said yes as well."

London held up her hand, "See Mom, of course I would say yes when he asked me if he could marry you!"

"Well then Emma, can I put it on you now, please?" Brody asked and knelt, "Marry me Em?"

"Of course" she smiled as he put the ring on her finger. Her mouth dropped slightly when she finally looked at it, and tears flooded her eyes. The five carat princess cut emerald ring with baguettes wrapped around the platinum band was so shiny and beautiful.

"Brody," she whispered in shock.

"It matches your eyes Emma, the ones I get lost in every time I look at you," Brody said and swallowed hard, "Look inside Emma."

Emma looked at the inscription WE ARE EACH OTHERS FOREVER 10 X 10.

"Brody I can't even put the words together," she said and let him put it back on her finger, "I love you, oh God I love you so much."

They hugged, and they held each other, completely lost in the moment. Emma pulled back and looked at him, and laughed as she shook her head, "I love you, Brody. Have I said yes enough, I mean after the stunt I pulled, have I said it enough?"

"It will never be enough," he laughed, "Will you marry me?"

"Yes," she giggled.

"Okay now more serious this time, Emma Will you do the honor of becoming my wife?" Brody said with a pretend serious face.

"Yes," she said and jumped up and wrapped her arms and legs around him.

"Come now Emma you can do better than that, marry me Emma?"

"Yes and any other question you have for me yes," she said and bit his neck lightly, "And Brody don't say that again unless you mean it," she laughed.

"Say what?" he asked laughing.

"Come now Emma," she whispered in his ear and they both laughed.

"This is wonderful, and all but dinner is going to get cold," Henry said dryly.

"Oh wow, sorry Dad, Mom, and London," Emma said, "London are you sure?"

"Mom seriously, I love him, check out my bling" she laughed.

"London did you thank Brody?" Emma asked in a motherly tone.

"She said yes, that is thanks enough," Brody smiled at London.

"Manners are very important," Emma said and shot him a look.

"I said thank you Mommy," London laughed.

"Did she?" Emma asked Brody.

"Of course she did Emma you have done a wonderful job raising her," Brody chuckled.

"Did you honestly have to buy such an expensive ring for a seven year old?" Emma asked, and he laughed, "What's so funny?"

"London will be my stepdaughter, Emma," Brody smiled, "If she wants something all she need do is ask."

"And then you will ask me, and we will discuss it, right Brody?" Emma said and locked eyes with him.

"Yes love," Brody smirked.

"So when will the wedding be Mom?" London asked.

"We haven't talked about it yet," Emma laughed.

"Well I think it should be soon," London said and looked at Brody.

"I think so as well, maybe this weekend?" Brody said and smiled.

"That's perfect!" London smiled.

"London, you get to see your father Saturday, remember?" Emma said and let out a big breath.

"Well then next weekend, or Halloween. A sleepy hollow wedding, in costume Brody!" London cheered.

"Wow, that sounds like fun," Brody said and laughed.

"Where will we live?" London took a bite of her soup.

"Well I have a few homes I would like to look at, I thought we could go tomorrow and check them out," Brody told her.

"You know you can stay here right?" Henry said his eyes fixed on Brody.

"Thank you Henry, that is very kind," Brody looked at Emma.

She looked up at him, and he winked. She looked back down and tried not to smile.

Brody and Emma got London to bed and sat on the couch.

"Can we talk about a few things?" Emma asked.

"Anything you want," Brody smiled.

"Do we need a house right now, I mean is it that important to you?" Emma asked.

"I thought it would be to you," Brody said confused.

"Well..." she began.

"Okay Em we have talked about this before, please just say what's on your mind, don't over think or try to take care of me, just tell me what you want to say," Brody smiled gently as he took her hand.

"Okay, I don't want to move London again, she just started school here," Emma quietly said avoiding eye contact, "And my mom works at her school and I just feel like she is safe. It was a big move for her, and for me."

"What else?" he asked and lightly kissed her hand.

"Well I need to tell Troy, not ask his permission but tell him. God Brody he doesn't even know about the cancer," Emma said and sat back closing her eyes.

"And you feel he needs to know everything," Brody stated.

"He is her father Brody, I can't change that ever," Emma spoke finally looking into his eyes.

"Alright I understand. I don't like it, but I knew all that before I asked you to marry me," he said and pulled her closer to him.

"I want to go tell him, with his therapist and not with London. I want him to have a couple days to process it before he sees her. I just think it will be better for both of them," Emma stopped and waited for him to respond and he didn't, "Please don't shut down, please talk to me."

"I am just mulling it over in my head, I am not shutting down," Brody thought out loud.

"If Troy is aware he won't be reactive when London is there. She won't see his anger or hurt or whatever it is he will feel at first. I just want him to have a heads up ya know," Emma hoped he would see her side.

"Alright I understand. Why don't you go Thursday after work?" Brody suggested.

Emma's gut reaction was to tell him she didn't need him to tell her how to do it. It was going to be difficult having someone around that was a true partner and not just part of the furniture. Emma loved the way Brody was with London, and she wanted to be sure to not hinder or weaken that relationship.

"Would you ride with me?" Emma asked. "I mean if I set it up and you are available, would you like to go?"

"Yes and I will make sure that I am available," Brody said, "Emma, are we finished, is there anything else pressing?"

"Ya, I kind of what to know what homes you had wanted to look at," Emma asked quietly.

"To see if I had considered London in this decision?" Brody asked.

"Well, yes and I want you to know how perfect it was that you asked her before asking me to marry you. It was so amazing, you are absolutely amazing," Emma said trying to make up for doubting him.

"All the homes I want to see are a little bit closer to the city, by maybe ten miles, all still in the same school district. With one, exception, I know that she could still attend school there I would just pay tuition, I could take her to school every day," Brody smiled pleased with himself.

"I love you. I am sorry I asked, I just have to think of her in every decision I make," Emma said looking at him.

"I know, just know I am doing the same thing Em, okay?" Brody asked.

~

Emma sat in the small office waiting for Troy and his therapist. Her stomach was in knots. Regardless of what he had put them through over the last eight years of their marriage she still didn't want him to be hurt. Troy was here getting help for his alcoholism and trying, and now she was about to set his recovery back.

"Emma," Troy smiled and hugged her when he walked through the door.

"Hello Troy," she smiled politely and returned his hug coldly, just like his hugs over the past several years.

Joe Login smiled at Emma. He was about five foot ten and had very short black hair and kind brown eyes.

"Troy have a seat, Emma it's truly nice to put a face to a name I have heard a lot over the past few weeks."

"Thank you for taking the time to do this for me," Emma said returning his smile.

"Nice ring Emma," Troy said with forged smile.

"I guess we should just jump right into this," Joe gently acknowledged.

"Brody has asked me to marry him Troy…and I accepted." Emma blurted out as her face reddened.

"Okay," Troy said trying to hide the anger or sadness in his voice.

"How do you really feel about that?" Joe asked.

"I guess I knew it was coming but not this soon. I worry about what he will be like as a constant influence in London's life, and Emma's. I know I have no right to ask her to wait," Troy said looking at Joe.

Wow, my ex-husband expressing feelings. Like he used to, like the man I married, this is not good, Emma thought.

"Emma do you have anything to say?" Joe asked.

"He is good to London and me, Troy has nothing to worry about," Emma said giving him a reassuring look.

"Okay Emma why so soon?" Troy calmly asked.

"It's just right for us," Emma said wishing she could figure out how this all happened so quickly.

"Okay", Troy looked lost.

"There is something else Emma needs to tell you," Joe said looking at Troy and then back to Emma.

"London is coming for a family visit on Sunday, and I want you to know what has been going on in our lives, everything. Troy you're her father always and I want you and I to be friends, maybe not best friends but I don't know, we have her, and she is the most important thing in either of our lives. We will forever be bound by that," Emma said and let out a breath.

"I know that now Emma, I wish that I had before. But we can't change the past, and I understand that now," he said looking emotionally drained.

"Been a rough few weeks?" Emma said and squeezed his hand.

"You have no idea?" Troy answered in a distracted tone.

"Emma, you have something else to tell Troy?" Joe said redirecting the conversation.

"I have had a really horrible few weeks as well," Emma smiled and told him the whole story about the cancer.

Emma finally looked up at Troy when she finished. Troy's face was full of trepidation and tears fell down his face.

"Oh, please don't do that," Emma said.

Emma remembered the only other time she had seen Troy cry. It was after the premature death of his father while they were at college. They were in his room studying when he received the call that his father had been in an accident and that he had died instantly. It was also the first night Troy and Emma had sex. She realized now that she had done it to try to ease his pain.

Troy laughed as he wiped his tears away, "Oh sorry I forgot, crying does something to you huh Emma?"

"It does, maybe, not in the same way your thinking but I don't want you to hurt," Emma explained gently.

"Alright then, are you sure you are ok?" Troy asked sincerely.

"Yes, but this made so many things become even more critical to me. If something happened to me Troy," she stopped. "You have to stay healthy for her, as healthy as you can anyway, sober and strong Troy," Emma said intensely.

"I will, I have one request Emma. I want to speak to Hines," Troy said, and Emma could tell there was no budging on this one.

"Okay when?" Emma took a deep breath.

"As soon as possible," Troy answered.

"Now?" Emma asked, "He is waiting for me in the car."

"No time like the present," Troy smiled and looked at Joe shaking his head.

~

"Back so soon?" Brody asked, and he stretched stepping out of the car and and grabbing her hand pulling her into him and kissed her.

He is so damn yummy, she thought lost in his kiss.

Emma pulled away smiling shyly, "Not really," she said stepping back and kicking the imaginary stones at her feet.

"What is it Emma," Brody said cupping her face in his hands.

"Troy wants to talk to you," Emma said still looking down.

"Good," he grinned mischievously.

"Brody can you be nice, he is trying," Emma protested.

"I hate him Emma, the way he spoke to you, the way he had absolutely no regard for London's safety and well being…" Brody said and his eyes were dark and full of hate and disgust.

"He is trying, and you Brody look so far away right now," Emma said astonished.

"I am full of anger right now. Let's go get this over with," Brody said taking her hand and dragging her behind him.

Everything had gone so well with Troy and now Brody is pissed, actually pissed, what the hell just happened? How am I going to get him to fucking calm down, why is it my job to make this better for everyone on the damned planet, Emma screamed in her head.

Emma released his hand harshly and stopped dead in her tracks.

"STOP," she yelled and stood with her arms crossed in front of her.

"Are you alright Emma?" Brody asked and walked back to her feeling her head.

Emma let out a deep breath, "I am doing the best I can…" she started and the dam broke, "I can't keep trying in vain to make this better for every person in my life, and you are scaring me right now!"

Brody looked at her confused and tilted his head as he studied her, "Emma?"

"I will meet you at the car, I will deal with this…this shit!" Emma screamed.

Brody jumped when she yelled, "Emma, damn it talk to me. Tell me what you need from me right now because I thought I was doing exactly what you wanted ME TOO!"

"Fuck you Brody," she said under her breath.

"Excuse me?" Brody asked in shock.

Emma scowled and looked down, Brody's eyes lit up in amusement, "It's not funny."

"Emma go sit in the car, I will take care of this," Brody said in his direct tone.

Emma laughed, "I don't think so."

"Go Now!" Brody snapped, and she didn't move.

Brody quickly swooped her up, tossing her over his shoulder and smacked her ass all in one swift move, she was in the car, and the door shut before she even had time to protest.

Emma tried to open the door, and it was locked.

"Open the damn door," she yelled.

The privacy window lowered, "Ma'am did you say something, do you need anything? A drink maybe?" Brody's driver Clive asked.

"No, but you can unlock the doors NOW!" Emma snapped.

"I am sorry ma'am, this new car has a security system, I honestly was just looking at the manual trying to read up on it, would you see if you can find it for me please ma'am?"

"Sure," Emma said quickly and grabbed the book looking at the index and thumbing through the pages. She read and found the security system information. She scowled up at him, "Push. The. Button."

"Really is that all there was to it? A button? Could you tell me where that button is ma'am?" Clive asked.

"How long have you worked for Brody?" Emma snapped.

"Ma'am?" he asked.

"I don't think he would hire an idiot, and I am very sure you are toying with me," Emma said with annoyance in her voice.

"No, he would not, I have worked for him for nine years," Clive answered.

"So you know him from England," Emma asked inquisitively.

"Yes, we have known each other for many years," he smiled.

"I should have known from your accent. I am pissed, let me out now," Emma stared into his eyes trying to intimidate him.

Clive jumped out and opened the door.

"Sorry ma'am." he whispered.

"I don't believe you, but if you do that again, you will be," Emma scolded him, and he tried not to laugh.

Emma waited as instructed by the receptionist rather impatiently in the waiting room. Joe, Troy, and Brody walked out from his office behind the glass wall. Emma watched as Troy and Brody shook hands and Brody walked out.

"What a pleasant surprise," Brody smiled roguishly and grabbed her hand.

Emma pinched his finger, and he laughed a deep mischievous laugh and she threw him a malevolent look.

They walked outside and around the corner of the building, Brody grabbed her by the waist and gently pinned her against the brick building, and she gasped. He leaned into her and pressed his nose roughly into her neck and nipped her ear.

"I played nice with your ex Emma. For London and for you," he kissed her throat, "I will until he fucks up, and then I will destroy him," he pulled her tightly into him, "You were supposed to wait for me in the car."

"Is that why he locked the fucking doors!" Emma yelled.

"Get your hot little ass back in there now," he said and rubbed his hand down her spine and squeezed her roughly on the ass.

Emma started to argue and he kissed her hard on the mouth, and she gasped.

"You're making a scene," she whimpered.

"You need to come Emma," he breathed in her ear and grabbed her hand pulling her behind him. She had to walk fast to keep up with his long strides.

I need to come? The audacity of this man is crazy, he makes me crazy! And I want him which makes me just as damn crazy, she thought. *Not going to happen I am not an on demand kind of girl!*

Brody slid in beside her and tried to grab her to place her on his lap.

"Oh no," she said pulling away, "I am pissed at you!"

"Emma, if you don't get back here I am going to come after you," he said in a dark intimidating tone.

"You need to listen to me..." Emma began, and he laughed a deep interrupting laugh and jumped up and straddled her legs and kissed her.

Emma pushed him and started to cry.

"I don't need to listen to you, I already know Emma, exactly what you need. In here," he said touching her chest and then wiped her tears. "And you know it, so stop please, stop trying to control everything when I know damn well that's not what you want. You're calling the shots Emma, I am listening and doing exactly what you need me to. You need to trust that I am going to give you exactly what you need."

"Well I don't need what you suggested," Emma snapped.

Brody smiled and looked her up and down, "Okay then," he said sliding off of her lap.

He grabbed his iPad and began working on something, and she sat tapping her foot still annoyed.

They drove for fifteen minutes, and she looked at him.

"Are you going to tell me what happened?" Emma sneered.

"No Em," he said and continued typing, "you need to trust that I did what you wanted, he was still breathing wasn't he?"

"Oh that's really mature," she snapped.

Brody bit his lip and tried not to smile and said nothing.

"Are you going to act like this the entire ride home?"

"Are you?" he asked and raised his eyebrow looking at her.

"Yes," Emma scowled.

His eyes twinkled, and he put away his iPad, he closed his eyes and sat back. She saw a grin creeping across his lips.

"Why are you so damn smug?" Emma asked.

"Are you done acting like an errant child Emma or do you need a spanking?" he asked his eyes still closed.

She didn't answer him, and he opened his eyes and looked at her mouth still dropped in disbelief, "Emma you need something?"

No way she thought, no way did I need that, Yes asshole but I will be damned if I am going to admit it.

"Listen to me and don't say a word. Your nipples are erect and want nothing more than for me to touch them and pull at them and take them in my mouth until your body starts to melt. You're wet and wild with desire, you may think you're pissed at me, but you are not Emma, you are so fucking hot and wet because I took care of something you needed me to, your body belongs to me and wants me so fucking bad it almost hurts. Regardless you also told me no, and I take that extremely seriously. So as, you sit there in flames desiring everything I can give you, you can thank yourself for the let down," Brody said and leaned forward lightly kissing her nose, "No means no Emma."

"Well obviously yours wants to please mine as well," Emma said looking smugly at his bulging pants.

"I was hard when you walked out of that office building after work Emma, you didn't need to be sidetracked. I was hard and waiting when you came out of the rehab center, your ex-husband's needs overshadowed mine, and I know you needed me to make it better for you. My body realized that Emma. When I came out I was hard as soon as you pinched me knowing that you needed to come, but you said no," Brody said and smiled as he looked away and she gasped.

Emma looked down and nervously played with her hands and tapped her foot.

"You're going to be fine Em," he said and took her hand, and she let him.

She sat waiting for more, and he just sat there, she lightly pinched his hand between her fingers and he looked at her out of the corner of his beautiful blue eyes.

"Emma?"

"Yes," she whimpered.

"Yes what Emma?" he asked cautiously.

"Yes please," she said breathlessly.

"Are you quite sure?" he asked and she was on his lap in a spilt second with her mouth on his and grinding in to him.

"Alright then," he said and lifted her off him.

"Please," Emma whined.

He moved his hand up her skirt, and rubbed her inner thigh and she spread her legs wide for him and moaned. He pushed her lacey panties aside and took a deep breath.

"So wet Emma, I want you so badly to taste you to lick you," he moved two fingers into her and circled her, and she pushed into him.

"Please," she panted.

"I think you should wait as long as I have," Brody said and slowly rhythmically pleasured her until she was on the edge and then he would slow down and pull out. "Is this nice Emma?"

"No, I want you, I want all of you," she yelled.

"Than have me you will, all of me, forever Emma?" he asked as he unbuttoned his black jeans and his erection sprang free.

"Yes, yes forever," Emma breathed out deeply as she bit her lip hungry for him. He knelt between her legs, "No I want you please Brody."

"You first love, this has got to be fast, we are almost at your parents," he said and winked as he went down and licked her until she was on the edge again and then he plunged his tongue deep in her and she climaxed. He laid her down and slowly entered her.

"Aww," she moaned as his thrust became deeper and harder hitting exactly the right spot.

"Emma come now," he said with urgency and her body did as it was told and he fiercely rammed into her until he came hard. Emma felt every time he jerked inside of her coming hard as he groaned her name.

He laid on top of her both of them panting and trying to catch their breath.

"Em we are almost there, we need to fix you up," he said as he watched her laying sprawled out.

"I can't move," she giggled softly.

She felt him start to wipe between her legs.

"Brody," she snapped.

"Shhh, I will take care of you, I love to take care of you," Brody said as he cleaned her.

"I don't..." she started.

"Emma when are you going to stop this insolence?" Brody asked and sounded hurt.

Emma sat up and looked at him as he looked down.

No, no, no, she cried inside, you are hurting him, for what? She wondered.

"Now?" Emma asked.

He smiled looking down and threw out the tissues and fixed his pants and sat back.

"You're not looking at me because I hurt you," Emma said and looked out the window.

"You have had a rough couple weeks," Brody said, his voice was quiet.

"That doesn't give me an excuse to lash out at you, I...I love you," Emma said and began to cry, "I just...I am scared, and you are so damn controlling."

Emma said as he sat closer to her and wrapped his arms around her.

"I love you, I won't lose you. I won't see you hurt. I need to know you trust me Emma. There is so much more that we need to know about each other, and if I know you trust me, in everything, we are going to be so damn perfect, so incredible for each other and forever. I know I have wanted forever with you from day one, and I fought it. I acted like an arrogant ass at our first meeting at Lila's, I didn't want to need you. You're the one fighting now, and I can promise you I will fight as dirty as I need to in order to keep you," Brody said through clenched teeth.

He held her so tightly it almost hurt. She knew he was scared to let go, and she was scared that he would if she continued to push him away.

"Brody, can we look at the houses tonight? The ones you like?" Emma gave up control.

"Are you sure?" he failed to mask his excitement.

"Yes," she said and turned and kissed him, "I don't want to hurt you, I love you. I want forever with you. You made me a bit nervous when you said there was a lot we don't know about each other, should I be?" Emma stroked his face.

He smiled down at her, "We are here, can we save that for another time?" Brody asked and pointed to London running towards the car.

"Of course," she said opening the door and London dove across them.

"How was Daddy?" London smiled.

"He was great and getting better for you. He also knows that I am going to marry your mom, and he is alright with it," Brody smiled at her.

"Good, less I have to deal with," London said dramatically, and they all laughed.
~
"So which one did you like best?" Brody asked Emma and London as the pulled back into her parents' house.

"The last one," they both said smiling.

"It's furthest away," Brody reminded them.

"Fifteen minutes from here, that's not bad right Mom?" London asked with wide hopeful eyes.

"No, it's perfect," Emma said and smiled, "A little big but perfect."

"Why is it too big Emma?" Brody asked as they walked in the house.

"I want you to make the final choice," she smiled up at him, "I trust you."

He returned her smile and looked at her and raised his dark thick brow in that way that turned her on. She shook her head and felt her face turn red.

"Feels good doesn't it?" he whispered in her ear.

"Yes, and knowing if we hate it you made the final decision takes the pressure off. Thanks for that," she smiled sarcastically.

"Hmm," he said and stared at her until she visibly squirmed.

"I am going to lay with London," Emma said and quickly walked away.

~

"When will it be available…okay I see… I put the offer in Monday what is the hold up…well could I pay more…I realize it's only two weeks, but I want it now…fine if that is absolutely the best you can do…if I don't hear from you by nine in the morning I will be using a different realtor," Brody hung up and growled and ran his hands through his hair.

Monday huh before I even said yes, Oh Brody you are going to make this so much fun, Emma thought.

Emma waited inside London's room until she heard Brody moving about. He stood at the kitchen sink deep in thought,

Emma silently walked up behind him and wrapped her arms around his lean and exceptionally defined waist.

"Hey London and I were talking, and I think we changed our mind," Emma said holding him tightly as she lightly covered his back with kisses.

His body stiffened, "About what love?" trying to sound carefree.

"The house, I think we liked the first one better. But it's totally up to you," Emma said putting her hands lower, gently rubbing the soft hair that lead to her happy place.

"Emma," he moaned and cleared his throat, "Let us talk about the house some more, come" he said grabbing her hand.

"Nope, my hands are extremely happy right here," she said and lowered them.

"Emma," he growled as she took him firmly in her hand, "Awe damn it Em," he said and slowly turned around.

"What's wrong? Something on your mind?" Emma asked Brody with pouty lips.

He laughed, "Emma could you let go for just a few minutes love?" Brody said and took her hand slowly off of him and closed his eyes as he gently kissed her hands. "The house Emma, what made you change your mind?"

"I don't know it just seems too vast," Emma said staring at him.

"Okay," he said and took a deep breath and sat in the chair across from her. He was looking down.

And he heard Emma start to laugh, "What's so funny Emma?"

"You are," she smiled.

"Really, this is funny," he gestured over himself.

"Yes you Brody, are you stuck on that house?" Emma asked smirking.

"Well I thought we all were?" he said softly.

"Did you think that Monday when you put the offer in and before you even asked me if I would marry you, and before we even…" Emma shrieked as he grabbed her up and hugged her tightly.

"I knew you would love it," Brody said elated, "And I knew you would say yes."

"Very confident huh? Arrogant maybe?" Emma teased.

"After the weekend we spent, I knew you still felt the way I did, and the house well I knew London would love it, and I knew because of that you would love it as well, are you mad?" he asked kissing her neck feverishly.

"I don't think you would care either way if I were mad, you would just drive me crazy with desire and make me feel like I am a fifteen year old irate girl," Emma said, and he looked surprised and then hurt at what she had said.

"Is that how I make you feel Emma?" Brody said with concern in his eyes.

"I guess sometimes, well a lot lately. Not before you…left," Emma said again realizing that she missed how he had been.

"I am sorry, so sorry. I don't want you to feel that way," he said and kissed her lightly, "I want you to feel cherished and beautiful, the way I see you, the way I feel about you."

"Okay, I'm sorry," Emma said looking at her feet, "I am tired, it has been a long week."

"May I lay with you until you do your little shake?" Brody said bending his knees so he could look into her eyes, "There you are, stop hiding on me."

Emma smiled and hugged him tightly, "I don't shake."

"You do, just like London," Brody said smiling and holding her tighter, "Let's get you some water, and that dreadful, I mean wonderful green shake your mother made for you, and get you to bed. Then I want to tell you another story."

There you are, right here with me. I adore this Brody, the sweet, kind, and funny Brody. But the controlling arrogant Brody can be so hot too, I wonder if he has mental health issues, Emma thought.

"Where did we leave off? Oh yes, since we last left the Princess her Prince had been chiseling away at her armor. So our beautiful, intelligent, strong, and sometimes stubborn Princess finally saw the Prince for who he truly was…" Brody began.

"And which one was this, the sweet, funny, charming, gentle, kind and loving Prince or the arrogant, controlling, sex fiend?" Emma asked smiling up at him.

"Well which do you prefer?" Brody stared down at her.

"Which one is real Brody?" Emma asked in a serious manner.

"Well all of them of course, whichever one the Princess needs him to be at the exact time she needs him, I hope anyway," Brody said deep in thought, "Which do you prefer Emma?"

"That is a hard question to answer," she said. "Which do you prefer?"

"I have never thought of myself that way," he laughed uncertainly.

"If I am honest with myself, I actually enjoy all of you. It is just harder with the later. Kind of takes me out of my comfort zone. Either way both are incredible sexy," Emma yawned and stroked his face, "But this is so nice."

"But this one bores you in bed, your yawning," he chuckled as he looked down at her.

"Hmm no, not bored. Just tired, and particularly comfortable right here in your arms," Emma said and began to drift.

"To be continued," Brody whispered and rubbed her back until she fell asleep.

Chapter 11

"You're sure you like it?" Brody's voice was shaky, and he was trying so hard to impress her.

"Of course I do, and love it, and I love you." Emma hugged him. Brody let out a immense sigh and Emma giggled.

Brody raised his eyebrow and walked towards her, "Are you laughing at me Emma?"

"No," she said shaking her head and smiling, "I certainly am not, I just like… no Love seeing you happy."

"You know what would make me happy?" he said grabbing her ass and lifting her up to him and biting her neck lightly.

"Getting London's room finished," she laughed as he tossed her on the bed.

"We have eight hours love, eight hours may not be two days, but it's eight hours Em," he laughed and kissed her again.

Emma smiled and took a deep breath, "I know," she said and tried to smile.

"Okay then," he sat back on his heels and pulled her up, "London is fine, your parents are supervising Troy's visit. He is in counseling, and they are building a great relationship. She loves you, and if I remember correctly she was the one who decided she wanted just to be with him today."

"That hurt," Emma whispered.

"Like hell," Brody said and held her tightly.

"I'm sorry," Emma said and held him close.

"Emma, she needs him right?" Brody asked.

"Yes," Emma said rubbing her hands through his hair.

"Yes," Brody pushed his forehead against hers.

"Boy are we a sorry bunch," Emma laughed.

"No, we are a family," Brody said, and his eyes went somewhere else.

"Hey, come back to me," she smiled and kissed him.

He looked down and closed his eyes tightly, "Fuck."

"Brody it bothers us both," Emma hugged him.

He pulled away, "Just need a minute Love alright?"

"No, it's not. Talk to me please?" Emma said, "Don't pull away."

"Just a moment, please," Brody stepped off the bed.

"No!" Emma snapped, and he quickly turned around and gave her a not now look and walked out the door. "Please!"

Brody stood in the hallway against the door and listened to her cry and got extremely angry and punched the wall, "Shit!" he yelled and held his hand.

Emma jumped up and walked out the door and found him crouched on the floor holding his bleeding hand. He looked at Emma and his jaw tightened, and he closed his eyes.

"Did that wall piss you off or was it me?" Emma asked as she knelt down and took his hand to look it over.

He flinched, "I am not mad at you."

"Okay so the wall then?" Emma forced a laugh as she stood up and pulled him with her.

"Sorry," Brody said his plump bottom lip sticking out.

"Okay you need to tell me what just happened Brody," Emma said as she led him into the master bathroom and washed his hand off as she examined it.

"Not now Emma," he said and flinched.

"Your hand looks fine, you're lucky," Emma said and walked out and went down the hall into London's room.

She stood in the middle of the floor and looked around the light pink room. London had picked a much brighter color pink and Emma swayed her into doing an accent wall in the Pepto Bismal pink instead of the whole room. *Okay Emma, she thought to herself, this is just a small issue easily overcome. He was upset just upset. Damn it why won't he talk to me?*

Emma walked out and past the master suite and went downstairs. The entry was grand and although she would never say it to either Brody or London she felt it was a waste of space. The dining room was to the right and was large enough to invite London's entire class of twenty kids for dinner. The living room was on the opposite side of the house and was huge. Brody, Emma, and London had agreed on a very pale yellow with the ceiling painted a shade darker. The furniture was enormous and fit the large room perfectly. The brown leather sectional was perfect for a family of ten, not just three, and there was a half bath off of it. The kitchen, pantry, study, and bathroom all were as oversized as the rest of the house and in the back of the house. The furniture had been delivered yesterday as a surprise to Emma. Brody wanted to keep her busy today, knowing she would be emotional, something happy to brighten her day.

"There you are," Brody said wrapping his arms around her waist from behind, she reached up and rubbed his soft stubble. "Okay?"

"Are you?" she asked softly.

"I am now, sorry about that," he kissed her neck.

"Brody, have you ever thought about adoption?" Emma asked softly.

He chuckled, "No Emma."

"Well I think it's something that could be considered," Emma turned around to face him.

His eyes widened, "Do you want another child?"

"I think you do, and if you do I want that as well," Emma said looking at the ground.

"Emma, I don't need that. You and London are enough," he hugged her.

"There are other ways," Emma said quietly.

"Emma do you want another child?" Brody asked lifting her chin and looking into her eyes.

"I want to give you a child," Emma said and looked at him, "I can't and I know what an amazing father you would be, I can't take that from you."

"I love you Emma, that upstairs was not about wanting a child. It's about my controlling tendencies. I don't want London to get hurt. That's it understand?" Brody asked.

"Yep, but..." Emma started.

Brody put his finger over her mouth, "Seven hours and fifteen minutes."

Emma looked at him, and his eyes were dark blue and slightly hooded.

"Plenty of time to get London's room done," Emma breathed out.

"How about we start in ours and work our way down the hall?" he asked as he pulled her closer into him.

Emma tried not to smile, "Why not start down here then?"

He smiled and kissed her gently, "Right here?" he asked rubbing down her back slowly as he kissed her neck.

"Uh huh," Emma said rolling her head to the side giving him further access to her neck.

"How about here?" he asked as he ran his finger tips across her breast that immediately responded to his touch.

"Yes," she moaned softly.

He slowly started to lift her shirt, and she stopped him, "Please not yet."

"Emma we have already been there, what's the problem love?" Brody asked as he reached behind her and unsnapped her bra one handed.

Emma pulled away slowly, "I look like the bride of Frankenstein, it's daylight and I just can't. Do you understand?"

"Nope," he said and took the right one in his mouth and Emma moaned when she really wanted to protest.

"The way I see it," he paused as he pulled on her nipple lightly with his teeth, "is very different from how you do," again he paused and licked her and lightly blew on her and she let out a breath. "This may seem perfect and don't get me wrong Em it is, pretty damn amazing, but I prefer this one." Brody slowly pulled her black lacey bra down and slowly knelt before her.

"Brody don't," she whispered.

"Trust me Emma this is by far my favorite, this little light pink mark," he said as he traced it with his tongue, "That is my favorite spot. What you see as monstrous I see as a blessing. This mark is where the doctors entered and removed a small lump that could have eventually taken you from me. This Emma is my favorite spot, and you're trying to keep me from it."

Brody stood and kissed her neck and up her face, and felt her moist cheek against his lips as he moved up her face.

"Did I overstep?" he asked softly as he leaned back.

"No, you did not, that was…" Emma started.

"The truth, you will not get anything else from me Emma. I may need a moment now and then, but I will always be honest and truthful," he said and kissed her soft wet lips. "I want to make love to you here Emma, may I?"

She shook her head yes and took his face in her hands and kissed him.

~

Emma sat up on the dinning room table completely exhausted. Brody smiled at her as he watched her and rubbed her bare back.

"Ready to move upstairs?" He asked.

"I can barely sit up," Emma giggled.

"Well we have five more hours to pass, and I actually want you in our bed," Brody said squeezing her rear.

"You have had me in every room and on every surface down here," Emma laughed "I don't think I will ever be able to wash dishes in that sink without turning red."

"You shouldn't have tried to run," Brody laughed.

"We need to clean up the floor, it's very slippery. Who would have thought the faucet sprayer could reach that far?" Emma laughed.

"I am so glad it did, that damn shirt needed to come off," he said as he sat up and wrapped his arms around her gently caressing her breast.

"Thank you," Emma whispered.

"For what love?" he said and kissed her neck.

"Everything, you are amazing and sweet and kind," Emma said leaning back into him, "And hard... again Brody?" she gasped as she felt him against her back.

"What do you expect, you're sitting naked on our dining room table, and all I can think about is what's down her for me to munch on," he laughed and grazed his long fingers between her legs.

"Oh Brody," she moaned and jumped off the table before he could grab her, "Meet me in that big old bed music man," she said running up the stairs.

He grabbed her before she got to the door and wrapped his arm around her and lightly bit her neck, "Gotcha."

"Well it seems you do," Emma said and turned toward him, "So now what are you going to do about it?"

Brody laughed his deep dark naughty laugh, "I am going to tie you up in bows love."

"I don't think..." Emma started, and he lifted her onto him and thrust into her savagely, and she cried out.

"No, you are not to think, just feel and do as you're told," Brody said pulling out as swiftly as he entered her.

Emma gasped, "Give that back."

"Demands will not be met at the present time, come I want to show you something," he said grabbing her hand and leading her to the closet.

Brody opened the door to his closet and pushed aside the clothes revealing another door, he pulled a key off of a shelf. He winked at Emma who was wide eyed with wonder. He opened the door and behind it was a small closet that had drawers and shelves that held boxes.

"Alright Emma why don't you check this out," his voice was controlled but she knew he was nervous.

Emma pulled open a drawer, and its contents made her gasp out loud. She picked up a small silver object, and her face turned red.

"Okay, just so you know, I am quite embarrassed right now and expect that you think I don't know what these are, but I do."

"What are they Emma," he wrapped his arms around her waist and slowly pressing his erection against her back.

"Bullets? Silver bullets, sex toys, and hand cuffs, and a vibrator," she moaned as he caressed her sex with his hands.

"Okay very good Emma, how do you feel about them," he said circling her with his finger.

"Well I have been to toy parties, I always bought the lotions," she said breathlessly.

He giggled and opened the next drawer revealing several lotions and oils.

"Yep like those," she said pushing into his touch.

He moaned, ", So you like those huh?"

"I think I will with you," she said her voice shaking. She reached down to the last drawer and he stopped it from opening with his knee.

"You aren't ready for that yet love," Brody said inserting a finger into her.

"Please," she moaned.

"Those boxes, the black one, is for now," he said and pulled his hands away from her and reached up to grab it, "Get in bed Emma."

His voice was gruff, and she felt excitement burn deep inside of her as she went to the bed and covered herself as she sat waiting and wanting all things Brody.

He bit the corner of his lip as he pulled the blanket off of her, "Give me your hand."

He gently tied it up and moved to the next, he didn't have to ask she just reached her hand out to him and squirmed a little and pressed her knees tightly together.

"You need me Em?" he asked stone faced as he cocked his head slightly to the left.

She looked up at him wide eyed and shook her head slowly.

"Of course you do," he reached over the headboard and pulled two rings attached to ropes from behind it and tugged forcefully checking that they were tight enough.

Emma gasped, and he released a soft deep haunting laugh that made her squeeze her legs together even tighter as he gently laid her down and attached her silk scarves to the rings. He was straddling her as he was tying her arm, in perfect position to take him in her mouth, and she did. He looked down at her mouth full of him.

"This isn't for me, yet," he grabbed a hold of himself and slowly dragged out of her mouth and moaned.

He lightly dragged his head across her lips and down her throat slowly as she followed with her tongue until she couldn't reach it anymore and she squirmed with a deep desire.

"I wasn't going to do this yet, but you're leaving me no choice," he said taking her ankle and tying it and then the other.

"How flexible are you Emma, should we see?" he asked as he raised her ankle to her arm.

"If any part of this bothers you you need to tell me and no or stop aren't going to work, your going to want to say those words and not mean it, I have heard you before, tell me what word you will say Emma if you ever truly want me to stop," he said pulling more rings from behind the bed.

They were longer, and he slid them firmly under her and tied her ankles to them. She could no longer squeeze her knees together.

"What's your word love?"

"I don't know, but I need you now I want to come for you please," Emma said panting.

"Not yet, pick a word," Brody demanded.

"Uncle?" Emma said trying to squirm.

He looked at her and tried to maintain his distant look, but she saw amusement.

"You can't laugh at me when you have me all tied up like this, it makes me feel..." she started.

Brody immediately went down, and she stopped and moaned.

He sat back, "No more talking Emma, or I will gag you," he warned. "You are so fucking hot, and you don't even know it, turn off that shit in your brain and feel," he said as he slid his finger in her and circled her.

Emma tossed her head back and cried out.

He propped her up with pillows, "You need to watch me make you come, see what I can do for you," he said as he took her again in his mouth.

She watched as he skillfully licked and sucked her, he used his fingers as he claimed her clit with his tongue and teeth, he looked up at her to make sure she was watching and slowly eased his finger out of her, and his tongue took it's place.

"Emma you taste divine, I want you to come for me, I want to taste you more," he said and she felt his tongue moving further south, and she gasped.

"No, don't please..." Emma said, and he shoved two fingers in her, and she felt her body tightening as he rimmed her and fucked her with his fingers until she exploded, screaming out his name.

He removed his fingers and savagely sucked between her legs thumbing her clit. Her orgasm lasted forever and when she finally finished he moved between her legs and thrust deeply into her, filling her totally. She couldn't move, and he didn't stop. She felt the release of her arms and legs and then his mouth was on her right breast and fingers on her left pulling and sucking her until she felt the tightening in her belly again.

"Oh, please, oh stop, aah" she cried out and came again.

Brody flipped her around on her stomach drawing her ass in the air and pushed into her again, this time slower and deeper until they both climaxed together.

Brody finally sat up and grabbed tissues off the nightstand and gently cleaned between her legs.

"I can do that." Emma said half asleep as she tried to stop him.

"My mess, I will clean it up. Rest now Emma because our next task is going to be as exhausting, we are going to talk about my past," he said quietly and kissed her inner thighs as he finished up.

"How do you suggest I rest now?" Emma asked sitting up and looking at him.

Brody smiled, "I will be right back, lay down."

What do I ask first? No, just listen Emma just listen, she thought to herself.

Emma jumped under the covers and went to put on her shirt when he returned with bottled water and sandwiches.

"Don't put that back on!" Brody yelled, and she jumped in response, "You have had those covered for a month now, I just got them back, and I really like them a lot," he said kissing her and sliding under the covers.

"Ok," she said quietly leaning into him as he took the top off her water and gave her a drink.

"Alright so my Mom left when I was eleven, we now know why, and I am in a good place with all that now. But we have yet to really discuss my father. So he began to drink a lot, Bobby and Rebecca kind of picked up the slack around the house and tended to me, the youngest. Dad simply drank and worked, he was not affectionate like my mother had been, and when he looked at us when he was sober he looked hurt. I get that all now as well. When we lost my childhood home we moved in with his younger brother, my uncle. His guest house actually. Uncle Bo was a bachelor and a party machine. He and Dad spent a lot of time together entertaining. His parties were epic. Wild women, booze, and drugs. I was fascinated by his lifestyle. It was unlike I had ever seen. My family didn't live that way when my mother was alive and well. We only saw Bo on New Years Day, I assume it's because the days after his big parties he was much calmer, hungover and used up," Brody laughed. "My mother kept us from all of that, which was the right thing to do. The last Christmas Mom was alive Dad dropped us off at my Aunt and Uncles in London for two days. You know I didn't even know she was sick, I was so pissed at her, so angry, I believe I hated her Emma and that must have hurt like hell, in her last days I hated her."

"Brody, she wanted what was best for you, not remember her as sick," Emma said and wrapped her arms around him.

"Ya not a good idea. I think we went through that huh Em? I also think because of your shenanigans I understand what she was trying to do now. I would have preferred her to have given me the opportunity," Brody sadly spoke. "Okay so she died, and Dad went from depressed to male whore overnight," Brody laughed. "He ended up moving in a much younger woman into the guest house, Betsy, I think she was just eighteen maybe nineteen. Well her sister would visit us a lot, we fed her. Her and I hung out a lot, Bobby left for the military and Rebecca ended up going away to school. So I was thirteen and very curious, so I would sneak out to Bo's on party nights and hide and watch the adults in their suit and ties and fancy dresses as they drank and did drugs and danced. They looked happy, so happy compared to the sadness I had lived for two years. Victoria, Betsy's sister, was sixteen. Well she followed me one night when I went to peek in the windows of the main house to watch the adults party, and I didn't know it. When I told her to go back to the house she said she would tell on me. So I let her come along. I was much braver with an audience, and well, we hide in my Uncle Bo's room. That night he had two women in his bed tied up, and he was fucking them forever. When he finished they practically fell to his feet. I remember being so happy when they finally left to get the hell out of there. Victoria and I didn't speak of that night for a week or so until she caught me sneaking out again. I told her if she followed me I would tie her up, and she said okay. That was my first experience. She was three years older than me and probably got sick of the fact that I couldn't last more than ten minutes, so being competitive I started making sure I would," he laughed, "Shall I stop Em?"

"No, please go on," Emma said kissing his chest.

"Well fast forward a year, Betsy moved out, and Victoria wasn't around, and Dad practically lived at Bo's. I went to London to try to get my head on straight and stayed with my Aunt and Uncle. I attended the music school my Aunt taught at, on scholarship and shockingly I excelled at piano, I then took to guitar and became fast friends with the other scholarship kids. All in my band, one my driver."

Emma smiled up at Brody, "I love you."

"I love you and trust me Emma I wish I could end there, but there is more. If I did not completely trust you, love you and know you feel the same I would end the story there. What I am about to tell you no one, I mean no one, except the guys know. This is how much I trust you, with my life Emma, I trust you with everything."

"I trust you just as much," Emma said and kissed him again.

"Alright, so one night I overheard my Aunt and Uncle quarreling over money. He was angry about her wanting to buy me a new guitar and he basically said he was fed up with the charity case she brought to their marriage. Again I know now he was just frustrated, and I am over it. Anyway I moved out, got a job at a pub, I was fifteen and looked twenty, you know tall with facial hair..."

"And hot," Emma laughed.

"My story remember?" he laughed and kissed her head.

"So I tended bar and played a bit of piano. Over the next year, I went from shit holes to the penthouse. When I wasn't tending bar I was playing gigs with the guys at all sorts of clubs. We got invited to a party, and it was wild. We fucked a lot and I used my teenage skill set on everyone I could. My boys don't know that, that's all for you," he laughed.

"Does Ariel know, I mean did you tie her up?" Emma asked.

"No, after Jemma died so did that part of my life," Brody said.

"Jemma?" Emma asked.

"Yes, we lived together briefly. She actually introduced me to the S & M scene, opened my eyes to what I had not learned from Bo's parties. But it was all promoted as control. They had no control, they had kids on drugs fucking, that's it. My first Dom was an older woman, not Jemma" Brody said sadly.

"I am sorry you lost her," Emma said softly.

"It wasn't like that, she wasn't someone I was in love with. She introduced me to drugs and I woke up tied up getting my ass beat at a party one night," Brody laughed, "Jemma was four years older than I was and very worldly. I was a toy."

"Is there more?" Emma asked.

"I think that's good for the night, unless you want me to talk about the Jemma years," Brody said looking down at her with a yuck look on his face.

"So it disgusts you, why still do it?" Emma asked.

"When done right without vengeance or perversion it's the most beautiful thing in the world," Brody said and closed his eyes, "With you it's beautiful and how I believe it should be."

"I guess I am confused," Emma said looking down.

"Okay how do I best explain this to you? When you are laying there wrapped in bows," he chuckled, "You're giving me complete control of you, you are trusting me completely, you know I won't hurt you or give you more than you can handle. That is the ultimate trust one could give another, trust, complete trust."

"So until then you didn't trust me or believe me?" Emma asked.

"Of course I did, or I would not have had you that way," Brody said rubbing her shoulders.

"So what do you get from it, I mean seriously, you could have your way with me anytime you'd like," Emma asked sincerely.

Brody laughed, "I get to please you, take you right to the edge without you crushing my face with your legs. I know you want me and desire me, I know when your frustrated you need that, I know when you do it is me you want, and to me I feel much better knowing I am the one who gets to do that to you, and if I didn't believe you before you said yes to my proposal I would know that you would be back for more."

"Really?" Emma asked.

"Yes, pretty confident about that. Should I not be?" she rolled her eyes at him, "Don't make me question myself or I could get out the whip."

"You really..." Emma started.

"No, I don't want to beat you that's twisted," Brody laughed, "But, there are many ways Emma."

"What's in the third drawer?" she asked nervously.

"Can you trust me enough not to need that answer right away?" Brody asked with a wicked little grin.

"If I have too," she groaned.

"Good, I want to talk to you about wedding stuff," Brody grinned and Emma smiled. "Big or small?"

"Whatever you want, we could do Vegas," Emma laughed.

"Done that," Brody laughed.

"Really?" Emma asked amused.

"Yep, corny huh?" Brody smiled.

"I have done big," Emma said.

"Yes you have," he said moving her hand from his chest down.

Emma laughed, "That's perfect after you know… you get me ready."

"Okay so no Vegas or big wedding, how about small and personal?" Brody asked.

Emma grinned, "Perfect" she purred and moved her hand lower.

"Hmm, a date Emma?" Brody moaned.

"Tomorrow?" she asked moving her hand up and down him.

"Emma, that would…be to soon…no time for planning" Brody moaned, "Fuck Emma," he said, and she winked at him and went under the covers.

Brody pushed the cover off and grabbed her hips and scooted down the bed. He lifted her above him, and she didn't stop. "Mine," he said and brought her down on his face.

"Mine," Emma said and sucked harder as he licked her deep, "Awe you need to stop. This was my idea, damn it!"

"Keep sucking love, please," he groaned as he continued pleasuring her.

Emma continued sucking him and licking the tip of his throbbing, hard, pleasure stick. She used her hand and sucked harder. She felt her body tighten up and wanted him to come first, she took him deeper in her throat than she ever had, letting it touch the back and he groaned deeply, and her body was on the edge as he came in her mouth and she followed suit.

She lay on top of him until her body stopped pulsing, kissing him until she could move as he gently rubbed her ass.

She sat up and turned around and looked at him and smiled, "Thank you."

"No love, thank you, again," Brody said shaking his head in disbelief.

"What?" Emma asked cocking her head to the side like he does and finally grinning.

"You like to do that huh?" Brody asked.

"I don't think Like is the right word," she said and laid on him with her chin on his chest looking up at him innocently.

"Oh no?" Brody smiled pushing her hair away from her eyes.

"Well as much as I would like to argue it is pretty amazing, but that's because it's with you," Emma said softly.

"In a loving, respectful relationship, it is more than I could have ever dreamed. Much hotter than I have ever experienced" Brody ran his hand across her chest. Emma smiled. "So you don't think I am a monster, you're not going to call me monster man instead of music man?"

Emma laughed a deep belly laugh, "I am the Bride of Frankenstein you can be my Monster Man."

Brody laughed, "Halloween is right around the corner, which by the way when is your birthday?"

"March third, wow when is yours?" Emma asked shocked that she didn't know.

"October thirty first," he laughed.

"Hmm, my monster man," she said and grabbed him firmly, "Mine."

"Oh yes all yours," Brody groaned.

They lay wrapped in each others arms exhausted, "We have two hours love, shall we shower and work on London's room?"

Emma giggled and sat up, "I think we should get that room done before we shower, we may not make it in there if we don't."

"Very true, let's go," Brody said and jumped up and turned and looked at her, "You coming Em?" Emma smiled and laughed.

Brody looked down at her with pride, "Perfectly fucked."

"From top to bottom, monster man," she winked.

"Rest, I am going to get started," he said and kissed her head.

"I am up," she laughed.

Chapter 11

"You're sure you like it?" Brody's voice was shaky, and he was trying so hard to impress her.

"Of course I do, and love it, and I love you." Emma hugged him. Brody let out a immense sigh and Emma giggled.

Brody raised his eyebrow and walked towards her, "Are you laughing at me Emma?"

"No," she said shaking her head and smiling, "I certainly am not, I just like... no Love seeing you happy."

"You know what would make me happy?" he said grabbing her ass and lifting her up to him and biting her neck lightly.

"Getting London's room finished," she laughed as he tossed her on the bed.

"We have eight hours love, eight hours may not be two days, but it's eight hours Em," he laughed and kissed her again.

Emma smiled and took a deep breath, "I know," she said and tried to smile.

"Okay then," he sat back on his heels and pulled her up, "London is fine, your parents are supervising Troy's visit. He is in counseling, and they are building a great relationship. She loves you, and if I remember correctly she was the one who decided she wanted just to be with him today."

"That hurt," Emma whispered.

"Like hell," Brody said and held her tightly.

"I'm sorry," Emma said and held him close.

"Emma, she needs him right?" Brody asked.

"Yes," Emma said rubbing her hands through his hair.

"Yes," Brody pushed his forehead against hers.

"Boy are we a sorry bunch," Emma laughed.

"No, we are a family," Brody said, and his eyes went somewhere else.

"Hey, come back to me," she smiled and kissed him.

He looked down and closed his eyes tightly, "Fuck."

"Brody it bothers us both," Emma hugged him.

He pulled away, "Just need a minute Love alright?"

"No, it's not. Talk to me please?" Emma said, "Don't pull away."

"Just a moment, please," Brody stepped off the bed.

"No!" Emma snapped, and he quickly turned around and gave her a not now look and walked out the door. "Please!"

Brody stood in the hallway against the door and listened to her cry and got extremely angry and punched the wall, "Shit!" he yelled and held his hand.

Emma jumped up and walked out the door and found him crouched on the floor holding his bleeding hand. He looked at Emma and his jaw tightened, and he closed his eyes.

"Did that wall piss you off or was it me?" Emma asked as she knelt down and took his hand to look it over.

He flinched, "I am not mad at you."

"Okay so the wall then?" Emma forced a laugh as she stood up and pulled him with her.

"Sorry," Brody said his plump bottom lip sticking out.

"Okay you need to tell me what just happened Brody," Emma said as she led him into the master bathroom and washed his hand off as she examined it.

"Not now Emma," he said and flinched.

"Your hand looks fine, you're lucky," Emma said and walked out and went down the hall into London's room.

She stood in the middle of the floor and looked around the light pink room. London had picked a much brighter color pink and Emma swayed her into doing an accent wall in the Pepto Bismal pink instead of the whole room. *Okay Emma, she thought to herself, this is just a small issue easily overcome. He was upset just upset. Damn it why won't he talk to me?*

Emma walked out and past the master suite and went downstairs. The entry was grand and although she would never say it to either Brody or London she felt it was a waste of space. The dining room was to the right and was large enough to invite London's entire class of twenty kids for dinner. The living room was on the opposite side of the house and was huge. Brody, Emma, and London had agreed on a very pale yellow with the ceiling painted a shade darker. The furniture was enormous and fit the large room perfectly. The brown leather sectional was perfect for a family of ten, not just three, and there was a half bath off of it. The kitchen, pantry, study, and bathroom all were as oversized as the rest of the house and in the back of the house. The furniture had been delivered yesterday as a surprise to Emma. Brody wanted to keep her busy today, knowing she would be emotional, something happy to brighten her day.

"There you are," Brody said wrapping his arms around her waist from behind, she reached up and rubbed his soft stubble. "Okay?"

"Are you?" she asked softly.

"I am now, sorry about that," he kissed her neck.

"Brody, have you ever thought about adoption?" Emma asked softly.

He chuckled, "No Emma."

"Well I think it's something that could be considered," Emma turned around to face him.

His eyes widened, "Do you want another child?"

"I think you do, and if you do I want that as well," Emma said looking at the ground.

"Emma, I don't need that. You and London are enough," he hugged her.

"There are other ways," Emma said quietly.

"Emma do you want another child?" Brody asked lifting her chin and looking into her eyes.

"I want to give you a child," Emma said and looked at him, "I can't and I know what an amazing father you would be, I can't take that from you."

"I love you Emma, that upstairs was not about wanting a child. It's about my controlling tendencies. I don't want London to get hurt. That's it understand?" Brody asked.

"Yep, but..." Emma started.

Brody put his finger over her mouth, "Seven hours and fifteen minutes."

Emma looked at him, and his eyes were dark blue and slightly hooded.

"Plenty of time to get London's room done," Emma breathed out.

"How about we start in ours and work our way down the hall?" he asked as he pulled her closer into him.

Emma tried not to smile, "Why not start down here then?"

He smiled and kissed her gently, "Right here?" he asked rubbing down her back slowly as he kissed her neck.

"Uh huh," Emma said rolling her head to the side giving him further access to her neck.

"How about here?" he asked as he ran his finger tips across her breast that immediately responded to his touch.

"Yes," she moaned softly.

He slowly started to lift her shirt, and she stopped him, "Please not yet."

"Emma we have already been there, what's the problem love?" Brody asked as he reached behind her and unsnapped her bra one handed.

Emma pulled away slowly, "I look like the bride of Frankenstein, it's daylight and I just can't. Do you understand?"

"Nope," he said and took the right one in his mouth and Emma moaned when she really wanted to protest.

"The way I see it," he paused as he pulled on her nipple lightly with his teeth, "is very different from how you do," again he paused and licked her and lightly blew on her and she let out a breath. "This may seem perfect and don't get me wrong Em it is, pretty damn amazing, but I prefer this one." Brody slowly pulled her black lacey bra down and slowly knelt before her.

"Brody don't," she whispered.

"Trust me Emma this is by far my favorite, this little light pink mark," he said as he traced it with his tongue, "That is my favorite spot. What you see as monstrous I see as a blessing. This mark is where the doctors entered and removed a small lump that could have eventually taken you from me. This Emma is my favorite spot, and you're trying to keep me from it."

Brody stood and kissed her neck and up her face, and felt her moist cheek against his lips as he moved up her face.

"Did I overstep?" he asked softly as he leaned back.

"No, you did not, that was…" Emma started.

"The truth, you will not get anything else from me Emma. I may need a moment now and then, but I will always be honest and truthful," he said and kissed her soft wet lips. "I want to make love to you here Emma, may I?"

She shook her head yes and took his face in her hands and kissed him.

~

Emma sat up on the dinning room table completely exhausted. Brody smiled at her as he watched her and rubbed her bare back.

"Ready to move upstairs?" He asked.

"I can barely sit up," Emma giggled.

"Well we have five more hours to pass, and I actually want you in our bed," Brody said squeezing her rear.

"You have had me in every room and on every surface down here," Emma laughed "I don't think I will ever be able to wash dishes in that sink without turning red."

"You shouldn't have tried to run," Brody laughed.

"We need to clean up the floor, it's very slippery. Who would have thought the faucet sprayer could reach that far?" Emma laughed.

"I am so glad it did, that damn shirt needed to come off," he said as he sat up and wrapped his arms around her gently caressing her breast.

"Thank you," Emma whispered.

"For what love?" he said and kissed her neck.

"Everything, you are amazing and sweet and kind," Emma said leaning back into him, "And hard… again Brody?" she gasped as she felt him against her back.

"What do you expect, you're sitting naked on our dining room table, and all I can think about is what's down her for me to munch on," he laughed and grazed his long fingers between her legs.

"Oh Brody," she moaned and jumped off the table before he could grab her, "Meet me in that big old bed music man," she said running up the stairs.

He grabbed her before she got to the door and wrapped his arm around her and lightly bit her neck, "Gotcha."

"Well it seems you do," Emma said and turned toward him, "So now what are you going to do about it?"

Brody laughed his deep dark naughty laugh, "I am going to tie you up in bows love."

"I don't think..." Emma started, and he lifted her onto him and thrust into her savagely, and she cried out.

"No, you are not to think, just feel and do as you're told," Brody said pulling out as swiftly as he entered her.

Emma gasped, "Give that back."

"Demands will not be met at the present time, come I want to show you something," he said grabbing her hand and leading her to the closet.

Brody opened the door to his closet and pushed aside the clothes revealing another door, he pulled a key off of a shelf. He winked at Emma who was wide eyed with wonder. He opened the door and behind it was a small closet that had drawers and shelves that held boxes.

"Alright Emma why don't you check this out," his voice was controlled but she knew he was nervous.

Emma pulled open a drawer, and its contents made her gasp out loud. She picked up a small silver object, and her face turned red.

"Okay, just so you know, I am quite embarrassed right now and expect that you think I don't know what these are, but I do."

"What are they Emma," he wrapped his arms around her waist and slowly pressing his erection against her back.

"Bullets? Silver bullets, sex toys, and hand cuffs, and a vibrator," she moaned as he caressed her sex with his hands.

"Okay very good Emma, how do you feel about them," he said circling her with his finger.

"Well I have been to toy parties, I always bought the lotions," she said breathlessly.

He giggled and opened the next drawer revealing several lotions and oils.

"Yep like those," she said pushing into his touch.

He moaned, ", So you like those huh?"

"I think I will with you," she said her voice shaking. She reached down to the last drawer and he stopped it from opening with his knee.

"You aren't ready for that yet love," Brody said inserting a finger into her.

"Please," she moaned.

"Those boxes, the black one, is for now," he said and pulled his hands away from her and reached up to grab it, "Get in bed Emma."

His voice was gruff, and she felt excitement burn deep inside of her as she went to the bed and covered herself as she sat waiting and wanting all things Brody.

He bit the corner of his lip as he pulled the blanket off of her, "Give me your hand."

He gently tied it up and moved to the next, he didn't have to ask she just reached her hand out to him and squirmed a little and pressed her knees tightly together.

"You need me Em?" he asked stone faced as he cocked his head slightly to the left.

She looked up at him wide eyed and shook her head slowly.

"Of course you do," he reached over the headboard and pulled two rings attached to ropes from behind it and tugged forcefully checking that they were tight enough.

Emma gasped, and he released a soft deep haunting laugh that made her squeeze her legs together even tighter as he gently laid her down and attached her silk scarves to the rings. He was straddling her as he was tying her arm, in perfect position to take him in her mouth, and she did. He looked down at her mouth full of him.

"This isn't for me, yet," he grabbed a hold of himself and slowly dragged out of her mouth and moaned.

He lightly dragged his head across her lips and down her throat slowly as she followed with her tongue until she couldn't reach it anymore and she squirmed with a deep desire.

"I wasn't going to do this yet, but you're leaving me no choice," he said taking her ankle and tying it and then the other.

"How flexible are you Emma, should we see?" he asked as he raised her ankle to her arm.

"If any part of this bothers you you need to tell me and no or stop aren't going to work, your going to want to say those words and not mean it, I have heard you before, tell me what word you will say Emma if you ever truly want me to stop," he said pulling more rings from behind the bed.

They were longer, and he slid them firmly under her and tied her ankles to them. She could no longer squeeze her knees together.

"What's your word love?"

"I don't know, but I need you now I want to come for you please," Emma said panting.

"Not yet, pick a word," Brody demanded.

"Uncle?" Emma said trying to squirm.

He looked at her and tried to maintain his distant look, but she saw amusement.

"You can't laugh at me when you have me all tied up like this, it makes me feel..." she started.

Brody immediately went down, and she stopped and moaned.

He sat back, "No more talking Emma, or I will gag you," he warned. "You are so fucking hot, and you don't even know it, turn off that shit in your brain and feel," he said as he slid his finger in her and circled her.

Emma tossed her head back and cried out.

He propped her up with pillows, "You need to watch me make you come, see what I can do for you," he said as he took her again in his mouth.

She watched as he skillfully licked and sucked her, he used his fingers as he claimed her clit with his tongue and teeth, he looked up at her to make sure she was watching and slowly eased his finger out of her, and his tongue took it's place.

"Emma you taste divine, I want you to come for me, I want to taste you more," he said and she felt his tongue moving further south, and she gasped.

"No, don't please..." Emma said, and he shoved two fingers in her, and she felt her body tightening as he rimmed her and fucked her with his fingers until she exploded, screaming out his name.

He removed his fingers and savagely sucked between her legs thumbing her clit. Her orgasm lasted forever and when she finally finished he moved between her legs and thrust deeply into her, filling her totally. She couldn't move, and he didn't stop. She felt the release of her arms and legs and then his mouth was on her right breast and fingers on her left pulling and sucking her until she felt the tightening in her belly again.

"Oh, please, oh stop, aah" she cried out and came again.

Brody flipped her around on her stomach drawing her ass in the air and pushed into her again, this time slower and deeper until they both climaxed together.

Brody finally sat up and grabbed tissues off the nightstand and gently cleaned between her legs.

"I can do that." Emma said half asleep as she tried to stop him.

"My mess, I will clean it up. Rest now Emma because our next task is going to be as exhausting, we are going to talk about my past," he said quietly and kissed her inner thighs as he finished up.

"How do you suggest I rest now?" Emma asked sitting up and looking at him.

Brody smiled, "I will be right back, lay down."

What do I ask first? No, just listen Emma just listen, she thought to herself.

Emma jumped under the covers and went to put on her shirt when he returned with bottled water and sandwiches.

"Don't put that back on!" Brody yelled, and she jumped in response, "You have had those covered for a month now, I just got them back, and I really like them a lot," he said kissing her and sliding under the covers.

"Ok," she said quietly leaning into him as he took the top off her water and gave her a drink.

"Alright so my Mom left when I was eleven, we now know why, and I am in a good place with all that now. But we have yet to really discuss my father. So he began to drink a lot, Bobby and Rebecca kind of picked up the slack around the house and tended to me, the youngest. Dad simply drank and worked, he was not affectionate like my mother had been, and when he looked at us when he was sober he looked hurt. I get that all now as well. When we lost my childhood home we moved in with his younger brother, my uncle. His guest house actually. Uncle Bo was a bachelor and a party machine. He and Dad spent a lot of time together entertaining. His parties were epic. Wild women, booze, and drugs. I was fascinated by his lifestyle. It was unlike I had ever seen. My family didn't live that way when my mother was alive and well. We only saw Bo on New Years Day, I assume it's because the days after his big parties he was much calmer, hungover and used up," Brody laughed. "My mother kept us from all of that, which was the right thing to do. The last Christmas Mom was alive Dad dropped us off at my Aunt and Uncles in London for two days. You know I didn't even know she was sick, I was so pissed at her, so angry, I believe I hated her Emma and that must have hurt like hell, in her last days I hated her."

"Brody, she wanted what was best for you, not remember her as sick," Emma said and wrapped her arms around him.

"Ya not a good idea. I think we went through that huh Em? I also think because of your shenanigans I understand what she was trying to do now. I would have preferred her to have given me the opportunity," Brody sadly spoke. "Okay so she died, and Dad went from depressed to male whore overnight," Brody laughed. "He ended up moving in a much younger woman into the guest house, Betsy, I think she was just eighteen maybe nineteen. Well her sister would visit us a lot, we fed her. Her and I hung out a lot, Bobby left for the military and Rebecca ended up going away to school. So I was thirteen and very curious, so I would sneak out to Bo's on party nights and hide and watch the adults in their suit and ties and fancy dresses as they drank and did drugs and danced. They looked happy, so happy compared to the sadness I had lived for two years. Victoria, Betsy's sister, was sixteen. Well she followed me one night when I went to peek in the windows of the main house to watch the adults party, and I didn't know it. When I told her to go back to the house she said she would tell on me. So I let her come along. I was much braver with an audience, and well, we hide in my Uncle Bo's room. That night he had two women in his bed tied up, and he was fucking them forever. When he finished they practically fell to his feet. I remember being so happy when they finally left to get the hell out of there. Victoria and I didn't speak of that night for a week or so until she caught me sneaking out again. I told her if she followed me I would tie her up, and she said okay. That was my first experience. She was three years older than me and probably got sick of the fact that I couldn't last more than ten minutes, so being competitive I started making sure I would," he laughed, "Shall I stop Em?"

"No, please go on," Emma said kissing his chest.

"Well fast forward a year, Betsy moved out, and Victoria wasn't around, and Dad practically lived at Bo's. I went to London to try to get my head on straight and stayed with my Aunt and Uncle. I attended the music school my Aunt taught at, on scholarship and shockingly I excelled at piano, I then took to guitar and became fast friends with the other scholarship kids. All in my band, one my driver."

Emma smiled up at Brody, "I love you."

"I love you and trust me Emma I wish I could end there, but there is more. If I did not completely trust you, love you and know you feel the same I would end the story there. What I am about to tell you no one, I mean no one, except the guys know. This is how much I trust you, with my life Emma, I trust you with everything."

"I trust you just as much," Emma said and kissed him again.

"Alright, so one night I overheard my Aunt and Uncle quarreling over money. He was angry about her wanting to buy me a new guitar and he basically said he was fed up with the charity case she brought to their marriage. Again I know now he was just frustrated, and I am over it. Anyway I moved out, got a job at a pub, I was fifteen and looked twenty, you know tall with facial hair..."

"And hot," Emma laughed.

"My story remember?" he laughed and kissed her head.

"So I tended bar and played a bit of piano. Over the next year, I went from shit holes to the penthouse. When I wasn't tending bar I was playing gigs with the guys at all sorts of clubs. We got invited to a party, and it was wild. We fucked a lot and I used my teenage skill set on everyone I could. My boys don't know that, that's all for you," he laughed.

"Does Ariel know, I mean did you tie her up?" Emma asked.

"No, after Jemma died so did that part of my life," Brody said.

"Jemma?" Emma asked.

"Yes, we lived together briefly. She actually introduced me to the S & M scene, opened my eyes to what I had not learned from Bo's parties. But it was all promoted as control. They had no control, they had kids on drugs fucking, that's it. My first Dom was an older woman, not Jemma" Brody said sadly.

"I am sorry you lost her," Emma said softly.

"It wasn't like that, she wasn't someone I was in love with. She introduced me to drugs and I woke up tied up getting my ass beat at a party one night," Brody laughed, "Jemma was four years older than I was and very worldly. I was a toy."

"Is there more?" Emma asked.

"I think that's good for the night, unless you want me to talk about the Jemma years," Brody said looking down at her with a yuck look on his face.

"So it disgusts you, why still do it?" Emma asked.

"When done right without vengeance or perversion it's the most beautiful thing in the world," Brody said and closed his eyes, "With you it's beautiful and how I believe it should be."

"I guess I am confused," Emma said looking down.

"Okay how do I best explain this to you? When you are laying there wrapped in bows," he chuckled, "You're giving me complete control of you, you are trusting me completely, you know I won't hurt you or give you more than you can handle. That is the ultimate trust one could give another, trust, complete trust."

"So until then you didn't trust me or believe me?" Emma asked.

"Of course I did, or I would not have had you that way," Brody said rubbing her shoulders.

"So what do you get from it, I mean seriously, you could have your way with me anytime you'd like," Emma asked sincerely.

Brody laughed, "I get to please you, take you right to the edge without you crushing my face with your legs. I know you want me and desire me, I know when your frustrated you need that, I know when you do it is me you want, and to me I feel much better knowing I am the one who gets to do that to you, and if I didn't believe you before you said yes to my proposal I would know that you would be back for more."

"Really?" Emma asked.

"Yes, pretty confident about that. Should I not be?" she rolled her eyes at him, "Don't make me question myself or I could get out the whip."

"You really..." Emma started.

"No, I don't want to beat you that's twisted," Brody laughed, "But, there are many ways Emma."

"What's in the third drawer?" she asked nervously.

"Can you trust me enough not to need that answer right away?" Brody asked with a wicked little grin.

"If I have too," she groaned.

"Good, I want to talk to you about wedding stuff," Brody grinned and Emma smiled. "Big or small?"

"Whatever you want, we could do Vegas," Emma laughed.

"Done that," Brody laughed.

"Really?" Emma asked amused.

"Yep, corny huh?" Brody smiled.

"I have done big," Emma said.

"Yes you have," he said moving her hand from his chest down.

Emma laughed, "That's perfect after you know… you get me ready."

"Okay so no Vegas or big wedding, how about small and personal?" Brody asked.

Emma grinned, "Perfect" she purred and moved her hand lower.

"Hmm, a date Emma?" Brody moaned.

"Tomorrow?" she asked moving her hand up and down him.

"Emma, that would…be to soon…no time for planning" Brody moaned, "Fuck Emma," he said, and she winked at him and went under the covers.

Brody pushed the cover off and grabbed her hips and scooted down the bed. He lifted her above him, and she didn't stop. "Mine," he said and brought her down on his face.

"Mine," Emma said and sucked harder as he licked her deep, "Awe you need to stop. This was my idea, damn it!"

"Keep sucking love, please," he groaned as he continued pleasuring her.

Emma continued sucking him and licking the tip of his throbbing, hard, pleasure stick. She used her hand and sucked harder. She felt her body tighten up and wanted him to come first, she took him deeper in her throat than she ever had, letting it touch the back and he groaned deeply, and her body was on the edge as he came in her mouth and she followed suit.

She lay on top of him until her body stopped pulsing, kissing him until she could move as he gently rubbed her ass.

She sat up and turned around and looked at him and smiled, "Thank you."

"No love, thank you, again," Brody said shaking his head in disbelief.

"What?" Emma asked cocking her head to the side like he does and finally grinning.

"You like to do that huh?" Brody asked.

"I don't think Like is the right word," she said and laid on him with her chin on his chest looking up at him innocently.

"Oh no?" Brody smiled pushing her hair away from her eyes.

"Well as much as I would like to argue it is pretty amazing, but that's because it's with you," Emma said softly.

"In a loving, respectful relationship, it is more than I could have ever dreamed. Much hotter than I have ever experienced" Brody ran his hand across her chest. Emma smiled. "So you don't think I am a monster, you're not going to call me monster man instead of music man?"

Emma laughed a deep belly laugh, "I am the Bride of Frankenstein you can be my Monster Man."

Brody laughed, "Halloween is right around the corner, which by the way when is your birthday?"

"March third, wow when is yours?" Emma asked shocked that she didn't know.

"October thirty first," he laughed.

"Hmm, my monster man," she said and grabbed him firmly, "Mine."

"Oh yes all yours," Brody groaned.

They lay wrapped in each others arms exhausted, "We have two hours love, shall we shower and work on London's room?"

Emma giggled and sat up, "I think we should get that room done before we shower, we may not make it in there if we don't."

"Very true, let's go," Brody said and jumped up and turned and looked at her, "You coming Em?" Emma smiled and laughed.

Brody looked down at her with pride, "Perfectly fucked."

"From top to bottom, monster man," she winked.

"Rest, I am going to get started," he said and kissed her head.

"I am up," she laughed.

Chapter 12

"So London, Halloween is coming up, what would you like to do?" Brody smiled at her.

"Well Mom told me it was your birthday, so it's up to you," London smiled.

"No, I remember how much you enjoyed dress up, so what would you like to do?" Brody said insistently.

London looked to Emma her eyes pleading for help, "Why don't we trick or treat early and then have a birthday party at our new home?"

"It's a Thursday night Emma," Brody laughed.

"I know, and you have the Today show the next day but I refuse to not celebrate your birthday," Emma grinned.

"I think that's perfect," London agreed as they pulled up to drop her off in front of her school.

Caroline met them at the car.

"Grandma big party Thursday night after trick or treat, it's Brody's birthday!" London announced.

"See you soon London," Emma said blowing her a kiss.

London caught it and tossed one back.

They pulled away, and Emma smiled at Brody, "I am only going to be six years older than you in a few days."

He laughed, "When will you let that go?"

"Never," she said sitting back and rolling her eyes.

"What do you want for your birthday Brody?" Emma smiled.

"You," he said looking out the window.

"What else?" Emma asked.

"Um...you," he smiled, "For my birthday I want you."

"Do you know how impossible it is going to be to figure out what to buy you? London has already asked me and well if you would be kind enough to help me out I would appreciate it," Emma said pouting.

"I want a party, with you and London and a few other people. Cheesecake is my favorite, you and cheesecake would make me extremely happy," Brody said as his eyes flashed.

"Okay, you can have me any way you want on your birthday," she smiled.

"Any way ?" he asked moving closer to her.

"Any way at all," Emma said and kissed him.

"Oh it's going to be my favorite birthday ever," Brody smiled.

"I hope so, could you please close the privacy window, I don't want him to get embarrassed," Emma nodded to Clive.

~

"Mom is Brody going to dress up with us tonight?" London yelled from the bathroom.

"I left that up to him, it's his Birthday, but I am all ready to go, check me out," she said and danced in circles.

"Mommy, we match," London laughed.

"Look at my two ladies," Brody laughed.

"Check you out Brody, you're Frankenstein!" London jumped up and down, "We all match."

Emma smiled and shook her head, and he kissed her neck, "My beautiful Bride."

"My monster man," Emma said trying not to smile too big, and he slowly stroked his nose across hers and pulled her bottom lip with his teeth.

"Ouch Mom, the flash!" Emma yelled and laughed.

"It is a beautiful picture Emma, well worth the momentary vision loss," Caroline smiled as London returned with her candy bag.

~
Brody, Emma, and London pulled in the driveway after Trick or Treating.

"There are lots of cars here," London exclaimed, "We need to get rid of these costumes, it's a birthday party now, what a fun day!"

Emma smiled and hugged London, and kissed her face, "You make me so happy!"

Caroline opened the door and took another picture and blinded them all momentarily.

"Mom!" Emma scowled.

Caroline laughed "Okay the back door, no one will see you, hurry up go get changed!"

"I will meet you ladies downstairs, my clothes are in the downstairs bathroom, and I know I will be changed before both of you," Brody smiled, and they started to walk away.

"Hey Emma can I see you for just a second?"

"Of course," Emma walked back to him.

"I love you," Brody kissed her.

"I love you more," Emma said and kissed him back.

"I don't know about that…prove it," he winked and kissed her.

"I will later, cheesecake and me and a lot of you," Emma kissed him and tried to pull away.

"Not so fast love," Brody said and lifted her up and spun her around, she wrapped her legs and arms around him and kissed him deeply, "Forever Em?"

"Nothing less," Emma said and kissed him again.

~

Emma walked into their room and took a deep breath and walked through to the bathroom. She washed her face and pulled her hairpins out and looked in the mirror, *you're a mess* she thought…*quick shower*.

"Emma, you have guests waiting dear," Caroline yelled in.

"I know, could you grab me my black slip dress please Mom," Emma said walking out in a towel.

"No, actually Brody asked me to give you this, and this," she smiled, "I wonder what is in this little bag," Caroline giggled.

Emma smiled and grabbed it, "Is London changed did all the makeup come off her face? I want this to be perfect for him," Emma said walking out of the closet, "Isn't this a little long, and I am starving, I can't wear this color," Emma laughed.

"Just do as he asks and get down there, he is waiting," Caroline smiled and walked out.

~

Emma walked down the stairs and looked at everyone all dressed in suits and evening attire. Emma scanned the room for Brody and he turned and looked at her, she smiled and he took a deep breath, he looked to London and grinned and she walked up to meet her Mom, and Henry followed behind her.

Emma looked at Brody, and he winked, she smiled and looked at her father who offered her his arm. London turned just before she got to Emma and started down the stairs dropping rose petals and then music rang through the surround sound. *Marry Me* by Train started playing and Emma gasped, and her eyes widened. Emma looked at Brody, and he smiled and cocked his head to the side. Emma smiled and looked towards her father.

"You ready for this?" Henry asked kissing her cheek.

"I have waited for him forever Daddy," Emma said and felt tears.

They walked down the stairs and up to Brody.

"Hi," he said and took her hand.

"Hi," Emma smiled as he wiped the tears off her face.

"Make this the best birthday ever?" Brody asked.

"Anything you want," she smiled and shook her head.

"Perfect," he kissed her gently, "Let's do this."

Emma turned and saw Lila and Mark sitting in the living room that was set up for the occasion. Brody's band was there, all of them. Her parents and she recognized his sister, the blonde from the photo. The pastor from her church was there, and Emma laughed and covered her mouth.

Brody laughed and took her hand, "You okay Em?"

Emma started laughing harder and hugged him burying her face into his chest.

He kissed her head, "Love did I drive you over the edge?"

"I am sorry, this is just so…how did you pull this off?" Emma asked.

"Em can we do this…thing first and then chat about the semantics?"

"Yes of course sorry," Emma said.

They walked up to Pastor Page, and he spoke. Emma heard nothing he said and just looked up at Brody smiling as he held her tightly against his side. One of his arms was draped around her waist the other casually in his pocket and his nose nuzzling into her hair.

"Emma are you ready for the vows?" Pastor Page asked again.

"Oh sorry, of course," Emma smiled.

They said their traditional vows, "With this ring I thee wed," Brody started and pushed the ring on her finger and Emma was smiling and quickly shook her head back and forth.

"What is it Emma?" Brody asked deeply concerned.

"I don't have a ring, Brody," Emma gasped.

"I got it covered love," he said and held up his hand.

Emma looked at his finger and smiled, "That is beautiful, I am usually, not into ink but…you had a ring tattooed on your finger Brody?"

"I had a wedding band, which is actually your name tattooed on my finger forever," Brody said, and she pulled his hand up to her mouth and kissed it.

"Always," she smiled and kissed it again.

"And forever Emma," Brody smiled, "You have given me everything, you and London are my more."

"I love you so much," Emma hugged him.

"I love you Always, don't you ever forget that. No more doubting, no more trying to push me away. I love you Emma, nothing will ever change that ever, not a million miles, not a million years. We are each others always." Brody hugged her.

"And forever," she said and jumped up and wrapped her legs around him.

"And forever," Brody kissed her.

Pastor Page cleared his throat, "Well I now pronounce you man and wife, kiss the bride I guess," he said with an exasperated smile, "Ladies and Gentleman may I introduce for the first time, Mr. and Mrs. Brody Hines!"

Brody laughed and Emma slowly lowered herself down and giggled, "Mrs. Hines shall we?"

"Of course," she followed him.

"Rebecca this is your sister in law, my wife, Emma," Brody smiled.

"Very nice to meet you Emma, I have heard a lot about you," Rebecca hugged her.

"I am so glad to meet you as well, how long can you stay, can you stay with us?" Emma beamed.

"I am staying in the city, big Today show interview, I had no idea I would be attending my baby brothers wedding," Rebecca smiled.

"Congratulations Mommy," London ran up and hugged her.

"Oh thank you, congratulations to you too, you now have a stepfather, and this is your step aunt Rebecca. Rebecca this is my daughter London," Emma smiled.

"London I have heard so much about you, I already feel like I know you," Rebecca said and hugged her.

"Who knew about this Brody?" Emma asked.

He nodded towards her parents, "Your parents and Troy."

"Troy?" Emma asked.

"I thought he should know, to be prepared right?" Brody asked.

"You are so amazing," Emma kissed him.

"Mrs. Hines if you keep kissing me like that I may take you right here love, control can only take me so far," Brody growled in her ear.

"Brody if you growl in my ear again like that I may come right here, love," Emma whispered back, and he gasped.

"I think we need to go upstairs for a few minutes," Brody said nuzzling into her neck.

"Not without cheesecake. Go talk to your friends," Emma laughed.

Emma and Brody cut the cake and gently fed each other bites, "Save room for more," Emma said and rubbed some on his lips and kissed it off.

~

"Do you have the lingerie on that I picked out for you?" Brody whispered softly in her ear.

"Uh huh," Emma said lying against his chest.

London would stay with Henry and Caroline while Brody and Emma went to the city to stay the night. He had to be at Rockefeller Center bright and early for his interview. Rebecca was staying at the same hotel as they were.

Brody swooped her up in his arms and carried her into their suite. There were candles flickering in the room and flowers everywhere. Soft music played in the background.

"This is beautiful," Emma whispered.

"It's insipid in comparison Mrs. Hines," Brody kissed her gently.

Emma caressed his face.

"Champagne?" Brody asked setting her down on the floor.

"Of course," Emma took the glass he offered.

"To you my wife, my love, my reason for being," Brody said staring into her eyes.

"Always," Emma said tenderly.

"And forever," Brody continued.

Brody smiled seductively at her and kissed her gently leaving her wanting more.

"It's your birthday," Emma smirked.

"The best ever," he pulled her against him.

"I have gifts for you, they're not all here," Emma said wrapping her arms around him.

"All?" he asked grinning.

"Well one is not something to open, I just thought you would like it," Emma said shyly.

"Alright but right now I want my wife, and cheesecake," he said turning her around and unzipping her dress, "You look amazing in satin Emma. Satin on silk skin, hmm." Brody kissed her neck.

"You look amazing, I have never seen you in a tux, so hot, so perfect," Emma gasped as his hands gently caressed her body.

Brody turned her around and looked her up and down, his eyes filled with desire, and she began to undress him, slowly.

"Shall we keep this tie out?" Emma smiled.

"No, not tonight," Brody smiled gently.

"Okay," Emma said removing his shirt planting soft kisses on him lower and lower. She unbuttoned his pants, and they dropped to the floor. She smiled up at him and slowly moved down to her knees.

"Emma..." he whispered trying to stop her.

"It's your birthday, and I have daydreamed all day about being on my knees in front of you, please just enjoy the moment husband," Emma said and took him in her mouth and took her time adoring his body with her mouth.

"Emma," he yelled out as he finished.

Emma stood and turned to walk to the bathroom.

"Where are you going?" he grabbed her.

"To brush my teeth," she giggled, "just give me two minutes."

"One," he yelled from behind her.

Emma brushed her teeth and went to the bathroom. She quickly washed all the important parts and took a deep breath, *why am I nervous* she thought. She took several deep breaths and finally emerged from the bathroom.

"I was wondering if you would ever come out," Brody smiled as he patted the spot beside him on the bed. Emma stood and looked at him shaking her head, "Everything alright?"

"Perfect, you are perfect and beautiful and..." Emma began.

"Would you get over here," he laughed uncomfortably.

"I want to look at you," Emma beamed.

Brody grabbed her by the waist and threw her down on the bed, "I want to taste you and cheesecake," he grabbed the box they had brought from home, and untied her bustier. He unsnapped her garter belt from her panties and slowly pulled them down with his teeth, "What have we here?" he asked with a boyish grin.

"Do you like?" Emma asked.

"Ya I like, when did you wax?" Brody asked kissing her belly button and moving down.

"Last night," Emma said breathlessly, "I wanted you to have a particularly clean plate for your birthday cake."

"Mmm Emma, I like the plate that has served me so many times before but the new plate is so smooth," he said as he ran his soft stubble across her bare pubic area and she moaned. "You're going to be even more sensitive now love," he said and he nipped her inner thighs lightly, and she moaned.

Brody grabbed the cheesecake and spread it across her, "Mmm mm mm," he said as he licked it off and with each sound the vibration sent her spiraling into the most sublime orgasm she had ever had.

"Wow," she breathed and looked up at him in shock, "What did you do?"

He laughed, "I will never tell, my secret."

"Will you do it again?" Emma asked.

"Anytime Mrs. Hines," he laughed.

"Now?" Emma asked.

"As you wish?" Brody said going down again.

Emma could not keep still, and this time was even more intense which made her more vocal.

"I need you now Em," Brody said as he hovered over her.

"Anytime," she moaned almost inaudible.

He kissed her hard on the mouth, and moved into her swiftly, and they both yelled out, "Emma keep still please or this isn't going to take long," Brody said through his teeth.

He pulled back and looked at her through deep lust filled eyes.

He grabbed her by the waist and sat her on him, and she bit into his shoulder, "Fuck Em!"

"Sorry, I'm sorry..." she moaned and began to wiggle.

"You are very hot right now but damn stay still," Brody laughed with warning.

"Shut up and lay down," Emma said laughing and pushed him back.

"Emma," he growled as she moved up and down him.

She took his hands and placed them on her breast and he squeezed her nipples between his fingers and she moved faster, and she felt her body tense.

"Oh God, Brody awww..." Emma yelled.

He sat and rolled her over and moved fast and hard into her until she screamed out his name over and over again. Brody came and rammed into her as he filled her with all of him.

He laid on top of her breathing heavy still inside of her. He began to slowly pull out, and she grabbed his ass and held him there.

Brody laughed, "You are unbelievable."

"Again please," Emma asked.

"Anything for you," he said, and she felt him harden inside her. Emma giggled, "What are you laughing at?"

"It's like Brody on demand," she said squeezing him.

"What was that?" his eyes danced.

"Kegals," she laughed, "muscle building exercises."

"Please do that again," Brody moaned and she did, "Emma fuck," he said and began his magical movements between her legs until they both climaxed together.

After awhile he moved out of her, "We need a shower, holy shit I am soaked, you made me work tonight love, on my birthday," he laughed and smacked her ass as she stood.

"Do that again," she laughed as she bent over in front of him.

He gasped, "What has gotten into you naughty girl?"

"You," she said and walked to the bathroom giggling, "I love you. Naughty," she mimicked his accent and laughed as she walked away.

When they finished their shower they lay in bed wrapped in each others embrace.

"Will you go with me tomorrow?" Brody asked.

"If you want me too," Emma said snuggling closer into him and yawning.

"I do," he said kissing her head.

"I do," she smiled and fell asleep smiling.

~

Rebecca waited in the car with Lila for Brody and Emma.

"Are you ready for this?" Lila asked Rebecca.

"I think so, I just have to sit and smile right?" Rebecca laughed.

"I am sure, this is going to be hard for him," Lila said looking over her notes.

"Good morning," Brody said holding the door open for Emma.

"Wow look at you two," Lila laughed.

Emma beamed, "Good morning."

"Has it been?" Lila asked, and Emma gave her a silly look as Rebecca smiled.

Brody sat and pulled her closer to him and buried his nose in her hair and closed his eyes.

"Brody could you give me your attention for a few moments," Lila demanded snapping her fingers in front of him.

"Sure," Brody smiled lifting his head away from Emma.

"There is no way in hell to hide this so…" Lila began.

"I am not going to hide this," he laughed and kissed Emma.

"Well even if you wanted to that stupid school boy grin would give it away," Lila scolded him, "So during the interview it would be best if you answer their questions honestly, I have photos on this disk from your ceremony, that way it's right there, no one will have to dig for them. Keep it short, sing your ass off and then be done."

"Eye eye captain," Brody chuckled.

The car pulled in front of the entry and Lila and Rebecca got out of the car and into the streets and crowd of screaming masses.

"You ready for this Mrs. Hines," Brody asked kissing her quickly.

"Not really," she said as he stood outside the car and held his hand out for her.

Emma stood out and looked up at him nervously, he smiled and wrapped his arm around her as he waved to the crowd with his other, smiling that sexy as hell smile that made her squirm.

They snuggled in the green room waiting as Lila spoke to the crew.

When she walked in she smiled at them, "Will you be going on with them Emma?"

"No!" Emma snapped.

Brody laughed, "She isn't ready for all this, hell I still am not. She can stay with you. Is that alright Mrs. Hines?" he said kissing her head and she shook her head yes.

~

"Welcome back Brody Hines," Matt smiled.

"Thanks for having me," Brody said shaking his hand and unbuttoning his jacket before he sat.

"So you made quite an entrance," Matt pointed to the monitor, "Who is that with you?"

"That is Emma, my wife," he smiled.

"Wow, that's a surprise," Matt smiled.

"It was to her as well," Brody laughed.

"When did you two tie the knot?" Matt asked.

"Last night, a surprise ceremony she knew nothing of," Brody laughed.

"It was your birthday as well?" Matt asked.

"Sure was, maybe that's why she didn't put up a fuss," he laughed.

"She is the woman you were photographed with?" Matt asked.

"Yes," Brody smiled.

"You brought us exclusive photos?" Matt asked.

"I guess we did?" Brody chuckled.

"You haven't seen them?" Matt asked.

"No, I haven't, let's see them," Brody shifted to look at the monitors.

The first was a picture of the London, Emma, and Brody dressed up for Halloween.

Brody laughed, "That's great, although it's not the wedding photos."

"Well tell us about it," Matt laughed.

"My step daughter likes Halloween, apparently her mother dresses up with her every year," Brody laughed again.

"So you had to do this huh?" Matt chuckled.

"No, actually they had no idea, and I didn't know what they were going as either, perfect right?" Brody shook his head and looked towards the green room.

"Very nice and this one?" he asked.

"That one, is at our home, Emma coming down the stairs and being surprised by the event," Brody looked pleased.

"She looked pretty shocked," Matt smiled.

"That she was," Brody said seriously as he gazed at the photo. The screen changed, "And this was her laughing, I assume it was nerves, but it took a bit of time to calm her down," he smiled softly and lovingly at the picture and the next was of her wrapped around him, Brody's eyebrow raised, "The I do's, there was a bit of improvisation there if you look you can see that her Pastor may have been a bit frustrated by that," Brody took a deep breath and sat back very relaxed and lost in the photos.

"She is beautiful Brody and appears to have a very calming effect on you," Matt acknowledged.

"She is perfect for me, and I for her," he said rubbing his lip still lost in the photo.

"What is this?" Matt asked pointing to his finger.

"Oh my wedding ring," he laughed, and the camera closed in on it. "It's her name and Always."

"Did she make you do that?" Matt chuckled.

"No, another surprise, I have been wrapped around hers since I first saw her, and now she is wrapped around mine," he looked at it.

"Wow that must have pleased her?" Matt laughed.

"I hope so," Brody smiled shifting again and laughing as he looked at his hands.

"So I have to ask, M&M's still your favorite candy? I mean so much has changed since you last stopped by," Matt chuckled.

"Of course," Brody said biting his cheek trying not to smile.

"Let's take a break, and we will be back with more Brody Hines," Matt smiled at the camera.

Brody shook his head and laughed, "You're an ass."

"Sorry I could not resist, congratulations by the way," Matt stood and shook his hand, "May I meet her?"

Matt and Brody entered the green room and Emma sat quietly reading, she looked up as they walked in, "Em this is Matt, Matt my wife Emma."

"Pleased to meet you," Emma said and held out her hand.

Matt shook her hand, "Pleased to meet the calm to this storm."

"This is Lila my publicist and my sister Rebecca," Brody introduced them and looked back at Emma and winked.

Emma smiled at him, and he walked over and hugged her.

"Sorry we are interrupting the honeymoon," Matt joked.

"I can tune you out," Brody rebounded.

"Well let's get out there, the stage is ready," Matt said and walked to the door.

"Come out with me Mrs. Hines," Brody asked as he held her tightly against him.

"If you want me too," she smiled.

"Emma don't smile like that, fuck we need to get out of here," Brody growled as he kicked the door shut behind him and lifted her up by her ass and kissed her. Emma gasped, and his tongue swiftly entered her mouth.

"Brody," Emma said and pulled back.

"Are you telling me no?" Brody gasped.

"I am telling you there is no way right now you need to be on stage in, I don't know, now?" Emma said as he pulled her panties to the side and slowly pushed into her and she gasped and grabbed his hair.

"Em, this is going to be really quick, I will make it up to you, but I need you now alright," Brody said with wild eyes and his jaw clenched.

"Of course," she said and finally breathed out.

He pinned her against the wall and fucked her expeditious and hard.

"Oh Brody," she moaned loudly and he covered her mouth with his as she held tightly to his hair, her body began to pulse, and he knew she was ready and quickly she began to relax and he came.

"God I love you, thank you," Brody said grabbing Kleenex and cleaned himself, and she did the same.

"I love you, and just so you know that wasn't just…" Emma started.

"I am well aware of that, damn you're responsive, so fucking hot," he kissed her again, "Let's go Mrs. Hines."

They walked out hand in hand, and he ushered her towards Lila.

"Sorry," he said as he brushed past Matt and hopped on stage.

"What the hell were you doing?" Lila snapped. Emma bit her cheek and raised her eyebrow, "Seriously?"

"It's my honeymoon," Emma laughed.

Brody stared at her as he sang and she tried don't to convulse. He smiled when she crossed her legs and closed her eyes. He was a lot of fun to watch, his ass was perfect, his body long and lean and the fact that she had just had him made her want him more and now.

The crowd cheered, and he signed a bunch of autographs as Rebecca talked about London's Child and the plan of bringing it the US.

Brody made his way towards Emma.

"You ready?" he asked breathlessly.

"Anytime," she giggled.

"Are you hungry?" Brody asked as he kissed her hand.

"Always," Emma smiled.

Brody let a low moan, "Love, we should go eat with Rebecca and Lila, is that alright."

"Sure," Emma said and smiled at him.

"Do you realize how agreeable you are to everything I say this morning?" Brody asked.

"I do," she said looking down.

"I like you this way," Brody hugged her.

"Exhausted and perfectly fu..." Emma began, and he kissed her.

The crowd cheered loudly, and Brody pulled away slowly, "Not cool."

"Sorry I..." Emma started again.

"Don't be sorry Emma, just please stay in front of me," he laughed, "Let's get out of here."

They waited in the car for Rebecca and Lila.

"I think you two need to go hide out in your bedroom until you can control yourselves," Lila snapped as she climbed in the Limo, "Do you know there are cameras in the green room?"

"Are you fucking kidding me?" Brody yelled.

"No, I am not," Lila shouted back, "But I took care of it, you owe me big if I get arrested you better figure it out," she snapped as she threw the disc at him.

"Is that the only one?" Brody growled.

"All except the one I am keeping to blackmail your ass with when I lose my damn job and am broke and living in the fucking strects!" Lila growled.

Emma started laughing and looked down, Rebecca laughed as well.

"Are you two out of your minds!" Brody snapped.

"Yes," Emma laughed.

"If you weren't so fucking agreeable that wouldn't have happened," Brody said and threw himself back.

"Sorry?" Emma said and looked out the window.

"We are going to eat breakfast, do you think you can..." Brody started.

"What say no to you? Probably not," Emma started laughing hysterically.

"What the hell has gotten into you Emma," Lila shouted.

Emma laughed harder and tears started coming out of her eyes.

"Holy shit, you have lost it," Brody said and held her tightly against him and laughed, "I love you."

"I love you," Emma smiled up at him.

"Enough," he hissed.

"Sorry," she said and put her face into her sweater.

"Nice hair by the way Brody," Lila snapped again.

"Why what's wrong with it?" he asked and grabbed the mirror, "Emma," he scolded.

She kept her eyes closed as she looked towards him, "I had nothing else to hold on to," she said and tried not to laugh.

"What is wrong with you, you have just gotten married if you choose to make love in the middle of the day you should. But don't be ugly at each other," Rebecca laughed.

"This is not ugly this is…" Brody stopped, and Emma chuckled.

They ate breakfast in uncomfortable silence. Lila was dropped off at her apartment. They drove Rebecca to the airport, and she and Brody discussed ideas about London's Child. They had already raised over a million dollars from the song which was still number five on the Pop charts. As they neared the airport. Brody looked down, and Emma was asleep on his chest.

"Will you be going on a holiday?" Rebecca asked.

"I don't think right away, London is in school," Brody said and sat back.

"Will you come visit for Christmas?" Rebecca asked politely.

"I don't think that will go over well with London's father, I sure wouldn't want to be without her on Christmas," Brody admitted.

"Will you have children?" Rebecca asked.

Brody explained Emma's situation, and Rebecca smiled sadly, "I am sorry, you would make a wonderful father, the way you look at London, well it's quite amazing."

"She is an amazing girl," Brody stated.

"Well if she had ovaries she could still produce eggs and you could do in-vetro right?" Rebecca asked.

"I don't know about any of that. I literally just found out what a hysterectomy was," Brody said dismissively.

"I would be a surrogate for you, just think about it, don't dismiss it. You will be amazing," Rebecca smiled.

"We could adopt, Emma mentioned that before, she tried to push me away with that as well, believing I would need to be a father," he laughed.

"You sell yourself short, I love you brother," Rebecca said and smiled.

"You as well, I think you should come here for the holidays," Brody suggested.

Emma opened her eyes, "Oh excuse me I didn't mean to fall asleep, how rude, I apologize Rebecca," Emma said sleepily.

~

Emma lay across Brody's lap sound asleep when they pulled into the driveway, "Wake up love," Brody whispered in her ear.

"Mmm," Emma smiled slightly as she stretched her back over her lap. He lightly skimmed his fingers teasingly across her chest, and she smiled. He did it again a little harder, and she moaned. He smiled down at her as she began to squirm, and he laughed softly. She opened her eyes.

"Good dream love?"

"Yes," she said and sat up.

"Well let's get you in the house while you are still so agreeable," Brody smiled.

"Please," Emma laughed.

Chapter 13

"He agreed?" Brody smiled.

"He did, and I want you to tell her. She is going to be so excited to go to England!" Emma smiled and hugged him.

"When will she be here?" Brody said hugging her.

"An hour, why what did you have in mind?" Emma said looking down at him.

"Em, I would like to have a chat, come sit," he said biting his cheek hiding his smile. Emma sat and smiled at him, "Do you want more children?"

"Wow, do you?" Emma asked.

"I think so, I know you wanted more and, well do you want another?" he stared at her.

"If you do yes, but if you're doing it because you think I need that to be happy please don't. I have London, and I have you," Emma said looking into his eyes.

"Well Rebecca said something about if you had ovaries egg production was still possible, she even offered to be a surrogate," Brody told her smiling.

"Okay will she move here while she is pregnant?" Emma asked nervously.

"Probably not, why?" Brody asked.

Emma took a deep breath, "I just don't know."

"About having another child, one that is part you and part me?" Brody asked confused.

"Okay you have had some time to think about this, could you please give me the same?" Emma stood up to leave.

"Emma, please just tell me what your reservations are," Brody said grabbing her.

Emma took a deep breath, "I can't have my child or yours grow inside someone else's body and not be part of that Brody, there is so much I would miss and I can't."

"Alright, calm down, I'm sorry," he held her, "So this is a no?"

"No, it's just it would have to be someone who would let me go to appointments and be there every step of the way, Rebecca lives so far away," Emma explained.

"So we find someone here?" Brody asked.

"Ok, if that's what you want," Emma said finally breathing out.

"Shall we ask London how she feels?" Brody smiled.

"No, I am sure we already know her reaction, she has mentioned it enough. I also think we may…" Emma started.

"Want to wait until we know it works?" he smiled and hugged her.

"Yes, Brody there is also one more thing, we need to talk to Mark," Emma said softly.

"Oh," he paused, "Emma if we can't we can't alright, I am sorry I didn't even consider it. Very thoughtless of me, I am sorry," Brody hugged her and kissed her.

"Please don't be, I just don't want to disappoint you," she whispered.

"Damn it don't think like that. Why the hell did I…" Brody said in a dark angry tone.

Emma looked up at him, "I shouldn't have said anything, this should be exciting for you, for us."

"I am calling him now, I want to know," Brody said grabbing her phone.

"Slow down, I also need to speak to a fertility specialist, and we need to find a trustworthy surrogate," Emma said gently taking his hand, "I am so sorry it has to be like this for you, Brody."

"Stop! We can both feel like shit about this and carry around a lot of guilt, but the truth is regardless we knew what we were getting ourselves into and it would not have changed a damn thing, agreed?" Brody asked sternly.

"Yes," Emma said.

"Like you mean it Em," Brody begged.

"I do," Emma said looking down and taking a deep breath.

"Okay, then. I am calling Mark first, no arguments. You are my life Em, now go make me and London dinner," he snapped and smacked her on the ass.

Emma smiled and walked into the kitchen to start dinner, she turned on the iPod and cranked up the music, and she cooked pasta and sauce. She made a salad and garlic bread and kept herself busy so that she could try to avoid the *damn* thoughts floating around in her head. The miscarriages, the hurt and pain of four years, the cancer, and disappointing this beautiful man who wanted everything she ever wanted and loved her better than anyone had or could ever.

"Em," Brody said looking at her as he stood in the doorway and tears burst out of her eyes.

"Please, I am sorry, I am so sorry, but I do have good news," he lifted her face and kissed away her tears, "We can move forward with this Em."

"I don't know if you understand what hell this is going to play on your emotions Brody, it is horrible and awful. When you try and lose and try again and have a little hope because the pregnancy is a few weeks longer and then you lose, and it sucks so bad," she sobbed, "You question everything, you wonder what the hell you did to deserve all this. I would not wish this on anyone ever and certainly not you, I can not bear to disappoint you."

"Emma, please, please I can't see you cry like this and know I have made you feel this way, please," he held her tightly.

"Shit," she said pulling away and pulling the overflowing pot off the burner, "Damn it!"

"Let me have a look at that," Brody kissed her burned hand gently, "Do we have a first aid kit?"

Emma cringed, "Yes."

"Could you tell me where it might be?" Brody asked scrunching up his nose.

"I will get it," Emma walked away, and he grabbed her and set her on the counter, "I want to."

Brody set the kit on the counter, "Good Lord Emma, this is quite a kit, should we put wheels on it, it's a bit heavy," he smiled and opened it. "Is all this necessary, I think you could perform surgery with all the items in here."

Emma smiled and blew on her burn. He took her hand and lightly licked across the red area and blew on it.

"Does that feel better?" he asked looking up at her through his startling long dark lashes.

"It makes me feel something," she gapped at him.

"Oh yay?" he smiled.

"Yes and London will be here soon so please," Emma said quietly.

"I know what you need Emma," Brody smiled as he sprayed the burn cream on her hand.

"Don't," Emma snapped.

"Shh," Brody said as he wrapped her hand.

Emma scowled at him, and he bit his cheek, "You're not funny you're being..."

"Shh, love shhh," Brody said concentrated on wrapping her hand, "What you need to realize is that without you, I would be empty, you are my life Em. With or without any extra," he kissed her hand and smiled looking at it.

Emma looked down and laughed, "You are perfect," she wrapped her arms around his neck and kissed him.

"We are, together, do you like the bow?" he smiled.

"I love the bow," Emma laughed, "I am burning dinner."

"You are sitting on mine," Brody whispered as he walked away.

~

"Thanks for coming out," Lila smiled and hugged Emma.

"I miss you," Emma said.

"Can you believe how well those two get along?" Lila asked looking at Brody and Mark sitting at the table deep in conversation.

"Thank God," Emma laughed.

"We ordered drinks," Brody said as he pulled out the chair for Emma to sit.

"Thank you," Emma smiled as she sat.

"So Mark says all your blood work came back perfectly," Brody said and kissed her hand, "Do you know what that means?"

"That we are good to go," Emma said taking a drink.

"Have you found someone?" Lila asked.

"No, we have another appointment next week at the fertility clinic," Emma said looking over the menu.

"Emma is a bit picky," Brody laughed.

"I just need to be sure, it's important," Emma scowled.

"I agree with you Emma, there are crazy's out there," Lila laughed, "She will be carrying Brody Hines child, what if..."

"Lila, she doesn't need anymore to worry about," Brody cautioned.

Emma looked up at Lila, and they exchanged a nervous glance.

"I will do it," Lila said quickly.

"What?" Mark gasped.

"Why not, I am healthy, and she is my best friend in this world, Emma I will do it," Lila smiled.

"Lila you don't have to do this," Emma laughed, "We will find someone."

"No, I want to, I want to do this for you," Lila said with conviction.

"Lila you should truly think about this and discuss it with Mark," Brody said kindly.

"It's my body, and I say I want to," Lila said defensively, "Besides, I certainly don't want your child, you won't have to worry about me flaking out."

"You have a career, and a life, don't be so quick to offer to do this. It isn't something to take lightly," Brody stated.

Lila laughed, "I can think about it, but I think everyone sitting here knows when I have made up my mind about something it doesn't change," Lila glanced at Mark who sat quietly looking down.

"Brody can you dance with me?" Emma asked as she stood.

"I would love to wife," he laughed.

Brody and Emma danced and held each other, the song changed, and another slow song was on.

"You needed to give them a minute?" Brody whispered in her ear.

"Yay, he looked upset. This is the longest relationship that Lila has had in years, they are perfect together, this shouldn't come between them," Emma said resting her head on his chest.

"Ok but she would be perfect," Brody said and kissed her head.

"She needs to worry about her," Emma said looking up at him.

"I know, sorry." Brody kissed her nose.

Their dinner was at the table when they returned. They ate quietly, Mark laughed and looked down shaking his head. Emma looked at him and smiled, and he closed his eyes and sat back. Lila stood abruptly and stormed towards the bathroom, Emma knew to give her a few minutes.

"Sorry Mark," Emma whispered.

"Emma this isn't your fault," Mark smiled.

"Well it kind of is," Emma said uncomfortably.

"Hey," he said and grabbed her hand, "Honestly it just shocked me, kind of messed up my plan for this evening."

"What do you mean?" Emma whispered.

Mark took a box out of his pocket and showed her, "I thought she and I were in a different place."

"Oh my goodness Mark, don't you even think about what just happened with us you…" Emma hugged him and laughed.

Brody scowled at his plate and Mark laughed.

"Is something amusing, is there something I am missing?" Brody said trying to retain his anger.

Emma sat and smiled and turned to Brody, "He was planning to propose tonight. We screwed that up."

"Oh, oh Mark I am so sorry," Brody said apologetically.

"Don't be, it probably just saved me a ton of embarrassment," Mark blushed.

Lila returned and began to eat and stopped and looked at them, "I am doing this, Mark do you have a problem with that?" she snapped.

"No dear," Mark said and looked at her, "I actually think it's a wonderful thing to do for someone you love."

"Okay so I will go to your next appointment with you so I know what's going on…" Emma began to interrupt, "It still gives me a few days or you all a few days, I am ready to do this. Emma I know you would do this for me."

Brody smiled down at the table and squeezed Emma's hand. Emma continued looking down and saw the ring box still sitting on the table and gasped.

Lila followed her eyes and saw the box, "You get a new ring Emma?" Emma's eyes widened and she looked at Mark, and he laughed. "What's so funny?"

"What the hell," Mark laughed and took the box, "Lila dear, I have known you for a few months now, I love every moment spent with you, even uncomfortable ones like these, and I wanted to ask you something tonight."

"Oh my God," Emma said and covered her mouth.

Mark went down on one knee, "Lila will you marry me?"

"My God get up," Lila gasped and looked around, "I am doing this for them Mark, so if this is some sort of…"

"You're a stubborn pain in the ass, I have had this for a week, but our schedules never seem to allow this to happen and apparently they won't for the next nine months or so. I love that you want to do this for your friends, our friends, and I love you. Marry Me?"

"Fine!" Lila snapped and then laughed and covered her mouth.

Mark hugged her and put the ring on her finger, and they kissed.

"It will have to be a long engagement, I want a big wedding, and I will have a baby for them first," Lila said in her authoritative voice.

He laughed, "You win on that one, but you're going to have to start at some point realizing this will be a partnership."

Lila smiled, "I love you, thank you."

~

"Wake up love," Brody said, "I need you now."

"You need me all the time," Emma giggled.

"I do but in a much different way today," he smiled.

Emma sat up and smiled, "You're happy."

"Yes Mrs. Hines, and you should really try it. It seems the only time you smile these past few weeks is when London's around or when, well when I am about to attack you," he kissed her neck and moved slowly down.

"Hold up there hot stuff, you need to save your swimmers for later," Emma laughed.

"Awe I see, point made. You're going to make me come, in a very public place, do you know how hot that is?" Brody growled, and he moved his hands swiftly down between her legs and she moaned.

"Brody," Emma breathed out.

He smiled and whipped the covers off of her and lifted her shirt as he looked down at her, "You have breakfast ready Emma it would be rude of me not to eat."

~

Emma's fertility treatments had started almost two weeks ago. When Emma had done the treatments before she had given herself the injections, Troy would not. She didn't argue or fight about it, she just handled it herself. It was completely different this time, Brody gave her the shots every day.

"Good morning Em," he kissed her, and she sat up, "Oh no lie down love."

Emma laid down, and Brody pulled up her nightgown and kissed her belly. He opened the alcohol pad and gently cleaned the injection site.

"Okay Emma I am very sorry about this, just a little pinch, followed by a burn, I am so sorry love," he said as he pulled out the needle and set it on the table and covered her belly with light kisses.

Emma laid back and smiled. It was the same every time, the kisses, the gentle cleaning, the step by step narrative, and more kisses followed by...

"Oh God Brody..." Emma moaned.

His tongue spread her softly, "Like silk," he purred.

Brody circled her clit with his tongue, avoiding applying pressure, bringing her to the edge and slowly sucking ever so gently so that she was almost there and he then moved lower plunging his skilled tongue inside her lapping upward skimming her g spot and then back to the teasing until she could not take it anymore and then in an instant he would push inside her, letting out a groan that's sound alone could cause her to go off.

"Em," Brody winced and pulled back.

"Sorry, oh damn....stop stop stop," Emma moaned.

Brody handed her a pillow, and she screamed into it and felt him jerk inside of her.

"Emma," Brody breathed rolling to his side.

"I am sorry, I love you," she said between breaths.

Emma took to biting a pillow to muffle her moans so that she would not wake London and when one wasn't available she sometimes used Brody.

"I love you Em," he laughed and pulled her into his arms.

Brody was there every step of the way, he even scheduled his upcoming tour around the possible date of the baby that may be theirs one day soon and around London's school schedule.

~

Emma picked up a magazine from the rack in the sperm collection room at the fertility clinic.

"So this is fun, we could watch a movie," she said and picked up the bin of blurays sitting next to the television.

"We should have brought our honeymoon video," he smiled and hugged her.

"You said not until our anniversary," Emma laughed.

"We have never watched Porn," Brody said flipping through the bin smirking.

"What's so funny?" Emma asked.

"Well how about Assman and Throbbin," Brody laughed, "Oh no this one might work, Raiders of the Lost Womb, huh Emma?"

Emma laughed and so did he.

"Oh I have just the one Assvengers, Skyballs, oh how about the Dark Bone Rises," he laughed loudly.

"Maybe that's not a good idea," Emma giggled.

Emma watched his expressions as he looked through the movies. His facial expressions were so expressive when it was just them, she did not wonder what he was thinking. It was much different from when they had first met, the mask he adorned was held in place then. Hiding from everyone his true self. Emma thought it must come with the territory. In the public eye, he was a mystery, just as he had worked so hard to be. But day by day he was coming out of his shell.

"What the hell decade are these from, honestly these women seem to literally have monkeys upon their laps, Emma do they not know about wax or hair removal or just trimming?" He looked disgusted, and Emma laughed.

"Step away from the Porn Music Man," Emma laughed.

"No, this is classic stuff Em, do you think we could get the receptionist to bring us some Popcorn?" Brody smiled, "Make it a movie Date?"

"Do you see deep throat in there?" Emma asked quietly.

Brody smiled at her amusingly, "You've watched …"

"No, but I am sure I could improvise you know, over here," she walked towards the couch.

"Emma how many blow jobs do you think have been given over there?" Brody smiled.

"Revolting," Emma said.

"Exactly," Brody pushed the buzzer and the nurse knocked and came in.

"Could we take this to my car?" Brody said holding up the collection container, "I fear I may have performance anxiety in this room."

Emma giggled and covered her face.

"I suppose, um you could use the back door," the receptionist blushed.

"Wouldn't that taint the…" Brody began.

"Alright thank you, we will be right back," Emma laughed and dragged him out the door.

They laughed the entire way to the car.

"Emma we could make better Porn than that," Brody laughed.

"Okay let's start now," Emma undid his pants.

"You really can recover from that so fast?" Brody asked as she released him from his pants.

"Um, we have a job to do here Music Man," Emma said took him in her mouth.

"Emma stop let me…" Brody started.

"You are going to get a blow job and empty in this cup," Emma began again.

"It's going to take awhile," he laughed.

"Do you want a baby Brody?" Emma said and sat next to him obviously frustrated.

"This can't be a job Em," he said scowling.

"What's wrong? You do know what we are here for right?" Emma smiled.

"Just…. Not what I am used to Emma…" Brody ran his hands through his hair.

Emma smiled, "Well you couldn't give me control just once could you?"

"What?" he asked confused.

"Sex Brody, couldn't let me make you come once without being in control. So here's the deal," Emma said hiking her skirt up, "I am going to get myself off right here, right now, and there isn't a damn thing I am going to let you do about it."

Emma stuck her finger in her mouth and sucked hard hollowing her cheeks. Brody's eyes widened, and he started to move towards her, "No."

Emma pulled her feet up on the leather seat and pulled her panties aside and continued sucking her finger. She saw Brody start to harden and slowly reached down and began to rub her clit.

Brody growled, "Emma."

She raised her eyebrow and let out a breath, "Brody?"

"My God," he gasped.

Brody lunged forward and put his hand under hers.

"You seem ready now," Emma moaned.

"You seemed to have made me that way," his mouth crashed over hers and his fingers pushed into her.

"Brody, damn it," Emma moaned.

~

"Good morning Lila," Brody said opening the car door for her and handed her flowers.

"Really Hines?" Lila laughed.

"Yes, Emma insisted that if we are implanting you today we better at least give you flowers, right Emma?" he said sitting next to her in the car.

Emma smiled, "If you have changed…"

"Emma," Lila smiled, "I only ask that you do one thing in return for me."

"Anything," Emma smiled.

"You will be my coach and my workout buddy after I give birth," Lila laughed.

"I will do both, and I will cook for you to," Emma said hugging her.

~

Emma, Lila, and Brody sat in the Doctor's office waiting to be called in.

"Well the blood work came back and it appears Lila's HCG levels are very high meaning the home test was accurate even if it was a couple days early," Dr. Stork scowled.

Brody looked at Emma and smiled. She hugged Lila, and they both cried.

"We will do an ultrasound to see how many babies we are looking at," Dr. Stork smiled.

~

When Emma and Brody were alone in the car, he looked at her and smiled again. Emma smiled back and looked out the window.

"Em, what is it," he asked pulling her towards him.

"Nothing, I am happy," she smiled and put her face into his chest. *And very nervous and scared to be happy for one minute because what happens if…*she thought hiding her face against him.

"Me too," he kissed her head, "Three huh?"

Emma giggled, "Yep."

"Does that worry you love?" Brody asked.

"No, I just won't get that much sleep," Emma smiled up at him, "Well worth it."

"You won't be alone Em, I am in this as deep as you. Midnight feedings, diaper changes, all of it," he smiled and kissed her nose.

"I will remember you said that," Emma nuzzled into his neck.

"You won't have to it was not an empty promise Emma, I want this as much if not more than you," Brody held her tightly.

Emma returned his embrace and stayed in his arms.

~

The phone rang at two in the morning and Emma reached for it blindly in the dark. Brody shifted in his sleep as she scrambled off the bed.

"Hello," Emma whispered as she walked into the bathroom so she would not disturb Brody.

"Sorry to call you at this hour Emma, I don't know what to do…" Lila began to cry.

"Lila are you okay?" Emma was stunned.

Lila was not one to cry. She was always so strong and levelheaded. She thought things through and did not act without doing so before hand.

"Emma I am bleeding, I am so sorry. I knew you would want to know. I called you before calling Mark because these are your babies," Lila apologized softly.

"Okay, but it's your body Lila, call him if you need him okay?" Emma said quietly.

"Emma," Lila said softly.

"I can come now," Emma started.

"Ok, but you better tell him Emma, first okay?" Lila instructed her.

"Okay, I will be there soon," Emma hung up the phone and sat on the bathroom floor and silently sobbed into her knees.

When she finally stopped she grabbed a washcloth and wet it under the water. She looked in the mirror and saw Brody standing in the doorway.

"Em, come here," he said and opened his arms and walked towards her.

"I am so sorry, I knew this would happen. I have been through this, I never wanted to hurt you or Lila this way," she cried, "I am so sorry."

"Shh, come now. I knew what could happen and so did Lila. I am so sorry you're reliving this," he held her tightly and kissed her head.

"I just need a few minutes," Emma tried to pull away, "I will be fine, I am sorry."

"Don't do that Em," he held her tighter, "It's us together, we do this together."

Brody held her and let her cry. Emma was not sure if she could not stop crying because of the hurt she was feeling for herself, or for Brody or Lila. She could not stop it though, and she realized she was crying for all of them and for the babies she had lost before. Brody held her and let her cry.

Chapter 14

After the appointment with the fertility specialist, all three of them had decided they would wait it out Lila's body to naturally miscarry instead of surgical procedure that had been suggested. Mark had agreed it was a good option considering any surgery was risky.

"Your HCG levels have lowered but not considerably. We are going to make sure everything has passed and do a vaginal Ultra sound," Dr. Grear explained.

"Would you like us to wait outside," Emma asked Lila.

"You stay sorry Hines, but that means you're going to have to leave," Lila smiled.

Brody understood, he certainly didn't need to be in the room, but he still wanted Emma to be alright. She had not completely distanced herself from him, but when he walked in a room he often saw her looking out a window deep in thought. His normal reaction was to hug her and ask her if she was alright or what she was thinking. He had stopped doing this when he realized it was incredibly repetitious and she was probably getting tired of telling him the same thing over and over again. He would not ask her to go through this again and had even looked into the adoption process deeper. Not that he felt it one hundred percent necessary to have a child, but he wanted her to be happy. Hell he wanted that connection with her. Brody knew that Troy would forever have her love, because of London and at times that made him squirm. Not that he was jealous, he knew her heart was forever his.

The door to the exam room opened, and he looked up at Emma's face. She had tears coming down her cheeks, but she smiled.

"Em," he went to hug her.

"Don't, I want to show you something in here," Emma smiled as she wiped her face.

Brody looked confused, and she laughed, "Cover your eyes, Lila doesn't want to give you a peep show."

He started to protest, and she giggled, "Just do it!"

Emma led Brody to the head of the exam table. The nurse had draped a blanket covering Lila's private area.

"Open your eyes," Emma said with a smile.

Brody opened his eyes, and the ultra sound technician enlarged the screen.

Emma took his hand, "Well look really carefully, and you will see that little flutter inside what looks like a peanut."

Brody shook his head, "Yes I see it, does this mean we have to have Lila go through…"

"Brody, one of our babies is still growing inside her, that little flutter, that is its heart," Emma beamed, "We are going to have a baby still, you are going to be a Daddy!"

Brody watched silently for a few seconds, and a smile began to creep across his face.

"You are quite sure?" he asked peeling his eyes off the screen and finally looking at Emma.

"We are at eleven weeks," Emma beamed, "Almost…"

"We can tell London at Christmas Em, we can still do that," Brody lifted her and twirled her around and kissed her.

"Yes, yes we can," Emma said slowly pulling away.

"Thank you!" Brody exclaimed and kissed Lila and then the nurse and finally looked up and said, "Thank you," to God.

Chapter 15

Before they left for England Emma and Brody gave London a package and he and Emma sat back and watched her.

"What's this for?" London smiled.

"Just open it," Brody laughed.

London pulled out a shirt and read it, "Big Sister…big sister?"

"Yes," Brody was about ready to burst.

"Is Mom…no she cant be. Mom?" London asked

Brody and Emma gave London the PG version of the pregnancy. London cried. Brody though that she was upset and looked devastated. Emma laughed, "Happy tears Brody."

"Very happy tears," London pounced on him and hugged him.
~
Emma and Brody sat in front of the fire place in his home in England, it was their first night, they had planned to spend two weeks, London's entire Christmas vacation there.

.Troy would be joining them on Christmas Eve with Caroline and Henry. Emma had been surprised when Brody had suggested it. He knew it was weighing on her heart being away from her family and keeping London from her father on a day like Christmas.

"You tired Em?" Brody asked as he walked in catching her yawning as he set a glass of wine on the floor next to her.

"Sit with me?" she smiled.

Brody sat with his back against the couch and pulled her back against his chest and held her.

"It's beautiful here," she smiled up at him.

"I have always enjoyed it, truly peaceful and relaxing. I have literally fallen asleep in front of this fire at least twice during each holiday I have taken," he said gazing down at her.

Emma smiled and pulled his arms tighter around her waist.

"I have always wondered what it would be like…" Brody stopped.

"Go on," she rubbed his hand gently.

Brody smiled, "What it would be like to have someone to truly share this with."

"But you and Ariel spent time here right?" Emma looked at him over her shoulder.

"Sure, a few times. When I spent time here she would normally be working. It wasn't lively enough for her. To me it's peaceful, it's home. I feel much the same comfort here as I do at our home in the states. It's always brought me tranquility when I have been here alone. But with you and London here I have that same peace, the serenity, but it's so full in here Em, so full," he sighed as he held his hand to his heart.

Emma felt her eyes warm and a pain in her chest. She could not possibly ask for anything more than Brody was in a man. Brody was beautiful, funny, deeply emotional, protective and absolutely, completely, the love of her life.

Emma knew there were parts of him that were still a mystery to her, they had only been together for three months, still she knew him. She knew his heart, and she knew he had given it to her to hold and cherish forever. Emma planned to do just that forever and as sure as she was about that she knew he too would hold and cherish hers.

When Emma looked up again, Brody smiled down at her and kissed her lightly, "Em don't be unhappy. None of that amounts to anything any longer. I am literally happier than ever before. I hope to do the same for you."

Emma kissed Brody and went to pull away. He gently cupped her chin and pressed his nose to hers and closed his eyes. He moved his hand down her throat lightly skimming his fingertips across her collar bone and to the back of her head. He kissed her gently and ran his tongue across her jawbone and then lightly nibbled her ear. Emma turned her body around to face him, and he ran his hand down her spine.

"You imbue my soul, my spirit, Emma," he whispered kissing her lips softly.

A whimper escaped Emma's mouth, and Brody ran his tongue across her lower lip and pulled her onto his lap. He held her arms to her side and kissed down the front of her cotton tee shirt. Emma breathed out a breath she had been holding. Brody held her tight to his body as he kissed her, stroking his tongue up and down hers mimicking how his tongue pleased her in other ways, causing her to push into the growing bulge in his cotton pajama pants

"Em," his low voice vibrated against her cheek.

Brody released Emma's hands, and she held his face lightly as she kissed him. Her tongue entered his mouth as his hands lightly cupped her rear. She ran her fingertips gently across his unshaved face, and her hands moved to his head lightly holding his hair and turning his head slightly to the left. She kissed down his neck and then back up.

Brody's hand skimmed up her back and gently fisted her hair and did the same to her neck as her back arched slightly, pressing her breast against his chest. He sat back and looked into her eyes as she pulled his shirt over his head and he did the same to hers.

Brody looked down at her black lacey bra and let out a breath before he kissed her shoulder and let his tongue run underneath her strap before pulling it down over her shoulder.

Emma grabbed his face and stroked his face as she kissed his again. She was on fire, his taste, his smell, combined with her need brought her body to a place she never knew existed. She had experienced multiple orgasms and mind blowing sex with Brody every time, but right now as she kissed him and he was holding her lightly she felt for the first time that she was giving as much as he was and that was mind altering.

Emma pulled his pants over his hips as he stroked her back and ran his hand lightly down the back of her underwear. She took him in her hand, and he snarled. She felt the heat of his body against hers rise ten degrees and then pushed her panties to the side and guided him into her. She circled her hips slowly filling herself with him inch by glorious inch. Brody sat up and pushed into her further, and she felt the pressure in her belly button as she continued to circle her hips, she started to slow down feeling the pressure everywhere including in her bladder. Brody began circling her and hitting her g spot with each move.

Emma began to pull away, and he kissed her hard on the mouth and pushed into her hitting perfectly on that spot with each thrust. Emma couldn't think or stop, but she felt her body explode, and she began to feel like…

"Em, damn," Brody held her against him and bucked wildly until her name vibrated across her neck.

"Brody I…" Emma's face was crimson, and he pulled her against him.

"Wow, Em," he said breathlessly.

"I am so sorry I don't know why that happened," Emma said softly.

"I can't wait until it happens again Em…damn," Brody said sitting back, his eyes on fire.

Emma's eyes were closed, and he was confused.

"Em look at me," Brody chuckled.

"Nope," she said squinting her eyes tightly together.

"Why," he laughed.

"Brody I think I just p…" Emma began.

Brody was laughing out loud now, and Emma opened her eyes and scowled at him.

"It's called female ejaculation Em, you didn't give me a golden shower," he smiled and kissed her cheek.

"That's happened to you before?" Emma asked.

"No love I have the wrong parts for that," he laughed.

Emma slugged him.

"I have heard of it, never experienced it, but it was hot as hell Em. How are you feeling?" Brody cupped her chin and looked at her.

"Fine," she whispered.

Brody kissed her, and she let out a breath.

"Fine, that's it Em?" Brody prodded.

"No, it was great but, that can't happen again," Emma said standing up.

"Like hell it won't!" Brody stood and grabbed her.

Emma scowled and turned away from him.

"You need to get over this," Brody grabbed her by the waist.

"No, I need to clean up," Emma snapped.

Brody brought her back harshly against his chest, "I love you, next time it'll be in my mouth!"

Brody nipped her neck and covered it with kisses.

Emma looked at him and shook her head slowly back and forth.

"Fucking hot Em," Brody kissed her head.

"Ya real hot, we should probably go through mattresses every other day," Emma turned back and walked towards the bathroom as Brody laughed.

~

Christmas morning was beautiful. London woke early, and Brody heard her outside the door and got up and tiptoed to the door.

"What are you doing young lady?" Brody smiled.

London jumped and covered her mouth, and he chuckled.

"I just wanted to peek and see what Santa brought, Mom said I needed to wait until seven, its almost seven right?" London said sweetly.

"Well actually its five Miss London, but I am also extremely excited. Maybe we could sneak down together but then right back up here okay?" Brody grinned.

London and Brody snuck down the stairs slowly and tip toed into the large living room.

The tree was lit in white lights, silver tinsel, and deep red balls. The room was glowing and beautiful. London giggled and walked quickly to the stockings hanging on the fireplace mantel.

"Can I look?" she whispered.

Brody smiled, "As long as you don't move anything, your Mother may be upset if she were to miss seeing your beautiful face taking this all in."

"Hey London would you help me hang these?" Brody asked pulling out a box of deep red bows.

"They are very pretty, I would love to," London smiled.

Brody and London finished hanging the bows and Brody snickered.

Brody looked up and saw Troy walking into the room.

"You are in so much trouble kiddo," Troy beamed.

"Don't tell on me Daddy," London giggled.

"I don't know, you even have Brody here sucked in," Troy grabbed her and hugged her, "Merry Christmas London."

"Merry Christmas Daddy," London hugged him back.

"I will go wake your Mom," Brody said as he slipped out of the room.

All the gifts were opened, and everyone was sitting down at the dining room table when the doorbell rang. Brody walked to the door and opened it.

"Rebecca," Brody smiled and hugged her.

"I brought someone," Rebecca whispered into his ear.

"Hello Son," Robert Hines smiled at his son.

"Father," Brody extended his hand and shook his father's hand.

"I heard you were home and that I have a daughter in law," he said as he looked down.

"Come in please," Brody opened the door wider allowing them in.

Emma walked into the foyer and smiled, "Rebecca Merry Christmas."

"Em, this is my father Robert," Brody forced a smile.

"A pleasure to meet you, finally," Emma smiled and hugged him.

"The pleasure is mine," Robert responded softly.

"Well come in, meet everyone, dinner is almost ready to be served," Emma smiled as Brody kissed her head.

"I will help you," Brody said softly.

"You should introduce your family to everyone, I can handle this," Emma smiled.

Brody introduced Robert to Henry, Caroline, London, and Troy. They all shook hands, and Henry went into the kitchen and carved the Prime Rib.

"Robert looks a lot like Brody doesn't he?" Henry smiled politely to his daughter.

"Sure does," Emma agreed.

"Do things seem off between them?" Henry asked inquisitively.

"I don't know, I have never met him Dad so I will reserve judgment," Emma smiled and kissed him swiftly on the cheek, "Let's go it's dinner time."

"Alright Princess," Henry smiled, "I still have one last gift you know."

"Of course, could we do it after dinner?" Emma asked.

"Sure Emma," Henry followed Emma into the dining room.

Everyone appeared to be having a great time. The food was great and conversation flowing. Troy and London played with her new toys as Rebecca and Robert watched and laughed. Brody was helping Caroline clean up from dinner.

"Emma got a minute," Henry asked grabbing a leather bound book and then her hand.

"Of course," Emma smiled sadly.

Each year since Emma could remember Henry and Emma would take time to remember Elizabeth. The book was full of photos from Elizabeth's birth through the holiday and every special moment in between. Emma's favorite photos had always been of the two of them playing on the floor in front of the family Christmas tree. Henry had an artist do composite sketches of what Elizabeth would look like each year. Through the years, they looked less ere and more like photos.

"She is beautiful Daddy," Emma said as they turned the pages.

"She is Princess," Henry agreed.

Caroline and Brody walked into the room and stood behind them looking over their shoulders as they turned the pages. Starting at the beginning over and over again. Henry held Caroline's hand and kissed it.

"Look at her, she was beautiful then," Henry said softly.

"I am sure she is just as beautiful now, sitting up in heaven with the angels," Caroline wiped a tear.

Brody looked at Emma and smiled, he knew this must be her sister that had been taken years ago. Caroline and Henry excused themselves and Brody sat next to Emma and smiled.

"She is beautiful Emma," he kissed her head.

"Yay," Emma said and wiped a tear away, "Okay let's go back."

"Em if you need a few minutes that would be understandable," Brody rubbed her hand.

"This happens every year," she smiled, "I am fine with it. I wish I could fix it, change the past, but I can't. But we have family in there, and we should get back."

Brody continued looking at the album and Emma left the room

~

"Do you three think you can come to Uncle Bo's New Year's party?" Rebecca asked as she walked into the study.

"I think it best if we didn't," Brody smiled looking up from the leather bound album.

"What's this?" Rebecca asked looking over his shoulder.

"A photo book. Emma's sister Elizabeth was taken from a shopping mall years ago. Henry has sketches done each year so they can see what she would look like today," Brody answered.

"Wow isn't that morbid?" Rebecca whispered.

"Well I guess if it is the way they choose to grieve it should be supported," Brody answered sitting back in his chair running his hands through his hair.

"May I?" Rebecca asked.

"Sure," Brody smiled.

"Why won't you come to the party?" Rebecca asked as she looked through the book.

"It's not a place London should be," Brody laughed.

"Her father is here, and Grandparents, you could skip out for a bit," Rebecca prodded.

Brody turned to the doorway and smiled at Emma.

He walked up and kissed her cheek.

"If you want to we can," Emma whispered into his ear.

"We can discuss, yes?" he whispered back.

"Of course," Emma said and kissed him.

~

"You're sure about this," Brody smiled as he drove, "We could always skip it and I could show you a few places."

"I am fine if you are," Emma rubbed his hand.

"I told you about his parties Em," Brody warned again.

"Yes I am aware. Brody I have kept you all to myself for months now. I don't want to keep you from the people you love," Emma giggled.

"I am with the people I love, you and London, you are not keeping me from anything Emma," Brody said as he pulled up the long winding driveway.

He got out of the car and handed the key to the valet and opened Emma's door. Emma watched him and knew he was uncomfortable.

"Brody," she said and stopped dead in her tracks tugging lightly at his hand holding him back, "We don't have to do this, you seem…"

"Brody!" A tall older handsome man in a tux stood at the top of the stairs leading to the mansion before them.

"Too late now love," Brody said looking nervously at her.

"Bo this is Emma, my wife," Brody introduced them.

Bo grabbed Emma and hugged her tightly and kissed her on the mouth. Emma pulled back and looked at Brody.

"Bo…" Brody's voice carried warning.

Bo laughed, "I couldn't help myself she is exquisite, come."

Emma held tightly to Brody's hand as Bo led her into the party by her other hand.

The party was in full swing, there were at least a hundred people in the ballroom. Emma noticed that most of the men were her age or older and women were all beautiful and young. Brody held her tightly against him.

"Dance," Brody said with his arms around her waist walking through the crowd to the dance floor.

Emma looked up at him, and he knew she was uneasy.

"We will be leaving very soon," Brody said holding her tightly against his chest as they danced.

"I am fine Brody," Emma smiled.

"That's a fake smile Em. I knew this was a bad idea damn it," Brody scolded himself.

"Brody stop. I have always been a bit socially awkward, I am fine okay?" she said and kissed him gently.

"I love you Em," Brody rubbed her back.

After a few songs later Emma felt a tap on her shoulder, "May I cut in?"

"My wife and I are dancing Bo," Brody said with his brow raised.

"It's okay Brody," Emma smiled.

It took a few seconds for Brody to release her and then when he did he glared at Bo.

"You are beautiful Emma," Bo said smiling at her.

"Thank you," Emma blushed.

"How did you meet my nephew?" Bo asked.

"Through a friend," Emma answered.

"So you like Rock stars huh?" Bo chuckled.

"I wasn't aware he was at the time," Emma said scanning the room for Brody.

Emma saw Brody arguing with Rebecca and grew concerned.

"He thinks I am going to try to get you upstairs," Bo laughed, "But you don't seem like the type."

"No, I am not… whatever that means," Emma still watched Brody, "I should go."

Rebecca grabbed Brody's hand and dragged him to the dance floor.

"He is fine," Bo said with a laugh, "Always has been quick tempered."

"I haven't seen that side of him, protective yes but never without reason," Emma said sticking up for her husband.

Bo waved to a waitress nearby. "A drink for you."

Emma needed a drink, something to take the edge off, she wanted Brody to have a good time and thought he may not be because she was nervous. She wanted desperately for him to never feel like she was trying to keep him from his family. She knew how she would feel if she could not be around her family and he went out of his way to make everything so perfect for her, always.

"Well look at you," Bo laughed and motioned for the waitress again, "Have another."

"Thank you," Emma smiled and tossed it back.

Brody saw her and stormed over towards her.

"Emma are you alright?" Brody said cupping her face and searching her eyes.

"I am," Emma smiled and wrapped her arms tightly around his neck and kissed him.

"Slow down love," Brody pulled her against his chest.

"What the hell did you give her to drink?" Brody snapped at Bo.

"I don't know just something the waitress brought," Bo patted his shoulder and laughed as he walked away.

"Hey Music Man," Emma slurred, "Is that Ariel?"

Brody looked up and saw Ariel walking down the grand staircase.

"What in bloody hell is she doing here!" he snapped.

"I don't know," Emma laughed.

"Em are you alright?" Brody asked lifting her face to his.

"No, I am…" Emma's eyes closed and he felt her body become weightless.

~

"What the hell did you give her!" Emma heard Brody yelling at someone.

"I gave her a drink, two drinks actually," Bo snarled back.

"What the fuck was in it Bo?" Brody yelled again.

"The wait staff brought it…" Bo snapped.

"Well I suggest you go find out what the fuck it was Bo before I do it myself," Brody threatened.

A door shut, and Emma heard another voice.

"Is she alright Brody?"

"She fucking better be!" Brody growled.

"Hey Brody did your wife have to much to drink?"

"Rebecca, what the fuck is she doing here?" Brody said through his teeth,

"Ariel comes every year Brody," Rebecca explained.

"He knows," Ariel laughed.

"Rebecca get her the fuck out of here!" Brody's voice was harsh and direct.

Emma heard a door shut, and then felt him lift her onto his lap.

"I am so sorry Em," he said as he kissed her head over and over again.

Emma's head was clearing, and she began to open her eyes.

"Em?" Brody said cupping her face and looking into her eyes.

"Hi," she whispered, "I am tired Brody."

"Okay love, rest a bit then we will leave," Brody's eyes showed hurt, "I am so sorry."

"I took care of it Brody," Bo said as he walked in the room.

"Took care of what, do you care to fucking fill me in?" Brody snapped quietly.

"Her drinks contained additives," Bo began.

"You drugged my wife?" he yelled.

Emma kept her eyes closed and snuggled in tighter to Brody.

"I did not DRUG your wife. The wait staff said someone was putting a small dose of a liquid drug called Forget Me Not into the drinks. They have been dismissed and dealt with," Bo snapped at him.

"I want to know what the fuck it was," Brody began to shake slightly.

"I will have it analyzed but there wasn't enough to do any permanent damage. I can assure you she will be fine," Bo looked down at Emma.

"From what I understand in high doses she could be out for a couple days, but it wasn't a large dose Brody and I am sorry," Bo explained.

"You are sorry, what the fuck BO! You're sorry!" Brody was tense and shaking.

"You need to calm down Brody, there is nothing else I can possibly do, I have taken care of it," Bo snapped.

Emma sat up and looked at Brody, and he let out a deep breath, "You're awake."

"I am, and I am going to be fine. I would like to go home Brody," Emma whispered.

"Okay I can change our flight," Brody said holding her tightly.

"No back to your…" Emma began.

"Ours, Emma, our place," Brody kissed her and stood up.

"I am very sorry Emma," Bo said softly.

"Okay," Emma said quietly.

Brody let go of her hand to grab his jacket and turned back to her and saw panic in her eyes. He pulled her into him and held her.

"I am not going to let this go," he snarled at Bo.

"It would be best if you did Brody. I will handle it. You take your wife home now," Bo looked at Emma, "I am truly sorry Emma. You need to think about your family and keep him in check."

Brody let go of Emma and lunged at Bo. They struggled and fell back into the doorway causing the door to the ballroom to swing open and the crowd to break apart as Brody and Bo tumbled onto the floor.

Emma ran to them and tried to pull Brody off of Bo. Rebecca grabbed her and held her back as two security men pulled Brody off of Bo.

"You better not make threats you fucking prick!" Brody screamed.

Bo spit a mouthful of blood onto the floor and took his handkerchief from his jacket pocket and wiped his face.

"It was not a threat Brody, but now it's a warning. Get him the hell out of here!" Bo's voice boomed through the now quiet ballroom.

"You need to remember who I am Bo, I don't easily scare," Brody laughed.

Emma grabbed Brody's hand, "Please Brody, please I want to go."

Brody looked at her and saw tears welling in her eyes and felt her tremble. He pulled her into his arms and kissed the top of her head and glared at Bo.

"Brody, get her out of here," Rebecca said pushing him towards the door, "I will call in the morning, go home."

Brody's body encased Emma as they walked through the crowd. He stopped for a moment and looked up at a woman in front of him. She quickly disappeared through the doorway, and he continued walking briskly until they reached the car, and he put Emma into the front seat.

~

Brody and Emma drove silently for ten minutes. She watched as his thumb thumped nervously on the steering wheel.

"Brody," Emma whispered and took his hand.

"Not now Em," he said as his nostrils flared and he rubbed her hand gently.

"Then when?" Emma asked pulling her hand away.

Brody downshifted and quickly pulled over. He jumped out of the car and paced back and forth as Emma sat in the car and watched him. He loosened his tie and clenched his fists. Emma stepped out of the car and cautiously walked towards him.

"Brody, please," Emma said and began to cry.

He grabbed her and held her tightly and she felt his heart beating hard and fast against her chest. After a few minutes, he began to relax.

"It is not your fault," Emma said and kissed him.

Brody let out a breath and opened his eyes and looked down at her, "I should not have taken you there."

"It was my fault, I thought I was keeping you from your family," Emma cried.

He grabbed her face and wiped her tears with his thumb, "YOU are my family Emma. You and London and our child, you are all I need."

"I am so sorry," Emma wrapped her arms around him.

"Don't you dare be sorry, I took you there this is my fault," Brody yelled.

"No, it isn't Brody, no it isn't. I should have listened, I felt you had reservations I should never have pushed," Emma continued to cry.

"I will take care of this. Everything will be alright Emma I promise you everything will be fine love," Brody softly whispered into her neck.

The phone rang as they neared the town.

"This is Brody," he snapped as he answered.

"Hello it's Henry I just wanted to let you know your father is here," Henry said quietly.

"Alright, have him sit still we will be there in less than an hour. Thank you Henry," Brody hung up the phone, "My father is at our home."

"Brody I don't want my father to know what happened, he over reacts…" Emma began.

"It would not be over reacting Emma, but I understand. If you change your mind I will talk to him," Brody kissed her hand.

"I just don't want him to worry, he has been through enough with everything that happened to Elizabeth. I have you and I know we will be fine," Emma was sincere, and he knew it.

"I will always make sure you are alright, I promise you that, until my last breath Emma I will keep you safe," Brody's voice was deep and angry.

"Thank you," Emma said squeezing his hand.

"I don't know why he is at our house, but I need to speak to him alone," Brody said softly.

"Okay, I am tired anyway," Emma began.

"How tired Em…you know we should get you to a hospital," Brody began to slow down as if he was changing directions.

"I am seriously just tired if I feel any differently I promise to tell you okay?" Emma interrupted.

"Promise me Em," Brody said as he pulled over.

"Of course," Emma smiled.

~

Brody tucked Emma in and kissed her, "I will be back soon."

"Brody I don't know what the relationship is with your father, and I hope you understand when I say this, he is your father. Regardless of what has happened in the past, please don't be angry at him He is going to be our child's grandfather, people can change Brody they just need reasons to. Look at Troy, he is trying," Emma hugged him, and he kissed her cheek.

"I will be back soon Emma," Brody walked out the door and down the stairs and found his father in the study looking through the music library.

"Father," Brody said as he approached.

"Son," Robert smiled, "Are you alright? Is your wife alright? I was on my way here to talk when Rebecca called, I was literally shocked to hear you went to your Uncle's."

"Everything is fine for now," Brody wanted to say more but stopped.

"No, Brody, not for now, you have to let it go. Bo has changed. He isn't right, he is ..." Robert stopped.

"Why aren't you there father, you never missed a party, not since mom became ill. Or as you told us, left you," Brody snapped.

"I can't change the past Brody, but I do understand that what I told you was wrong. She would not let me take care of her. She did not want you all to know she was sick...It killed me Brody.

God do you know what it's like to let someone walk away knowing..." Robert stopped and stood up and walked towards the fireplace, "I am truly sorry son."

"Alright Dad, alright," Brody walked over to him and patted his shoulder.

"What I did after was inexcusable, I did not understand that until later. I was angry at her, so angry. I think that's why I leaned on Bo and his lifestyle. She hated him and all that he was, and I truly felt I hated her at that time. I know it was wrong now, I..." Robert wiped away a tear, "I loved her so much. I turned away from all my family could have offered our family because I knew it was all corrupt and that living with nothing but her love was more than enough. And then you all came..."

"Dad, I understand alright, I do. I forgive you," Brody hugged him. He understood what loving someone truly could do to you, finally he knew.

"Thank you, thank you so much," Robert and Brody hugged for a long time.

"Can I get you a drink," Brody said stepping back and drying his eyes.

"I don't drink anymore," Robert smiled.

"Excellent, tea then?" Brody asked.

"I am alright, but if you need something go ahead," Robert sat next to the fire, "And then we need to talk."

"I am fine, tell me what's on your mind," Brody sat in the chair next to him.

"Stay away from Bo. I am serious Brody. You have started a wonderful thing, London's Child will help so many, stay away from him," Robert warned.

"I have no intention of going back there. But he made a threat…" Brody began.

"Dad…" Brody began.

"Just let it go," Robert was visibly upset.

"Has he threatened you?" Brody snarled.

"No." Robert stood up and walked away.

"Dad, I want you to come to the States, we would like you to stay with us, we have plenty of room," Brody offered.

"Okay," Robert smiled, "Let me tie up a few things around here. I am going to be a Grandfather huh Brody?"

"You are," Brody smiled.

Brody and Robert talked for another hour before they hugged and Robert insisted on leaving. Brody went upstairs, and Emma was in the bathroom.

"You alright Em?" Brody asked as he walked in the bathroom.

"Of course, I just had to use the bathroom," Emma smiled, "Are you alright?"

"Wonderful actually, Dad has agreed to leave here and move to the States. He is sober, and I understand why things turned into such a mess for him. I could not imagine what I would do if I lost you Emma," Brody grabbed her face and kissed her.

Emma knew he had a rough night and that he needed her.

She pulled back and let out a breath, "I want you."

"Than have me," he said and grabbed her and kissed her hard on the mouth.

Emma wrapped her legs around him, and he carried her to the bed. She slowly began to unbutton his shirt as he kissed down her neck. As she struggled trying to unbutton his shirt he lifted her shirt over her head and grabbed her breast and squeezed it gently. Emma moaned and continued unbuttoning his shirt.

"Fuck it," he snarled and ripped his shirt off and continued kissing her.

Emma released him from his pants and began to stroke him. Brody gasped and bite down on her nipple as he rubbed the other between his fingers. He pulled her up off the bed and pushed her up against the wall and wrapped her legs around him as he licked and sucked her breast. He moved into her slowly and she moaned.

"I will never lose you," he groaned in her ear, "I love you Emma, you are my life."

Brody continued kissing her neck and pounding into her as she hung on for dear life.

"Brody," she moaned and felt her body explode.

Brody lay her on the bed and continued slamming into her until she came again and he finally finished and lay on top of her.

"I love you," he said against her cheek, "So much Em, I love you."

"I love you more," Emma said right before she fell asleep.

~

"Rebecca what time is it?" Brody asked when he answered the phone.

Emma sat up and looked at Brody and saw his face in the moonlight, his expression turned from confusion to pain immediately.

"I will be right there," Brody hung up and jumped out of bed.

"Brody?" Emma asked following him into the bathroom.

"Em," he grabbed her and hugged her and quickly pulled back, "There has been an accident, I need to get to the hospital, it's my father."

Emma grabbed him clothes as he washed his face and brushed his teeth. Emma dressed quickly and walked out of their room and woke her mom to tell her they had to leave and that she would call when she could.

Brody was grabbing his coat when she ran down the stairs, "Em you don't have to go. I will call you."

"I am going with you," she grabbed her coat.

Brody stopped and looked at her and let out a deep breath.

"Brody if it were my family you would insist so don't bother, let's go," Emma grabbed the keys and walked out, he followed behind her.

"I can drive Emma," he snapped.

"Get in," Emma said and started the car.

Emma held his hand as they walked into the hospital and Rebecca met them at the desk of the Emergency Room.

"Brody, he isn't good," she cried.

"I want to see him, take us to him," Brody and Emma followed Rebecca into the exam room.

Brody stopped short at the door and turned to Emma, "You don't have to be in here."

"Brody stop," Emma whispered and gently stroked his face.

Emma took Brody's hand and walked to Robert's side. Brody cringed when he looked at him. Robert's eyes were swollen and purple, his face had several lacerations and a blood stained bandage was wrapped around the entire top of his head.

"Mr. Hines, I am Doctor James. I would like to discuss your options, would you care to have a seat?" Brody sat down, and Emma stood beside him with her hand on his shoulder. His face was expressionless as he looked at Robert.

"Your father suffered a great deal of trauma to his head. He has what we call countercoup injury. The force of the impact from the accident caused severe brain damage to the opposite or left side of his brain. He has also had a fractured skull, the blood you see is from his ears, his pupils are uneven. From the scans, we have run it is only a matter of time before he passes. We would like to know if you would consider allowing us to harvest his organ…"

"Get the fuck out," Brody screamed and stood up.

"I understand that this is a horrible…" Doctor James continued.

Brody took a step towards him, and Emma stood in front of him, holding him back.

"Now is not the time Doctor," Emma said holding Brody's hands tightly around her waist.

"But it's a time sensitive…" Doctor James started.

Brody tried to release his hands from Emma's grasp.

"With all due respect, get the hell out, get out now," Emma snapped and the doctor left the room.

Emma turned to Brody and grabbed his face and looked into his eyes, "Sit, Brody sit down over here."

Emma dragged a chair next to Robert's side, and Brody sat, "Hold his hand."

Brody closed his eyes and held his hand. Emma started to walk away.

"Em…" Brody started.

"I am not going anywhere," Emma looked at Rebecca who still stood in the doorway.

Emma pulled a chair next to Brody's and took Rebecca's hand and walked her to the chair where she sat next to Brody.

Emma stood behind them and kissed them both on the head. They sat for close to an hour, and the heart monitor started to beep loudly causing a team of nurses to rush through the door.

"Clear the room," the head nurse yelled and brought a crash cart into the room.

"Brody, Rebecca, we need to let them work," Emma said softly and pulled them both into the hallway.

No one said a word.

Emma held their hands as they leaned against the wall.

Emma heard a woman crying in the room across the hallway. A stretcher was being brought out of the room with a child on it attached to a ventilator.

"We can't lose him," the woman cried into what appeared to be her husband's chest as he rubbed her back.

"We have to be prepared," he held her tighter.

"No," she cried.

Doctor James walked past them and nodded.

"Anything?" the woman grabbed his arm.

"I am sorry," he said and patted her hand.

Emma closed her eyes and did not want to see Brody's reaction.

The nurses exited Robert's room and Emma looked up.

"Go ahead in," the nurse said.

"Could you tell us anything?" Emma asked.

"You don't have a lot of time, his heart is giving out. His brain waves are slowing down. He is only alive because of the machines. You should be prepared to say your goodbyes," she rubbed Emma's back and walked away.

"Rebecca, you go ahead in, we will be in momentarily," Brody said and kissed his sister.

Emma hugged Brody, and he hugged her back.

"Please tell me what I have to do, I can't make that decision Em," he said quietly.

"You have to, you and Rebecca have to make the decision together," Emma kissed him.

"Brody Hines?" the woman who was crying earlier looked at him.

"Yes," he said quietly.

"My son is a huge fan, he will be back soon. He doesn't have long, but it would mean a lot to him if you said hello," she said and cried.

"Of course," Brody smiled softly.

Brody looked at Emma and shook his head and pulled her tighter into him.

"If he were ours…" Brody started.

"He isn't," Emma ran her hands through his hair.

"My father is not going to wake up," Brody said searching for answers in Emma's eyes.

"No," she said in barely a whisper.

"I need to talk to Rebecca," Brody said pulling her head against his chest.

"I will give you a few minutes alone," Emma offered.

"No, I need you Emma unless…"

"No, unless, I just thought you may want a few minutes, of course I want to be there for you," Emma took his hand and they walked in.

"We need to make a decision," Brody said and hugged his sister.

"I think we both know what we need to do Brody," Rebecca said, her facial expression unchanged, "He isn't here."

"Emma would you go speak to Doctor James please," Brody asked.

"Of course," Emma said and hugged him.

All the paperwork was signed and they began to wheel the stretcher out of the room.

Brody held his hand tightly to his chest, and a look of panic crept into his eyes.

Emma could not stop the tears from welling up even though she tried.

"Stop," Brody's voice echoed down the hall as he ran to the stretcher and held his father, "I love you, I love you."

He looked at the monitors hoping for a change, and nothing had changed. Brody stepped back and watched as the operating room staff took him through the doors and they shut behind them. Brody crouched down and leaned against the wall and hugged his knees.

Emma ran down the hall and knelt down in front of him and held him as he cried.

Another stretcher passed them as they held each other.

Brody stood, and Emma wiped away his tears, "Get me out of here," he whispered in his ear.

"Mr. Hines!" the woman yelled.

Brody turned to see the woman motioning her into a room, he closed his eyes and took Emma's hand and walked towards them.

"This is my son Johna," she smiled.

"Hello Johna," Brody shook his hand.

"Wow, it really is you, are you here to see me?" Johna asked.

"I am," Brody smiled.

Dr. Green entered the room and looked curiously at Brody. "Johna we have some great news for you, we have a match, you're getting your transplant."

Johna's mother cried and fell to her knees in prayer. Emma held Brody's hand tightly.

"That's good news, I mean I am happy but someone died? Mom I don't know if I can," Johna said with tears in his eyes.

"Johna, you don't have a choice darling," his mother said as she stood and held his hand.

Brody stood and stared at the floor, "Mr. Hines what would you do?"

"Well Johna I would take it, you have many years ahead of you. Things happen for a reason. Think of it as a gift from God," Brody smiled and kissed his head.

"Okay, are you sick? Why are you here?" Johna asked as curiously as any eight year old would.

"I am here to see you, and now that I know you're going to be okay I can leave," Brody smiled.

~

Brody, Emma, and Rebecca walked into the house, and Henry met them at the door, he looked at Emma and at Brody.

"What can I do to help?" Henry asked.

"Thank you Henry but there isn't much we can do at this hour. Rebecca why don't you go rest, call our brother and Bo. You and I will make arrangements and get back to them," Brody looked at Emma, "You should rest, we can't do anything for a couple more hours."

"I will when you do, I am going to make some tea," Emma kissed him and disappeared into the kitchen.

~

The funeral service was small and private, held graveside. It was held two days after Robert's passing. Bo, Bobby, Rebecca, and Brody stood together quietly. London and Emma behind them and Caroline and Henry were there as well. The minister read several passages and shook their hands before he walked away.

"Emma, Dad and I are going to take London back and get lunch set up," Caroline said hugging Emma.

"Grandma I want to stay with Brody," London said and started to cry.

Emma hugged London, "We have to let him grieve London. We will be there very soon okay?"

London looked up, and Brody took her hand, "London, thank you."

London hugged Brody tightly, "Brody I am so sorry."

Brody scooped her up in his arms and held her, "Me too."

"Do you need me to stay?" London asked.

"I need you all the time, but maybe Grandma Caroline needs your help setting the table," Brody wiped London's tears as he put her down, "Sometimes I wonder if she knows where the fork goes."

"I know where it goes," London smiled and wiped his tears.

"I know you do," Brody kissed her finger.

"Okay but if you need me Brody," London said raising her eyebrows.

"I know where to find you and I can promise I will need extra hugs this evening," Brody smiled.

"Okay, like a hundred?" She asked.

"Maybe a hundred and fifty," Brody winked.

Brody took Emma's hand and walked towards Bobby and Rebecca.

"Bobby this is Emma, Em this is my brother," Brody introduced them.

"I am so sorry for your loss," Emma said and shook his hand.

"Thank you, I am sorry this is how we had to meet," Bobby smiled slightly.

"Me too," Emma said softly.

They stood looking at the grave quietly, "Well he is with Mom now."

Bobby shook his head, "Yay, what the hell happened? Did he have a heart attack, was he drinking?"

"He had not drank in awhile, he left our home and hit a tree," Brody said scowling down.

"He stopped drinking?" Bobby asked surprised, "What caused the accident?"

"I haven't had time to get a copy of the accident report," Rebecca said quickly.

"We have been busy, Rebecca it's alright," Brody said and hugged her.

"I will look into it, I know a few people in the police department," Bo offered.

"No, I can do it," Brody scowled.

"Brody let him, you guys leave in two days. I will call you as soon as we know anything," Rebecca patted his back.

"Fine." Brody let out a breath.

They all drove back to Brody's and ate. Bobby was staying the night and Bo and Rebecca left shortly after dinner.
~
"He stopped drinking?" Bobby laughed.

"Yes," Brody smirked.

"Well I guess miracles do happen," Bobby laughed.

"So tell me how are things with you?" Brody asked.

"Great, busy but great," Bobby smiled.

"Do you hear from Claire anymore?" Brody smiled.

"Not in awhile, I kind of messed that up huh?" Bobby chuckled.

"I guess you did," Brody laughed.

"I am settling down, work has me very busy, not a lot of time to get into trouble. And you are married… again," Bobby winked.

"Yes, this one is forever, we are having a child, and then there is London. It couldn't be any more perfect. Dad was here before the accident, he was going to move to the States with us. He and I talked, things were good," Brody said staring into the fire.

"I am glad that you two patched things up. He hurt for many years and then there was Bo," Bobby looked at Brody.

"Yay about that, father was no longer a fan of Bo's. Do you know why?" Brody asked.

"Well if he was sober maybe he saw what truly was going on around him," Bobby scowled.

"The parties?" Brody asked.

"Yay the parties," Bobby laughed.

"What am I missing?" Brody asked.

"From what I remember nothing, you were ass deep into the lifestyle until Jemma's death," Bobby rolled his eyes.

"Things change Bobby," Brody looked away.

"I am glad, none of the Hines family want anything to do with him anymore, he is out of control. They cut him off. I have no idea how he is able to afford that place and that lifestyle anymore and honestly I don't want to," Bobby sat back, "Stay away from him Brody."

"Well what about Rebecca?" Brody asked.

"She is running that charity for you now, she knows better," Bobby patted his brother's knee.

"And you are knee deep in Hines family business now," Brody laughed.

"It's legitimate Brody. And you're a Rockstar," Bobby smiled.

Chapter 16

It had been a few weeks since they had returned from England. Brody and London had been working on a piano piece, writing it and practicing every day for London's end of year recital. Emma was busy with work and Lila.

~

"You are sure you don't want to find out what we are having?" Emma smiled as they drove into the city for Lila's ultrasound appointment.

"I though we had agreed Em, but if you want to we can," Brody kissed her head and pulled her closer to him.

"No, that's fine, how about names" Emma smiled up at him.

"You choose," he smiled.

"No, I want to discuss it, I want you to tell me what you want," Emma rubbed his chest.

"I want you, all the time," he kissed her lips.

"Focus Brody, names, let's have it. I am sure you have some ideas, I want to hear them," Emma smiled.

"Lexington Avenue is where I bought the ring, Lexington Grace, Grace after…" Brody started.

"Your mother. Brody it's perfect. Lexington Grace, Lexi and London," Emma's eyes danced, "Yes?"

"Yes," Brody kissed her gently on the lips.

Emma laughed, "Okay and for a boy name?"

"Robert Henry?" Brody asked.

"Yes, it's perfect. God I love you!" Emma kissed him.

Brody laughed, "The nursery?"

Emma laughed, "Whatever you want will be perfect, just like you."

"I have a surprise," Brody smiled.

"Okay, I like surprises," Emma sat up and turned towards him.

"Your birthday is the same week as London's mid winter break from school yes?" Brody smiled.

Emma shook her head, "Well I bought you a present and well I want to take you both to see it that week."

"Okay tell me," Emma sat on her knees in front of him and clapped.

"Oh no, you'll have to wait," he smiled.

~

"Brody wake up, Brody please wake up," Emma shook him.

Brody sat up and looked around, his body was drenched in sweat, and he shook slightly. He looked around the room and then at Emma. He held her tightly against him and let out a breath.

"Damn it Em, I am sorry, I am soaked, I need a shower," Brody stood up quickly and walked into the bathroom.

Emma followed him, "Do you remember this one?"

"No," he said and turned on the shower.

"Brody…" Emma began.

"I don't remember," he snapped.

Emma turned to walk away, and he grabbed her hand, "Sorry Em, it's just…I don't remember."

"Okay," she said pulling her hand from his, "I am going back to bed."

~

Emma walked down the stairs and into the kitchen. She began making London's lunch and felt Brody wrap his arms around her from behind.

"Good morning," he said and kissed her neck.

"Good morning, I had a late start, I need to get this done sorry," she said and pulled away from him.

Brody quickly turned her to face him, "Emma I really don't remember. I am sorry I was rude."

"Okay," she said and started to pull away again.

"Em, I love you," Brody kissed her.

"Gross, do you two ever stop?" London laughed as she walked in.

"Good morning London. We are running late, let's go get those teeth brushed, and wow look at that hair," Brody laughed, "Alright back up those stairs, get dressed, I will be up in a minute. Mom will finish making you lunch, wild one."

London laughed, and Emma hugged her quickly before she continued making her lunch.

"Em…" Brody began.

"I am not mad Brody just worried. You have had those dreams, nightmares since we got back, I am just worried," Emma smiled and turned back and finished making London's lunch, "Since your Dad."

"I know, it'll get better. Maybe it's a good thing I don't remember," Brody kissed her, "Wish me luck, I am off to try to tame the wild one's hair."

Emma turned and smiled, "I love you."

"Much better Em," Brody kissed her again and ran to the stairs, "You better be ready Miss London!"

~

"It's so beautiful," London squealed and clapped.

"No fair I can't see," Emma laughed.

"It's your surprise, you're not supposed to see," London laughed, "And it's a very big surprise, wow Brody it's amazing!"

"Perfect huh?" Brody laughed. "Do you think she will like it?"

"You two are horrible and extremely lucky I don't take this off," Emma laughed.

"If you try I will pull over and tie your hands up Em," Brody snickered.

"You wouldn't dare," London laughed loudly.

"I would," Brody smiled and looked over at Emma who was holding her breath.

"Breathe Em," he said smiling.

Emma felt the vehicle stop, "Are we here?"

"Yes, London would you like to go have a peek before I bring your mom?" Brody asked.

"Oh yes!" London ran ahead.

Emma felt him take her hand and help her out. Brody pulled her close to him, "Emma your daughter is out of ear shot and sight. You look completely fuckable right now."

Brody kissed her hard on the mouth, and she moaned into his. His hand skimmed across her chest and he leaned down pulling her shirt up and pulling the cup of her lacey pink bra down, he bit lightly on her nipple and her breath hastened. His hand grabbed the other and released it from her bra and did the same.

"I want you so fucking bad right now," Brody kissed her again.

"Okay," she whimpered.

Brody laughed, "Company Em, but tonight I want you in bows. HEY LONDON come back here. Breathe Em."

Brody quickly licked both nipples before pulling her bra to cover them, his breath was hot on her neck as he turned her and pulled her back to his chest and walked her to the steps.

"One, Two, Three," Brody turned her to him and untied the blindfold and looked at her eyes.

Emma blinked and looked up at him and closed her eyes and took several breaths. Her eyes were wet and not from tears.

"Emma," Brody clenched his jaw.

She wrapped her arms around him and hugged him tightly, "Sorry, but it's your fault."

Brody laughed, ", And this is yours, you better stay in front of me until I can get you alone, damn it woman!"

Emma giggled and pulled back and looked down and then up at him.

"You ready?" he asked.

"Very," she smiled.

Brody threw his head back and laughed deeply and turned her around, "Happy Birthday Em."

"Oh My God!" Emma gasped loudly and started towards the steps.

Brody quickly grabbed her and pulled her back against him and laughed, "Don't you dare expose me."

Emma laughed and turned around and kissed him, "Not helping EM."

The cabin was amazing, it sat on Lake Winnipesaukee.

"Was it worth the five hour drive Em?" Brody asked as he watched her walk around smiling.

"Absolutely, Brody this is amazing. How long are we staying?" Emma smiled.

"A week this time, but in the summer I thought we could stay here as often as possible," he smiled, "It's ours."

Emma gasped, "You bought it?"

"Yes, I hope it makes you happy," Brody said anxiously.

"Yes happy, very, very, happy," Emma threw her arms around him, "I like the fireplace, it reminds me of England."

Brody groaned, "Your parents will be here soon. But right now you need to stay away from me."

Emma laughed and turned away, "London, show me the upstairs?"

"I am up here," London waved from the balcony, "Five bedrooms Mom!"

"Five?" Emma laughed as she ran up the stairs.

~

"They will be gone at least an hour, show me the room you picked," Brody smiled.

"Well I picked the one London told me you had picked. You two are sneaky, how long have you been working on this?" Emma smiled.

"Since we got back from England. I promised you a happy life and well I am trying Em," Brody frowned.

"What does that mean Brody?" Emma asked rubbing his face.

"Honestly, you have had cancer, two lost children, my Uncle…God Emma…then my father. It hasn't been that wonderful, but it will be. I have put you through a lot," Brody pulled her hair back away from her face and lifted her chin, "And now I have made you cry."

"Brody, I am cancer free, you helped me through all that, I have a man who wanted a child with me, who adores and loves my child, your Uncle is an ass, and your father passed away, none of those are your fault, none of it." Emma kissed him, "I am happier than I ever imagined. We all have pasts, but each day with you erases the hurt from my past. You don't just make me happy Brody you make me whole."

Brody kissed her harshly on the mouth, and his hand floated softly down her back, "I have never felt more cherished Em, not ever."

"Me either, I love you," Emma kissed his neck softly and pulled his shirt off. She undid his pants, and they fell to the ground, "God I am so glad you don't wear underwear."

Emma took him in her mouth quickly, and he gasped, "Em stop....fuck."

Brody took her hair in his hands and guided her head. She stopped and grasped his shaft and stroked gently as her tongue flicked across his tip causing him to twitch. She cupped his sack and tugged gently as she sucked hard on him. Brody moaned and threw his head back.

"Emma," he hissed trying to hold back his release.

Emma moved faster and she felt him tense and release into her mouth, and he held the back of her head and thrust into her mouth cursing loudly.

When he was empty he stammered back against the counter, "Damn Em."

Emma smiled and stood up and watched him try to regain his composure. She took a picture with her phone of him leaning against the counter running his hands through his hair and his mouth slightly opened trying to catch his breath.

He opened his eyes and smiled, "Do you have any idea how amazing you are?"

"Yes," Emma beamed.

Brody laughed, "Do you have any idea what I am going to do to you?"

Emma's jaw dropped, and she froze, Brody pulled his pants up and peered up at her through his dark lashes and raised his eyebrow. Emma gasped, and he took a deep breath and ran his hands through his hair. He stood back and leaned on the counter and looked her up and down, slowly he licked his lips and ran his tongue across his plump lower lip. He cocked his head to the side and glared at her.

"You may want to run Em," his voice warned as he slowly took a step towards her.

"What?" she whispered as her eyes grew and jaw dropped.

He laughed wickedly, "Three, two…"

Emma jumped and ran up the stairs as he followed her, she dove into the bed and pulled the covers up to her chin and watched him come in the room giving her an intimidating glare.

"You don't scare me," her voice squeaked as he got closer.

"Oh this won't be scary, but you're going to feel boneless for the rest of the day," he warned.

Emma's eyes lit up, and Brody laughed a deep dark laugh.

He grabbed a box off of the self in the closet and brought it out.

"Brody they will be back…" Emma began.

"I would stop talking if I were you," Brody warned.

"But…"

Brody stood up quickly and gave Emma a look that made her stop talking immediately.

He grabbed his phone from his pocket and dialed a number, "Caroline, Emma has decided she would rather not cook tonight…no she doesn't want you to either, Emma wants Prime Rib, only the best cut. There is a place we passed about twenty miles out of town, would you mind terribly? The drive up tired her out, and I think she is going to rest a bit and then when you get back she would like to eat, she is going to be extremely hungry. Thank you."

"Brody…" Emma began to protest.

"It would be best if you would just shut that hot little mouth of yours Em, fair warning, not a peep," he advised his brow raising.

Brody opened the box and took out several silk scarves and smiled and looked at Emma.

She sat with her knees to her chest with the blanket pulled over her nose and her eyes wide.

"Stand up and take your clothes off Emma," Brody instructed.

Emma didn't move, "Do it now or I will do it for you."

Emma stood up quickly and did what he asked. Brody let his pants drop to the floor and stood with his back to her.

"Kneel on the edge of the bed and sit back on your heels," He instructed and turned towards her with his erection in hand slowly moving his hand back and forth.

Emma moaned, and her nipples tightened and peeked.

"Look at your tits Emma, begging for my mouth to suck them, look at them Emma," Brody's voice was gruff and hot.

Emma looked down and closed her knees tightly.

"Spread your legs now," he said pumping himself harder.

Brody walked over and grabbed two candles out of the box and set them on the dresser and lit them.

"You're not going to talk, just listen and understand that I am going to fuck you until you can't take anymore. These candles might seem romantic, but that hot wax is going to be a bit uncomfortable dripping over those pink aching nipples," Brody warned.

"Do you have any idea how hot…"

"Emma don't," Brody said harshly.

"I know exactly how hot you're getting, I see your tight little pussy is swollen wanting me, your perfect tits need to be sucked hard, and you're getting wet, soaked actually. It started downstairs as you sucked greedily on my cock until I filled your mouth with my come, and then with each warning it gets slicker and wetter and needs me even more. I promise you you'll come Emma, harder and longer than ever before," Brody blew out the candles.

"I am going to let that sit for a moment so that I doesn't burn you…" Brody started.

"I want you too," Emma panted.

"Shh Em, no you don't and I don't want to hurt you," Brody took a scarf and wrapped it around her waist and tied it loosely.

"Spread your knees further I want to see that clit," Brody instructed.

"Use your hands on yourself, spread and rub," Brody said softly.

She did as he asked and he stroked himself at the same time.

"STOP."

Emma jumped, "I need you, please, I need you."

Emma started squeezing her knees together and Brody stood between them so she could not. He leaned into her and tied two scarves from the waist band to her ankles so that she couldn't move them and then tied two more to her wrists and attached them to her ankles.

"Look at you, so beautiful," he rubbed his cock lightly against her clit and she groaned loudly.

He stepped back and looked her up and down, "Breathtaking," he whispered.

He grabbed the candle and slowly poured little drops on to her left nipple, and she yelled out his name, he repeated it on her right.

"You're going to get so turned on your nipples are going to grow even more and crack that wax after it's hardened," Brody blindfolded Emma.

"The way you wanted me in the car, unable to see me, just the thought of me, my voice talking about tying you up Em, it's the anticipation. You couldn't wait to be on your knees sucking this," he stroked himself and moaned loudly.

"I see your nipples responding to me Em, they are so in need of my mouth, my teeth, my breath," he blew cold air onto them, "I can't wait to have them in my mouth."

Brody rubbed from her knees to just below her groin, "And then there is this," he bent down and blew on her, and she moaned.

She felt the blindfold release, "You have cracked the wax Em, I think I should get rid of it now."

Brody ran his teeth slowly across her nipples peeling the wax away with his mouth and repeated on the other side.

"Oh God," Emma screamed and she felt herself starting to orgasm.

"Damn Em," Brody released the scarf around her waist and flipped her on her stomach and pushed into her.

Emma screamed out with each thrust and tried to pull away.

"Hell no," Brody flipped her to her back and shoved two fingers into her as she peaked his mouth covered her as she let go, holding nothing back until she lay limp.

"Sorry," she whispered.

"Fuck Em," he pushed into her and she let out little cries of pleasure until she came again and he did so with her.

"How are you feeling?" he asked when he finally pushed himself off of her.

"Perfect," Emma whispered.

"You tasted perfect, that has to happen every time," Emma rolled to her back and hid her face in the pillow, Brody smacked her ass, "Got it, no holding back on me, I want it like that every time."

Brody pulled her up, "Shower with me, my fucking hot amazing wife!"

Emma looked up at him and scowled, he was beaming.

"I wasn't even in you yet, that's unbelievable. When you went off... I am so glad I had my mouth...damn Em, you taste amazing... hot damn!" He twirled her in a circle and kissed her.

Emma buried her face in his neck and giggled.

Brody cupped her chin and looked at her and smiled, "You are glowing. We are so good together love."

Emma felt him growing against him and looked up, "One more time and then a shower, they'll be here soon."

"Brody!" she yelped when he threw her over his shoulder and smacked her bare butt

Chapter 17

Brody woke from his dream and gasped, he looked over and Emma was still asleep. He got out of bed and washed his face and took a deep breath. He walked downstairs and got a drink and sat on the couch and thought about what he had remembered.

A blonde woman, she reminded him of his first experience with a Dom, and he sat back. Why the fuck am I dreaming about this, he wondered. She had a tattoo, it looked more like a brand. He remembered the bar he was at before he was married, with Rebecca when Ariel showed up, the bar maid had the same tattoo, so what, he told himself. He stood and paced the floor and remembered he had seen it again and froze. No big deal, but why the dreams damn it! He asked himself. It's not like it matters anymore Brody get a grip.

Brody sat on the couch and tried to stop his brain from going back to his dream. He looked down and grabbed the leather photo album and started looking through it. He came to the last page and froze.

"Oh my God," Brody gasped.

"Everything okay out here?" Henry asked walking past him into the kitchen.

"Yes, everything is fine," Brody's voice shook.

Henry walked over and looked at him as he stared down at the pictures, "Brody?"

Brody shook his head back and forth, "It's nothing Henry."

"It doesn't seem like nothing Hines, you look white as a sheet," Henry said and sat.

"It's nothing I have just been having a rough time lately, not a lot of sleep," Brody forced a smile.

Henry studied his face, "When you're ready to talk about it son I am here, is Emma alright."

"She is exceptional, wonderful. I love your daughter very much Henry, I always will," Brody said softly.

Brody climbed back into bed, and Emma sat up, "Are you okay?"

"I am Emma, I love you," he lay down and pulled her onto him.

"I love you more," she smiled and wrapped her arms around him.

They spent the week in the snow. They cross country skied, snow shoed, and ice fished. London had a great time, and so did Emma. Caroline and Henry were taking London home with them so that she could have her visit with Troy in the garage apartment.

~

"You haven't had any nightmares this week," Emma smiled and kissed him, "Maybe we should move up here."

"And forget about the outside world, and responsibilities. I think you prefer it away from home as well," Brody smiled.

"Why would you say that, I love our home," Emma asked looking up at him.

"You seem to let loose more away from home…squirt," Brody chuckled.

"You did not just…" Emma snapped and he covered her mouth, and she pulled it away, "Or do that!"

"Hmm I did," Brody's eyes danced.

"Just so you know that embarrasses me Brody," Emma said quietly.

"Why?" he gasped.

"It's not normal," Emma scowled.

"It's a fucking gift Em," Brody turned her towards him.

"Please don't call me that," she looked down.

"Make a deal?" Brody kissed her gently, "Don't hold back on me and I won't, but Em I was not poking fun at you okay? I would never."

Brody hugged her tightly, and she began to relax.

"Emma, I have to go back to England for a few days to wrap things up with my father's estate, as well as do a couple interviews before our tour. I would like to get that out of the way as soon as possible so that I can get back here for our child's birth. Would you like to go?"

"I would love to, but London is in school," Emma said softly.

"I know, I should only be gone a few days, I will have Lila work on it, but I want to do it soon is that alright?" Brody asked.

"Okay," she smiled up at him.

~

Brody and Emma stood at the airport waiting for his flight to be called. Emma sat playing with her hands, and he grabbed them and kissed them.

"Would you stop?" Brody smiled at her.

"Sorry," Emma smiled.

"No, Em, I am sorry. I wish I didn't have to go, but I must. When I come back it's happy from here on out okay?" Brody wiped away Emma's tear and held her tightly.

"I don't mean to…Brody you are my happily ever after. It hurts to think you don't know that. I Love you and us and our life, I wish you understood that. You are my more," Emma held him tightly.

"You are mine as well love," Brody kissed her, "Listen let's be happy we have five minutes before I leave, I want to see you smile Em," Brody kissed her face.

Emma smiled at him, "That's better."

"Just a few days?" Emma held his face in her hands.

Brody smiled, "I will be back before you know it."

Brody kissed Emma and pulled her up and hugged her tightly.

"The nursery looks good right?" Brody smiled.

"It's perfect, I can't believe you did all of that," Emma smiled.

"We will do more when I get back," Brody kissed her again, "I need to get going, customs, uugghh!"

"I love you Brody, see you soon," Emma smiled broadly.

"I love you Emma Hines, see you soon," Brody kissed her quickly and turned and walked away.

Brody walked through the gate, and his heart pounded, he did not relish the idea of not telling his wife the other reason for his trip. But it had to be done, he couldn't go on ignoring what his gut was telling him.

Brody walked through customs and walked to his gate. He looked around to see if his travel companion was waiting. He smiled shyly and sat down.

"Thank you for meeting me. I am sorry about all of this secrecy I just don't want to hurt her," Brody put his head in his hands.

"I understand Brody, I don't want to hurt her either. I am glad you trusted me enough to open up to me about everything. I will not hold anything against you if this does not pan out, I will not say that I am not only hoping but praying things will go well."

"I know, but I don't think I am wrong, and it scares the hell out of me. Emma is going to be hurt, I just don't know how the hell this happened. Never in a million years could I have ever imagined something like this. Unbelievable," Brody sighed.

Their flight was called, and they walked onto the plane and sat.

"It's going to be a wild few days, I hope you are ready for it," Brody laughed nervously.

"I am ready, we should rest on the flight over, I don't think we will get much sleep if we are to get this all wrapped up in a few days. If it takes any longer they are both going to be suspicious."

"I agree," Brody turned toward the window, "I should have just told her, damn it. It's going to crush her."

"Why? If nothing comes of it and you did tell her she would be even more devastated. She does not need to know until we figure it out."

"Okay," Brody said and closed his eyes as the plane took off.

~

Emma cried the entire way home. She couldn't shake the thought that something was going to go horribly wrong. The first time he went to England they nearly broke up. The second time she was drugged, and his father died. She couldn't shake the feeling that he was hiding something from her or that something horrific was about to happen.

~

"Em, I am in London," Brody said softly.

"Okay…Brody is everything alright? I can come if you need me. I love you," Emma began to cry.

"Shh Em, I love you. Everything will be fine, I miss you already," Brody said softly.

"I am going to come, Mom and Dad can watch London, I should be with you…"

Brody cut her off, "Emma I won't be long, you need to be with London and Lila. I want you to know I wish you could be here as well, but it will be just fine. When I come home it will be a very long time before I ever leave you again. I love you more Em. Kiss London for me, I will see you soon."

~

They walked into the bar that he had first seen the tattoo. Brody ordered drinks and sat in the booth.

"Do you see the tattoo on that woman's neck?" Brody asked.

"I do."

"It's the same one Henry," Brody shook his head.

"Well let's get the ball rolling if Elizabeth is alive I need to know," Henry said with restrained urgency.

"We will go to the hotel, and I will make the call," Brody said.

Brody slammed his drink, and they left.
#########

A bit of Wrapped in Armor

My Dearest Brody,

I have had a difficult day. I hurt thinking of what may have happened to you. I hurt knowing that wherever you are you are unable to get back to us. I hurt knowing that I have failed in finding you. I hurt so much missing you. I hurt knowing that I am either crazy believing that you are out there somewhere and I hurt thinking you are not...It has been eight months without you and I know when I smell your pillow, it truly is not your scent I smell but the memory of it. People say memories fade and that scares me senseless. I never want to go a day when I don't remember your smile, your smell, your touch, your voice or the way you loved me.

Yours Always and Forever,

Em

~

Brody laughed as he walked in, "Feisty little thing isn't she." He kissed her neck, "Why won't you give poor Rupert the day off?"

"He is staying on full time. And he is my employee," Emma said glaring at him.

"Do we fight after sex a lot?" Brody asked cocking his head to the side. Emma turned and gasped. "What's wrong love, Clive bought the condoms, Rupert watched London, what do you think they thought was going on? So anyway do we? I mean you sounded like you enjoyed yourself and you tasted..."

Other Titles by MJ Fields

The Love Series

Blue Love

New Love

Sad Love

True Love

The Wrapped Series

Wrapped in Armor

Look for **Wrapped Always and Forever** book three in the MJ Fields Wrapped series

coming in May 2013

A Young adult series is also in the works and will be available

In the Summer of 2013!!!

mjfieldsbooks@gmail.com

www.mjfieldsbooks.com

https://www.facebook.com/pages/MJ-Fields-books/514446948612589

Made in the USA
Charleston, SC
08 May 2013